American Fiction

American Fiction

Volume 17

The Best Unpublished Stories by
New and Emerging Writers

Editor: Bruce Pratt
Finalist Judge: Colin Fleming

n RIVERS e PRESS w MSUM

First Edition
Library of Congress Control Number: 2018962679
ISBN: 978-0-89823-387-2
e-ISBN: 978-0-89823-388-9

New Rivers Press is a nonprofit literary press associated with Minnesota State University Moorhead.

MINNESOTA STATE UNIVERSITY MOORHEAD.

Cover and interior design by Samantha Albrecht
The publication of *American Fiction Volume 17* is made possible by the generous support of Minnesota State University Moorhead, the Dawson Family Endowment, and other contributors to New Rivers Press.

NRP Staff: Nayt Rundquist, Managing Editor; Kevin Carollo, Editor; Travis Dolence, Director
Trista Conzemius, Art Director
Interns: Alyssa Berry, Olivia Carlson, Sarah Ernster, Alex Ferguson, Laura Grimm, Aubrey Johnson, Lauren Phillips

American Fiction Volume 17 book team: Sara Barone, Alyssa Berry, Dana Casey, Sarah Ernster, Belle Hausladen, Emily Lauinger, Katelyn Martinson, Delaney Noe

Printed in the USA on acid-free, archival-grade paper.

American Fiction Volume 17 is distributed nationally by Small Press Distribution.

n RIVERS e PRESS w MSUM

New Rivers Press
c/o MSUM
1104 7th Ave S
Moorhead, MN 56563
www.newriverspress.com

Contents

Editor's Note

Bruce Pratt

Years ago, I heard a man declare that, "People take more baths in surveys than bathtubs." His evidence was a survey where nearly 100 percent of the participants insisted, they bathed or showered every day. "None of them ever got sick and stayed in bed for a few days?" the fellow added. I have no idea how that survey was conducted but it's not difficult to parse the results. No one wants to be thought of as indifferent to personal hygiene. Think of the old saw, figures don't lie but liars figure. Or, more benignly, think of how we often give the answer we believe our interlocutor wants to hear.

Fiction can be like that, too, when a writer assumes that every one of his or stories need be fraught with despair and dripping with dire and daunting challenges for their characters to overcome. This is far too often the modus operandi for creators of contemporary short fiction.

One in ten Americans will develop severe dementia. One in five Americans will die from cancer and about four in ten will have some form of the disease in their lifetime. Three-hundred and seventy-five thousand Americans will die this year from heart disease. Yet, many more will succumb to old age, and simply wear out after a good run. I wish I met the latter more often in contemporary short fiction.

A year or two ago, I read a story where, in the opening paragraph, a twice-divorced, thirty five-year old woman whose teaching position had been eliminated was driving back to her hometown with her ailing dog in her unreliable fifteen-year old Subaru to take over the care of her father, afflicted with Alzheimer's, because her mother, whose breast cancer had reappeared, was no longer up to the task. A rich but feckless brother offered no help. Then it got worse.

Great fiction does arise from the struggles of characters onto which the author piles sorrow after sorrow, but from characters readers can imagine as real people and in whom they are invested. I believe you will discover and embrace such characters here—compelling and believable—but most of all human. While many of them struggle to stay afloat in a frenetic and sometimes dangerous world, many of these stories arrive at places of joy, hope, and redemption. Never formulaic, these narratives engage and enlighten. Chosen from an unusually impressive short list of semifinalists, the stories in this anthology were each a pleasure to read and re-read.

I know that it was an even more difficult task for our Finalist Judge, Colin Fleming, to make his choices, and deeply appreciate him bringing his prodigious skills to this task, as no one I know is a more prolific contributor to American letters, or as well-versed in film, music, and literary criticism.

Introduction

Colin Fleming

This was the first contest I've judged, and, I must confess, it was both a relief and a pleasure.

I anticipated wading through a clutch of MFA-machined stories that would serve as mental emetics of the same old, same old. The formula. The pretentiousness. Lifelessness. Caution. But lo, how wrong I was, and I am grateful for the errors of my preconceptions, for these stories—even when they reached and didn't quite to the place where hands were aimed—shared a bond with each other in trying to reach readers. Sounds simple, right? But we don't see a lot of that these days. And, for their efforts, I wish to commend everyone in this anthology.

I was surprised how many stories dealt with sports, which is usually a no-fly zone for writer-types, sadly, but that made a certain amount of sense, as nary a work here suggested to me that its author found an easy home in a mold. And there were a number of stories about faith, which was heartening. Not because on wishes to thump the drum of religiosity, but because the actions that we make, and the choices we select, are always matters of faith in the most important endeavors, be they ones of love, of friendship, or or honest storytelling.

As for the three winners: I wish to say that "Barn Find" by Matthew Finch had voice and verve. I felt like I would know the cut of this voice's jib if it took on human form, donned clothes, walked around in the world. At the Starbucks, listening to this voice-person order a latte, I'd have a good idea it was the voice from the story.

Charles Duffie's "Catalina" made me think that the forces that drove this story were out there. I just hadn't experienced them firsthand yet. But they were of, and out in, the world, and now I would be better served to come upon them.

David H. Fuks's "Distinctions" took the top prize, but I went round and round. My feeling was that if Fuks had been the last man on earth, like in a bad Vincent Price horror film, he would have worried less about acquiring food and water than he would have about completing this fiction account. Make me read so that I feel that it matters to you, because you tried so hard to give characters dimensionality, as hard as you try to give anything in your life dimensionality. Harder. Then harder than that, and more. I felt that Fuks understands this for his readers.

Do that, and you, the writer, is removed; the autonomous story is what remains, the story with legs, that story gets up and goes. Here's a clutch of them, each surprising in its way, each a reason to put your expectations aside, as each made me do.

Hand-Picked

DISTINCTIONS

David H. Fuks

While some people eat with impeccable manners, others attack their food with an animal aggression. My father, Sam, was of the latter while his friend, Simon, was of the former. Sitting with the two men at Katz's Delicatessen in Detroit, I observed this stark difference with a studied indifference. I chose the venue for our meal together so that we might sit in the shelter of one of the high booths. By sitting next to my father, I was also obscuring his lack of grace and manners from the view of other patrons. Simon sat opposite us. His herringbone sport jacket and natty tie reflected the style of the college professor that he was. My father wore the clothes of a laborer. Denim pants and a blue work shirt under a crew neck sweater which now had splatters of sauerkraut and coleslaw that he wiped away with his napkin when he noticed my glance.

"I'd leave the food there in case I want a snack later," Sam said laughing. "But I wouldn't want you to be embarrassed."

My father laughed at my discomfort as he took another enormous bite out of his Reuben sandwich. I was always afraid that he would choke when he ate like that. He seemed to be able to swallow the meat, bread, and sauerkraut like a python. Sam wiped his chin and took a long drink of beer and then burped and winked at me.

Simon acted as though he didn't notice. He took a delicate bite of his blintz and sipped his tea and wiped his mouth with his napkin before speaking to me. "Marvin, you should join my son, Irving, and come hear my lecture next Thursday at Wayne State. I'm speaking about the impact of the Holocaust in literature. I'll be discussing Elie Wiesel, Primo Levi, and Victor Frankel. I expect that you will find it interesting."

"You should go, College Boy," my father said to me while inadvertently spraying little projectiles of his sandwich as he spoke.

"From me you can learn how to make cars, but from Simon you can learn how to make distinctions." Both men laughed.

I wiped a few flecks of food from my shirt and smiled at these old friends. Simply sitting with them was an opportunity to make distinctions. Both men had endured the Buchenwald Concentration Camp. They had known each other as boys and had their differences but, in the context of their enslavement, they supported each other and somehow managed to survive. Sam had emerged with a shell of fierceness around him and Simon with an erudite passivity that he wrapped with an intellectual mask. "I'll be happy to attend," I said to Simon. "How about you, Pop?" I asked my father.

"Don't be ridiculous. I don't watch Simon lecture and he doesn't come to the factory to see me on the line. We just get together for lunch every few months to celebrate that we're still alive. Who knows maybe next summer we'll take you boys to a Tigers game so we can pretend we're just regular Americans." My father looked at his friend. "What do you say, Simon? We can bring our wives and have a few laughs."

Simon looked uncomfortable for a moment. His smile had something false in it. "We'll see," he said as he slid out of the booth and dropped some money on the table. The two men nodded and Simon turned and walked past the deli counter and out the door without looking back. My father smiled at me and finished his beer.

....

I sat in the front seat of the car between Sam and my mother, Ruthie. Irving sat in the back seat between Simon and his mother, Sophie. We were driving downtown to see a Tigers game. Instead of looking out of the window and being a little excited about the outing, my mother was looking at some photos that she had just picked up from the drugstore and getting ready for her favorite pastime . . . expressing disappointment in me.

"Why are you making a face in this picture?" she accused me. Then turning towards her best friend, Sophie, she explained, "My Marvin, he's always fooling around. I wish he could learn from your Irving how to present himself as a gentleman."

I didn't even need to look into the backseat to see what was happening next. Sophie put her arm around Irving's shoulder and pinched his cheek. "He's such a good boy and so handsome."

My mother added, "My Marvin looks all right when he's not making faces."

"Mom, I'm not making a face in that picture," I defended myself. "That is my face. You and Pop made that face. I'm sorry if I can't be pretty like Irving."

I heard Irving snort. "Don't hate me because I'm beautiful!" he said. I didn't hate him. I just didn't like him that much.

The Tigers were playing in the old Briggs Stadium. Renaming it Tiger Stadium hadn't made it more attractive. But I loved the place—it was gritty and a bit dirty, but it was real. This was the place that right fielder Al Kaline graced . . . that Rocky Calovito and Norman Cash were giants in . . . where "Hammerin' Hank" Greenberg hit so many homeruns and refused to play on Yom Kippur.

That day, Mark Fidrych was pitching. They called him "The Bird." I loved the guy, not because he was having a great year, but because he was nuts. He would get excited and groom the mound and the crowd would go wild singing "The Bird is the Word."

My father found a parking spot on the street a few blocks away from the stadium. A fellow was sitting in a lawn chair about ten yards up the street. Pop walked up to him and handed him a five dollar bill. "Watch my car would you?" he asked. "I'll give you another five later if it's okay."

Simon objected, "This is a public street. What are you paying this guy for? This is extortion!" He seemed agitated.

"It's a service," Sam responded. "This fellow is doing me a favor."

The man in the lawn chair said to Simon, "I'd do a favor for you, too, if you needed it."

"Well, you're a nicer person than I am," Simon said as he stomped away.

"I suppose I am," the man in the chair said with a smile as Pop patted him on the shoulder and we all walked to the stadium.

We sat in the bleachers. The game seemed very far away, but I didn't care. The Tigers were playing the Yankees, and everyone in the crowd was screaming their heads off, enjoying the rivalry. Irving took out a program and a pencil and started tracking the status of every play, delighting in the statistics. My father bought me a kielbasa, my mother a kosher dog, and himself two beers. Sophie had packed a lunch for her family, and Simon sat stiffly drinking tea from his thermos.

"This is a game of situations," Simon remarked.

"Who cares?" countered Sam.

Ruth and Sophie looked at each other and laughed.

Simon looked at them suspiciously, like they knew something he didn't. Sam teased him. "Take it easy. Let them have a good time. Don't worry, they're not talking about you."

Simon turned to my father with inordinate anger. He spilled hot tea on himself, which made my father laugh. Simon screamed in pain or frustration. "You bastard!" he yelled and stomped away to find another seat and nurse his grudge.

....

Over the years, there weren't many encounters between our two families. Sam socialized with his friends at the Workman's Circle Branch 227, a sort of Jewish Socialist-Bund Elks Club. He loved going to the meetings where he could drink vodka with his friends and sing. He also loved the energy among these Eastern European Jews who had moved a bit to the right to become Democrats and enjoyed yelling at and taunting each other.

Simon engaged more frequently in university politics at Wayne State and, when he did attend an event at the Workman's Circle, he made it clear that he was doing so to indulge Sophie's desire to spend time with Ruthie. (The women had grown up together and loved each other.) During these encounters, Simon looked at the Bundist crowd as a group of misguided peasants. "Don't worry," my father teased him. "I won't tell them that you voted for Eisenhower, and then for Nixon."

At a New Year's Eve party, Simon announced that his family would be moving to Lawrence, Kansas. He had been offered a philosophy professorship. "Are there Jews in Kansas?" my mother asked.

"Of course, it's a university town. There are always Jews at universities," Simon reassured Ruthie.

"I suppose they also have furniture stores. Perhaps you will find Jews there that you can look down your nose at," my father joked. Simon's smile was more of a sneer.

"Don't worry, Ruthie. We can travel to visit each other . . . and go on vacations together." Sophie put her hand on my mother's arm to reassure her.

Simon looked at Sam as if to say, "Don't count on it."

We did visit once. Irving had just graduated from MIT with a degree in engineering. I was invited along for this important celebration. My recent MFA in theater arts did not similarly impress the need to celebrate upon my parents. They were convinced I would likely starve to death.

"Marvin, maybe you can teach," my mother said.

"Learn to act normal," my father advised.

My presence at the gathering was a duty I didn't relish. My father was glad to have my company so that he could have an audience for his anti-intellectual wisecracks. My mother, no doubt, took some pleasure in having an opportunity to share her disappointment in my achievements as she compared me to the handsome and brilliant Irving.

It surprised me that Irving was actually glad to see me. He had entered college prior to his parents' move and had few friends in Kansas. Irving invited me into his father's den to see what he had been working on at MIT. He held a small box with a keyboard on his lap. "It's a new kind of computer. We're teaching it to talk," he said with pride.

I was impressed. Computers, at the time, were generally huge and not being used outside of university or military settings. Teaching them to talk seemed amazing to me. "What can it say?" I asked.

Irving typed and pushed a return key and the machine said, "Burp." He repeated the process and the machine said, "Fart." We both laughed. For the first time, I actually liked this guy.

"Irving, I'm glad to see you're making such good use of this technological advance," I teased.

"Marvin, I just wanted to make sure that I was using words that might be in your vocabulary," he said. "Would you like to try?"

I typed and pushed the return key. "Screw you, Irving," the machine said.

....

"The proper thing to say to someone in mourning is 'May you be comforted among the mourners of Zion,'" my mother advised me. Five years after our families parted, we were flying back to Kansas for Simon's funeral. He had died from esophageal cancer.

"I'm sorry for your loss," my father said. "That's simpler. The main thing is not to say too much, but to be present."

". . . and kind," my mother added.

Ruthie sat next to Sophie during the funeral and I sat next to Irving. My father stood in the back of the chapel. Sam was not fond of religious services but attended for Ruthie's sake. "Thanks for being here," Irving said to me. "We'll need you for a minion at the house, later." Finding ten Jewish men for an orthodox minion in Lawrence was, apparently, a bit of a challenge.

At the gathering at Irving's parents' house after the funeral, I stood next to my father in the back of the room. I fumbled my way through the liturgy and noticed that Sam was shifting back and forth next to me without a prayer book in his hands. "I hate this crap," he whispered.

My father and God were not on speaking terms. "I get it," I said.

After the service, we entered the parlor where Ruthie and Sophie were sitting together. They sat on chairs without cushions. The mirrors were covered with cloth. People were lining up to express sympathy to Sophie as Ruthie sat quietly holding her friend's hand.

There was a table with fruit, cold cuts, and soft drinks. Irving stood nearby talking with a few of his father's university friends. Sam paced uncomfortably and then walked over to me. "Come on, Boy, let's go to a bar," he said.

It appeared I was to be the designated driver. I nursed a bottle of Rolling Rock beer while my father drank two double shots of Stolichnaya vodka. His face had a bit of a blush as he began to relax and talk. "It's no surprise to me that Simon died of cancer. When you carry secrets and fears, they eat at you," Sam said.

"From Buchenwald?" I asked.

"No, that hell was straightforward. The Nazis used us as slave laborers. They killed randomly and with pleasure. If you had a skill like Simon's, they used you to keep their records. If you were a brute like me, you spent your days mucking out latrines and burying the dead. In that place, Simon and I watched out for each other. He could get a little extra bread, which he shared with me, and I could keep bigger men from taking the bread out of his hands before he could eat it. He always ate too slowly. Simon was always trying to protect his dignity. I was simply trying not to be killed. No, the secrets came after the war."

I was intrigued by my pop's openness. He rarely spoke about the war. "What happened when you were liberated?" I asked.

"Simon and I were separated towards the end, and I was forced to join a death march to Auschwitz. A few of us tried to run away. The others were killed, but I ran into the woods and kept running for three days and then collapsed. When I awoke, I was in a chair, face to face, with a Wehrmacht Lieutenant. I lied and told him I was a prisoner of war. I was hoping to be sent to a Stalag and not to a concentration camp to be killed.

'Shut up, Jew,' the Nazi officer hissed. I thought right then that I was a dead man. Then he surprised me. 'We are losing this war,' the

Lieutenant said. 'For me, the time for killing needs to end.' He then sent me to a Stalag where I was placed among Russian soldiers. This was lucky because Polish soldiers would have killed me."

"And Simon?" I asked.

"He was liberated from Buchenwald, and when he was stronger he made his way back to Lodz. I ran into him there. We embraced like brothers. But it was difficult in Poland. We decided we couldn't stay."

My father ordered another double shot and swallowed quickly. He shuddered a bit and smiled bitterly. "You see, the Poles were not so excited to see any Jews coming home. 'You're alive?' they asked, but not with pleasure. Perhaps they were afraid we wanted our homes and old lives back. But I already knew this was impossible."

"Impossible?" I repeated.

"First, what did I have? My parents, my brothers and sisters, my wife and daughter had all been killed. My so-called friends in the labor movement had been the people who betrayed me. I went back to Lodz because I had no idea about how to move forward. Second, the Poles were making pogroms against those of us who had returned. I felt that to stay was to die. I had done nothing but drink for two weeks and then I ran into Simon. Having a friend gave me some hope."

"So what about the secrets and the fearfulness?" I asked.

"Be patient, Boy. I'll get there." Pop laughed at my rapt attention. "Simon told me he had met two girls in Prague. 'One is for me,' he said. 'You should come with me and meet the other one.' So I agreed and we went to Prague. The two girls were Sophie and Ruthie."

I smiled at my father. It made sense to me. Mostly, it was the young and the fit who had survived. Many were without roots and families. They were displaced persons left to wander about and, if they were lucky, find each other and find a way to make a new start.

My father leaned forward sharing a confidence with me. "Loving Ruthie saved my life. She gave me the ability to start over. It surprised me to meet two innocent girls. They had been in Oberalstadt in a slave labor camp and, although they were pretty, they had been left alone by the guards. This had to be difficult. There were some who would do anything for a crust of bread and some guards who would have thought nothing of raping a pretty girl. But there was randomness to survival. Maybe it was because they were friends or maybe because of some other reason beyond my understanding, but these two girls survived five years as slaves. They were beautiful and wanted husbands and to make families.

"So Simon and I found a rabbi and asked him to help us marry these girls. The rabbi hesitated. He said, 'You were both married men. Who knows if by some miracle your wives might be alive? Put up a notice with the Allies refugee agency and wait thirty days. If no one responds, then I will marry you."

"That sounds reasonable," I said.

"Those were not reasonable times," my father responded. "Simon started to weep. I got angry. I said to the rabbi, 'Listen, I'm not such a religious Jew, and I can sleep with whoever I want. I don't need a rabbi for anything. So, if this sweet girl gets pregnant and has no husband, let it be on your head.'"

I stared at my father in amazement. He was, after all, talking about my mother. "So, what did the rabbi say?" I asked him.

My father laughed, "He asked what time the wedding should be."

I remained mystified. "So, you all got married and made families. How was this a problem for Simon?"

Sam continued. "We went to Landsberg, in Bavaria, to a displaced persons camp. It was in the American sector of occupied Germany. We all wanted to come to the USA. We two couples were sharing a small apartment. One day, I went with Simon to buy coffee beans. We walked into a shop and, suddenly, Simon turned and ran out the door. I didn't understand why until I saw Rifkah, Simon's wife. She had survived! Simon was married to two women."

"Oh God!" I said.

"If there is a God, he has a wicked sense of humor," my father said. "So Rifka approached me. 'Where did Simon go?' she asked. 'I don't know,' I replied. 'He married again, didn't he?' she asked me. 'I don't know,' I lied. 'Well, I know and you can tell him for me that I don't care. I don't care if I ever see him again,' she said and she walked away. Simon was waiting for me outside of the apartment building where we lived. He begged me not to tell Sophie or Ruthie. He wept and wailed until I agreed."

"And you never told anyone, not even Mom?" I asked.

"I'm only telling you now because Simon is dead. I want you to know how a secret and a lie can kill a weak man's soul. You must never tell anyone," my father instructed. "As long as we are alive, you must never say a word."

"But why not tell Ruthie?" I asked.

Sam's voice was sweeter and gentler than I had ever heard it. "Your mother has an innocent soul. We must protect it."

"Is there anything else about you that I should know?" I asked my father.

He ordered another vodka. "No, Boy. You could never understand," he said.

CATALINA

Charles Duffie

I drove west with my brother's flag riding shotgun. The flag lay inside one of those triangle-shaped frames designed to hold a soldier's final colors. I kept glancing over at the brass hinges, the glass lid, the sharp corners. It always bothered me, how the flag had been folded to show only stars through the glass, as if my brother had gone into space instead of the ground.

He came home wrapped in that flag fifteen years ago, summer of 1970. I was fourteen the day we buried him. A pair of soldiers in dress blues and white gloves folded the flag between them, pulling tight on each turn. Thirty people sat in a portable outdoor chapel, rain tapping slow on the blue tarp; all around us, hundreds of bronze plates floated on wet, rolling grass like the remains of a shipwreck. Back home, I opened the glass lid on the frame, tucked the flag inside, closed the lid and turned the latch. That night, while mom stared at *My Three Sons*, I took the frame to my room, placed it on the bed, and slid a gallon-sized freezer bag from under the mattress. A K-Bar combat knife lay sealed inside. The blade and handle were dull black, the way blood looked in old movies. I hid the bagged knife under the flag and closed the frame. When mom was asleep, I took the frame to the garage and soldered the latch shut.

I spent the next fifteen years running up and down the coast, carrying that frame from San Diego to Santa Rosa, but always tumbling back to the L.A. basin like a hole I couldn't crawl out of.

Now it was summer of '85. I was twenty-nine, six years older than my brother had ever been. One of his old Vietnam buddies, Mike Somebody, called last week. He must have got my number from mom, but it felt more mysterious than that, like someone had found me in my wilderness, the way the grace of God was supposed to feel. His VA group was holding a flag rally on the beach, protesting Reagan's war in Central America. He asked me to bring my brother's flag. He talked about peace like it was something you could wrap around you. I hung up on him.

Then last night I stood in the sea, baptized by waves and woke sucking air. I took the frame from its shelf, pried the latch with a butter knife, and raised the glass lid for the first time since closing it. I pressed my hands on the stars until I stopped shaking. For a moment I felt the absurd hope that maybe I had imagined it all. But when I lifted the flag, the knife was there, preserved in plastic. All the times I had almost buried it in the mountains, thrown it in a landfill, turned it over to the police, and it was still here, with me.

By morning, the drive had taken on the weight of a pilgrimage. I'd visit the old neighborhood and say a prayer at my brother's grave. Then I'd head west to the flag rally, lay his colors on the sand, swim past the waves, and drop the knife and the past into the sea.

....

My first stop was our old house in Hollywood. It was a duplex now, the avocado tree gone, bars on the windows. My brother and I loved to climb the tree up to the roof. Sometimes mom would get the ladder and join us. "Know why I picked this house?" she'd say. My brother and I, knowing our cue, would chime, "Because you can see the Hollywood sign from up here."

That summer, I invited Shane over for the first time. We were going into 6th grade, though I was a year younger. We sat on the roof and read comics. When I scrambled down for snacks, my brother and mom were at the kitchen table. He read a psychology textbook, prepping for his second year at Los Angeles City College. She chain smoked while flipping through the latest issue of *Modern Screen*; Liz Taylor lay in full color across the glossy spread.

Mom smiled as I walked in. "Your pal looks like Steve McQueen in *The Blob*."

I loaded cans of ten-cent Shasta in a backpack: Grape, Lemon-Lime, Root Beer.

"Your big brother?" mom said, slapping his shoulder with the back of her hand, "B-movie Monty Clift. Look at that smile. Me, I'm more of a Donna Reed knock off."

"Which one?" my brother asked, grinning.

Mom laughed. "*Eternity*, smart ass." She lit another cigarette. "No one would cast me in *Wonderful Life* anymore." She squinted at me. "And you . . . ? *Rebel Without A Cause.*"

I liked that. "James Dean? But he had blond hair."

"No, baby, the other one."

"Sal Mineo?" I stuffed a bag of Lays into the backpack. As I walked out, she called after me, "How about Johnny Crawford from *The Rifleman*, ka-pow, ka-pow!" but I kept walking.

Mom and her movie stars.

Shane stood on the edge of the roof, watching as I climbed the tree. "Let's jump," he said.

I stretched across from branch to shingles. "Why?"

"To scare the shit out of ourselves."

"You'll break your legs."

"It's only like ten feet."

I turned to put down the backpack. When I turned back, Shane was gone—then I heard a chicken clucking my name. I thought of Sal Mineo and jumped.

We spent all afternoon crouching on the roof, paratrooping through the air, bending our knees, rolling in the grass, crawling under enemy fire to the sidewalk. In those life-and-death scenarios, Shane really did look like a sixth-grade Steve McQueen, and I suppose I did look like Sal Mineo. My brother and mom came out and sat on the porch. The day faded, and still we fought the good fight, my brother making sound effects in the darkness, the red arc of mom's cigarette moving from her knee to her lips like rescue flares.

....

I drove through the old neighborhood. Lemon Grove Park was still on the corner, a tall fence around it now. My brother and I used to play basketball here, but the court had been replaced by a jungle gym. 7-Eleven had taken over the Martinez Market, and the dirt lot where we built cinder block forts was a little apartment building.

Ramona Elementary School looked like an abandoned factory, blinds pulled down, doors chained shut for the summer. Shane and I had been sixth grade flag monitors here. I'd untie the rope and he'd sing the flag down, clapping *Mrs. Robinson* or *Fortunate Son.* One day Mr. Glick, a retired Air Force sergeant and our new Vice Principal, summoned us to his office.

"Gentlemen," he said, "if you can't respect the flag, I *will* relieve you of duty."

Shane snapped to attention, hand to brow in a crisp salute. Mr. Glick stared down with the full weight of his authority—but what could he do? He had to return the salute.

On the way home, Shane saluted everyone we passed. Earlier that week, mom and I had visited my brother in boot camp where we swore allegiance to the flag as if our lives depended on it. But nothing was sacred to Shane, not even the flag in wartime. He was like one of the characters in my comic books—the bullets of the world just bounced off.

Shane stopped and saluted me, holding the pose until I returned it. And just like that, we were both saluting strangers as we marched down the street. I felt free, unafraid for the first time since visiting my brother. When there was no one to salute, we saluted each other, right handed, left handed, karate-chopping ourselves across the foreheads, laughing.

A black Lincoln Continental pulled to the curb like a civilian tank. Mr. Glick climbed out, came around the hood, and slapped me so hard I spun in the air. Black light flashed, loud thrums pulsed in my head, and I found myself face-down on the hot sidewalk. Mr. Glick was gone. Shane stood over me, laughing. One side of his face was red, and blood dripped from his nose. He had been slapped even harder but he just laughed, like it didn't hurt. Like bullets bouncing off. As I sat up, he saluted. I laughed and returned the salute.

....

I drove to Hope Lutheran, one of my brother's sacred places. The sign outside now advertised vacation bible school in English and Vietnamese.

After Dad passed, Mom had no use for Jesus, and refused to let me go to church. "God had his chance," she said, "and he chose to let your dad fade out in a hospital bed." But my brother kept going. He finished boot camp about the same time I started junior high.

The Sunday before he shipped out, he asked if I wanted to be baptized. I didn't know what I thought about God, but I had no doubts about my brother. That morning, the pastor told stories that made me feel better, like comic books that might turn out to be true. I knelt and bowed my head over a golden bowl. The water lay so still, I would have thought the bowl was empty, if not for my reflection. The pastor's hand came into view, scooped the invisible water, and disappeared. I closed my eyes and held my breath. A moment later, the cool promises spilled over my head, and I felt something, I really did.

Walking to school, I told Shane about it. "The pastor had this story," I said, trying to get him to feel what I had felt. "There was a storm on the ocean. The disciples were in a boat, and were getting knocked around by the waves. They look up and see Jesus walking on the water—"

Shane cut in. "I heard this one! One guy, Petey, climbs out of boat."

"Peter, yeah, he—"

"He thinks he can walk on water too." Shane acts it out. "But what happens? Petey takes a few steps . . . and starts to sink! He has no mojo! No abracadabra! He yells, "Help me, Jesus, help me!" But Jesus is pissed. He taught Petey all his tricks and now the asshole can't even walk on water? So Jesus lets him drown to teach the other guys a lesson."

Shane laughed and walked on.

"That's not how the story goes," I said, running to catch up.

....

I parked across the street from Le Conte Junior High. The first letters arrived when I was in 7th grade. My brother had been selected for an officer training program and wrote home about the "psychology of combat." Mom hated the promotion. In the movies, officers always got it first.

While my brother was gone, Shane and I became unlikely best friends. "The wallflower and the clown," Mom called us. Shane recited the Pledge of Allegiance like a TV evangelist, smuggled firecrackers to school in Band-Aid tins, punctuated his recital of the Gettysburg Address with, "N'yuk, n'yuk, n'yuk," and when old Mrs. Bell assigned a book report on *The Grapes of Wrath*, Shane wrote about *Stranger In A Strange Land*, saying, "Okies, aliens, what's the difference?"

Our moms worked, so we hung out at the after-school program, playing tether ball. One day, Shane's older brother, Robert, showed up. I hated that he had a college deferment.

"Hooyah," Shane said, punching the tether ball. "Joe Chicken Shit, I mean, Joe College." Robert snatched the hard yellow ball out of the air. "Where is it?"

Shane tried to look innocent. Robert bounced the ball off Shane's head. "What?" Shane shouted, pushing Robert away.

"Where is it?" Robert said, palming the ball, stepping back.

"Where's what?"

Robert pulled him into a headlock and pounded him with the ball. "Where *is* it where *is* it where *is* it where *is* it?"

Shane stuck to his story, shouting "What? What?" until Robert shoved him to the asphalt. A small cut leaked blood along the edge of his eyebrow.

"If I find out you took it," Robert said, "I'll make you dig your fucking grave."

When Robert was gone, Shane wiped the cut over his eye like it was nothing but sweat. "Come on," he said, grinning.

He led me behind the big auditorium. We squeezed between the back of the building and the ivy-covered chain link fence. With my left hand pressing on the hot concrete and my right trailing through cool leaves, I felt like I was being led into a secret place. Shane crouched, felt around in the ivy, and found something wrapped in a white dish towel. When he unrolled the bundle, I saw the knife for the first time.

"1953 K-Bar Marine Combat Knife. The real shit."

"Are you crazy?" I said. "You stole that from your maniac brother?"

"This was my dad's. It belongs to *me*, not to that Spam-in-a-can draft dodger." Shane passed me the knife. The leather handle felt soft, like human skin. I thought of Shane's dad dying in Korea. I thought of my brother fighting in Vietnam.

The pilgrimage was becoming more about Shane than my brother. I told myself that was the last thing I wanted and turned the key, but the car wouldn't start. I squeezed the steering wheel, pressed back into the hot vinyl, and stared through the windshield. Far off, the Griffith Park Observatory stood high in the foothills. My brother and I loved that place. We'd hike up five, ten times every summer, tired and dusty and happy, sweat cooling on our skin as we walked the marbled halls like kings.

....

Mom always drove her red Mustang convertible with the top down. She said she looked younger with wind in her hair. I explained the flag protest on the beach, and my plan to stop along the way like my own Stations of the Cross. I didn't mention Shane.

We parked in Hollywood High's empty lot and stared at the mural of famous graduates painted on the gym wall: Carol Burnett and Carole Lombard laughing arm in arm, Alan Hale Jr. glancing nervously at Lon Chaney Jr., Judy Garland walking with Mickey Rooney under a rainbow that curled like a wave, Ricky Nelson drawing a six gun and firing at the world.

Mom lit a cigarette. "So, was I on your memory lane tour, or did you just need a ride?" She checked herself in the mirror, pressing the wrinkles. "I was Natalie Wood when I graduated from this dump, you believe that? *Splendor in the Grass.*"

We walked across the empty campus. Homecoming signs hung from gray buildings, but otherwise the place was cleaned and prepped for the next wave. Neither of us said a word.

In ninth grade, the letters changed. "I've never seen" became my brother's new mantra: *I've never seen rain like this, I've never seen the night so black, I've never seen good guys go so crazy, I've never seen men love each other so much.*

And I never told Shane about the letters.

One day, Cheryl Parker noticed the flag sewn on my backpack. I told her my brother was in Vietnam. When her eyes welled up, it felt like the day I had been baptized, like light in my lungs. Cheryl had been crowned Junior Homecoming Queen the week before. She started wearing a lot of make-up that year; Shane said she had a college boyfriend. She was so out of my league, our orbits only crossed in homeroom. But every Monday she knelt by my desk and asked, "How's your brother?" I had this crazy fantasy about him coming home and marrying Cheryl.

I never told Shane that either.

....

It was mom's idea to stop by the Campus Theater, which had been converted into a church a couple years ago. The marquee read *THIEF IN THE NIGHT.*

"God, I loved this place," she said. "Saturday matinees. You, me, and your brother. This is where we saw *Out of the Past*, remember? Robert Mitchum and Jane Greer. Jesus."

"Butch Cassidy, too."

"Newman and Redford, Christ." She took a drag. "From hundreds of gods and goddesses to one God and a virgin."

I laughed.

She looked at me and grinned. "What?" I said.

"I don't hear you laugh much, that's all. Maybe if you visited more I wouldn't be so surprised."

"How much more do you want me to visit?"

She exhaled. "How much is more than never?" I laughed again, and this time she laughed too.

In 10th grade, Shane got a job cleaning pinball machines at the arcade. Sometimes he pried centerfolds from the *Playboys* in the manager's office and pasted them inside my textbooks. One day I opened *Modern Geometry* to find Miss August staring back at me. The manager at the arcade paid in tokens, which Shane traded to an usher at the theater. They showed revivals all summer, like *Invasion of the Body Snatchers* and *Kiss Me Deadly.* Those were my favorites, but Shane loved the R-rated stuff, *High Plains Drifter, The Exorcist.*

One weekend they ran an Elizabeth Taylor festival. Shane and I sat in the balcony watching *A Place in the Sun.* Mom was right: my brother did look a little like Montgomery Clift. And Liz—I stared at her the way you stare at something you can't believe is real.

"Thinking of Cheryl?" Shane said. I turned, the spell broken.

He grinned. "Go ahead."

"What?"

He glanced around. "No one's here. Pull it out and get to work."

I didn't know what he was talking about. He laughed and turned back to the screen.

But when Liz leaned close to Monty, her dress dipping open, and whispered, "I'll be your pickup," I knew exactly what Shane meant.

The next time Cheryl knelt by my desk, I wasn't thinking about my brother.

....

We sat on a hillside at Forest Lawn. I gave Mom a look when she lit another cigarette.

"If it didn't bother them when they were alive," she said, "it won't bother them now."

She ripped tufts of grass away from my dad's name plate. "Your dad could have been Jack Lemmon's little brother. God, he knew how to laugh. That's one of the couple of million things I loved about him. He died the same day as Judy Holiday. You didn't know that, did you? I loved Judy Holiday. Christ, that day. Like the sun going out. Then just when things start to brighten up, those two boys in blue knock on the door and shoot out the lights. Ka-pow. Like Johnny Crawford, remember? *The Rifleman.* You loved that show. Chuck Conners, always standing up for justice. Ka-pow, ka-pow."

She turned to my brother's name plate, pulling grass from the edges.

"Jimmy Stewart is buried around here somewhere," she said. "Your brother loved *Harvey*. The one with the 6-foot-tall rabbit only Jimmy Stewart could see? Your brother used to pretend Harvey was *his* imaginary friend too. It was always, Harvey and me are hungry and Harvey and me want to go to the park. Swear to God, I started to see that stupid rabbit myself. Then you came along, and he never mentioned Harvey again. You were good for him."

I felt that in my chest. "I always thought it was the other way around."

"Yeah? That's what the guys in the script department call dramatic irony." I put my arm around her.

"I ever tell you why I picked this spot?" she said, dabbing her eyes with her pinkies. I smiled at my cue. "Because you can see the mountains?"

"Who cares about mountains?" She pointed down to the huge lot across the highway, sound stages lined up big as airplane hangers. "You can see Warner Brothers from here."

....

Maybe my pilgrimage was about Shane all along, because here we were, parked outside his house. "If his mom's still around," I said, "maybe I can get his phone number."

Mom lit another cigarette. "I wonder if he still looks like Steve McQueen. Remember *The Sand Pebbles?* God."

I walked toward the house, the frame under my arm. Nothing much had changed. Patchy lawn, yellow stucco walls, stacks of empty flower pots. I followed the driveway to the old garage and stared into the backyard. What had been a wild garden was just weeds now, with a sad square of concrete by the back door. An uncovered jacuzzi sat on the slab, blue plastic shell faded by the sun. I heard kids laughing somewhere, and the splash of a pool.

I walked back to the front of the house. Mom leaned into the passenger window, gesturing, *Well?* I waved her off and went up the stone porch, pausing to glance at our 6th grade handprints indented in a concrete step.

The front porch was shaded from the street by ivy trellises. Empty pots stood in uneven stacks on a little table; Shane's mom had been crazy for flowers. A "No Soliciting" sign hung from the mailbox. I left the frame on the table, but before I could knock, Shane himself opened the door.

"Son of a bitch," he said.

Mom would have been disappointed. This soft, thick thirty-year-old looked nothing like Steve McQueen. He barely resembled a used-up version of himself.

He pulled me inside and we sat on those same wood chairs in that same dining room. Shane did most of the talking, just like when we were kids. He told me how he ran the arcade, how he spent four years in the Merchant Marines, how his mom had passed three months ago. It hurt to look at his puffy face. I doubted any bullets had bounced off in a long time.

"Oh, shit!" he said, clapping his hands. "I have something you gotta see!" He hustled down the hallway and came back with a metal briefcase, the kind photographers used. He thumbed the combination and flipped the latch. "You'll never guess, but guess."

All I could think of was the silver box in *Kiss Me Deadly*, the one with the shining end of the world inside.

Shane leaned forward like Alex Trebek. "Wonder. Woman. Naked."

"What?"

"It's a hint, man. Forget it. Just sit back and enjoy."

Shane opened the briefcase to reveal a stack of porn magazines. He carefully picked one off the top and held the cover outward like a holy book. A beautiful young woman lay on her back, one arm hiding her breasts, her bare legs stretching up as if propped on the edge of the magazine. Her other hand pressed an apple to her open lips. I felt sick before I knew why.

"It's Cheryl Parker!" Shane crowed.

I turned my head like I was taking a punch.

"Cheryl Parker," he said, "revealed at last." The sound of glossy pages made me nauseous. "You hear she killed herself? I got every spread she ever did. These are mint."

I stood and stepped away. Shane followed, sliding pages.

"Her boyfriend got her into all kinds of shit. The All-American Girl." He pulled me around and opened the centerfold. "This'll turn your water into wine."

I shoved him hard in the chest, knocking him against the china cabinet. The plates sounded like chimes. We stared at each other, then Shane dove at me, shoulder in my gut. I flung him off, wrestled him around, and ran him back into the cabinet. His forehead cracked the tall mirror and plates broke like fragile bones deep in the cupboard. He fell to his knees then lunged up, grabbing me behind the thighs and heaving. We tumbled onto the floor. I wrapped an arm around his neck, pulling him against my chest. He yanked sideways, throwing elbows into my ribs. His legs pedaled, tennis shoes kicking and squeaking on the wood. He bucked up but I yanked him back like I was trying to drown him.

We stopped and lay there, gasping like we had held our breath all these years. He raised his hands. I let go; the wet skin of his throat peeled from my forearm. Coughing, he crawled to the magazine and smoothed the glossy pages.

I was almost to the car when mom called, "Where's your brother's flag?"

Adrenaline carried me a few more steps before I turned back to the porch. The frame lay on the table. I pulled the baggie from under the flag. Prying it open, I caught a puff of stale air, like dust. All the things I had thought to do all these years… and in the end I just tipped the bag upside-down and shook. The knife *clanged* into the white mailbox.

As we drove to the beach, mom asked what had happened. All I could manage was that Shane's mom had passed and someone else was living there now.

....

In tenth grade, Shane's backyard was an enormous garden, an overgrown half acre that became a jungle at night. Armed with a flashlight, I eased between thick tomato bushes, hid behind dwarf citrus trees, climbed over cucumber vines, hunting for Shane who hunted for me, blasting bullets of light which gave away my position, forcing me to move again, ducking into knee-high zucchini leaves, pressing flat into cool ivy. Wild herbs grew everywhere; the air changed as I crept through the war zone, peppermint and sweet basil, cilantro and sage.

I loved Flashlight War, pretending to be my brother, deep in the Communist jungle, fighting for freedom. Maybe that's why I won most of the time, but even when I lost, we just laughed, counted silently to twenty as we took up new positions, and started again. We only played when Shane's mom and Robert weren't home. The bursts of light on the windows made her nervous, and Robert made us nervous.

One night Robert showed up and forced himself into the game. Shane's .22 caliber flashlight drilled Robert in the chest and back, but Robert never called himself out. His five-battery Mag Lite lit up the yard, shotgun blasts of white that were never quick enough to find Shane.

Robert strutted through the garden, kicking down bean tripods, ripping guide wires from their eyelets, punching wood slats from trellises. Every few minutes he popped another can of beer and continued the hunt, heckled by Shane's voice in the dark.

"Here, chick-chick-chicken shit! Private Chickenshit, report to the latrines!" From the ivy, I saw Robert stumble up the steps, through the screen door. "Shane!" I hissed. "Let's go! Shane!"

But Robert was already coming back. He kicked the door so hard the top hinge broke loose; the screen hung open, tilted at an ugly angle.

Ch-clack ch-clack ch-clack.

His pump-action BB gun. I sank deeper in the ivy as the Mag Lite swept the yard.

Pop! Pop! Pop!

I heard Shane run, leaves crunching.

Pop! Pop! Pop!

Shane yelped, soft like an animal. I saw him scramble through the busted doorway into the house. Robert staggered behind him, arm ratcheting the pump action.

Pop! Glass tinkled inside the house. *Pop! Pop! Pop!*

I crept from the ivy but couldn't make myself go through that black hole of a door. I heard Robert's voice, then something like furniture falling over. I pictured Shane on the floor,

Robert's foot on his chest. I took a step—when Shane stumbled through the door carrying a bundle under his arm. I followed him out of the yard and up the driveway. He walked with a jittery stride, barely able to keep from running. He glanced around at the empty street, the bright porch lights. I recognized the towel-wrapped bundle.

"Shane, what happened?"

At the corner, he broke into a run. I chased after him.

He wouldn't say a word until we got to my house, two blocks over. It was past 11, the windows dark. He led the way to the garage and we ducked through the side door.

Shane clicked the bulb over the sink. I stood behind him as he unrolled the towel. He had to peel away the last wet folds, then shook the knife loose. Blood that was invisible on the dark blade splattered red on the porcelain. He twisted the faucet. Water poured over his hands onto the knife, churning muddily round the drain without seeming to go down.

He looked at me, dirty face cut with tears. "It was an accident, swear to God." He clutched the edges of the sink. "Robert kept saying, 'gonna put out your eye, put out your eye' . . . shit!" He picked up the knife. "Get a sponge or—fuck!"

I handed him a rag. He scrubbed the knife but blood kept tinting the water as if the blade was still cutting. Noticing a thick splotch on his t-shirt, he stripped it off and threw it in thesink. Three purple welts rose on his back, close together like holes in a target.

"I got the knife, just to scare him off." He was half sobbing now. "But I didn't know where he was. So I snuck into the kitchen . . ." Shane tapped the back of his neck. "Then I felt . . . He put the barrel . . . I spun and swear to God the knife just went in . . ." He blinked like he was coming out of a trance. "Fuck him. Come on. We gotta clean up. We gotta be ready."

"Ready for what?" I said.

He looked at me like I had lost my mind.

We hid the towel and his clothes in the garage, cleaned everything, scrubbed our hands, then cleaned everything again. We checked his sneakers but they looked OK.

Mom was asleep on the couch. We went down the hall to my bedroom. Shane put on jeans and a t-shirt. They were a little small but who would notice?

I refused to touch the knife, and didn't want it touching anything else, so I crept past mom into the kitchen and got a gallon-sized freezer bag. On the way back, Mom touched my hand. I jumped a little, turning as she looked up from the couch.

"Aren't you at Shane's tonight?"

I thought of what I should say. "He's sleeping over here, remember?"

She shrugged, already half asleep. "Yeah, that's right. Don't stay up too late, baby."

Back in my room, Shane eased the blade inside the bag, zipped it closed and slid it under the mattress.

"What're you doing?" I said.

"It has to stay here. They'll find it at my house. They can match it to—"

"So let's bury it or throw it in the trash or—"

"My mom's gonna be home any second. She's gonna call. We gotta be *here*. Asleep." He slapped the light switch and we lay down on the floor.

"You gotta swear," he said. "Swear you won't tell."

"But it was an accident."

His voice shook. "You gotta swear."

"OK," I said.

"No OK." He was crying now. "Swear on your brother's life."

I was crying too. "I swear."

"On your brother's life."

"On my brother's life."

Ten minutes later, the phone rang. We pretended Shane had spent the night, like he did half the summer. It never occurred to anyone that we were involved. Shane called it karma.

Robert, he said, had it coming. A week later, when two soldiers knocked on our door, karma rolled back the other way.

At Robert's funeral, I stood with my mom across from Shane's family. As the priest made promises, Shane and I kept looking at each other over the casket, looking away, looking back. A few weeks later, when it was my brother's turn, I told mom Shane couldn't handle another funeral. But the truth was, I didn't want him there. After the service, I opened the triangle-shaped frame for the first time, slid Shane's knife under my brother's flag, and closed the lid. I was fourteen. I didn't know what else to do with death except keep it all in one place.

My grandmother invited me to spend the rest of summer at her house in Rialto, a desert town thirty miles east of L.A. In the fall, mom allowed me to start on my GED. I never went back to high school, and I never saw Shane again, until today.

....

Twenty, thirty people had gathered on the beach. They held banners, made speeches, arranged flags end to end on the sand—but as a war protest, it was a bust. No crowds, no reporters, no TV vans, just a lanky L.A. Times photographer who had run out of things to shoot.

"Hey," Mom said. "There's Mike."

An African American man in an old army jacket walked out to meet her. As they embraced, I kept moving, carrying the frame until I reached that soft ledge of sand that sloped down to the water. My brother taught me to body surf out here, showed me how to trust a wave by the way it broke. I stripped to my boxers, but just sat there, staring at the ocean.

Mom walked up and sat next to me. The sand felt warm and the breeze raised goosebumps on my arms.

She opened the frame. "You're shivering." She unfolded the flag then wrapped it around me. "There. Like Captain America in *Easy Rider.*"

I looked at her. "Didn't he die at the end?"

"Don't be so literal." She touched my face. "You look a lot like him, you know?" "Captain America?"

"No, smart ass. Your brother." She gazed out at the waves, then pointed. "Look." An island waited twenty miles offshore like a new world. "You can see Catalina from here. God. I lived in L.A. all my life and I've never been to Catalina. Can you believe that?"

"Let's go," I said, standing up.

Mom smiled. "What, now?"

"Right now."

"You going to walk on water or swim across?"

Holding the flag around my shoulders, I stepped into the ocean. Mom laughed, and I glanced back like a little boy. When I was chest-deep, a swell lifted me to my toes—then the Pacific washed over my head. I held the flag tight and pushed to the surface; the world sounded loud and light burned my eyes. I swam farther out.

Someone called my name. Treading water, I turned and saw Mike swimming after me. He led a dozen people, swimming past the waves, trailing flags like capes. Maybe they thought this was part of the protest, loss as performance art. They bobbed around me like fallen super heroes.

The photographer danced in the surf, snapping with a zoom lens; Mom stood with both hands cupped over her eyes.

I slipped the flag off my shoulders, pressed the stars to my forehead, and let go. We watched the colors lay down in the dark, then everyone did the same, kissing flags as their lips dipped underwater, murmuring names like prayers, waving empty hands at the sun.

Then we just stayed out there, drifting west.

BARN FIND

Matthew Fitch

Thane cranked his head to look at the sunlit saltbox house and its barn rising behind.

His tongue clicked in his mouth.

"I think she's hot. Dju think she's hot?"

"Yeah, she's hot." I was sleepy.

"Wonder what she's doing in there," he mused. "Maybe she's in the shower."

From the other direction a car whispered beyond the rise in the road.

"Maybe she has a *pulsating shower head*," said Thane.

I looked down at my sneakers, sodden with cut grass.

It was the end of our first day tending the grounds. We waited on the wall by the quiet road. The afternoon sun spangled the blacktop through the shade of giant maples.

A black caterpillar dropped from a bough. Thane snapped his eyes and pinned it by its hind end with a twig on the stone. It reared its bubble head.

"Don't," I said.

"*Don't,*" he mimicked.

The caterpillar flailed; it flared its jaws in a silent roar. It twisted around on itself, clamping its legs upon the maroon twig.

"Quit it." I reached to yank the twig where it poked from Thane's hand. He worked it like a joystick. I swatted his hand. The caterpillar curled and fell off the wall.

Thane lived up the street from me. We were friends from grade school days. Now we were fifteen, and he allowed that he might *do* anything that moved.

"You're a pussy," he said and breathed hard out his nose.

....

That morning my mom dropped us off by a splash of tiger lilies by the wall at the road.

We walked the drive beneath the maples.

"Money," Thane said. "These people got *money*."

The house was a slate-topped saltbox in periwinkle clapboard. Behind the house was a parked Mercedes station wagon; beyond, a tidy red barn with a glassy cupola. A cockerel weathervane lorded over hayfields.

"Who puts a barn on a hill?" said Thane.

"Maybe it was there," I said.

A bushy tortoiseshell cat sat square in the middle of the lawn. A tall woman was at the door to the ell behind the house, our moms' age—younger—in a rough ankle-length skirt, billowy blouse, and tiny geeky glasses. She held the telephone receiver to her ear and covered it with her hand.

She smiled.

"Hello, boys," she said softly.

I said, "Is Mrs. Holcomb home?"

"I'm Mrs. Holcomb." Still smiling. She beckoned us in.

She went back to her conversation.

Thane cupped his hand at my ear and rasped, so hot it stank, "Second wife." Our sneakers clunked hollow floorboards. My eyes had to adjust. Mrs. Holcomb hung up the phone. She sat us at her table and explained the job to us. Thane blinked blue eyes at her, through lids astonished and lazy.

". . . and you'll find the mowers and the garden tools in the shed out back," she finished.

Through a door I saw a tufted leather chair, a polished copper pan, and a painting of a chicken with an oversize, squarish body.

Outside she showed us around the shed at the end of the ell. She showed us rusty garden dusters, a rumpled sack of poison, canvas garden gloves, and polypropylene safety goggles.

We went back out. "And here's for you to drink," Mrs. Holcomb said of a spattering well pipe jutting from the lawn.

Behind the drive and the ell rose the barn on its fieldstone pilings. She pointed.

"I must ask you to keep away from there," she said.

"Yes, Mrs. Holcomb," we said.

She went back inside and we went to work. We knew how to push junky mowers around.

....

Tuesday we weeded.

"Fuck weeding."

"Least it's not tobacco again," I offered.

"Fuck tobacco."

Thane spit in the mulch.

We waddled through the terraced shrub beds behind the house, dropping sad weedlings in weathered bushel baskets.

"I bet she doesn't even notice the difference."

Thane stood up and looked down at the house.

"What about him?" I said, standing and cracking my back.

"Who?"

"*Mr.* Holcomb."

"He's at Crestboro." Thane's eyes widened at me. "Cancer. For the *duration*."

Thane let his eyes roll up, lolling his tongue in the morning sun. He sliced his finger across his neck.

"*Chemo*," he continued. "It makes you barf up your guts. Makes you a skeleton. Makes your teeth stick out like fangs."

He muckled his mouth to show his teeth.

"And then you bite it anyway," he concluded.

"And you wanna *do* his wife," I sniggered.

"Damn right. And you should too, pussy."

He unbuttoned the top of his cutoff jeans. "I should flash her. Dare me?"

"Don't."

"I bet she sees *this*."

"No, don't."

"OK, pussy."

We picked up our bushel baskets and were hard by the creosote slats of the barn.

"We should break in," said Thane.

"She said to stay out."

"*She thaid to thtay out.*"

We weeded. The sun pressed the back of my t-shirt like a waffle iron.

"I can't," I said, tumbling to available shade.

"Gahh me neither," huffed Thane. He plopped in the shade of a holly. "This job sucks."

The cat stalked the garden behind us, sniffing freshly weeded soil. Thane threw a pebble. The cat crouched, otherwise unmoved.

We looked at each other in the woodsy quiet and heard from below,

"*Boi-yoys,*" Mrs. Holcomb called to us. "*BOI-yoys.*"

We poked from the shrubbery. The cat scuttled away through the shrubs at her voice.

There she was on the back drive beside the Mercedes, the strap of her bag on her shoulder. She waved above her head, smiled.

She called, "*Dju think you can get after a yellowjacket nest today?*"

"*Yes, ma'am,*" called Thane.

The cat rubbed her legs. Her smile grew broader and she waved again.

"*Yes, Mrs. Holcomb,*" I echoed.

"*Great! It's in the wall out front.*"

The car door was open. She clambered inside and swung her bag after her. The car door closed, *whump*. I saw her roots through the sunroof as she fumbled the key on the end of a silver train of baubles, feathers, and string. The car burbled.

"Diesel," said Thane. He watched her pull away. His lips parted the air as she rounded the house and slipped under maple boughs by the road. A gay blast from the car horn as she motored off.

I sat back at the edge of my shade.

"Yellowjackets," said Thane. "Eff." He sat and lay back in the mulch.

We sat another minute.

We dozed off on the mulch.

....

"Eff," Thane said again. "Yellowjackets. Hey."

I started from sleep.

"OK." He got to his feet.

Was it afternoon? No.

"Wakey. We're doing this."

We shambled down the garden slope and clomped to the shed behind the ell.

We went to the rumpled sack of powder in the shed depths. With a garden trowel we broke pinky-sized cakes from the dried-up mass inside. We pulverized them with the trowel handle on a workbench, wiping our noses and eyes.

We sluiced the powder into the rusty garden duster reservoirs.

We strapped polypropylene safety goggles around our heads, donned our sweaty garden gloves and marched down the drive through the gap to the road, turned left and paced along the wall.

"This is it," said Thane.

And it was. Wasps loitered in the air above the lilies.

"But these ain't no yellowjackets."

And that was for sure. Some flew close to have a look at us. They were glossy, blue-black, with eyes so strangely keen.

We drew our duster piston handles and plunged them slowly. Wasps trickled from the wall. We pushed the handles to the hilt, fluffing a yellowish, primitive aerosol through the air. Wasps streamed from the wall.

Wasps were behind, below, and above; they flew wide around our aerosol of death. Something alighted *thwump* behind my ear. Frantic fishhook feet wandered my t-shirt and thighs. A many-jointed thing clambered blue-sky polypropylene in front of my eye, tapping the plastic with its urgent rear.

The stings came after, not too long after. My feet slapped the gravel of the drive in boiling panic. Thane outpaced me.

At the pipe behind the shed we slathered cool water. But cool relief was a mirage.

"Anhh," Thane mouthed, waving off pursuers. His face puffed like Elephant Man's. "*Phone,*" he mouthed to me. I heard only *roar*, the blood in my head, a parade of C-5s parting my hair down the middle. *"Phone."* No phone. We rattled, rapped and scratched at the door of the ell even knowing she was gone, gone for the day.

....

Wednesday it rained, and we stayed home.

Thursday we were back on the horse. We would trim.

And in the cool of the shed in the morning, Thane said, "I think I know a way in."

He spoke low in the shed, almost whispering, "Next time she leaves."

I tested my shears. "Way in where?"

"The barn, numbnuts."

"OK. Why?"

"There's something in there. They don't want us in there."

The screen door of the ell creaked. The house door clicked and we heard her keys and baubles.

"There you are."

Mrs. Holcomb stepped into view on the lawn in the open door frame, followed by the tortoiseshell cat, gingerly stepping in the dewy shade.

"Good morning," she said.

"Good morning," we said.

She was dressed for town. She was a little made up. She asked, "How did you make out the other day?"

Her bag strap was on her shoulder. Her key-string dangled from her hand. The bit of the Mercedes key slanted where it just touched the ground.

"Okay," Thane ventured.

"Really?" said Mrs. Holcomb.

"We got *stung*, Ma'am," said Thane.

"Yeah we got *stung*," said I.

Mrs. Holcomb bent in a little at the shed door to see us better.

"I'm so sorry," she said, inspecting our faces. She smelled beautiful. Like a garden: soil, roses, rain, and everything. "I hope you'll get them next time." She looked at us one to the other, her eyes now adjusted, big and brown and round. "But I would really like you to take care of it."

"They're not *yellow*jackets," complained Thane through his teeth.

"You'll do fine," she said, retreating out the door to where the light was. "Back in a bit!"

She turned and walked away from us, pawing through her bag as she went. We heard the car door unseal, the bag heave across the seat, the keys and baubles. The car started and burbled.

Mrs. Holcomb drove off. Thane went to the shed door, gave double middle fingers after the noise where it trailed the corner of the house.

He kicked the dirt floor of the shed. The cat bolted from view.

"Pssh."

He gave his middle finger to the dusters on the bench.

"OK," he said. "We really are doing this."

"She didn't say *when*," I said. "Maybe we can wait. We can ask our moms."

"*We can ask our moms*. Do you ever get tired of being such a wuss?"

He breathed hard out his nose.

"Not *that*."

....

On the far side of the barn Thane's face was half in the dirt. His ass was in the air.

"Under here. I saw the cat go in once. You can squeeze."

"Uh-uh," I said.

"*Uh-uh,*" Thane mimicked.

"Just put your feet in," he said. "I'll push and you slide. Then unlock the door."

"Why me?"

"Because you're skinny?"

Thane thought himself muscular. I guess he was. He wore a puka choker.

"What if she comes back?"

"*What if she comes back?* We're fifteen, dipshit. Are they gonna arrest us?"

"She'll fire us? My dad'll kill me. I can't do tobacco again."

"We're done no matter what. We can't keep this place up. They used to have landscapers. She fired them. He's about to croak and she's selling this whole place off."

"Wh- how?"

"You don't know anything! My mom saw the listing. Her friend works for the agent. *Shit!*" he finished.

Thane was almost panting.

"You don't know anything," he said again. "Just get under there."

"And do what?"

"*And do what?* Let me in, for fuck's sake, if you're good for nothing else."

I looked at the hayfield across the track beside the barn. I looked at the dirt depression by the wall.

I was out of things to say.

So I did it. I lay down on the dirt and put my face under the slats of the barn.

"Head first?" said Thane. "Suit yourself, then. Scoot in. Wiggle."

"No. This way." I turned over on my back.

"Figures. Fine by me. Now scoot. Go."

I pressed my palms in the dirt at my sides, wiggled and scooted into twilight. The smell changed. The slat ends were on my collar bones. I saw the wooden mass of a beam above my face.

"I'm gonna push. Tell me when."

I imagined antennae, legs, webs, and lacy wings in the world around my head. I shuddered with a chill.

"Anh! Ew!" I cried, and turned my head and slapped the dirt, my hands still outside.

Thane was muffled: "*OK!*" He shoved his palms hard on my sneaker soles. The air went dark. The slat-ends scraped my sternum, pulled my t-shirt collar down.

"*Annhh*!" I slapped dirt again.

"*Breathe out*," Thane said, muffled. "'*Pshoo*,'" he mimicked, helpfully.

I breathed out and Thane pushed. The slats scraped my bottom ribs and then I was through to my middle.

Again Thane pushed.

"Anh! Quit it!"

"*You alright?*"

I leaned up on my elbows, my knees still under the slats. I sat up and pulled my feet inside. I stood up in the murk, reached around to brush my back and made a cloud of dust and motes.

I lifted my shirt and saw dim welts from the slats. I smelled peat. Sheets of sun sliced the air through the slats of the barn's far wall. A thing loomed through the murk like a shipwreck.

Whoa, I said.

To myself.

....

Thane squeezed between the barn's wide doors, the cat on tiptoe behind.

"Holy schnikey, that a *Rolls?*"

The car's huge headlamps loomed like spectacles through the tea-colored dark. Its billowy canvas cover lay carelessly beside it.

"It is, holy fuck."

It was green and tall like a bus, long as a train. It had an open-top cab for a top-hatted driver. It had chocks beneath its wheels. We walked around it like it was booby-trapped, a rhinoceros that might gore us.

At long last we touched. We ran our hands along panels and fenders, tapped glasses of windows and lamps. We squeezed tires, paced its long running boards. We fumbled at latches and creaked open a side of the long hood. We inspected handles and dials.

"I've seen this," Thane said, snapping his fingers. "I've seen it at shows."

I knew I had too, at the weekend car shows of summer.

"So that means it runs," Thane said. "Let's take it for a ride."

"Take it *where*?"

Thane jerked his thumb.

"The field. Out back. Who the fuck's gonna know?"

"Since when can you drive?"

"I can drive. My dad lets me drive on his weekends."

"What if she comes back?"

Thane ignored me and climbed in the cab. I stood on the running board and leaned in at the door.

"How come no key?" I said.

Thane played with the choke; gasoline fumes seeped from somewhere. "They didn't have em back then."

"So anyone can just take it?"

"What do *you* think." He pressed a button and the giant car bucked beneath our bodies.

"*Fuck!*" we whinnied, and laughed.

....

"What if she comes back?"

Thane took pause, for once. He squinted up at the rafters.

"You can look out."

I let my eyes follow his up through the dim blocky rafters. The sun glowed around the eaves of the cupola.

"I'm not—"

But Thane was already in action. He gimped up the rough ladder rungs on the wall to the loft, then up a leaning ladder to a narrow ledge around the cupola sides. He braced his hands against the cupola wall and walked up the top rungs. The ladder rails trembled, flexed.

"I can see your *house*!" he said. "There's mine!"

"No you can't—"

"I can. I swear. C'mon!" he said.

Up I went. On the wobbly ladder I hesitated. It was old: gray-brown, dusky wood. Thane bent at the knees and reached his hand to me.

He pulled and I walked up the ladder end. My hands met the wall. He shuffled sideways and gave me room.

Our heels hung in space. I held the windowsill to keep from falling.

"Wow," I said. The glittering green tops of the massive maples rolled away like a cloud bank along the roadside below. I glanced right. The saltbox house, the ell, the shed and the yard looked like models in a diorama.

"*Thought it would be hot,*" I murmured, but a sweet peaty updraft blew, wheezing through louvers above. The window glass was cobwebby yet clean. At each wheeze and draft the cockerel wind vane creaked on its mast above.

"So what's the signal?"

Thane tapped the glass. He glanced left out the window over the hayfields. He reached behind him with one hand, pulled off his t-shirt and put it in my free hand.

"Just put the shirt in the window," he said. "I'll pull it back in. It's quiet, right? Rollses are quiet?"

"So they say."

"So she won't hear. Or I ditch it out back. She can get it herself. I'll get home through the woods or on hitchhike. Fuck me."

He let himself around me on the ledge, stepped on the rung of the lean-to ladder and clambered down to the loft.

"What about the *dust* cloud?" I called after him.

"I don't *care*," he called back. "And don't move," he said up at me from the planks of the loft, gripping the ladder rung in front of him. I saw his hands tighten around it. His shoulders flexed, and he yanked, slapping the ladder top down upon a rafter below. Below me in space.

"Just stay up there," he warned. "I'll go and I'll be right back."

Thane gave me a last look and clambered down the wall to the Rolls. He went back to study its complicated controls.

I looked out; I looked over. Across the hayfields I could see a mile to the wooded side of the town's traprock ridge. I could see the netted fields where we sweated the summer before, the sheds where we and the other tobacco-army kids hung it all up to dry.

The draft rose and ebbed around me like a bellows. The sun slanted in at one side.

Thane tinkered below.

I thought of past predicaments with him. There were slushy adventures on spring ice, a vial of pure sodium lifted from chemistry lab, firecrackers in soda cans. I looked down and met eyes with the cat who twitched its tail on the floor, and I decided this was nothing.

I studied the Rolls's length. I felt calm in its magnetism, its brass-and-nickel put-togetherness, its sheer rightness. I took in its wooden dashboard covered in gadgets and gauges.

It was not a normal car.

Thane, for his part, listened to its internal music, swinging and toggling every pressure switch and lever. *This* one caused a sump to plunge somewhere in the machinery, *that* one the smell of oil to rise all the way up the air to reach my nose. Still others hummed electrically.

Thane got down from the cab. He rolled the barn doors wide. He pulled the chocks from the wheels.

He mounted the driver's bench and pressed the starter. The massive car rolled along on one dud turn of its mighty crankshaft. Its nose poked out the door. The air carried a waft of burnt gasoline. Thane muttered.

"*Wait. I can do it.*" He finagled the clutch. He hit the starter again; no take. He choked it again and dialed the spark a few degrees.

Something made me twitch my head. I glanced out the cupola but there was no Mercedes, no Mrs. Holcomb, no nothing.

The car started. I barely knew it except for the smell of rich exhaust. From my place it sounded almost like nothing, *vsh-vsh-vsh-vsh-vsh-*

Thane sat straight on the driver's bench. He smiled up at me, giving me thumbs-up. He hit the klaxon horn; it vibrated through the barn and me to the very weathervane above. His eyes glittered, and this happened:

The car's gears choked on each other like my dad's table saw the time it hit a hidden reef of nails;

The car lurched from view out the door; it reappeared bounding sideways down shimmering terraces of shrubs and grass, on course for the trees by the road;

A tall wraith was on the sunny lawn behind the saltbox house waving skeleton hands frantically in air; its fierce sunken eyes were damning, accusing; the front of its black robe parted to show a bony rib cage and pelvis from which a surprisingly large and meaty donk swung between stick thighs clad in tight white hose;

From my place I could see Thane's hands, wrists and fingers doing frantic dances in the open-top cab of the Rolls, but the cause was lost; it was like the Hindenburg going down. The car would wreck across the wall like the corny flying machines of early film. So it did: it bounded past the house and its ample ass rose in the air; it collapsed the flat stone wall ahead of its weight and smashed its front corner against a horny maple there by the road

I saw Thane spin sideways through the air in a coma of blood and thick chunks of sparkling glass, *smack* like a ragdoll against the trunk of the tree;

My mouth moved to cry, but my eyes were stuck on the maple's giant canopy gyrating slowly hither and fro. The wraith hobbled at the wreck, its open robe waving behind, its floppy donk heaving the June air and then;

then I heard the tortoiseshell cat chattering at me from the floor of the barn—I saw dark; I felt myself carried away; I fell and now, *now*—

Now my palms are sticky with tobacco sap. My scalp tingles under heat of sultry nets and I'm back picking shade where they don't ask a lot of questions, another pair of hands is always needed, they never heard the words *grief counseling* and the fat green caterpillars have horns but at least their bite is soft.

Secrets

WINTER GRASS

Ramona DeFelice Long

The lock on the gate is rusty and old. Orange flakes float down as Tom slips in the key and opens it. His wife, Marybeth, would fuss at him to get a new one, would say for the umpteenth time that it's ridiculous the way he hangs onto things that are falling apart, and point at the red smear across his palm as proof. But Marybeth has not been back here in a long time, so Tom hangs the open lock onto the loop. He's never seen the sense in throwing away something just because it gets worn down or ugly.

He drags the gate across the crushed oyster shells that top the road to his cattle pastures and walks back to his truck, shells crunching under his boots. He doesn't hurry. The sun is high and the shells are blinding white. Ahead, his barn glows a dull red. Beyond the barn, the shell road is almost luminous as it cuts into the dark green grass he's been growing since late summer.

It's hot. He lets his truck's air conditioning blast onto his face. He doesn't mind the heat, but as he shifts into drive, he thinks that it's a shame it's in the 80s, one day before Christmas. He hopes the church is cool tonight for Midnight Mass. It's bad enough the service will last so long—almost two hours last year—because Marybeth's ankles will swell if she has to sit in the heat for that long. The older they get, the harder it is to get through these holiday services, but convincing Marybeth to miss mass would be like arguing with the sky.

He drives to his barn. The herd has been in the back pasture for two months now so the winter grass can grow. Tom squints ahead but sees no cows. They must be hanging toward the side fence, closer to the canal. Smart, in this heat. People think cows are dumb, but Tom knows better. He's spent his life raising Heifers. He understands them, respects them, more than he understands and respects most humans.

At his barn, he unlocks a newer, bigger lock and slides open the rattling wooden door. He backs the truck inside and sniffs for the musky smell of mice, or the more disturbing smell of cigarettes. He has an intense, almost irrational fear of fire. He can leave the front gate unlocked and wide open, but he'd never do that with the barn. It is full of temptation—his ATV, his boat, cords of barbed wire, racks of tools, his tractor, a couple of shotguns for copperheads. All of that he could stand to lose; it's all insured. But in the corner is an anvil and the old sharpening stone he inherited from his grandfather. A fire taking his valuable farm equipment would hurt, but losing family heirlooms would pain him in a different way.

There's also hay, piled high on one side, stacked there in August by himself and the other cowboys who help each other with the baling. It would piss him off mightily if all his hard work went up because some kid snuck in here to smoke cigarettes or pot.

The back of the barn is cool. He opens the tailgate of his truck, puts on heavy gloves and, with a grunt, lifts a bale of hay and heaves it onto the truck bed. Another grunt and he shoves it as far back as he can. He rests a moment, leaning against the truck. He doesn't feel any strain, but he's seventy-two and takes his time with the strenuous stuff. Not that he has trouble lifting a bale of hay, but there's no rush, and he's not out to impress anybody.

He steps forward and bends over another bale.

"Tom. Hey."

Tom whirls around. He squints at the man walking up alongside his truck.

"Randy," Tom says. "Shit. You almost gave me a heart attack."

Surprise isn't the only reason his heart rate ticks up, but Randy's in jeans and a t-shirt, and through the open barn door, Tom can see a red pickup. Not a sheriff's cruiser, so it's not an official visit. At least he hopes not, anyway.

"Sorry," Randy says. They shake hands. Randy nods at the hay. "You need help?"

Tom pauses a moment before he nods. "Sure. You need gloves?"

"Nah," Randy says. "I'll tough it."

They chuckle awkwardly. Tom bends over the bale again; he grabs the twine on one end and Randy grabs the other. They toss it into the truck and then a couple more. Without being told, Randy hops into the truck bed and shoves the hay forward. He hops down again and they work silently, until Tom says, "Thanks, I think that'll do 'em."

It's only been a couple of minutes but the outside heat has crept in. Randy's face is pink and sheeny with sweat. He removes his ball cap and wipes his forehead.

"Can you believe it's this hot?" he says. "Jackie's been complaining all morning. She bought the girls sweaters to wear to mass. They're gonna roast."

Tom slams the tailgate shut. "How old are your girls now?"

"Christina's seventeen, Robin's thirteen, Missy's eleven."

Tom winces. Hearing those ages aches more than saying his own. "You all going to Midnight Mass?"

"No," Randy says. "We go in the morning. We're going to Mama's tonight to open presents. Then we're at Jackie's folks for Christmas Day, straight after mass."

"We got the whole crew coming here tomorrow morning," Tom says, then mentally corrects himself. *Not the whole crew.* "How's she doing, your mama?"

Randy shrugs. "All right, I guess. Good days, bad days. It's hard. They were together a long time."

"Long as us," Tom says. "Longer. I stood in their wedding, couple of months before ours." He'd been best man for his best friend, and hung over from taking the groom-to-be out for his last night of freedom. Tom had sweated through that wedding as if it was a hot day baling hay. Randy's dad had suffered, too. It had been a miserable wedding, but the marriage had been happy, far as Tom ever knew.

"Fifty-two years," Randy says. "The other day, Mama said it flew by. One minute they were newlyweds, then the kids came, then Daddy was gone, just like that." He snaps his fingers.

Tom winces again, noticing with a pang how much the young man before him resembles his father, but not so young anymore. Randy's hairline has been gone for a while. Now his hair is shaved close, not quite a cue ball, but short, like all the cops and soldiers seem to favor. Tom's own hair is still thick and dark. Mostly. His sons' too. They inherited that from him.

They're good sons, his three boys, just as Randy is to his own family. For a moment, Tom is tempted to tell Randy that he made his father proud, but he holds back. It isn't his style, especially now, guessing why Randy has come here this morning.

The jump of fear he felt before has quieted down, replaced by a drumbeat of dread.

"And what about you and Jackie?" he asks. "Think you two will make it fifty-two years?"

Randy laughs. "We made it twenty so far. I think she can put up with me for another thirty-two." He glances up at the second floor of the barn, empty now except for tools Tom never uses. Randy tips his head at it. "And to think, it all started right here. You remember that?"

"Remember it? Damn, boy, I nearly shot the both of you."

Randy laughs harder. "God, Jackie was so embarrassed. We weren't even doing anything. Not compared to some others."

"Don't remind me," Tom grumbles, and he means it. His barn was the secret lovers' spot for half the high school, and he never knew it until he caught Randy and Jackie making out. Tom had been so busy worrying about his hay, checking for cigarettes between the bales, that he never thought he should have been upstairs, checking for rubbers.

It still rankles. It must show on his face because Randy says, "Hey, I made an honest woman of her."

"That you did," Tom agrees, glad to let it go. He looks Randy up and down. It's a shame he didn't become a cowboy like his dad. It's not like being a deputy is a bad thing, but he's still not a cowboy.

He juts his chin towards the truck. "Thanks for the help," he says, like a dismissal, and he hopes that Randy will walk away, that all this is a stop to wish him Merry Christmas.

"No problem." Randy doesn't move, and Tom knows it is time.

"What is it?" he asks, and holds back a shiver. There is sweat on his neck, but his hands, still in the heavy work gloves, suddenly feel like ice.

"Car wreck," Randy says. "Hit and run. My deputy friend in Mobile recognized Cara's name in the police report, so he called me. He said there was a little piece in their newspaper." Randy says it like a recitation. Blunt. Just the facts.

Tom clenches his fists inside the gloves. "Was she hurt?"

"Minor injuries. She was treated and released at the hospital, same day. That was Monday. She probably just got bumped around some."

Tom breathes in, deeply, inhaling hay along with his relief. She's all right. She's all right.

He'd like to slump against the truck, but he doesn't want to do that in front of Randy. "So, hit and run?" he says. "What does that mean? Jail?"

He doesn't say *again* but he thinks it, thinks of the other times he's had bad news about his granddaughter, on holidays and other days. Drugs. Shoplifting. Running away. Breaking into cars. More times than he can count. Rehabs, therapy, and probation—they've been through it all.

It's been three years since she left. No word, no contact, no messages. The last time she called, it was from jail, to ask for bail money. Tom had listened to his granddaughter begging in one ear and his wife sobbing in the other. And he had said no. That's what his son Dennis, his oldest, told him to do. It was the only hope that she might stop, Dennis said. Giving her money wasn't helping: it was enabling. Tom had never heard that word before, but he heard the desperation in his son's voice. He had no choice, he'd told Marybeth. He couldn't go against Dennis. In the end, it had seemed like the wise thing, because she got a court-ordered rehab. Residential, six months. She was lucky, the public defender said, to get a placement. To everyone's surprise, she stayed in. Did the whole six months, no slip-ups. In the end, Dennis was right about saying no, and Tom was relieved he hadn't gone against him.

But no one had warned him—or any of them—that Cara would disappear. That she'd do her time and get placed in a halfway house to get clean, and then move away and cut herself off from the family.

Three years. Tom knows where she lives, that she has an apartment and a grocery store job. After the first year, without telling anyone in the family, Tom sold a few head of Heifers through a slaughterhouse he didn't generally use and hired a retired cop to locate his granddaughter. Randy had pointed him to the guy, all legal. And then, as luck would have it—Luck? Ha! Whoever thought luck would ever find them when it came to Cara?—Randy happened to know a cop in Mobile. He said he'd give Randy a heads up if he ever saw Cara got into trouble.

And now she had, and here is Randy breaking it to him in his barn on Christmas Eve.

"How bad?" he asks, but Randy shakes his head and says he's sorry.

"No, no, Cara's not in trouble. She got hit. The other car ran a stop sign, t-boned her car and then took off. The only reason my friend called was he saw her name in the newspaper."

Tom needs a moment to process this. Randy waits, as if he understands okay news is almost as difficult to grasp as bad. "So, she's all right? And she's not in trouble?"

"No. None at all. But . . ."

There's always a but. She'll clean up her act, but she'll divorce herself from the family. She's strong-willed enough to kick the drugs, but too stubborn to go back on her last words to him: "I'll never speak to you again! I hate you! I'll never forgive you for this!"

"But what?" he asks Randy.

Randy runs a hand along the side of the truck. "She wasn't by herself. There was a child in the car with her. Her child."

Tom feels his face freeze. It must look alarming because Randy immediately adds, "The baby's all right, too. She's fine."

Tom has to swallow before he can speak. "Cara has a baby?"

"A girl, five months old," Randy tells him. "They're both all right."

They. Cara has a baby girl. His first great grandchild. Now he leans against the truck, letting joy-shock-worry-hurt-surprise-insult-gladness-relief wash over him, rippling over one another so quickly he hardly has a chance to feel one thing before something else replaces it.

He straightens up, clears his throat. "Does Dennis know? About the baby?"

Randy frowns, and begins to say, "I don't—" but Tom holds up a hand to stop him. What a stupid question. How would Randy know what Dennis knows?

"Never mind," Tom says. "Thanks for telling me. Thank your buddy, too."

"Just keeping an eye open," Randy says. "That's all he can do. If we could do more . . ." He shrugs, and lets it die off.

"Thanks," Tom says, again. He removes his gloves. He feels…he doesn't know what he feels. Shock. Relief. Shock again.

Randy is making no move to leave. Tom can't decide if he wants him to go or not. Finally, Tom tosses the gloves onto the dashboard of the truck. "You wanna help me unload that hay? You got time?"

"Time? Are you kidding?" Randy scoffs. "I didn't tell Jackie where I was going, and she's already had two meltdowns about the girls' sweaters and why she always has to be the one to bake the ham. She'll probably go apeshit on me the second I walk in the house."

Tom smiles. The cows are waiting, but they're not going anywhere.

Randy smiles back. "Hell, yeah, I got time. Head 'em up. Move 'em out."

....

There are two fences between the barn and the back end of Tom's property. The first fence is just beyond the barn, to keep the herd from being near his equipment. The second is a quarter mile down the road, closed now to keep the cows out of the new grass while it is still tender and growing. When Tom's sons were little, they took turns climbing out of the truck to open and close the fence gates. Three boys, three gates—worked out perfectly. Every time he drives down this road, Tom pictures his little fellas tugging on the gates. His boys fought like demons in the house, but never in the pasture.

Now they are grown men with their own kids. None of them raise cows. None of his nephews either. After nearly two centuries raising cattle on these same flat pastures, when Tom sells off his last Heifer, the family business will die away.

"That grass looks good," Randy says. "You'll have some happy cows in February."

"Not in February," Tom says, without meaning to. "Tomorrow."

"Tomorrow? Why?"

Tom feels his face grow hot. *Why did I say that?* he thinks, and then just as quickly amends it with, *Who the hell cares?* But he hears the defensive note in his voice when he explains. "I let the herd in on Christmas. Just for the one day."

Randy's eyebrows rise. "Like, as a present?"

"Something like that."

Randy nods, but he turns towards the passenger window and Tom sees the smile playing around the younger man's face.

The truck hits a rut in the shell road and lurches. Randy's hand shoots out to grab the dashboard. Tom curses.

"Sorry," he says. "Time for a new load of shells." Up ahead, the road is pock-marked with puddles that weren't there even two days ago. It looks bad, as if he has been neglectful.

"How many head you got now?" Randy asks.

"Eighty, ninety, thereabouts."

"Not a big herd."

"Big enough to keep me busy," Tom says. "But only over the winter. I don't keep any over the summer anymore, other than a few bulls."

"Daddy did the same thing," Randy says. "I guess you know that. He didn't want to have to worry about the cows during hurricane season." He gazes out of the window as they drive past the small corral where the herd is brought up for shots and branding.

"Man, I remember that spot," he says. "You and Daddy and the other cowboys, on horseback, bringing them up, hollering and whipping to get them in the chutes. Just like in the movies. Exciting to watch if you're a boy."

"You were pretty good on a horse," Tom says. "I know you like being outdoors. You ever thought about getting yourself a few head?"

"Nah," Randy says. "I mean, I thought about it a few times. I'm up for early retirement in five years. I'll barely be fifty. Jackie says I can't retire until I have a second job lined up."

Tom laughs. Randy laughs with him.

"But I never felt the cow love like you and Daddy. They're just dumb beasts, you know?"

"They're not," Tom says, surprised at the rush of emotion that bubbles up inside. Randy should know better. It's like he's speaking ill of his own father.

Tom slows and nods curtly at the windshield. "Get the gate, would you?"

A minute later, Randy's back in the truck, his face red from heat and Tom is sorry.

"Not everybody's meant to be a cowboy," he says. It's the best he can do for an apology, and he's relieved when Randy shrugs.

"I know Daddy was disappointed," Randy says. "It just wasn't my thing. I like working with people."

People. He means criminals, Tom thinks. Silence fills the cab. The sun is glaring off the shells, but in the distance is a black and white blob, the Heifers huddled close near the water.

"I do miss riding horses," Randy says. "Though I guess it's all ATVs now. Cattle prods instead of whips and 'yee-ha's.'"

"That's right," Tom says. He dislikes the cattle prods. "Just like that thing you use now, to shock people. What do you call them?"

"Tasers? Yeah, a Taser's basically the same as a cattle prod."

"I bet your people don't like them anymore than the cows do."

"Nope." Randy suddenly laughs.

"What?" Tom asks. Did he miss a joke?

Randy laughs again and says, "Don't tase me, cowboy."

....

The cows hear the truck. Through the windshield, Tom sees it happen, spots the moment one head raises after catching the sound. The cow turns toward it and lows. In moments, the black and white blob is on the move, *en masse*, lumbering towards the truck. It never fails to thrill Tom, to see them move as one.

"Here they come," Randy says. "You want me in the back?"

Tom hands him the gloves. "Sure. But let me turn around first."

He goes a little farther and then steers and backs up, back and forth, on the narrow road until the truck is aimed back at the front. He idles while Randy climbs in the back and, with a grunt Tom can hear through the open back window, throws a bale onto the ground. It explodes on the listless December grass, hay shooting out sideways and into the air like sunbursts.

Randy knocks twice on the roof and Tom drives slowly forward. He checks the rear-view mirror, sees the cows coming faster, sees Randy's legs, backwards, leaning against the cab. He stops the truck, and Randy throws out another bale. It bursts on impact like the first one.

They do this until the hay is gone. By then, the herd has reached the first bale. Cows cluster around it, but some move on ahead. They know the shell road will be lined with food.

Dumb beasts, Tom thinks. *Ha.*

Randy's shirt is wet at the collar, and the smell of sweat fills the cab when he climbs back into the truck. *It's a man smell, a good smell*, Tom thinks. You can't be a cowboy if you can't handle sweat, and cow shit; piss and blood and the hot scent of placenta during calving; and seared hide during branding. Growing up, Randy smelled all of that, but at his job, he must have smelled worse. Seen worse: drunks and overdoses, bloodied women, beat-up kids. Things Tom doesn't want to think about.

Randy's smiling like a kid after a ball game. He turns around to watch the herd, now splintering into small groups to gather around the bales.

"They knew you were coming," he says.

"They know the sound of my truck coming."

"I hear that. Some of my people know the sound of my car coming, too."

It's a joke, but Tom suddenly feels cold again. Would Cara recognize the sound of a police car coming?

When they get to the first gate, Randy goes out to close it, but the picture that comes to Tom now isn't one of his happy sons, but of his grandchildren on Christmas mornings. He grips the steering wheels as he remembers Cara, his first granddaughter, her hair in a mess of curls, her sweet smile lighting up her face as she ripped wrapping paper off her presents.

It's not my fault, he thinks. *I did what Dennis said we had to do.*

Randy climbs back in. "You said everybody's coming tomorrow?" he asks, eerily almost reading Tom's thoughts. Tom grips a second longer before answering.

"Yup. Fourteen at the table."

"That's a lot of work for Miss Marybeth."

"Yeah, but she loves it. As long as she can stand over the stove, she'll be making Christmas dinner."

He wonders if his grandchildren feel as enthusiastic about the visit. They're growing up, graduating college, moving away. He wonders if any of his sons have to say, *They're getting older, this could be the last time*, to guilt the grandchildren into coming out to the country for the holiday.

Tom suddenly blurts, "It's your first Christmas without your dad," and is sorry when Randy flinches.

"Yeah," Randy says. He opens the truck door even though Tom is not at a complete stop before the next gate.

"I'm sorry," Tom says, soon as Randy's settled back in. "I just meant . . . I'm glad you're going to your mama's tonight. Tell her Merry Christmas for us."

"Sure will," Randy says.

They're back at the barn. Tom pulls alongside Randy's pickup. Randy opens his door, but Tom stops him. He needs to thank him. He wants to say how much he appreciates Randy's help, today and other times, too, but when he puts a hand on the younger man's arm, he can't speak. His throat is closed up, and it's not from heat or hay.

Randy's face is neutral. "I'm sorry I had to do this on Christmas Eve," he says. "I hope I didn't ruin your holiday."

Tom clears his throat. "No, I appreciate you coming out. It's just . . . it was a surprise."

Randy slides out. Heat shoots in through the open door. Randy starts to close it and then opens it up again, hesitating.

Tom leans forward, frowning. "What?"

"It's not my business," Randy says. "You told me not to tell anybody when you were looking for her, and I didn't. Not even Jackie. But I'm just wondering. Did you ever tell Dennis you'd done that?"

"No," Tom says. He knows what Randy will ask next. "I have to tell him now, don't I?"

Randy shrugs. "If it was me, one of my girls, I'd want to know. Definitely about the baby. 'Cause when you have a kid, things change.

You grow up. Cara might want to hear from you now. She just might not want to make the first move."

"Maybe so," Tom says, impressed at Randy's insight. Which he should not be. Randy said it himself, he likes to work with people. A cowboy might not know what makes people change, but a cop would.

"Thanks," he says, and starts to say more, manliness and his usual taciturn ways be damned, but Randy jerks and reaches into his pocket for his cell phone. He grimaces at it.

"I'm dead meat," he says. "Tell everybody hey for me tomorrow, and have a Merry Christmas."

"Will do," Tom says. "And you tell your mama we'll come see her soon. Or come get her to have supper with us. We should do that. It's been too long."

Randy says that would be nice, and then he's gone, holding a hand against the glare until he climbs into his pickup. He waves out the window once and then speeds off.

Tom pulls up to the barn. The door is wide open, gaping, unlocked. He shakes his head, stunned that he forgot to lock it. He can't remember the last time he was so careless.

He slides the barn door shut, locks it. He turns back towards his truck, but keeps going, walking past it, and hops the ditch that runs alongside the road. His knee—the one a cow kicked while in labor—twinges as he lands, but he doesn't stop until he reaches the fence. He leans against it, panting, one elbow resting on the post, while he waits for his heart rate to tick down.

He stares at the dark green grass while his head floods with questions he didn't ask Randy. Not that Randy would know the answers. Is Cara married? Was there a man, her boyfriend or husband, in the car? He'd met one or two of Cara's boyfriends. His hands go cold at the thought of one of those guys with his granddaughter, and a small child.

Barbed wire is stretched across the top of the fence. He grips it with his free hand. Other thoughts come, practical ones mixed with worry. *Does she have enough money? If her car was totaled, will her insurance pay for a new one? What will she do if she can't pay her bills? Is his great-grandchild safe and cared for properly?*

He could help her. He could sell a couple of cows again. Like Randy said, she has a baby now. Maybe she'd take the money if he asked her to, instead of the other way around.

He lets go of the fence. No. He has to tell Dennis. It seems cruel to break it on Christmas, to his boy who has already suffered so much, but how can he not?

A breeze blows across the pasture. The grass gently undulates and then settles back into stillness. Tom watches. It is so beautiful, it hurts to see it, the same way it hurts to remember Cara as a happy child on Christmas morning.

Three years. *How much longer*, he wonders. *How much longer will she make them wait?*

He pulls away from the fence, walks back to the gate and opens it. He crunches along the shell road for a few feet and then wades into the grass as if he's walking into the gentle waves of the Gulf. Under his boots, the ground feels soft. The sun is glaring, but the grass is so soft and lush that he can feel it tearing beneath his boots.

He walks parallel to the road, going too fast, He is old and it is hot and his blood is hammering in his ears, but he reaches the next gate and opens that one, too.

The herd is still eating hay. They're not dumb, but they have food right in front of them, so they won't seek more when they already have plenty.

He cups his hands to his mouth and calls, "Ya! Ya!"

A head raises at the call. Tom calls again and more heads turn, and then they move, just as they did when they heard his truck. He calls until his throat hurts and they get closer, not fast, not panicky, just lumbering along because he called them.

He walks to the corner of the fence. He bends, knees soft like he's ready to haul up a bale, and grabs a fistful of grass. He yanks it out and runs his fingers through it The grass is bright, soft, and cool. Unspoiled and nourishing.

He leans against the fencepost, feeling old and worn. He holds the grass in his hand, squints against the sun, and waits for his cows.

THE OWLS OF EL CENTRO

William Burtch

The father of the boy recalled his childhood neighbor, Bustone, a durable old brickyard laborer who crossed up corn liquor with a shotgun one fevered night. Bustone's judgmentally inclined spouse, Francine, blasted point blank into a frigid mist. Her last words uttered in her native Italian. She was soon joined by what had been a good rabbit dog.

Colder and stiffer than the bars that had contained him, Bustone was dragged decades later from his dank cell in the bowels of the penitentiary. Discarded like a moldy furnace filter. Shriveled to a translucent shell, held intact by a patchwork of scars and scabs.

Informed by this cautionary recollection, the father of the boy smuggled no booze to this desert hunting outpost. Brought no temptation. Only the shotgun his son had borrowed for him. He could last it out with the bottled water in the Styrofoam cooler for a night and a day. Just his son and him.

The landscape they faced was otherworldly with rattlesnakes and tarantulas lolling and crawling about, leaving odd telltale trails in the sand. The Imperial Valley was a parched and near endless expanse of California wasteland in 1973, hemmed in by the Colorado River to the east and the San Andreas Fault to the west. The Colorado sprang forth in the upper passes of the Southern Rockies but, after quenching the thirsty irrigation ditches of this California desert valley, it became a trickle if it reached the Sea of Cortez at all. The son's appreciation for this terrain, and all strains of the natural world, belied his thirteen years. Rivers, to the boy, were the great sculptors of the earth, chiseling works such as the Missouri Breaks and the boulder formations of the lower Susquehanna. But he was affected most by the Colorado's magnum opus, the grandest canyon of them all.

In hours the sun would rise and resume scolding the baked desert and the checkerboard produce fields that defied nature. Brilliant tapestries of green, edges shaped to perfection, and laughably out of place. The boy knew his father did not want to be in this desert valley. Knew he would rather have been home in his den, comfortable, in the place that only his gin, that warm seductress he had hidden all about the house, could transport him.

This was the boy's first dove hunt. He had beseeched his father to partake, but it was a trepid curiosity more than anything that had brought the old man into the fold. They had arrived from L.A. in the family's now sand-covered station wagon, backing the wood paneled beast into a remote pocket of gnarled brush. Creosote and mesquite. A few hard miles outside of El Centro, after the sun had long set. Other reveling dove hunting camps in the near distance could be heard jostling about, laughing and whooping in anticipation of the morning's hunt.

The backseat was folded down and sleeping bags were unfurled in the station wagon cargo space. Both of them were flat on their backs, on top of their bags. They sweated and they stank and they stared at the unlit dome light as the coyotes chorused in concert harmony. Neither had ever shot a game bird. The boy had an intrepid attraction to adventure, which repelled his equally unadventurous father. The iterative consequences of the old man's gin thirst wedged them yet further apart. The son shielded his few friends from the binge drinking spectacles and the family's innate and ceaseless chaos. Kept the whole mess guarded as best he could. He did not wish to display his family as a carnival exhibit, or the tangled and complicated mash-up of dependencies and secrets that it was.

Like a bloodhound, the boy sampled the air for gin, which he did not detect. He saw the whites of his dad's eyes as he stared, preoccupied, at the ceiling of the station wagon. He'd seen that look before, during the San Fernando earthquake two years prior. A jarring and traumatic early morning awakening. The boy had staggered, as though tossed in a storm at sea, to his bedroom door frame and remained there until the jolting subsided, all the while screaming out to his family. He then advanced down the hallway and checked on his sister who was crying in shock. When he reached his parents' bedroom at the end of the hallway his mother was hysterical and scrambling out of bed. With both hands his father grasped the covers over his face except for his eyes which were terrified. That was the moment the boy knew his father was not a protector. That he lacked that paternal gene code. Such were the eyes he saw in the back of the station wagon, parked there in the desert, hidden by the brush.

Neither had yet achieved a true sleep state in the car.

"Jesus Christ it's hot," the father said as it closed in on midnight.

"Yeah. I guess."

"I thought the desert was supposed to cool off at night."

"I think it did. A little, maybe."

"What, to ninety seven from a hundred and two? Christ."

The boy smiled. "I can't think of anything but sunrise. Shooting birds. Too excited to sleep," the boy said.

The father only mumbled.

"Maybe you'll get some doves, Dad. Mom could cook them up. I can get a recipe."

"I'm telling you I can hardly breathe. Goddamn. I don't know about this," the father resumed.

"It's stuffy," the boy agreed.

"Can you reach a bottle of water for me?" the father ordered more than asked.

The boy stretched to reach the cooler at their feet. He popped the lid open and retrieved two bottles of water, handing his father one and twisting open the other. In silence they both splashed the cool contents down the backs of their parched throats. His father farted. They both chuckled.

"I know there are some motels out on the highway. With air conditioners," the father said. His eyebrows were raised.

"I think I can make it here okay."

"A motel room won't make any sense in another hour or two. So we should decide now."

"I think I can make it."

"I'm not sure I can. I'm soaked in sweat. This goddamn car. It's like a pizza oven."

Just then there were two distinct and sharp avian hoots in the thick darkness about twenty yards from the car. The boy sat up on his elbows.

"Did you hear that?" he asked.

"Owl."

"Owl?"

"I read about them in the *L.A. Times*. Burrowing owls. Native to the Imperial Valley. Sleep in holes in the ground. Old holes of other animals. Won't dig them themselves."

The boy thought all of this through in the darkness.

"They've got long funny goddamn legs. Can run like hell or fly, day or night," the father went on.

"Really?"

"They act all silly one minute then hiss like a rattlesnake the next."

"Hiss?"

"They hoot and they hiss. They can imitate a rattlesnake when they're pissed off."

"Burrowing owls?"

"Maybe the article was just blowing smoke. But that's what it said. Shit, I've made up our minds. We need to find a motel room," the father said.

The boy was too hot and keyed up to argue. They scrambled out the back of the station wagon and climbed into the front seat. In the distance all about them they could see faint flickers of campfires.

"Why in the hell would they have fires, for Christ's sake?" the father asked as he turned the ignition.

"Maybe they cooked something."

"Too goddamn hot to cook."

"They gotta eat."

"That's why we have Burger King."

After bouncing a mile or so on the desert access road, driving only by the light of a slim crescent moon, they reached the highway. The father popped the headlights on. They could see the hazy golden glow of El Centro's business district ahead. The car air conditioner pierced them with what felt like tiny shards of ice, and their sweat soon evaporated, leaving white salt streaks on their skin like maps.

"A nice shower then cool sleep," the old man sighed.

The boy said nothing.

After another mile a motel sign lit the night. *No Vacancy* flashed in tacky purple neon. Pickup trucks were lined up in front of every room of the motel. A few shadowy figures leaned against the truck beds, smoking and talking.

The father said nothing and drove on.

Just outside of El Centro another electric motel sign appeared but the neon flickered in a frenetic state of disrepair, the vacancy status a mystery. The father guided the car onto the gravel lot and parked, leaving the engine running.

"Stay here with the guns and everything until I get us checked in," he said.

The boy watched his father enter the small adobe office where he saw an old gray Mexican man behind the counter. Soon the Mexican shook his head, then laughed and waved his arms. His father turned and scowled as he approached the car.

"*No hay vacantes, Señor*," his father mockingly parroted the motel keeper. "No vacancy. Shit. Said we wouldn't find a room between Coachella and Mexicali. Opening day of dove season tomorrow. Hunters crawling out of the goddamn cracks."

The boy just looked at him.

"What do you want to do?" the father asked.

"If we go back to L.A. now it will be daylight by the time we get home. No sleep," the boy said.

"But we would be in an air conditioned car."

"I know."

The boy gazed at the bright sliver of the early September moon, still a couple of weeks from the Harvest Moon and the equinox. He rubbed his eyes and avoided looking at his father.

"What do you think?" the father asked.

His son lowered his head.

"Dad, I'm sorry I brought you out here. You could be home in a cool bed instead of soaked in sweat."

The father said nothing.

"But I'd like to hunt a little bit in the morning, I guess," the boy said. "I mean we drove all the way down here. Bought the shotgun shells and all. Mom packed the coolers. Won't be long before the sun starts to rise. The doves will be flying."

The father held the wheel and looked back into the motel office window at the old gray Mexican. He gripped the wheel to hide his shakes.

"We'll try to find that spot again and park the car," he said.

They retraced their path back to the desert access road and bounced along until they managed to find the same spot they had occupied before. The station wagon was again backed in between the creosote bushes. They stretched out on to their backs on top of the sleeping bags and stared again at the dome light. The boy rummaged two more water bottles from the cooler. They each held them to their faces and let the condensation crawl down their cheeks. Silently they waited on the sun.

....

What woke them was not the sun. What woke them were shotgun blasts. Shotgun blasts that soon rained thousands of shot pellets onto the desert floor all around them.

The doves were flying.

Without speaking, both scrambled out of the back of the wagon's lift gate. The boy threw on his hunting vest and cap and unsheathed his pump shotgun. His father walked to the edge of the brush to urinate. His eyes were alert as he searched for snakes and then scanned the horizon. It was still more dark than light.

"How the hell are they even seeing to shoot?" the father asked.

"Look for motion in the sky," the boy replied as he loaded shot shells into his gun. "They fly fast."

"Can you get my gun ready while I piss?" the father asked.

The boy reached for his father's shotgun case and unzipped it. He got his father's vest ready and loaded the twenty-gauge pump-gun with number eight shot. Made sure the safety was on and put a few extra shells in the vest.

"Which way should we go?" the father asked, looking to the sky.

After handing his father the vest and shotgun, the boy looked around, his adrenaline surging.

"Let's cut through those bushes and see if there is a good spot to wait. We don't want the doves to see us standing here or they'll swerve around us."

"Let's not hide so fucking good that the other hunters don't see us."

They pushed their way through the scrubby brush. Critters of the desert floor darted about. Dead greasewood and mesquite snapped under their boots. Both were already scraped and bleeding but they pressed ahead.

It was just as they broke through the final snarls of tangled bramble, the sun still a blip on the horizon, when the whirl of wings burst forth, shattering the stillness. The bird materialized as a strumming silhouette against the charcoal sky, loud and frantic.

The boy, stunned, witnessed the fluidity with which his father shouldered his shotgun, released the safety and swung to a lead just ahead of the bird. Then shot. A curt thump of lead shot slamming feather and flesh. Feathers that then showered down as if so many dried maple leaves were blowing in an autumn wind. The lifeless thud of the bird on the hard packed desert floor, like a sack of flour dropped on the kitchen tile. But what was seared into the deepest crevices in the boy's mind was his father's face. He saw an expectant plea for approval in his father's eyes. For *his* approval. For the approval of his long dead forebears and of other souls for which the son had no frame of reference.

"Son-of-a-bitch," the father yelled. "Son-of-a-bitch. I got him."

The boy flailed for his father in an attempt at a supportive pat or some kind of awkward arm hug, but he missed.

"I'll get him, Dad. Let me get him. Open up the game pouch in your vest. Keep it open. There's gonna be more. I have a feeling there's gonna be a lot more."

With his gun pointed to the ground, the son almost skipped out to the barren sand upon which the bird rested, as still as a rail spike. As he got within five feet of the bird he slowed. He then stopped mid-stride. Holding his breath, he absorbed the scene, the lifeless bundle of feathers and beak. The tiny crimson blood pools that specked the sand.

"Bring him here," the father yelled from over the boy's shoulder.

The boy remained frozen in place. Quiet. With the butt of his shotgun he then rolled the bird over. Staring back at him were not the black shiny ovate eyes of a dove. Staring back were round eyes. Round and dead as marbles. The eyes of an owl. Yellow and still and lifeless, meeting the boy's gaze in a suspended state of horrified shock.

"What's the matter?" the father asked, ceding to confusion.

The boy was struck by the latent morbidity of sobriety in his father's face.

"Christ, what's the matter?" the father asked as he approached his son. Then he spotted the owl's eyes. The first rays of the young morning sun falling across the face of the bird, which looked to be alone in its tragic predicament, solitary in the world. A spectacle.

"Oh Jesus Christ," the father said.

The boy stopped a dry heave mid-throat.

"Oh shit an owl. Oh Christ I'm sick," the father coughed.

"It's okay Dad. Dad, don't get upset."

They stood motionless. The father looked at his son with an expectant scowl.

"We need to hide the bastard," the father blurted. "It's a goddamn five hundred dollar fine."

With his boot the son nudged the bird, this burrowing owl of the Imperial Valley. Then he nudged several more times, until it was situated under the scraggy brush. Dropping to his knees he used his bare hands to rifle into the ancient desert earth, throwing sand scattershot. When an adequate hole emerged, he lowered his eyes and beheld the owl. There was brief stillness. He then placed the bird into the hole and covered it, patting down the fresh mound. He scattered dried greasewood and tumbleweed remnants over the spot. All vestiges of the fallen owl were then gone, save for what will remain forever in their shared memory.

The boy would not speak. The father held his shotgun as though it were a baby with a loaded diaper. The boy took the weapon from him. The father stood motionless.

Overhead the doves darted, as fast as arrows, through the now brilliant desert sky. Shots rang. Then more blasts. Jarring the stillness around the boy and his father was a torrent of shot pellets kicking up tiny explosions of sand where they struck.

"Christ a few of those just hit me!" the father yelled. He searched all over his arms as if stung by a swarm of bees.

The boy looked at his father. Round terrified orbs peered back at him. The boy thought of the youthful joy he had witnessed in his father. Fleeting and precious.

"I'm sorry Dad," he almost said. "Sorry to subject you to any of this. To my life at all."

But he did not speak those words. He lifted his face as if to feel the sun.

There was a familiar nothingness. A reversion to the boy's mean. A comfortable vacancy of the senses near entire.

Only the now abstract pops of the dove guns of El Centro.

....

The coyote shivered as it emerged from the brush. It stopped as if it heard something but there was nothing. It sniffed the night air up high, and then lowered its nose to the dry desert floor. Its ears were giant, and its fur was matted in spots and sparse in others. A kind of irascible imp of the wastelands. A complete, if crude, chronical of the desert's indifference to all things living.

In a lanky gait the coyote approached the dried blood droplets of the owl, at the point where its lifeless body had slammed into the earth. It was dark at this late hour, but the sliver of the moon coaxed the droplets to glisten. After a thorough sniffing of the area, the animal tasted a blood droplet, raising its head to the sky, as though to howl.

But it remained quiet. Nose back to the ground, it advanced its investigation along the path upon which the dead owl had been nudged by the boy's boot.

The small and still fresh mound then rose up as if in an offering to the nose of the coyote. The sparse spattering of dried twigs that had been placed upon the mound was not a foil, and only for a moment did it confuse the animal. The human scent. It again looked to the sky as if in search, and it panted. Seeing nothing, it dropped its head and resumed sniffing the mound with a now ravenous eagerness.

When the razor talons ripped into the shoulder of the coyote it released a pathetic yelp. By instinct it flipped to its back and bore its teeth to defend. To fight for its life. Blood had been drawn. The coyote soon determined the identity of its adversary in the darkness. Its attacker was circling in the sky, streaking past the blue glow of the moon.

Again, it entered into a dive, talons splayed, its wild eyes yellow and furious.

MAGICIAN

Rosanna Staffa

Her father had a tight smile as he stood in the doorway on a Sunday morning, new glasses and hair cut so short that his ears stuck out. It had been months since the divorce. He stood in the pale sun, wearing the scarf and gray coat she remembered but somehow seeming different. She wondered if entering the house could change that, and he would become his old self amidst the familiar clutter. But he waited for her at the door, his hands in his pockets.

One time walking down the street Biba had seen a man who looked like her father. She followed him around Park Slope, but after a few blocks noticed that he walked differently and was too young. She turned back, but at home she told her mother that she had seen him. For a moment, she had.

Her father had arrived by subway but they took a taxi into the city. Against the light of the window, he looked like a sketch of the father she had been imagining, with a lightness to him that was unsettling. She wondered if there was a link between the way people appeared and their wish to be seen or unseen.

They had lunch at a diner where they used white paper tablecloths you could draw on. They sat there for the longest time, eating a burger with fries and drawing with crayons. Cats, a tiny moon. They did not say much. Biba wanted to have good stories to tell him and thought about it, but fourth grade was boring. It seemed like they were waiting for the waiter to tell them that they were done and could go.

At school she had worked for days on a secret card for him that she ended up misplacing. It said that she wanted to live with him: her mother talked too much, she was too sad, rustling about the house like a restless bird.

"What do you want to do?" her father asked Biba when they left the restaurant.

"I want to become a magician," she said. She liked that magicians were so graceful but had the upsetting ability of making things appear and disappear, rendering nothing and something interchangeable.

"I mean today, now," her father said.

"Of course. Teasing you," she lied.

They walked to Chinatown and went to the back of an old store with faded Buddha posters, into a room with a low ceiling where a chicken paced in its cage. A dirty light came from a tiny window. Her father put two quarters in a slot to start the music, and the chicken danced, taking steps back and forth until the song ended. She told her father that she liked it; he had always been pleased to witness her wonder at something he had come up with.

"I want to go to the zoo," Biba said, as there was a familiarity to animals, a silliness even.

They both used to scream in fright at the bat cage and burst out laughing. Both her fear and attraction were not pretend.

They went to the zoo. The monkeys were inside, the bears were outside; their fur had yellow tufts sticking out. Her father was shivering, his hands in his pockets. Again she wasn't sure what they were waiting for. He just lowered his head and sang under his breath, the way he used to in the shower.

She started to wonder how it would all end. When her mother read to her she refused to let Biba guess how it finished, as she thought it ruined everything. On the contrary, Biba was relieved by endings, as then a different story could start. She liked very much the crescendo of a narrative gearing up to its conclusion, like a noise of traffic swelling in the distance, and still utterly surprising when it appeared.

"Biba," her father said, "do you want to see my place?"

She had no memory of him leaving and taking things with him; it had happened when she was not at home. The event felt dramatic but somehow illegible, as something written in a foreign language nobody spoke well.

"Sure," she said.

She was puzzled, but knew from her books that the good part always started with an unexpected event.

....

They took a bus. She kissed her own lips in the reflection of the window, a thing her mother forbade. Her father kept looking outside, saying nothing.

They walked to a little apartment in a building with no elevator. The entrance was freshly painted and inviting. Her father's place was at the ground floor and it had only sparse furniture, an odd assortment that created the impression the space was still practicing being a home. The breakfast things had been left on the table: a bowl, a spoon, a box of cereal. There was nothing on the walls, but a few framed paintings she recognized were leaning against a tall bookcase, where only two shelves were filled. The space suggested a kind of loss of heart in the person who lived there, a hesitation in carrying through something started.

"What do you think?" her father said.

"It's nice," Biba said.

She told him that she was a bit hungry, even if it wasn't true, and he found a bag of peanuts. She expected an apple. At home for a snack he used to peel one for her in one long strip she could play with. She loved the handling of such a delicate thing without breaking it, while he watched with his chin resting on his palm. Her father always used to have a gentle interrogation in his eyes, and even his body emanated a soft, receiving quality. One evening she had asked him if the spirit left the body at night and floated about, like a boy told her at school. He waited a while and then said 'That would be tempting.' And she stopped worrying about it.

The phone rang.

"Would you like to meet my daughter?" her father asked the caller. Then he sat on the sofabed and looked outside. His hand was clasping the armrest.

"You'll meet a friend of mine, Biba," he said. "We're good friends." He stood up and paced. Then he sat at the table across from her while she still held the peanuts untouched. "It'll be nice."

She said, "Okay."

The stories she liked best picked up with a wish, the appearance of a special object, the clicking of a door.

Her father put some coffee on. He placed the dirty bowl and spoon in the sink, attentive, like when he helped her put her bear to bed. They waited. He drank coffee looking outside.

"My friend might not come at all. Is that okay?" He stood up and paced.

"It's okay," she said.

The first night her father had not come home, she heard her mother walk incessantly, with a ferocity in her steps she only had when late to work, determined to shove people out of the way if necessary.

"How's school?" her father asked.

"Fine."

"Do you like science? I liked it."

"I don't have science yet."

"Oh, you don't."

She knew what he was going to do. He always did it when he didn't know what to say after making a silly mistake. He was going to tickle her. She giggled.

"What's funny?" he asked. They waited some more.

Her thoughts went to her mother, probably practicing yoga on her blue carpet at this very time by the large window in the living room. At the end her mother relaxed in the final pose, *Shivassana*, enacting one's death, lying flat on the back, arms open. She explained to Biba that her thoughts were little waves of nothing then. She motioned with her hands, fingers fluttering. During *Shivassana* everything vanished, for a bit anyway.

....

Her father's friend had the key. He walked in with fast steps, his large eyes curious. He had a schoolboy's haircut and long legs. He carried a small paper package and a folded newspaper.

"My, oh my," he said showing tiny teeth in a quick smile. "Here's your little girl." He looked at her father saying it, and he blushed. The friend put the little package on the table, took croissants out of it. "I hope these work."

"Of course . . . thank you . . ." her father said.

"My name is Oliver," the friend said, leaning in very close to Biba. His lips were small and full, like a doll's. "What's your name?"

"Biba," said her father. He came close too. He seemed nervous.

"Biba," she repeated to Oliver's face. He smiled. He had fine lines at the corner of his eyes.

"Biba, would you like a croissant?" he asked.

"Yes," she said.

"I woke up in a foul mood," Oliver said to her father. "I had to call. I was hoping you would be back already."

"We just got here."

"My sister is moving to town," Oliver said. He threw his coat on a chair. "Come on."

"She has talked to my mother about it. The whole family agrees." Oliver put the croissant on a plate. He set the plate on the table. There was a familiarity to both gestures. "Is there any coffee?"

Her father was very calm now.

"Sure." His hands went from cup to cup in the cupboard before choosing the right one.

He poured coffee for his friend.

"Thank you," Oliver said.

Her father looked at her. His eyes were warm. "Biba, would you like anything else?" he asked.

"Oh, no," she said, "thank you." She felt like being real polite. "Thanks so much."

Everybody seemed to do better. Oliver said something in a whisper; her father had to lean over the table to hear.

"I have no patience left," Oliver said, a little louder.

Her father took his wrist; held it. It looked like he was feeling Oliver's pulse to see if he had a fever, and Biba felt sorry for him. They stood perfectly still, her father feeling Oliver's pulse, Oliver looking at his cup, seemingly worried about his temperature.

"Let's get out of here," Oliver said.

They both stood without looking at each other. Her father handed Oliver his coat. He tried to help Biba put her's on, but she did it herself. They all walked out in the street with their hands in their pockets.

"I'm sorry," said Oliver. "I shouldn't have come."

"You did the right thing," her father said.

They stopped to look at the window of a toy store. "What would you like?" Oliver asked.

Her father was standing with his hands in his pockets, watching. "Nothing," she said. "Thank you, Oliver."

He laughed.

"The pink elephant, maybe? It's a beautiful elephant. Yes?" He had noticed how she looked at it.

He took her hand and walked firmly into the toy store. Her father followed them slowly. "Oliver . . ." he said.

"We would like the pink elephant," Oliver said. "Don't wrap it. Thank you." He looked at her father. "Do you like it?"

"Oh, I don't know." Her father held the elephant, "It's cute."

"It's beautiful," said Oliver.

They walked outside and to the park. They stopped at the merry-go-round. It was closed, and covered with tarp. Oliver took her father's scarf and wrapped it around his neck. They looked at each other. Oliver smiled, balancing himself on one foot, then the other.

A few sparrows hovered briefly around their heads, then took off. Pigeons floated down, possibly expecting food. The pink elephant had a surprising weight, but there was something cozy in feeling it in her arms with such total, if stolid, abandon.

Her father looked around in silence, then up at the sky. Something disturbing seemed to be on his mind. She hoped he would not tear up or do something strange like her mother now often did around this time of the day.

The wind died down. There was an intensity to her father's stare on her, and she sensed the budding of some kind of request. She did not want him to propose dinner together or anything like that.

In the stories her mother read to her a conclusion was expected as a resolution was reached. The person who had taken charge of the moment usually said something pleasant to that purpose. The stories varied in tone and intention, but this never changed. Biba shifted the pink elephant slightly to find a more erect posture.

"I had a very nice time," she said to her father. "Thank you. It's time for me to go home." Her tone was warm but formal. It had finality.

Every evening at home, when the end of a story was reached, it was Biba's task to close the book and put it on the shelf. She always did it with a swift decisiveness her mother admired.

THE SHABBOS GOY

Kathleen Ford

1953

My uniform jumper smelled like dried sweat and my blouse didn't smell good either. After yanking off my bowtie and blouse, I saw that the armpits were yellow and the Peter Pan collar was gray. Well, there were only two more weeks of school and next year I'd be done with the jumper and the stupid clip-on bowtie that looked like a dead bird was stuck to my collar. In seventh grade I'd wear a pleated skirt, and my blouse would have a pointed collar instead of a round one. Besides, Uncle Jimmy said by next September every Catholic school girl would be wearing a new sort of blouse that was made with a special fabric called Dacron that you didn't have to iron.

My sister and I were the models for the blouses Uncle Jimmy said would make him a millionaire. My uncle paid the Chinese tailor to make four sample blouses and every Saturday for two months Ellie and I modeled them in different parishes. In rectories and principals' offices we stood as straight as hat stands while Uncle Jimmy took the "demonstration items" out of his case. The items were: a small wash basin, a jar of water, a cork-topped bottle of liquid soap, two clothes hangers, two small cloth towels, and a paper bag. After pulling the blouses from the bag, he gave them a shake. The small Peter Pan-collared blouse was like the one Ellie was wearing. The pointed-collared blouse was like the one I wore.

While the priest or the principal watched from behind a desk, Uncle Jimmy took an egg timer from his pocket and spread the towels on the floor in front of us. Then he swished the soap in the water and twirled the blouses around in the basin. After counting to five, he took the first blouse from the water, squeezed it over the basin, and hung it on the hanger that he gave to Ellie. He did the same with the bigger blouse. We stood perfectly still holding the hangers above the towels as Uncle Jimmy turned over the egg timer on the desk. Then he started talking about cleanliness being next to godliness and how Dacron blouses could be washed every night. Best of all, he said, they needed no ironing.

Uncle Jimmy said that if he talked for fifteen minutes the blouses would be dry enough to give the parish priests and the school principals the idea. If the priest or the sister wasn't restless, he'd talk for longer and the blouses would be dry.

After Uncle Jimmy packed up his demonstration items into the sales case he slid a holy card of the Sacred Heart onto the desk along with one of his business cards. He told the priests and the principals that the diocese would be accepting recommendations for new uniforms by the end of the school year, and that his company—James K. McGuire Uniforms—was in a perfect position to provide blouses to all the grades. If orders were placed by the end of June, his no- iron, wrinkle-free blouses could be ready by the Feast of the Assumption on August 15th.

....

I kicked the smelly jumper under the bed and pulled last summer's pedal pushers from the dresser drawer. Tonight, it wouldn't get dark until eight-thirty-three, which meant that if Nana would let me leave right after dinner, I'd have more than an hour to visit with Mrs. Levy before I turned on her lights and went home. I took the bracelet Mrs. Levy had given me out of the box under my bed. It was a circle of blue and white beads on an elastic string, and when the old lady gave it to me she said it was just a "tchotchke" one of her daughters had bought ages ago at the Beth Sholem Bazaar. The bracelet wasn't any different from the bracelets Ellie made with the beads she got last Christmas, but even if it wasn't fancy or valuable, I liked it.

After sliding it onto my wrist I looked for hair. My arms and legs had been getting a lot hairier lately, and there were hairs growing on my cheeks too. I snapped the bracelet before taking it off and shoving it in my pocket. I didn't want Nana or Ellie to see it—not because I had secrets with Mrs. Levy like I did with Uncle Jimmy—but because I wanted to keep her to myself. I loved having a grown-up job that no one else had anything to do with, and even though Nana knew I went to Mrs. Levy's house on Friday evenings, she didn't know more than that. She'd never met Mrs. Levy, or Mrs. Levy's daughter, who paid me fifty cents to turn on the lights for the Sabbath. And though Nana had spoken to Mrs. Levy's daughter twice, those conversations had been on the phone when Mrs. Singer called to remind me what time sundown was. Both times, when she called, I already knew when the sun set. The third time she called I told her I'd made my own sundown chart and that I'd glued it into my notebook.

....

I met Mrs. Singer in early March, when she stopped me on my way home from school. She asked where I lived and where I went to school, and when I told her I was a sixth grader at Our Lady of Good Counsel and that I lived around the block, she asked if I wanted a once-a-week job helping an old lady. I said "yes" right away.

"My mother lives in this house," Mrs. Singer said, pointing to the dark green clapboard that stood at the top of four concrete steps. Another house, exactly like it, was next door; then came a skinny alley. The whole street was packed with twin houses sitting side by side. Each pair was painted in green, brown, or gray. I'd been walking to school since starting at Good Counsel but just then I realized how strange it was that all the houses were painted in matching sets.

I left my books on the steps and followed Mrs. Singer to the rusted metal chairs on the porch. "I don't know if you know anything about the Jewish Sabbath," she said, "but it starts when the sun goes down on Friday, and lasts until the sun goes down on Saturday." Her shiny eyebrows looked like they'd been brushed with oil and when they rose to her forehead I smoothed out my own brows with my finger. Like my arms and legs, my eyebrows were definitely getting hairier. Last month when I plucked three hairs in the space above my nose, my face turned red and my eyes watered for half an hour.

"Jews are forbidden from turning on lights during the Sabbath," she said.

I nodded so it would look like I knew what she was talking about, but the only time I ever said the word "Sabbath" was when I recited the commandments, and I didn't know anything about Saturdays or turning on lights. Still, as Mrs. Singer rattled on about what people could and couldn't do on Saturday, I remembered Nana telling me and Ellie that we shouldn't run around like wild Indians on Sunday. I also remembered a Sunday last spring when Nana looked out the window and clucked her tongue because Mrs. Amato, our backyard neighbor, was beating her rugs.

I knew Jewish people went to a synagogue instead of a church, and that they bought their meat at Katz's Butcher Shop which had Hebrew writing on the window. I also knew that Jewish boys studied Hebrew, and when Sister Mary Alberta told the class that Jewish people had a great respect for education, I thought about those boys dragging their book bags to the Union Street synagogue every afternoon when regular school let out. Sometimes they pushed one another onto the dirt strip next to the sidewalk which made the passing cars honk like crazy.

I knew Jesus was Jewish. I knew Abraham was Jewish and that he talked to God. Abraham was going to kill his son Isaac because he thought that's what God wanted him to do, but when God saw that he was really going to do it, He sent an angel to stop him. Anyway, even though I didn't know much about Abraham, I knew he'd lived before Jesus, and that when Jesus came along the Jews didn't accept Him as God.

Catholics believed that Jesus was God. We believed He was as much God as God the Father, and as much God as God the Holy Ghost. And even though when you said they were all God, and that there were three of them, you couldn't believe there were three gods. God the Father, Jesus, and the Holy Ghost were "Persons," and the catechism said there were three "Persons" in one God. It was a mystery—the Mystery of the Trinity—and if you were Catholic you had to believe it. Anyway, Jews didn't believe it, so they didn't become Catholic.

Some Protestants believed in the Holy Trinity and some didn't, but the important thing to remember was that the Protestants got started with Martin Luther, a heretic, who disobeyed the pope and began his own religion. A number of other people also broke away from the Catholic Church, and they were called Protestants because they "protested" the original church which the catechism said was "the one, holy, catholic and apostolic church."

I'd been taking catechism classes since second grade, and for the past three years I'd won the end-of-year prize for best religion student. Next year, I'd make my Confirmation and become a Soldier of Christ. As a Soldier of Christ, I'd need to know my religion so well that I could stand up and fight for it if I had to. Sister said the public school kids who took catechism classes on Wednesday nights probably wouldn't learn enough to be confirmed, but I was jealous of them anyway. They got to go to junior high when we had to stay in the same school for another two years. But it wasn't just having two more years of elementary school that made me jealous. I was jealous of the pale brick building that sprawled on top of Tremont Hill. In certain lights it looked like a yellow sheet cake, and sometimes it had little sparkles in it. What's more, the school had tennis courts, a running track and big playing fields on its lower sides. I'd heard it also had an indoor swimming pool.

I didn't know anyone who went to public school, but Bernadette Flynn, my classmate at Good Counsel, said that all the girls in her ballet class were from public school. When I asked Nana if I could take ballet with Bernadette, she said she'd ask Uncle Jimmy for the money after I finished eighth grade. But it would be too late by then. Bernadette told me you had to take lessons for six years before you could dance on your toes like a real ballerina.

....

While Mrs. Singer and I sat on the porch a foggy darkness drifted up from the street. "What would happen if your mother *did* turn on the lights?" I asked.

"Nothing horrible would happen, but I know she'd feel bad about it."

I felt bad about copying Patricia's homework and signing Nana's name to school papers but I did it anyway. "Couldn't she put the lights on before the sun goes down and leave them on the whole time?"

"She doesn't want to waste electricity, and she forgets which lights to leave on so she's got lights blazing and then she can't sleep. I told her to leave the bathroom light on and keep the door to her bedroom open, but with only the bathroom light it's too dark for her to see where she's going. She needs the closet and the hall lights too so she can get herself into bed."

Nana didn't let me and Ellie keep the hall light on, so when she left the room we'd pull up the shades and watch the car lights zip along the walls. The lights whizzed on my wall before traveling to Ellie's, and if I slapped when the light passed my bed, Ellie would have to slap when the light reached her bed. If the traffic was heavy on Prospect Street the lights flew past before we could slap them and that meant we'd miss a point.

Some nights, after saying our regular prayers, we got back out of bed to pray for special intentions. We prayed Ellie would get ball-bearing roller skates, that Katie O'Rourke would invite me to her birthday party, that President Eisenhower would be a good president. Sometimes

I prayed for a secret intention—that I'd get a limp that didn't really hurt but would make people feel sorry for me. One night I prayed that I'd be blind—for a little while anyway—but then I realized that if my prayer was answered I wouldn't be able to see the people feeling sorry for me.

Some nights Ellie and I told each other what we'd eat if we could just have one thing in the whole world. Most of the time I wanted roast beef, but in summer I wanted cantaloupe. Ellie usually wanted lamb chops or rocky road ice cream.

....

"I can't get to my mother's house every Friday," Mrs. Singer said. "And since my sister moved to the shore she can't get here as often as she used to."

"I can do it, Mrs. Singer," I said.

"She refuses to live with me, and she won't move to the garden apartments near my house. She's lived in Vailsburg all her life so it's what she's used to."

I was five and Ellie was two when Mom died and we moved into Nana's house. I didn't remember much about the old house except that we had ants in the pantry and the back hall smelled like mothballs. I remembered sneaking downstairs one morning and finding birds banging against the windows. The laundry Mom had folded and left on the table was all messed up, and the clothes were covered with blood. After yelling for Mom, I hid under the sofa cushions and held my breath. By the time she pulled back the cushions my ears were ringing and I had pins and needles in my feet. I grabbed Mom's nightgown and followed behind her as she batted down the birds with a broom. Afterwards, she told me the laundry stains weren't blood but mulberry juice. She said the birds had been eating the berries in the tree that grew too close to the house and that they must have dropped down the chimney. "Like Santa," she said.

....

Mrs. Singer got up from the metal chair and jiggled a key into the door lock. "Ma, it's me," she called when the door opened. "Where are you?"

The old lady was sitting in a wing chair holding a magnifying glass. A magazine was in her lap and a floor lamp with a torn shade stood beside the chair.

"Ma, this is Margaret. She's going to be the Shabbos Goy."

The old lady pressed her hands into the chair arms and pushed herself up. She was short and frail and wore her hair in a tiny knot. "I don't need," she said.

"Yes, Ma, you do. I'm going to show Margaret around so she can see what lights she should put on."

"I don't need," Mrs. Levy said again.

"I'm afraid you'll fall, Ma. You're not so steady on your feet and you can't see very well."

"I don't fall."

"Margaret will come and check that you have enough light to see what you're doing. She can check the stove too."

I followed Mrs. Singer to the kitchen where the red linoleum had worn to pink in front of the sink. A newspaper with a picture of the Rosenberg spies was on the table. Mrs. Singer yanked open the back door then slammed it shut and locked it. "Ma," she yelled, "the back door wasn't locked. You didn't lock it."

Mrs. Singer showed me how to unscrew the light bulb in the refrigerator so her mother wouldn't turn on a light when she opened it. Then she showed me how the stove worked. She said her mother would probably have it on low when I came, but that I should check it and turn it off if her mother wanted it off. "Sometimes she puts it on before Sabbath, but you can check with her and see what she wants."

I stood behind Mrs. Singer as she stepped into the bathroom and moved a bucket from the tub to a spot under the sink. In the dark room across the hall the bed was covered with a crocheted bedspread that looked like Nana's Sunday tablecloth. Mrs. Singer opened the closet door and pulled the light string. "If you leave on the hall light, the bathroom light, and this closet light she should have enough to see where she's going."

"Ma," Mrs. Singer said, "Can you see your way around in here?" The old woman shuffled into the bedroom and rested her thick fingers on the edge of the bed. "Margaret will put on the lights so you can open and shut the doors if you need to make it darker or lighter."

Mrs. Levy sighed. "I see good."

"I'm going to show Margaret where I'll leave the money, and then I'm going." Mrs. Singer bent to give her mother a hug. "Remember, Margaret will come this Friday. I'll call to remind you so you'll let her in. Okay?"

I followed Mrs. Singer to a table beside the front door that held a doily and a pink dish trimmed in gold. "I'll leave two quarters here, Margaret. I'm here two times a week, so you don't have to worry about being paid."

"Thank you."

"Ma, don't forget to lock up after Margaret leaves," Mrs. Singer called to the air. "You hear me?"

"I hear." The old woman was standing in the living room doorway. "The girl comes at Shabbos."

"Ma, her name is Margaret."

"Sheyna meydeleh," Mrs. Levy said, before she hobbled toward me. "Like a princess."

"She likes you," Mrs. Singer said. "She says you're a pretty girl."

When Mrs. Singer opened the door, Mrs. Levy and I looked at each other. Mrs. Singer sighed, stepped through the door, and slammed it behind her.

Mrs. Levy took my hand into her sandpaper palms. "Like velvet," she said, "and so tall and strong."

"I'm the second tallest girl in my class," I said, feeling like a hairy giant.

Nana was my same height so I didn't tower over her the way I did with Mrs. Levy. And when I stood beside my grandmother I didn't see the U-shaped roll of hair that was pinned to the back of her head. But Mrs. Levy was so short and her hair was so thin, I could see her scalp through the strips of hair that were pulled back to a bun the size of a teabag.

"You study good?" She let go of my hand and began patting my back. Uncle Jimmy patted me too, but then he ran his hand down my chest to see if my "titties" were growing. He said it was a shame that my no-good father had died, but I was lucky to have an uncle who'd teach me about men.

"I study a lot," I said, but after saying it, I realized the only thing I studied was the catechism questions I memorized every night.

"So smart in school and pretty . . . a scholar." She put her hand on my face.

Once Sister Alberta told the class that there was a difference between a "pupil" and a "scholar," but I couldn't remember what she said about each one—only that the scholar was better than the pupil.

"I have to leave, Mrs. Levy," I said. "My grandmother will worry if I'm late." Nana wouldn't worry for one minute. The only thing she worried about was whether or not Uncle Jimmy was coming for dinner. Uncle Jimmy said his new apartment had a view of New York City, but none of us had ever seen it, and we didn't know why he came to see us if he could look to the city lights whenever he wanted. Most of the time Nana didn't know when he was coming so she had to hustle around and make a special meal, because, as she said a million times, "We'd be in the poor house if it wasn't for your uncle."

"You come tomorrow?" Mrs. Levy asked.

"No. I'll come in three days . . . on Friday." After closing the door, I listened to hear if she'd locked it. It was dark enough that I had to hold the railing as I climbed down the steps to get my books. Spring would be here soon and Ellie had already seen a robin, but my nose felt like an ice cube and the tops of my ears were numb. I hugged my notebook and walked as fast as I could. When I saw the whale shape in front of my house my stomach tightened but a moment later I realized it wasn't Uncle Jimmy's Buick, but the Packard that belonged to Mr. O'Toole, who lived across the street.

....

The pedal pushers that were too big last summer were a little tight but when I looked in the mirror I saw my rear end was still skinny and flat. I brought my face close to the mirror and found three hairs in my right eyebrow that were standing straight instead of laying flat. While I was deciding if it would hurt too much to pluck them, Nana called for me to come and set the table.

"Your uncle is coming," she said when I reached the kitchen, "and I still haven't made his favorite dessert." I pictured Nana's tapioca pudding, which was thick enough to stand a spoon in..

"Where's Ellie?" I asked.

"I don't know where she goes."

My sister didn't answer when Nana called so that meant I got stuck with all the work. Still, sometimes I didn't mind because I'd pretend people were watching me from the ceiling, and when they saw me hobbling because of my crippled leg, or bumping into the chairs because I couldn't see right, they'd feel sorry for me for having to work so hard. When Ellie was around I didn't imagine people on the ceiling. The one time I hobbled when she was there she kept asking why I was faking.

I dragged the step stool to the pantry to reach the crème de menthe, and after I put the bottle on the kitchen counter, I crept my fingers along the cabinet shelf until they touched Nana's little glass goblet that came from Ireland. I put the goblet and the bottle on the sideboard so I'd be ready to pour the green liquor when Nana brought Uncle Jimmy his coffee. When Uncle Jimmy came to dinner he liked to have his coffee and his crème de menthe at the end of the meal—at the same time Nana hovered beside him asking if he wanted more pudding.

The smell of cabbage and fish turned my stomach but at least there was a plate of celery sticks and bowls of apple sauce and stewed tomatoes. I'd just brought the bowls to the table when Uncle Jimmy came to the front door and called for me.

"Look at the bathing beauty!" he said when I went to the hall. "What would the nuns say if they could see you in those pants? Turn around." He grabbed my shoulders and turned me to the hall mirror. Then he stood behind me breathing onto my neck. "Those titties are getting bigger every day." Sometimes I was able to stop hearing him by imagining a black velvet curtain, but now my mind wasn't blank enough and instead of seeing a curtain I saw a girl with eyes as flat as paving stones. For an instant, I didn't recognize myself.

The first time Uncle Jimmy touched me was in Saint Joseph's Church right after Ellie and I had modeled the blouses in the rectory. As we walked to the car Uncle Jimmy dropped his hand on my neck and said he wanted to show me a statue in the side chapel. Ellie ran ahead swinging the sales case and didn't look back.

The church was cold and smelled of incense and ashes. Eight wrought iron chandeliers hung from chains on either side of the main aisle, but the side chapel had one lone ceiling lamp and a single pew with a torn kneeling pad in front of it. Uncle Jimmy stood beside the holy water font, and after I blessed myself he patted my backside and ran his hand down the front of my blouse. "You'll have to start watching out for the boys," he said as a drop of holy water ran down my forehead. "And tell me if any of them puts a hand on you." He squeezed my right breast. These titties are for me, and don't go talking to your grandmother or anyone else about what we do. We've got our secret, don't we?"

I felt as if I'd swum the length of a pool without breathing and now that I'd come up for air my lungs wouldn't work. The inside of my body was frozen as I watched Uncle Jimmy stick his hand in the holy water and bless himself. He nodded to the statue of Saint Patrick that was shiny with new paint and stood on a pedestal. "That statue took a big fall," he said, "but they fixed it up and now it's like new." I followed him to the vestibule and after he went out the heavy door I stared at the metal rack that held the church bulletins. A hand-printed sign said a novena to Our Lady of Sorrows was starting on Monday.

I don't know if I would have told Nana about what happened in the church if Uncle Jimmy hadn't told me not to. Anyway, when I told her, she froze just like I had. But then she clucked her tongue. "I don't know, Margaret," she said. "There's nothing wrong with a little 'kanoodle' now and then. Your uncle has been very good to us. You know he pays for this house and everything we eat. I couldn't have taken you and Ellie in if it hadn't been for him."

....

A second after Uncle Jimmy turned my shoulders away from the flat-eyed girl in the mirror, Ellie crashed through the front door. One of her braids was undone and for some reason she was wearing her Brownie beanie though it wasn't her meeting day. It was pinned into her hair with criss-crossed bobby pins. "O Captain! My Captain!" she boomed. "Our fearful trip is done."

Ellie had been picked to recite the Walt Whitman poem at the end-of-school convocation and now that she'd memorized it she said it whenever she saw me. "Stop!" I held up my hand like the crossing guard. "Uncle Jimmy," I said, "Ellie is going to recite a poem for the whole school. She knows 'O Captain! My Captain!' by heart."

When Ellie saw that she had a new audience she took Uncle Jimmy's hand and led him to the living room. After he sat down she returned to the doorway and knitted her fingers into a ball. Then she pressed the ball to her waist and lifted her chin to the ceiling so she looked like she was receiving a message from heaven. I'd heard the poem a hundred times, but seeing her knot her hands was new, and I wondered if everyone at the convocation would laugh at her. Uncle Jimmy kept nodding and when Ellie was finished he clapped. He was still clapping when Nana called us to the table.

After we said grace, Nana told us the Christ Child Society was going to be sewing Communion dresses for poor children in the South and that her group had promised to send two dozen dresses to Atlanta by Labor Day. Ellie said Mrs. Edwards, her Brownie leader, was going to give the troop sewing lessons so they could sew their patches onto their uniforms when they became Girl Scouts. The sewing lesson would be after their visit to the roller rink next week.

Uncle Jimmy said he expected to hear from the diocese about the Dacron blouses by the end of the month.

I pushed the fish around my plate and tried to figure how much longer we'd be at the table. If we finished eating in fifteen minutes, I'd be able to clear the plates and serve the pudding before seven. With any luck, I'd leave for Mrs. Levy's by seven fifteen.

For the past few weeks—because the sky stayed light longer—I'd been arriving at Mrs. Levy's an hour before sunset so we had time for tea. Mrs. Levy put orange juice and lots of sugar in the tea. After we sipped it we went to the living room sofa so she could look through her photo album. "Ah," she'd say, "Uncle Irving," before tapping a picture with the rim of her magnifying glass. I'd bend forward to get a better look at the bearded man sitting so straight he could have had a broomstick up his back. In four of the pictures—those of Uncle Isaac, Uncle Hyman, Uncle Abe, and Uncle Benny, a bearded man had a short woman standing beside him, resting a hand on his shoulder.

....

I was boring my eyes into Nana so she'd tell me to clear the table when Uncle Jimmy tilted back his chair and stared at Ellie. "Ellie," he said, "you'll come with me tomorrow. I'm going back to Saint Rose of Lima. Father McNulty wants another look."

Nana's eyes darted to Uncle Jimmy then back to Ellie. "You're not going to take Margaret?" she said.

"Father has an eye for the little gals, especially ones with freckles."

My heart split in two then traveled to my ears so all I could hear was the pounding. "DON'T LET HER GO!" I screamed to myself, but when I spoke I wasn't yelling, but talking in a normal voice to Uncle Jimmy. "Don't you want me to come?"

"No, just my little sweetheart this time," he said. "Father McNulty will want to hear that poem of hers."

Nana swished her eyes around the table before standing to collect the fish platter and the applesauce. I followed with the stewed tomatoes which sloshed around like baby hearts in watered-down blood. "Nana," I whispered when we were in the kitchen, "Please don't let Ellie go by herself."

Nana pushed her lips into a pucker so her cheeks hollowed out. "I might talk to him about it, but in the meantime help me get the pudding on the table."

After pouring the crème de menthe I squeezed the bracelet in my pocket. On Fridays, I left after putting the plates in the dish pan, but with Uncle Jimmy here I worried that Nana would make me stay at the table and be "civilized."

"What do you think about the Rosenbergs, Mom?" Uncle Jimmy said.

"It's tonight, isn't it?" Nana asked.

"They're finally going to get what's coming to them."

Ellie and I looked at each other. Mrs. Edwards had given Ellie a magazine with pictures of the Rosenbergs but Nana said we were too young to be thinking about spies and bombs. And she didn't care that Sister Alberta let us talk about them or how they gave secrets to the Russians so they could build an atomic bomb. Ellie and I had to hide in the closet with the magazine and a flashlight so we could stare at the Rosenberg boys. Michael was two years younger than me, and Robert was two years younger than Ellie and they were three years apart just like me and Ellie. They wore the same brown oxfords too. In the picture they were standing in front of the White House fence which was made of spikes that had arrow tips on top. It was exactly like the fence that went around Holy Angels Cemetery where Mom was buried. The caption under the picture said that Michael had written a letter to President Eisenhower. The letter asked the president to spare his parents from the electric chair.

"They'll burn in hell," Uncle Jimmy said.

Sister Alberta said that if our souls didn't have mortal sin on them we shouldn't worry about the atomic bomb. She said there'd be a flash first and that we'd be dead so fast it might not even hurt. She also said that we couldn't be sure who was going to hell because no one, except God, really knew for certain.

"Well," Nana said, "That will put an end to it."

"I don't think it's the end. There are Commies all over. Jews mostly," Uncle Jimmy said, "You can't trust them."

"Jesus was a Jew," I said, but Uncle Jimmy kept talking about how the Commies were everywhere.

When he stopped talking, Nana turned to me. "You can go now, Margaret," she said.

"Where's she going?" Uncle Jimmy asked.

"She has a babysitting job," Nana said. "She'll be back soon."

I looked at Nana and Ellie who stared back at me without saying anything. Then I left the table and went out the back door. It was still light and I had more than an hour to be with Mrs. Levy.

I slipped the bracelet on my wrist and thought about Michael and Robert, and wondered if I could meet them. When their parents were dead they'd be orphans like me and Ellie. People would probably feel sorry for them because, even though their parents were spies, they were electrocuted and hadn't died from cancer or a bad heart. People would probably be nice to them, and tell them they were wonderful because they'd written to the president. The closest I got to having people tell me I was wonderful was when Mrs. Edwards said that next year I could help with the Brownies. "The Brownies will look up to you as a strong role model," she'd said.

It took a long time for Mrs. Levy to come to the door and when she did we didn't go to the kitchen for tea but straight to the living room. She sank onto the sofa and patted the cushion next to her. The photo album was on the chair cushion and her spyglass was on top of it. A newspaper with a headline saying, "Spies to die in electric chair" was tented over the sofa arm.

"Don't you want to look at your pictures?" I asked.

"You want?"

"No, it's okay." I had a hungry feeling as if my stomach was empty, but I didn't want to eat.

She wrapped her hand around my fingers and squeezed. "Are you sad about the Rosenbergs?" I asked.

Mrs. Levy reached her other hand across her lap and ran it up and down my arm. "Soft like a baby," she said. Her hand was rough, but I didn't pull away, and after a few seconds I slouched lower down in the sofa and put my head on her shoulder. "My uncle keeps touching me," I whispered. My voice was soft, and I didn't know if she heard me.

When my shoulders began shaking, I lifted my head. My face kept wrinkling up and collapsing, but I didn't cry. After a while I started counting my breaths and my shoulders relaxed.

"My sister and I have been praying for Michael and Robert," I said. "They're our special intention." For the past five nights Ellie and I had knelt by my bed and raced through three Our Fathers and three Hail Marys with our eyes squinted tight.

"Such sadness," Mrs. Levy said.

I put my head back on her shoulder.

"So strong," she sighed. Mrs. Edwards and Mrs. Levy both thought I was strong, but I wasn't. Sometimes my arms felt so weak I was afraid to move them. Other times, I felt my insides were held up with a yardstick so even though I looked tall and strong, if someone tapped me even a little, I'd fall right over.

I took a breath and my chest shivered when I let out the air. "I feel sad about the Rosenbergs," I said, and just then I felt so sad I wished everything would stop and stay still and nothing more would ever happen. Sister Alberta had told us the Rosenbergs weren't supposed to be executed on the Jewish Sabbath, and since the prison didn't want to execute them on Sunday, they'd be killed before the Sabbath began.

"It's now, isn't it?" I whispered. My own words surprised me because even though Sister had said what she did about the Sabbath, and even though Uncle Jimmy and Nana had said what they did about the execution, it hadn't sunk in. I hadn't thought the Rosenbergs would be executed when I was with Mrs. Levy. In a way, I hadn't thought the Rosenbergs would be killed at all.

"It's happening right now, Mrs. Levy," I said. Mrs. Levy squeezed my hand.

I squeezed back before she lifted my hand and kissed my fingers and I let out a big sigh.

KALO LIVADI

Jennifer Lee

On the way to Mykonos, seagulls glide just off the rail of the ferryboat, swiveling their greedy eyes at us. Troy hops from foot to foot in his ungainly way, his arms outstretched wings. When he is excited he makes an open-mouthed grimace, his lips pulled over his teeth in a strange parody of a baby animal. When he is excited he makes a cawing sound, like a crow. It is his expression of joy, of speechless wonder at the world. Troy has some words, but there isn't much he can say.

Ian is more patient with Troy than I, more accepting of what our life is because of him. He follows Troy around the ferry and meets the eyes of people who stare. He stretches out his arms with Troy and together they caw at the birds.

Ian is forever saying we should live our lives, and that sounds good in theory, but then I imagine us a few years down the road, Troy a hulking teenager who can't dress himself, and I panic. Ian tells me not to do this, not to think of the future, but what else is there to think about?

When we were in college we fantasized about a trip to Greece. We would lie on our crummy futon mattress and imagine our future. Ian liked thinking about the future then; it is only now that things have caught up to us that he has changed his mind.

Last year we got a postcard from my sister. She had gone on an Aegean cruise, and the picture on the postcard was the white-washed mills of Mykonos. Ian pinned it to the refrigerator and stared at it all winter. People say children like Troy don't recognize other people's emotions, but that isn't true. The picture of Mykonos slid down the door of the fridge until it was eye level with Troy. The paper began to curl at the edges from his handling of it, and each morning Troy kissed the postcard, a special ritual, and made his cawing sound at the mills. Troy didn't care about the picture; the postcard from Mykonos was a proxy for his father. It was Ian, after all, who taught our son to kiss.

Ian is a more affectionate parent than I am. I don't know how he does it. In the back of my mind I am sure there is something wrong with me, that I will fail the greatest test a person can face. People say God doesn't give anyone a burden too great to bear, but that isn't true. Every day Troy breaks my heart. How long am I supposed to bear that? I don't know how Ian can love me and Troy the way he does, as if it is easy and natural and full of fair returns.

Troy is still sleeping when we get on the bus for the hotel. People look at me and smile. Troy is a long-limbed child and he looks heavy, but there is a secret people don't know, something I cherish about my boy. My son is as light as an angel. His chest, pressed against mine is warm air, and I can feel him lifting up, even as his lips press against my collarbone. I never want him to wake up when he's like this. I sway from side to side, a human hammock, as the bus crosses the dry island hills.

The Hotel Archipelago is in an area called Kalo Livadi. There is a white sand beach and a tavern nearby. We were told Kalo Livadi is a good place to go with children; no crazy nightlife like Mykonos Town. The sea is shallow and calm and the hotel has a swimming pool and a playground.

Our room is L-shaped with a double bed and a sitting area. In the short arm of the L there is a twin bed for Troy. Glass doors open onto a patio where bougainvillea hugs the walls and geraniums fill the pots. The plants give the space privacy, but the view of the sea is unobstructed, framed by the flat white roofs of the buildings below us. There is barely any movement, only a slight breeze that wobbles the paper flowers of the bougainvillea. Ian touches my shoulder and kisses my neck and at our feet Troy traces a pattern of round pebbles in the mosaic floor.

One of the hardest things to learn once Troy was with us, and perhaps this is true for parents of all children, I don't know, was how to be still. Before Troy, I would have stared a few minutes at the view and then changed into my suit and headed for the beach. I feel that desire now, that restlessness. We will only be on Mykonos three days and I want to experience everything. Already I am planning when we will go see those famous windmills.

But Troy is discovering this place. Like a labyrinth, the mosaic floor will hold him for hours with the variety of shape and size and color in its stones, the complex swirls of its patterns. He crab walks about, jabbering to himself as he touches. He squawks with fury when I slather sunscreen on his arms and the back of his neck. Ian and I read our books as the sun moves lower, heading west behind the hills of the island. This has never happened before, that Troy is awake and we are both reading for pleasure. We don't mention it, in case we jinx it, but Ian catches my eye and winks.

At eight o'clock Ian says, "I'm going to the restaurant to see what we can do about dinner."

He glances at Troy, his hand on the garden gate, and frowns. He is wondering what we will feed our child. Troy eats food he knows and nothing else. Even ice cream. If it isn't a vanilla scoop on a cake cone he won't touch it. When we talked about travelling to Greece, one of the marks against the trip was the daunting task of feeding Troy. "What will he eat?" I said. "I don't think they have hotdogs in Greece."

"The Mediterranean diet is the best in the world," Ian said. "We will find food for Troy. I'm sure they have French fries. It's only for a week. We can do this."

Ian comes back with a menu. Everything looks excellent and we quickly decide on a grilled sea bream, greens, and an octopus and polenta dish. What we spend our time on is the children's menu. There is macaroni and cheese listed, Troy's favorite, but we are not fooled. Our first night in Athens we ordered macaroni and cheese for Troy, so pleased, thinking the food issue was going to be a piece of cake. But what was served was a plate of spaghetti with grated cheese sprinkled on top. Troy let out a wail and slid under the table. We gave him chocolate milk for dinner that night, two glasses full. The Greeks make very good chocolate milk.

From the patio we watch a waiter climb the curved path to our bungalow. He carries a bottle of white wine and a bucket of ice. As he pours the wine he speaks to us in perfect English. Our waiter's name is Benito, and he suggests the melitzanosalata as an appetizer. "And your son? What would he like for dinner?" he asks.

"We're not sure what he will eat. Troy is very picky," I say.

"Does he like mac and cheese?"

"Yes, but the American kind, where the cheese is in the sauce, and with macaroni, not spaghetti. I'm sorry to be fussy, but he won't eat it otherwise."

Benito grins. "Troy is not our only young American guest. There are two little girls here with exactly the same preference. Does Troy like a hotdog cut up in his mac and cheese?"

"He loves hotdog in his mac and cheese!" Ian blurts. You would think he is the one wanting to eat this dish, he is so excited.

"And does Troy want his food to have an obnoxious orange color?"

"Oh, you are good," I say.

"Perfection is in the details," Benito says, and he pulls the cork from the bottle. "I will be back in a moment with your appetizer."

When he brings the melitzanosalata, a puree of eggplant with minced parsley and red peppers, Benito also brings a small bowl of potato chips. "This is for Troy, if he likes."

There are five chips in the bowl. None of them are broken. Troy loves potato chips, but he won't eat broken ones. A shiver runs down my neck and I have goose bumps. I look at Ian. "This is perfect," I say.

....

Troy is placid and docile in the morning, relaxed in a way he rarely is. I hope things will stay this way, but I have no great expectations. Breakfast is beside the pool. There is a buffet, and Troy eats cornflakes without complaint. Ian refills our coffee cups and sits back, grinning. Troy is so well behaved anyone looking at us would assume we are a normal family. I want breakfast to stretch on and on, to last all day, but the table is covered in crumbs, and the sun, which was warm on my back when I sat down, has turned hot.

From the far side of the pool, a family of four approaches the dining area. The way we are seated at the table, Ian does not see them. He is playing with Troy, shaping patterns out of dry cornflakes. The family walking toward us is beautiful, the woman with long, dark hair and a flowing linen blouse. Her husband is fair and tall with the build of an athlete. The two girls wear sundresses, and I feel a pang of envy, looking at them. The older girl walks beside her mother, quiet and attentive, as if she is studying how to be a woman. She is maybe ten years old. The little one is rambunctious, skipping circles around her family. She is about the same age as Troy.

What makes this family unusual—stunning, perhaps—is that the woman is in a wheelchair. I try not to stare as her husband wheels her up to the table behind ours. Ian notices my attention and turns around to look. He meets the eyes of the little girl, and Ian, who is wonderful with all children, not just our own, says, "Are you the person who taught the chef how to make mac and cheese?"

The girl's eyes fly open with amazement, as if Ian has read her mind. "I am," she says, full of wonder.

"What's your name?" Ian asks.

"I'm Lucia."

Then she notices Troy and her expression turns to delight. She bounds over and stands beside him, smiling a glad greeting which Troy ignores. Lucia is unfazed, and bends her face toward Troy, who is concentrating on his cereal flakes. She scrunches up her nose and crinkles her eyes like a little rodent and says in a squeaky voice, "mousey eat, mousey eat," and snatches a cornflake and pops it in her mouth.

"Lucia," her father scolds, "Don't take other people's food."

I watch to see how Troy will react. This sort of thing could send him under the table. But Troy favors Lucia with his special smile, all lips and no teeth, and caws.

We do not go far, after that. My wish comes true, and breakfast stretches on and on. We move from the table to reclining chairs beside the pool and we talk with John and 'Lizabette. The girls, Caroline and Lucia, play with Troy in the water. Caroline pretends to be a princess and Lucia and Troy are her animal friends, Mouse and Bird.

They are from New York, the Upper East Side. 'Lizabette says, "New York is hell in a wheelchair, but Europe is worse."

She says this so naturally, mentioning the thing I most want to understand, but the follow up question sticks in my throat. She knows. Pointing to her thin, flaccid legs, she says, "It's ALS. I got the diagnosis a year ago. I got the chair this spring."

"Can you walk at all?" Ian asks.

She shakes her head. "Not anymore. We planned this trip in the winter, when I could still walk. Even knowing the course of the disease, knowing I was going to lose my legs, we didn't plan the trip with handicapped services in mind." She takes John's hand. "It wouldn't have changed anything anyway."

Lucia comes to us, leading Troy by the hand. My son is blue-lipped and shivering, his skin prickled with bumps. "Bird is cold," Lucia says, and then runs back to the pool.

I wrap Troy in a towel and nestle him in my lap. Swaddled like a mummy he shivers and I warm him with my body. 'Lizabette is saying how they will go to Egypt next, to see the Pyramids, but I am only half listening, distracted by the delicious weight of my child. The shivers decrease, the chattering of his teeth stops, and Troy relaxes in my arms.

John catches my eye and smiles. It makes me blush; he knows exactly the pleasure I am taking in motherhood.

Caroline and Lucia get out of the pool. It is their turn to shiver in towels. "We want to watch a movie," Caroline says. "Can Troy come?"

I feel a moment of panic. Troy has been so good all morning, eating breakfast, playing with the girls. I don't know if he can handle a movie. There are only a few he watches—early Disney films. Anything else and he ignores the screen like a potted plant. "Maybe," I say. "What movies do you have?"

Lucia rattles off a list: "*Cloudy with a Chance of Meatballs*, *Despicable Me*, *Snow White*, *The Lion the Witch and the Wardrobe*."

"Snow White." Troy says. "Snow White!" He wriggles his arms out of the towel and is opening and closing his fingers. *Snow White* is his favorite, and he is asking for his doll, a rag doll in a bright satin dress. He loves his Snow White, loves the feel of her satin dress between her fingers. Troy will not go to bed at night without his doll, so of course she is with us on the trip.

"I'll go get it," Ian says.

When he comes back, everyone makes appreciative noises over the doll—it really is a fine thing—and Troy smiles proudly, petting her dress. I've never seen this smile before, my son taking pleasure in the appreciation of others. Troy takes Caroline's hand and walks away with the girls. I realize I've been holding my breath.

"Caroline and Lucia are so good with him," I say. This is the opening line parents like me learn to use, words that prepare us to say the truth, that Troy is autistic, his impairment severe. We first suspected something when he was fifteen months old and the diagnosis was confirmed when he was two. It was another year before we understood the severity of his condition. We tell all this to John and 'Lizabette. We explain that Troy attends a special school where he learns to take care of himself and communicate with others as best he can.

The afternoon flies past on a current of conversation. *Snow White* lasts blissfully long and we order cocktails by the poolside. Benito tends the bar, crushing mint for mojitos, showing off his talent for perfection. It has been ages since Ian and I had company like this, another couple to talk to. It feels so good, like circulation returning to your limbs after a long night in the cold.

The sun has dipped toward the west when Caroline returns. Her cheeks are rosy from the sun, her hair stiff from the pool water.

"Is the movie over?" Her mother asks.

Caroline nods. "Troy fell asleep while we were watching it."

Ian stands up. "I'll go get him."

"You don't have to," John says. "He can sleep where he is."

"Oh, he won't wake when I move him. Once he's asleep he's a rock. And he'll do better waking up in his own bed."

"I should have a rest too," 'Lizabette says. "We're going into town this evening, to Mykonos."

So our party breaks up, and Ian carries Troy back to our room where he and I read our novels on the patio until dusk. When Troy wakes, we give him a snack pack of Goldfish. This is his favorite treat. Terrified we wouldn't find any in Europe, we packed a box of them in our suitcase.

The air has turned soft, pastel colors soaking into things. It is too early for dinner so we decide on a walk. Ian hoists Troy onto his shoulders. If we want to get anywhere with Troy, he needs to be off the ground. Otherwise he will stop to examine every conceivable object on our way and we won't move ten feet.

The Hotel Archipelago sits on a rise above the sea. A paved street to the right leads down to the beach. Along the way, little footpaths twist between rocks and scrub toward the shore. Ian heads down one of these, and we find ourselves on a narrow spit of sand beneath the cliff. The shore here is mostly rocks with patches of sand wedged in between. Ian kicks off his sandals and wades into the water, picking his way between the sharp rocks. The coast has hidden alcoves between boulders and the wall of the cliff, and we wander along, finding a string of miniature beaches.

"It's getting dark," I say. I have tender feet, and the stones are sharp in the water where I can't find the sand. We head back the way we came and continue down the road toward the beach.

A few bathers still dot the water, their heads floating above the surface like seals. On the beach, parents gather towels and toys. Some are heading toward an outdoor tavern lit by a string of bare bulbs. We had planned on dinner at the hotel, but Troy spots French fries. He points to a table laden with food and uses his extra polite voice, the rising cadence of the question exaggerated: "Dinner? Do I want them? French fries?"

We choose a table and a waiter brings a basket with bread and napkins and forks. There is no menu, but in a strange patois of European languages he rattles off a list of things they have. We order a few small plates, not quite sure what will be coming, except that there will definitely be French fries.

As we wait for the food, Troy discovers cigarette butts in the sand. They are all over the place, and he starts a collection. I put the ashtray on the ground and Troy fills it. A Greek woman at a nearby table tells me, "Don't let him touch this. It is dirty."

"He'll throw a fit if I stop him," I tell her. "Don't worry; I'll wash his hands before he eats."

She doesn't understand who Troy is, and she shrugs at me with disapproval.

When the French fries arrive with the other dishes—calamari, tzatziki, a plate of boiled zucchini—Troy clambers onto his chair, ready to dive in. Ian clasps his wrists with his long fingers, like human handcuffs, and I use wipes to clean Troy's hands, rubbing each little finger and making him giggle.

Troy picks up a fry and drops it on his plate. "Hot. Hot." He blows on it like a birthday candle. I move a few fries on to a plate—a Troy-sized portion—and spread them around so they will cool.

Ian and I are ravenous. Everything is delicious and I don't realize Troy is watching us until he says, "Dip? French fries dip?" One of the foods Troy will eat is baby carrots dipped in Ranch dressing. I am holding a French fry dipped in tzatziki half way to my mouth. The tzatziki is white, like Ranch. Troy picks up a fry and dips it in the tzatziki. Normally he sniffs new food, flicks it with his tongue like a lizard. Instead he stuffs it into his mouth and chews. "Yummy dip!" He says. We order a second plate of tzatziki.

Walking back to the hotel, the steep rise of the hill putting a pleasant stretch in our legs, Ian giggles and says, "He tried new food!"

"Yummy dip!" I say, laughing.

....

Late in the morning we meet Caroline and Lucia and John for breakfast. We sit together at a long table, the children at one end, the adults at the other. "Where is 'Lizabette?" I ask.

"Mykonos wore her out," John says. "She's sleeping in."

Lucia has brought an inflated boat to breakfast, her souvenir from town last night. She is dying to put it in the water. It is a sea toy, not a pool toy, and with a verbal exchange that would challenge a lawyer John convinces her to wait until we go to the beach.

"The girls can come down with us," I say, "and you and 'Lizabette can take your time." I want to go to the beach, and taking Troy in the company of Lucia will be far easier than trying to get him down there on his own. He has never responded to another person the way he has to Lucia. I wish I could take her home with us.

John agrees, and Lucia jumps up and down on her toes, but Caroline whispers something in her father's ear. He kisses her forehead and says, "Okay. Why don't you make Mommy a plate for breakfast." To Lucia he says, "You be good. Caroline is going to stay with me and Mommy. We'll be down a little later."

Troy rides on Ian's shoulders and I carry Lucia's dinghy. The children are sticky with sunscreen and Troy wears inflatable armbands. I ask Lucia if she has arm floats, but she tosses up her chin and says, "I can swim. My daddy is a life guard and he taught me."

We are moving at vacation pace this morning, and it is already a little past noon when we stretch out our towels in the sand. Ian holds the little boat steady while Lucia climbs in and then he lifts Troy and puts him in beside her. He squats down and pushes them around, making motorboat noises with his mouth.

I sit and watch them, my book unopened beside me, and imagine that I am the mother of two normal children. They would play like this with their father, laughing and splashing each other. When Troy was small and we were still reeling from the diagnosis, learning each day what autism meant for him, for us, we talked about having another child. We even tried for a few months, but we gave up. We found ourselves fighting over trivial things, shouting matches that began over nothing. Eventually we gave up for good, and Ian had a vasectomy. Seeing Lucia and Troy together, I wonder if we made the right decision.

John,'Lizabette, and Caroline arrive a few hours later. We are in the shade of a bamboo awning at a little cantina, Lucia and Troy eating ice cream cones. It is not the kind he likes, a cake cone with a scoop of vanilla. These are cooler bin ice creams with hardened, waxy chocolate encrusted on top. Lucia is having a ball with hers, lapping up melting streams and biting off the chocolate topping in slabs. Troy watches her as he tickles the white ice cream with his tongue, drips running down the cone to his hand and wrist.

My attention swings back and forth between Troy, eating new food for the second day in a row, and the three walking toward us down the hill. Caroline walks beside her mother, her hand on the armrest of the wheel chair. This is just as I first saw her yesterday morning when the family came to breakfast. Then I had thought she was acting the little lady; I understand her better now. Caroline knows what Lucia does not, that her mother will die. Her desire to be near her is both an act of nurture and a desperate attempt to keep her. I don't know what a ten year old can grasp regarding death, but I recognize in Caroline a grown up pain, a mirror of her parents' suffering.

Lucia sucks the last sweet slop from the bottom of her cone and squeals when she sees her family. She runs barefoot across the baked dirt parking lot and leaps into her father's arms. "Come swimming with me!" She says. "Come play with us!"

John and Ian and the children head down to the water, leaving me and 'Lizabette at a table in the shade. This is as close as she will get to the water; the wheels of her chair aren't made for sand. We order lemon sodas and watch our husbands play with the kids. Lucia rides her father's back and Troy rides on Ian's. They are bobbing around in the water like wild animals, clearly enjoying themselves. They look ridiculous.

"What are they doing?" I ask, a little embarrassed for Ian and his antics.

'Lizabette laughs. This is a game she knows. "Bronco turtles. You pretend to be a bucking sea turtle. The goal is to dislodge your rider. Lucia is so fierce; I don't think John can get her off without drowning her."

I don't even want to imagine the meltdown that would occur if Troy fell off his father's back. It was years of swimming lessons before we could get Troy comfortable in the water. He still doesn't love it. He hates putting his face underwater, and if he fell off, came up sputtering, the day would be ruined. Upsetting events cause a cascade of neural responses in Troy's brain, and not even Lucia could bring him back from such a meltdown. I can tell that while Ian is playing his part, bucking like a good bronco turtle, he has a tight grip on Troy's ankles.

Caroline is in the little boat, drifting away. A light breeze pushes her sideways, parallel to the beach. She is too big for the dinghy, her long limbs dangling in the water. She will be an adolescent soon, a teenager. My heart misses a beat when I realize 'Lizabette might never know her like that.

"Caroline is so mature," I say. "She really wants to look after you, doesn't she?"

'Lizabette has been studying Caroline too. "This is so hard for her. She knows everything. Way too much. Sometimes when I'm having a bad day, I pretend that I feel great, just so she can leave the house. If she knows I feel lousy she wants to stay home with me. She missed a lot of school in the spring when I lost my legs. We'd try to get her to go, but even if we got her out the door, she'd get sent home. She'd go to the nurse crying hysterically. They couldn't send her back to class like that, they couldn't even keep her in the health suite. The only way to keep her in school, the only way to keep her life normal, was to fake it."

I can think of nothing to say. For the first time, raising Troy seems easy.

When the sun begins to set, we head to the tavern where we ate last night. John and 'Lizabette have a better sense of the menu and order all sorts of things I haven't a clue about. And of course we get French fries and tzatziki.

Troy is animated, pointing and talking. "You eat this. You eat this dip, see?" He shows everyone how to eat French fries with tzatziki. It goes well at first, with everyone saying, "Pass the dip, pass the dip." We order more fries, more tzatziki.

We fill up on small plates while we wait for the grilled snapper, a big fish John and Ian chose from a box of crushed ice. Troy is full, he has eaten more than he usually does, but instead of winding down he is winding up. This is a sign of exhaustion. He has spent all day in the sun, and as he pokes his fingers into the tzatziki, shrieking with laughter, I know he is not going to make it through dinner.

Ian realizes this too. "I better get him out of here," he says. Ian does a much better job than me when dealing with imminent meltdowns.

"I want to go too," Lucia says. Her nose is sunburned, and she looks ready to cry. She, too, is exhausted.

The adults look around the table at one another. It is too late to cancel the fish order, but there is no holding Troy and Lucia in place.

"I'll go too," 'Lizabette says. "I'm tired as well. Ian, can you get me up to the hotel?"

"I'll help," Caroline says. She is already pushing back her chair.

"Wait," John says.

"No, you stay," 'Lizabette tells him. "You and Felicia have to stay and eat the fish."

I turn toward Ian. All this is happening so fast. He already has Troy on his shoulders. "Stay and enjoy the fish," he says. "It cost an arm and a leg; it would be a shame to waste it." He kisses me goodbye.

John and I watch our families retreat up the hill, Caroline and Ian each pushing a side of Lizabette's chair. There are no streetlights between the tavern and the hotel up the road and they are soon swallowed by darkness.

John fills our wine glasses. We had ordered another jug of wine just before everyone left, and so we have this to consume in addition to the fish. I am nervous; John is a very attractive man, a fact I could distract myself from when Lucia and Troy were about, but now there is nothing to hold my attention but him.

"Lucia tells me you're a life guard."

"Was. In college. At Jones Beach."

"I know Jones Beach. I had friends who had a little cabana there. We went every weekend for years. You were probably sitting on the guard stand ten feet from where we were sun bathing."

"Then you were probably right next to 'Lizabette. The summer we met, I think we spent three weeks staring at each other before either of us said a word. She was so brown, with her olive Italian skin. I thought she was the most exotic woman I'd ever seen."

I watch John's face, how it goes from a memory of youthful lust to deep sadness. When you live a tragedy it's hard to know what will trigger the pain. Jones Beach: Who would have thought? When I think of Mary Lee's cabana, the days we spent rinsing the sand out of our suits, water trickling from a pipe in the tiny shower walled off by a sheet of corrugated tin, I recall such innocence, such unawareness of all that the world held in store for me.

"You put on a good show," I say.

"What choice is there?"

The fish arrives and we busy ourselves with eating it. We drink more wine. I know we both want to talk about something that will make us happy, will make us laugh, but we just can't seem to do it. We make one false start after another, stopping when our conversation rings false. At last John asks me, "What's it like, raising Troy? What will he be able to do when he grows up?"

I've spent a lot of time imagining this. I imagine looking forward to the milestones Troy has a chance of reaching: living in a group home with care workers checking in on him regularly and a low-paying job with an employer who has a good history working with the severely autistic. I force myself to imagine these things, believing that acceptance is the first step. Inevitably I get angry, bitter, grieving at all he will not do. He won't attend college or go on a road trip with friends. He won't get married and have a family.

I tell John this, especially how it feels to me. "It isn't that I have trouble accepting Troy as he is. Troy is fine and I love him. It's when I think of the future that everything comes undone. Ian doesn't understand. He keeps telling me not to think about the future, but I don't know how to stop. I wish I could; the future makes me unhappy."

"I feel the same way. All the future means is that I'm going to lose 'Lizabette. Why would I want to think about that? And yet my life feels like a lie when I think of anything else. And she can't stand it, you know. She can tell by looking at me that I'm thinking about the future. I've tried looking in the mirror, to see my face when I'm thinking about her being gone, so I can understand what she sees and why it drives her crazy. But I can't see it."

I can. It is all over his face now that the others are gone. He doesn't look like he is going to cry, it is farther along than that. His handsome face, deeply wrinkled from the years on the guard stand soaking up the sun, looks like it is breaking and reshaping itself continually, as if the pain is a lava flow or glacial sheet, shifting just below the surface. I look in John's eyes and tell him what I see.

He listens to my description. "Suffering as an inexorable, geologic force. That sounds about right. Part of what drives me crazy, what makes me feel like you do when you try to imagine Troy's future, is that I can't see 'Lizabette's suffering. She hides it from me. I know her pain, at least when it's too much to hide, but she treats me like Caroline. I know that's what she needs, I know that's what she can stand, but I can't stand it.

"Did you watch her eating this evening? How she mashed everything with a fork, took tiny bites? Her hand was shaking, she could barely hold the fork. The doctors told us it was only a matter of time before the disease made it hard for her to swallow. She hasn't said anything about it to me, but that's what's happening, I'm sure."

John shifts in his chair. His despair has fermented into anger. I am familiar with that brew. "I know what you mean," I say. "Ian acts like it's a choice, whether I think about the future or not. I just wish he would look at it through my eyes for once, so he would know how I feel, what I need from him. I guess that's too much to ask from another person."

"I guess."

We finish the meal and put a stack of Euros on the table. Our conversation leaves us in a foul mood, but moving away from the table, into the starry dark, improves things. We walk slowly up the hill, admiring the stretch of Milky Way in the sky.

We come to a little trail leading down to the shore, the one Ian and I followed last night. "Come with me," John says.

He is half way down the path before I decide to follow him.

John stands on a patch of sand. He takes off his shirt and begins unbuttoning his pants.

"What are you doing?" I say.

"A night swim. A night swim to clear my head. Are you coming?"

"I don't think so."

John steps into the water, his white buttocks like twin moons. I realize that if a fire suddenly erupted on the opposite shore I would keep staring at this man's naked body rather than the inferno. I slip out of my clothes and into the water.

The water is cool, and I paddle my feet carefully, not knowing the depth. John is in front of me, his hair wet and slicked back like a cap. It changes how he looks, how I see him. He is a stranger.

He swims toward me, one strong kick beneath the water. We are maybe twenty yards from shore, far enough that the water is ink-black all around. John runs his hands over my waist, my breasts. He pulls me close and I feel his penis hard against my legs. He presses his lips against mine, pushes his tongue into my mouth. I am amazed that he can keep both our heads above the water; I am making no effort at all to stay afloat.

He rolls onto his back and with swift strokes pulls us toward the shore, toward a boulder and its shadow at the base of the cliff. Neither of us say a word as he presses me against the rock and enters me.

I come quickly, the first few strokes and I am electric, moaning, and John thrusts deeper and I feel him come. He pulls out, but late. I know he put seed inside me, and as I feel his semen slide down my thigh I come again, thinking about that.

He kisses me gently, one hand cradling my head and the other scooped under my ass. He pulls away so we can look at one another. His blue eyes are black in the night and the planes of his face reflect the light of stars.

We walk along the coast, picking our way between the rocks, just as Ian and I did the night before. I am not lucky this time, and in the dark I step on a sharp rock. I hiss, drawing in my breath, and John squeezes my hand.

I do not realize my foot is bleeding until we reach the hotel. I stand at the door of our room and look back at the blood spots I have left on the flagstones.

Ian and Troy lay curled on the double bed. I move quietly, taking a shower and changing into a dry shirt. I press a wad of toilet paper against my cut, and on my knees I wipe blood from the tile floor before I crawl into the tiny bed in the alcove.

....

Troy wakes early. It is seven a.m. and he stands on the bed in his underwear, frowning. This is not a good sign; when a day starts badly with Troy it usually stays that way.

"No!" he shouts. "No, No, No!"

We get him dressed and go to breakfast. Things do not improve. Lucia and her family are not around and Troy drops cutlery on the floor over and over, just to hear it clatter. We get irritated looks from nearby tables, looks that say, 'you are ruining our holiday.'

I fold cookies into a paper napkin for later—Troy has eaten nothing—and we spend a few hours at the pool. Ian plays with Troy in the water. I have a bandage on my foot, my excuse for sitting in the shade. Ian does not express any curiosity about my injury, for which I am grateful. I hope Lucia will arrive, rescue us from Troy, even though I am terrified to look at John. Like a child in the throes of magical thinking, I am sure that if we are together, people will be able to read the truth just by looking at us.

But they don't come. The pool is empty except for ourselves, and at last we give up. Ian goes to arrange a van into town. It is our last day on Mykonos, our ferry leaves the island tomorrow at nine in the morning; if we want to see the town, the time is now.

With Troy in a difficult mood, I know this is a bad idea. Ian and I hardly look at each other, and I know he is thinking the same thing. But sometimes you have to do things against your better judgment. Sometimes there are things you need and there is a price to pay for having them. That is how I see the mills of Mykonos, the postcard that beckoned us all winter, promising that we, too, could have what we wanted.

Benito drives the van. He chats with us as we head over the hills toward town. "What will you see?" He asks. "The mills and Little Venice?"

"Yes," Ian tells him. "Is there anything else you recommend?"

"Look for Petros, the pelican. He is the mascot of the island. You will find him near the waterfront. Do you like birds, Troy?" He looks at Troy in the rear view mirror. "You can pet him. He's very nice."

Troy isn't having any. His mouth has been in a frown since the moment he woke up. He scowls at the seatback in front of him.

I ask, "Do you have any children, Benito?"

"I have a little daughter, three years old."

"She must love living in Kalo Livadi. What a beautiful place to grow up."

"She doesn't live here. She and my wife are in Spain, with my wife's family. I won't see them until October, when the tourist season is over."

"That must be hard."

"It is. Last year when I went home she was only two. She didn't remember me at all. It was weeks before she trusted me again. This year we Skype every day. I think it will be better."

Benito drops us off at a hairpin turn near the end of the harbor. The sun reflects blindingly off the whitewashed buildings, and we dart for the shade of the narrow streets. It is mid afternoon, siesta time, but no one is resting in Mykonos. The shops are open and the streets, flagstone paths with each rock outlined in whitewash like a jigsaw puzzle, crisscross in a dense jumble. We are lost within minutes, following the flow of people as it ebbs through town.

Troy rides on his father's shoulders, whimpering. He hates this. The crowds, the narrow streets, the bright light on all the white—it is too much for him. At one point we find ourselves in an open square with a little ice cream shop and a few benches under which stray kittens play. Ian tries to lift him down. Troy pinches his knees against Ian's ears and pulls his hair. He doesn't want to come down for anything.

It is several minutes of cajoling, promising ice cream, before Troy permits his father to put him on the ground. We order ice cream, a cake cone with a scoop of vanilla for Troy, and this familiar treat calms him a little.

The square opens onto a street that curls around the harbor. A group of people are gathered at the water's edge. They huddle around something impossible to see. Then someone shifts and I catch sight of pale pink feathers.

Petros is enormous. He waddles about and tolerates the constant petting and the photographs. Troy loves birds, and people move aside so he can get close. He pets the sleek feathers and caws softly at Petros. He has one hand on the bird's back and in the other he holds his melting ice cream. The bird is not interested in Troy, but it does have an eye on the cone. Ian takes a picture. The photograph, I am sure, will tell a different story from the one we are living.

We hope after this interlude that we will be able to see more of the town, find the mills and the bars and restaurants that overlook the water, the neighborhood called Little Venice. We hope Troy will be in a better mood, but that does not happen. The streets are more crowded, and Troy grinds his knees into Ian's ears, making a whining sound we both know is a precursor to a full-on shriek. We are lost, completely turned around by the little streets, and though we know the places we want to see lie in the direction of the heaviest traffic, we veer away from the crowds. In a few minutes we are alone. We find a schoolyard, empty except for a rusted swing set and weeds sprouting between the cracks in the asphalt.

Troy loves swings, and willingly comes down from his father's shoulders to ride on one. We push him for what seems like hours, lulled by the creak of the chains.

"We can just head back, you know. We don't have to see the mills and all the rest." I am exhausted, my foot aches, and I know—we both know—that Troy will not get any easier.

Usually Ian is very accommodating. He is the first to let go, to accept defeat. But not today. "No. I want to see those damn windmills. I came all this way. I want to see them."

He doesn't sound like my husband. He sounds like a pouting child. He sounds like Troy, in fact, when he has set his heart on something and cannot let it go. Ian rhythmically pushes our son on the swing, just enough to keep them both calm.

A broad street leads downhill from the school, and in a few minutes we arrive at a restaurant with dozens of tables spilling out onto the street. "Look," I say, pointing a little further on. We have found the mills.

We walk toward them. To the right, restaurants crowd the waterfront, every one of them packed. The sun is setting and people are here for the event, the sea shining like glass. On our left a broad flight of stairs leads up to the little promontory where the mills lean into the Aegean. Long ago wind ripped the sails from the spars, and the wooden arms hang useless. There is nothing left to catch the wind, but it still blows fiercely here.

Ian lifts Troy down, despite his protests. "I'm going up there," he says, and bounds up the steps.

I want to call after him, make him wait. I want to follow. But I recognize that this is something Ian needs, to move away from us. He needs to be alone with the mills, without Troy riding his back. We have learned to recognize this in one another, like a sixth sense, knowing when the other needs something, even something forbidden, in order simply to go on.

The sun floats below the horizon and the light changes. Above us Ian becomes smaller and smaller as he walks against the wind toward the furthest mill. I watch him, but Troy does not. He presses himself against my leg, his arms wrapped around me like a vice.

A child comes toward us. He is dark-skinned and filthy, a gypsy, his neck and wrists loaded down with cheap, glow-in-the-dark bands. He looks at Troy. "Boy," he says. "Boy. You want? You want?" He swings his arms, making the colors swirl.

Troy lifts his arm to shield himself from this stranger, but the gypsy boy is relentless. He pulls Troy's arm down. "Hey, boy. You want? Three euro," he says, turning his eyes toward me.

Troy buries his face in my crotch and howls. The boy's touch has sent him over the edge. I pray for Ian to turn around and see, to know that we need him, but he is still looking at the windmills.

The boy with his necklaces stares at Troy as if he is a dog that has been hit by a car. He doesn't show pity, the way most people are trained to do. He looks at Troy with a mixture of revulsion and curiosity.

"Go away!" I yell at him. He shrugs his shoulders and leaves us to ourselves.

By the time Ian comes back, Troy is inconsolable. He won't ride on his father's shoulders. He won't take his arms from around my waist. I scoop him up and carry him like firewood.

There is a taxi stand on the square where we had ice cream earlier in the day. We stumble upon it after weaving through the narrow streets. Twenty people stand in the cue, and we wait ten minutes and only one taxi comes. Troy has the collar of my shirt between his teeth. This muffles his cries, though my neck is wet with his saliva.

"Call Benito, please." I say to Ian.

We return to the hairpin turn on the edge of town where Benito dropped us off. We stand in the loose gravel of the shoulder, the hill plummeting just a few feet away. My foot throbs with the beat of my heart. It is dark, and I cannot see clearly, but I imagine the soft canvas of my shoe stained with blood. I am certain the wound has opened. It has hurt all day, more with every step. It is a welcome distraction from the misery of Troy.

Benito arrives and we climb into the van. "Is he alright?" Benito asks.

Usually Ian answers question like this. Usually it is Ian who holds Troy through a meltdown. But Ian is staring out the window at nothing, and so I tell Benito, "It was too much for him. The crowds and the narrow streets; we should have known not to try."

We drive across the winding spine of the island, Troy's rhythmic sobs the only sound. I am lulled by the music of it, and don't notice at first that a voice has joined him. Benito sings in a soft baritone, words I don't understand, Spanish or Greek or Italian. Soon I realize Troy is listening too—his crying stops. In my arms I can feel the tension in his body, the fragile mind that had been a source of distress all day long, relax.

He is asleep when we reach the hotel. I lay him in the little bed and slip him out of the clothes he wears so they won't twist and discomfort him in the night. Troy's little bones lie perfect beneath his skin, and I marvel, as I have countless times, at the mystery of mind and body. Something in my child's brain is wired differently, it cannot be repaired, but you would never know it to look at him. In his body, Troy is an angel, a perfect creation. I smooth the hair from his forehead and go to wash my foot in the bathtub.

I was right; the wound has opened and blood stains the bottom of my shoe. The flesh of my sole is inflamed and I run warm water and soak it. It takes me a while to tend my injury, and I am surprised to find Ian awake. He lies on his side and watches me climb into bed. His eyes are dark pools in the night.

We face each other long minutes, not saying anything. The pain in my foot is insistent. "John and I went swimming last night. That's how I cut my foot."

"I know."

Ian's face seems to melt in suffering. It reminds me of how John looked last night, the way the tectonic plates of tragedy moved in him. But this is my own tragedy at work, and I strain to perceive what is before me. I told John that I didn't understand Ian's fortitude, his acceptance of the way things are. What I meant was that I love him, that my way is crooked and weak next to his.

"How can you love me the way you do?" I ask him. I want his secret. I want to make it mine.

"I don't know," he whispers.

I lean across the space that separates us and kiss Ian's lips, drawing his mouth into mine. I reach for him like a climber on a cliff's face. Ian, my rock, lets me hold him. Slowly his arms wrap around me, pull me close. This is love, and also something dire—the struggle to gain a purchase where we can make a stand.

SURELY GOODNESS

Jeremy Schnotala

On Wednesdays I get off the bus and I go straight to Mr. Turner's house. I mow the yellow grass or sweep the floor that ain't got nothing on it but dust or wash out the lazy dog's water bowl that's orange from the rusty well water. Even when there ain't a chore, I go to Mr. Turner's because he comes up with something. And I always leave with something—three crisp one-dollar bills that he pulls out of the pages of the big red Bible he keeps on his coffee table. He never reads that Bible. It's just a money machine for all I can tell. And every Wednesday when I'm done, like the fishes and loaves in that one story, out come those three dollar bills. And I take them home and roll them up real tight so they can squeeze through the little hole in my old Snoopy, right under his left ear. I cram them down inside the stuffing like I'm saving up to run away some day. And maybe I am saving up to run away someday. I just haven't decided yet. Or at least I ain't ready to tell anyone.

Every Wednesday—and I've only missed one in three years, when I had the flu so bad it was coming out both ends—I knock on the door and Mr. Turner asks me why I am knocking, you're old enough to just walk in, but I never do. "What's on the docket for today, Mr. Turner?" I say because I know he loves it when I use one of his crazy words like *docket.* "Oh we gots lots to do, boy," he always says.

And every week, Mr. Turner looks a little shorter and tells me how I've grown a little taller. Every week he sounds a little quieter and my voice is loud enough now to shout down the moon. Mr. Turner gets weaker and I get stronger. It's like standing in front of reverse mirror, even though I don't know if that's really a thing. Sounds about right, though. A reverse mirror.

Other than Mr. Turner himself, nothing else really changes. The rusty water bowl. The three dollars. The reverse mirror. At least not until the day I show up and knock and knock and knock and he don't answer. I know his hearing's going, so I knock even louder. But nothing. Then I put my ear to the door because I can hear through steel. Still nothing. I hear my ma's voice: *If you ever get there and that old man is slumped over in his chair, you come right home, Philip. You hear me. Don't you try to be some goddamned hero.* I don't even know what that means—*being a hero*—all I'm thinking about is poor Mr. Turner slumped over in his yellow recliner with that lazy dog snoring away at his feet not doing anything, so I just walk in. For the first time ever.

Mr. Turner ain't dead and that's a good thing. He's sitting in his recliner like normal, only he ain't normal. He's staring off into space and the rest of his body is frozen and his lips are moving like he's some old lady who's finishing up some nibble of bread she found in her cheek. Or like he's mumbling a prayer at church, though I know he don't pray because he told me once. "What do you pray for at night, Philip?" he asked me one day when I was sorting out his sock drawer.

"I don't know, sir. My mom. Peace on earth. Stuff like that." He turned me around and tapped me on the nose.

"Well, that's a lot for a young boy to pray for. Not me. I don't pray. Not no more," he said and I thought about that for weeks and weeks. Now he's sitting in his recliner, his lips mumbling something that ain't a prayer, and looking like he's lost in his own house.

I wave my hand in front of his eyes like you see someone do in a movie when their friend is in a trance. And I'm wondering if things are all blurring together in front of him like they sometimes do for me when I get stuck thinking too deep about things. Things like not praying or running away or other stuff I ain't ready to put into words. Moments like that, when everything is so heavy it all starts turning in on itself like you're stuck inside some giant kaleidoscope and someone's turning it a little at a time. Click. And everything shifts just a little. Click. And, well, you get the picture.

Mr. Turner doesn't see my hand. And he doesn't see me. He sees something, all right, but it ain't in that room. "Mr. Turner," I say trying to break him out of the trance. His lips keep moving without saying anything. "Mr. Turner. It's me," I yell.

"Who," he says. But not as a question. More like he's reading the word from a spelling list for little kids. *Who.*

"It's me, Mr. Turner. Philip." Then he turns away from the window and looks me directly in the eyes and that kaleidoscope rights itself.

"Oh?" he says, using the question mark he forgot earlier. Then we both just stand there and it's real awkward.

"Are you ok, sir?" I ask, but he don't answer. "Do you want me throw a load in the wash? Do you want me to clean up from last night's grub?" The lazy dog yawns and rolls over, but Mr. Turner still don't answer. Instead, he watches my face until it's like he finally gets an answer to something he's looking for. Then he turns back to the window, pinches his brows together until his wrinkles get deeper.

"Do you ever wonder why they chirp?" he asks.

"What's that?" I ask. "Why they chirp?" I listen, but I don't hear no chirping. "The birds, Mr. Turner? Why the birds chirp?" He doesn't answer. And the room gets real quiet again. So quiet I can hear the breathing of the old man. And the lazy dog. So quiet I can hear my own breathing. And my heartbeat. *Thump. Thump.* So quiet it's kind of scary.

And then, like it's sliding in through cracks in the walls or slipping in through tiny slivers in the ceiling, I hear it for the first time. The chirping. A faint *gleet gleet gleet* beyond the front window. So faint I'm surprised the old man can hear it.

"Them's crickets, Mr. Turner."

"Oh."

"Probably living outside the window under that rock pile you have me weed every spring. I guess I never noticed them before."

"Mm-hmm."

But Mr. Turner hadn't asked what they were. He had asked why they chirp. It's an odd question. I ask myself odd questions sometimes too. I have all sorts of odd questions that I try to answer. I just never say them out loud to no one. "I never really thought about why they chirp, Mr. Turner," I say, but the old man just stares with his mouth a little open waiting for a better answer than that. Just like a little kid who asks a parent what thunder is or why some people live on the street or what did God do with all the souls he ain't using. "Maybe they're just happy because it's so sunny out," I say. "Or maybe there's a big ol' garden snake out there about ready to gulp 'em up and they're warning their friends." I pause to wonder a little bit. I look out the window with Mr. Turner. "Or maybe they need their ma. And she's too busy to notice."

"Mm-hmm," he says. But it's one of those *mm-hmms* someone says when they aren't really listening to you.

"What do you think the reason is, Mr. Turner?" That's always the best way to handle a question you don't really have the answer to. Throw it back on the asker. The old man is leaning forward in the yellow recliner now and his lips are closed. Pressed tight. And he has worry written all over the wrinkles of his face. And suddenly I really want to know the answer. "Well, what is it sir?" I wait. He presses his lips tighter. The chirping gets just a little louder. The lazy dog lifts his head a little off the ground. We are all listening for the answer.

Then Mr. Turner rocks back once in the yellow recliner and uses that momentum to push himself up 'til he's standing as tall as he can in front of me. He repeats *mm-hmm* once more and then shuffles past me. He repeats *mm-hmm* again as he totters to the door. And one last time before he opens the door and walks out of the house into the sunshine.

The lazy dog drags himself off the floor and follows Mr. Turner outside. I follow too. Out into the yard, around the corner of the house, and straight to the decorative rock pile underneath the big front window.

"Help me down, young man," Mr. Turner says, and I let him lean all his weight on me as he crouches down and kneels in the grass. His bones creak and he grunts and breathes heavier than normal. And I wonder what it's like to have bones that make noises. The sun shines down on Mr. Turner's black skin as he settles in the grass and little beads of sweat start making it look even prettier in the shine. And I wonder what it's like to have black skin that don't burn in the sun. Mr. Turner leans forward and his curved fingers grope around the pile for a rock he can get a grip on. He finds one that fits perfectly in the cup of his hand. His fingers are gnarled and knotted like an old tree branch and they look even older against the smooth white rock he has in his hand. They look like they hurt, those fingers. And I wonder what it's like to have fingers that turn and twist like roots. The rock in his hand looks like a flattened baseball. Same dirty white. Same size only like someone run it over with a tractor. And just as I'm studying that rock and those fingers and the color of his skin in the sunlight, Mr. Turner chucks the rock over his shoulder and out into the yard.

"What ya doing, Mr. Turner?" I ask, but he just rakes out another rock with his knotty fingers and throws that one into the yard too. Then a third. And a fourth. He grunts with each throw and winces once it leaves his hand and then lets out a short gasp of air when it's done. *Whehhh* is what it sounds like.

"I'm not sure you want to do that, Mr. Turner," I say softly and then put my hand on his just as he's about to throw the next one. Next to his, my skin almost looks as white as the rock in his hand. He looks up at me, and I can see an angry purpose pinched in the wrinkles between his eyes. The skin on his fingers is dry and the wrinkles feel like folds of old fabric. I try to take the rock from his hand, and he struggles to pull away from my grip. I win the battle and take the rock out of his hand and let it fall back to the rock pile. "I won't be able to mow with all them rocks in the grass, sir. The blades'll snag 'em up and spit 'em back out like bullets."

"Mm-hmm," Mr. Turner says again and like a bad little kid grabs another rock before I can stop him and throws it over his shoulder.

The sun is on the same side of the house as the rock pile so I'm sweating by the time I catch up with Mr. Turner. He throws a rock and I run after it and pile it in the dirt patch under the tire swing that Mr. Turner hung up generations ago when he had kids around the place. Four boys that he loves to brag about, though I never saw a single picture of any of them. Matthew, Mark, Luke, and John. "My own little gospels," he loves to say. They were all grown up now, with kids of their own, and scattered around the country. I never asked Mr. Turner if they came to visit. I figured it might make him sad.

Mr. Turner is breathing heavily when he finally stops. And I'm so busy gathering the rocks and piling them under the tire swing that I don't even notice his hands. They're covered in dirt and dust. His nails are all chipped up too and one of them's bleeding. "You're all dirty, Mr. Turner. And you're bleeding," I say.

"Mm-hmm," he says and wipes the dust and blood on his pants.

"Don't you think you've done enough landscaping today? Let's get you inside to the watering hole for a drink," I say, but Mr. Turner doesn't laugh.

"I'm so close, Philip," he says as I'm standing him up. I'm glad to hear him use my name. Mr. Turner has a deep voice that sounds like coffee and thunder. I know that's weird, but that's just what it sounds like, and I like it most when he says my name. Once he's standing, he closes his eyes and breathes in real deep, like he's enjoying the aroma of a fresh baked pie or the thank you smell of a mown lawn, even though I don't smell nothing but sweat and dirt.

"So close to what?" I ask once Mr. Turner comes out of his trance.

He turns to me like I just asked the dumbest question in the world and that pinch appears again between his eyes. "Why. The chirping, Philip. The goddamn chirping."

....

I lay awake in bed a long time after my ma and stepdad are asleep. Long after the full moon moves past my window and tucks itself behind the big maple tree. I listen to the katydids and the tree frogs and the other night sounds. I think of the rocks and the tire swing, of Mr. Turner's sons and the colors of our skins. But mostly I think of that look on Mr. Turner's face. That pinch between his eyes. The goddamn chirping. It's the first swear word I ever heard the old man use in the all three years I been going there. Swearing doesn't bother me. My stepdad swears all the time. He says *shit* and *fuck* and *faggot* and all sorts of ugly words. Even *cunt* once when he was fighting real bad with my ma. But it's different with Mr. Turner. He never seemed like someone who needed to swear. Least not until the chirping. The goddamn chirping.

I don't sleep well at all. I toss and turn and have all sorts of strange dreams. Dreams with long wrinkled fingers clawing at white boulders. Sleek black legs and beady heads with antennaes darting deeper and deeper into crevices. And chirping. Louder. And louder. And Mr. Turner's deflated body drying up in the sun like that old black tire. And hadn't the chirping always been there?

....

"Hasn't the chirping always been there?" I ask Mr. Turner a week later when I get there. Mr. Turner's already sitting in front of the rock pile like a big kid and the yard is already splotched with dozens of white rocks here and there.

"What does it matter if it's always been there or if God just commanded them to start chirping this very minute. It's there all the same, isn't it? It's here. And I'm going to stop it." Mr. Turner coughs. A little at first. Then deeper and angrier and louder, like he's trying to cough out a curse. "Goddammit!" he shouts. Maybe at his old lungs. Maybe at me for asking such annoying questions. Maybe at the rock in his hand that he throws but can't throw as far as he wants to. Maybe at the chirping that seems louder than ever.

Louder than it was last week, I swear, even though I wonder how that's possible. Were there more crickets now? Dozens and dozens of the rocks had been ripped out of the area in front of the big window and I can see dimpled patches of dry, brown earth where the rocks used to be. Maybe the rocks had shielded some of the sound. I kneel down next to Mr. Turner and look close at the ground. The *gleet gleet gleet* pulses in my ear. It's like the rocks themselves are chirping. Like it's coming from the earth. *Gleet gleet gleet* times a thousand. Times a million. But I don't see a single cricket.

"Have you seen any yet, Mr. Turner?" I whisper, but Mr. Turner doesn't answer. "And what are you going to do with 'em when you find 'em, sir?" I ask. He doesn't answer that either.

"Goddamnit you ask a lot of fucking questions. Help me up. I have to piss," Mr. Turner says. "I've been out in this yard all afternoon. Why are you so late?" It doesn't sound like Mr. Turner at all. Sounds more like my stepdad. And I'm feeling a little bad because Mr. Turner's never talked to me like that before, but I help him off the ground and am about to help him across the front yard into the house to pee when he unzips his blue trousers, yanks down his boxers, pulls out his penis, and pees all over the leftover rocks under the window. "Take that you little fucking bastards," he says and laughs and coughs and laughs some more.

I want to laugh too, but the moment catches me off guard. I also want to turn my head away like you do in the boy's bathroom at school when another kid is peeing in the urinal next to you. But I don't. And there I am, staring at Mr. Turner's shriveled up penis that looks like a dried up mushroom in a bird's next. At first I'm thinking about how I'd love to take a piss in my stepdad's bottle one of these days when he ain't looking. Then I'm trying to remember if I've ever really seen anyone else's penis before in my whole life. I know I tried to see one last year when another boy in my class was climbing the jungle gym above me in recess. It was Brian and he was wearing red shorts and everyone had been joking all day that he wasn't wearing underwear.

"Brian's free balling it," one of the other kids had said.

"What's free balling?" I asked like some idiot.

"He's not wearing underwear!"

I had always thought Brian was pretty. His skin was a warm color and he had thick dark lashes and a few dark freckles on both sides of his brown face. And the thought of him not wearing underwear had made me feel happy for some reason.

"Faggot!" someone shouted. And of course everyone looked. "Philip's a faggot. He's trying to see Brian's dick." And everyone laughed. Deep laughs like coughs.

It was true, though I denied it.

"Are you a faggot?" Brian asked me himself. He looked around to make sure all the other boys had heard him. Like he had to ask me, even though he didn't want to. I shook my head no, but Brian knew. Everyone knew.

"Oh, fuck. I got it all over my pants. That's what happens when you get old. You always get it all over everywhere," Mr. Turner says and zips up his pants. And sure enough, he's got a big, round wet stain on the front of his pants. "Lots of things happen when you get old, Philip," Mr. Turner says and then stares at the leftover rocks. "I'm sorry I talked to you that way, Philip. It was wrong. That's another thing that happens when you get old."

The pee doesn't affect the chirping. The rocks glisten a little more and there are trails of wet dirt where Mr. Turner missed the rocks, but the crickets keep on chirping. "That's all for today," Mr. Turner says with a really tired voice. He seems sad and sorry and tired all at the same time.

He hobbles to the door, and the chirping gets a little louder as he leaves. He opens the door and goes inside without a goodbye. The lazy dog barks once and Mr. Turner opens the door to let him in. "Go home, Philip. That's all for today," he says and shuts the door. And the chirping gets a little louder again. Grows like a fever that I can feel in every part of my body. Pulsing with every chirp. Just like every part of my body has its own little heart that's beating separately. Beating heavy. Beating angry.

....

The next Wednesday, Mr. Turner is standing wobbily on the porch waiting for me. "Aren't you late?" he asks.

"No, sir. The bus lets us off at—"

"I don't give a shit about the bus. Help me off this goddamned porch."

I can tell he's gonna be mean again this week. I set my backpack next to the steps and grab his arm. "I think we're going to be lucky today, Mr. Turner. I feel like we're real close, don't you think?" He doesn't answer me and we walk silently across the front of the house to the half-destroyed rock garden. It's ugly to look at and I wonder what Matthew, Mark, Luke, and John would think if they saw their place now. Most of the rocks that are left are half buried in hardened dirt. I think about just telling Mr. Turner to sit in the shade next to the lazy dog with an iced tea and watch while I dig out the rest of the rocks with a hoe. I could chip away at them and pile them all into the old green wheelbarrow, and in one or two loads dump 'em all in the pile under the swing. I hate the crickets now as much as the old man does and part of me would love to do it myself.

"Don't think of it, boy," the old man says like he's reading my mind. "We have roles to play. Don't mess with roles," he says and settles himself onto his knees in front of the rocks, I don't know what he means by roles, but I know I'll be thinking about it for a long time.

I watch as he digs at the rocks first with a small garden spade. Then with a spoon from the kitchen. And when neither of them work, he goes at it with his bare hands. His hands are scratched and cut up and he can't get a grip on any of the last stubborn rocks. It's like the earth doesn't want to let go. Like nature knows that the crickets are right under those last few rocks, shaking in their shiny suits. Mr. Turner can feel it too and he claws at the earth with his nails. He grunts. He sweats. He curses. It's almost like he's a beast, sweating on his knees in the hot sun, trying to escape some cage he's penned inside of.

I feel like I'm inside that cage sometimes too. And when I am, I get mean too. I want to yell at people and swear and be rude. Maybe I can when I get old.

I go inside and bring back a glass of water and a pair of leather gloves from the hallway closet. They're women's gloves and it's first time I think about a woman ever being here at the house. Of course there had to be a woman if Mr. Turner had four sons. But somehow the image of a Mrs. Turner doesn't fit.

"Here, use these, Mr. Turner. Your hands are bleeding again." The sweat and dirt and blood on his hands are all mixed together. It looks like his hands are covered in guts.

Mr. Turner stares at the gloves like they hurt him to see 'em. "Get rid of those. I don't need a pair of gloves. I need a goddamn blitzkrieg!" And he goes back to his frenzied digging.

I don't know exactly what a *blitzkrieg* is, but I can imagine it's some kind of weapon. I picture Mr. Turner with one of those huge fire-launchers spraying blue fire all over the dirt and all over the last of the rocks. I picture thousands of little crickets finally crawling out from their holes, crusty little cinders, each carrying a tiny flame on their back. It makes me smile. I hold out the glass of water, but Mr. Turner won't take it, so I drink it myself.

"What do you do during the week when I'm not here, Mr. Turner?" I'm not really sure where my question comes from. I don't mean it to be rude and I'm not insinuating that Mr. Turner should be out here in this horrible sun alone, but it just suddenly dawns on me that Mr. Turner only exists on Wednesdays. Like he's just a one-day-a-week person in my mind. And it bothers me that I can't picture him on a Friday night or a Sunday morning. Like a full, seven-day-a-week person. Like my mother or her nasty husband. Or even Brian from school.

Mr. Turner stops scraping the edges of one of the rocks with the handle side of the spoon. He puts the spoon on the ground and wipes his black forehead with his dirty hand so that he's got guts all over his face. And then he turns to me and the sun washes out the color from his eyes and there's a long silence before he answers and I wish that sun wasn't so bright so I could see what the pinch between his eyes is saying. "I inch. A little closer to death. That's what I do. I inch a little closer to death each and every day."

....

I try to relive the moment in my mind that night when I'm in bed. Try to make it something else. I do that sometimes. Try to recreate things I did wrong. Or things I said that I shouldn't have. Or things I thought about that I know are bad. Like trying to see Brian's penis. Or telling my ma that I think of boys sometimes. I change it from boys to girls so that I don't hate myself so much and so she doesn't have to tell her husband and so he doesn't have to take out his ugly belt to fix me. I do that with my question to Mr. Turner. I change it to something nicer like, "Mr. Turner, do you watch TV at nights?" or "Do you get any other visitors during the week?" But each time, the old man turns to me with the same answer. "I inch. A little closer to death." And each time, he sounds a little more angry and a little more hurt. Until he starts saying my name, too. "I inch. Philip. A little closer to death." It growls from the belly of the old man like an infected cough. And my name is like a swear word. And I picture him as an old, wrinkled cricket with Mr. Turner's head on it, inching along in the dirt, each knobby joint as brittle as a seed husk. He's trying to find a rock to hide under in the rock garden where there ain't no more rocks. And the sun beats down on his black body. Beats down and down on that black crusty shell until he gives up. Finally. Until he lies in the middle of the dust, his body moving up and down. Trying to chirp. No. Trying to breathe.

....

The following Wednesday Mr. Turner isn't in the yard when I get there. And he isn't on the porch either, but I can see that he's been working at the rocks all week. By himself. The rock pile is whittled down to just a few rocks that look like they'll never come loose. And there are white splotches all around the yard. I feel guilty. I'm always feeling guilty about stuff.

Mr. Turner isn't in the yellow recliner either. "Mr. Turner?" I ask the dark house. "Mr. Turner?"

I find him in his bedroom, lying awake on top of his bedspread. He's naked, his clothes clumped up in a pile on the floor next to the bed—trousers, shirt, boxers, t-shirt. There are clumps of dirty clothes just like that one all around the room. And I can imagine Mr. Turner shuffling in from the sun, sweaty, exhausted. I can imagine him stripping off his button-up shirt, his t-shirt, trousers, peeling his boxers off and collapsing in the bed. Everything smells of sweat and underarms, hard work, and urine. Especially urine. So strong it burns your eyes.

"Mr. Turner. You want me to help you to the shower?" He doesn't answer. Maybe he can't, I think. "Are you sick, sir? You don't look so good." His black skin doesn't have its normal, pretty shine. He looks almost gray. And I know he's thinking about the chirping. About those goddamned crickets. They're so loud it's like they're right there in the bedroom, huddled under the pee-soaked clothes. I have to raise my voice a little louder to be heard over their chirping. "Don't you want to get rid of the rest of the rocks, Mr. Turner? I think we're real close to finding them, no?"

"Mm-hmm?" Mr. Turner says. Just like a little boy. Then he rolls his head toward me and his eyes are real sad. "You really think so?" he asks. His voice is so weak and so drowned out by the crickets that I have to read his lips which is real hard since they are covered up by some of his whiskers. And then out of some deep part, he inhales a really long, ugly breath through his nose and belts out, "Then get me out of this goddamn piss pile and let's get to work."

I help him out of the bed and into a pair of dry boxers that I find in the dresser. And then into a pair of his blue trousers that I have to button and zip up for him like he's a little kid. The whole time Mr. Turner's swearing "Goddamn bugs" and "Fucking racket this and that" and "Them bastards." His trousers are real loose so I have to find a belt and slide it through the loops and buckle it in the front. I pull a dingy white t-shirt over his head and direct his old arms through each hole while he keeps swearing. "Bitches" this and "Bastards" that. I put one of his blue, button-up shirts on him and button three buttons like he always does. "Motherfuckingbitchballbastards!" he says and I laugh.

"That's a good one, Mr. Turner."

"That's what they are. Motherfuckingbitchballbastards!" he says again. "It's today. Or it's never, Philip. You hear me?"

"I hear you, sir."

"Say it then."

"It's today or it's—"

"No. You forgot the Motherfucking . . ."

I finish it with him. "Bitchballbastards. It's today or it's never." That makes me smile. And it makes me sad.

Outside, Mr. Turner doesn't have as much gusto as he had sitting on the edge of the bed swearing. He stands and stares over the few remaining rocks and his shoulders kind of sink down. He looks defeated.

"There's not even a dozen rocks left, Mr. Turner. You can do it." Though I really don't know.

"What happens if we remove all the rocks and there aren't any crickets there? What then?" he asks me. Just like that. Like I have the answers to questions like that.

"Well, sir," I say to bide some time so I can think. Then he throws another one at me.

"What happens if we do find them? Find all of them? What happens if under the last rock there are swarms and swarms of them just cowering and huddling together, chirping like all get out? What then? What are we supposed to do then?"

I think about how I probably should have just left the old man in bed. Just covered him up with an afghan or a sheet. Told him I'd see him next Wednesday. But I didn't. I'm standing here now and he's my responsibility. And he's looking at me like he's desperate for an answer.

And, suddenly, I know he won't be around 'til next Wednesday. Somehow I just know it.

I grab his hand and I squeeze it. It's just like an answer. And I help him kneel down in the grass for what I know will be the last time. I guide his hand to a rock, and he don't know that I'm digging at it with my nails. He thinks he's doing by himself. And I feel his hand reach around that stone and a little smile pops up on his face when he lifts it out of the dirt. He's too weak to throw it over his shoulder, but he's got my muscles now, and we chuck it into the grass together.

It goes like that until there's nothing left but dirt in front of Mr. Turner's front window. Dirt and chirping. Mr. Turner looks sick and his pants are stained where he's wet himself again. "It's time to go inside Mr. Turner. The crickets are down in their holes getting ready to sleep," I say, even though I don't know if crickets sleep. I don't know anything about crickets.

He puts the palms of both his hands on the dirt. "Can't we dig up the dirt?" he asks. His voice is weak. He already knows the answer.

"No, sir. We can't do that."

He nods. And before he pulls his hands from the ground, he takes a deep breath. For a minute it looks like he's laying hands on the ground to pray. Like he's blessing the land. Like he's sanctifying the crickets hiding deep in their holes. "You know," he says. "It's only the male crickets that sing." He struggles then to push himself off the ground. I have to help. I have to lift his body. "And maybe—" he says, "maybe their song ain't all that bad."

I walk him back to the house. Real slow. Each step feels like the next one'll be impossible. Like we're walking through a swamp that's sucking us both down and don't want to let us go.

The lazy dog is waiting in Mr. Turner's bed when we get there. Keeping his spot warm. I shoo him away and set the old man down on the edge of the bed.

"You want me to help you get into your pajamas, Mr. Turner?" He doesn't answer me. And that's ok. I take his clothes off—his shirt, his t-shirt, his wet trousers and wet boxers. I fold them up and put them on the floor. I wet down a towel with warm water from the kitchen sink and kind of sponge Mr. Turner clean. His skin moves all funny when I wipe him. Like it's lost its will to cling to the body. I worry I might be hurting him even though I'm being real gentle. "Does this hurt, Mr. Turner?" He doesn't answer. I wash his face and his arms. I wash his chest. His legs. I even wash his privates. I want him to feel clean. I want him to feel refreshed. I want things I don't even understand.

There ain't no pajamas in his dresser, so I just put a pair of clean boxers and a t-shirt on him. Then I lay him down in the bed and make sure his head is comfortable in the center of the pillow. I cover his body with a clean sheet and the old, green afghan from the recliner. And then there's really nothing else I can do. Except kiss him on his forehead. He smells clean and his skin is warm.

"It's almost nighttime, sir. You need to get some sleep. I'm probably gonna get in trouble if I don't head home soon." He breathes with his mouth open. His eyes are open too, but they don't look like they're seeing anything. "The chirping sounds real nice now with all the other night sounds. Ain't that true, Mr. Turner?" I listen to the sounds of katydids and tree frogs, the hoots of owls and the rustle of leaves in the wind. The male crickets and their song. It's like we're out in the great, wide open. Like the walls of the house are gone and everything is just one beautiful song. "That's something real nice about the night," I say out loud. "Now you close your eyes, Mr. Turner, and sleep now, sir. You deserve it."

....

I don't remember the walk home. I don't remember that I told my ma Mr. Turner died. But I guess I did. I don't remember much. Except for how beautiful the night sounded. How free.

....

On Sunday, my ma digs out a black dress and a black raincoat from the basement. Of course it's raining out, I think. I put on a black coat and a pair of dress pants that are really just a dark navy blue, but they'll pass. My stepdad says he can't go to the memorial because he don't have nothing black and I'm glad. "Plus," he says, "I don't know why everybody's getting all worked up for that old, black queer anyway. You're lucky he never perverted your boy, Maureen," he says to my ma. "He ever pervert you, boy?" he asks me. Pervert ain't a verb, I want to tell him, but I don't really know if it is or isn't, so I just roll my eyes and get in the car. The whole ride there is quiet. Real quiet. Except for the squeaking of the windshield wipers. And my ma humming that sad church song "I Come to the Garden Alone."

"Will Mr. Turner's sons be there?" I ask my ma before we pull into the cemetery. "Mathew, Mark, Luke, and John?" My ma looks at me like I'm dumb.

"Philip, Mr. Turner never had any children. He was an old bachelor."

I reach into my coat pocket where I have a handful of white rocks I took from his yard. The rest are scattered around the lawn because it was too dark when I left to collect them and the others are stacked underneath the tire swing—the tire swing that wasn't really for his sons because he never had sons. "Well then who—" but I change my question. "Who will be coming to the memorial?" I ask.

"We'll see. We are," she says and the rest of the ride is just the squeaking of the wipers.

....

The rain makes everybody's clothes look shiny, their umbrellas sleek. I don't recognize a single person, except for Mr. Turner in his casket, but he looks all plastic and posed. I want to tell somebody he'd never wear a white dress shirt like that and an ugly red tie, but it ain't my business. So I just picture him wearing his typical blue, his skin rich and dark against the color. There are about a dozen or so people here and I'm happy about that. Mostly they're old men. Black men and white men and brown men. Skinny and wrinkled with wide eyes that look like they've been crying for years. Old men dressed up nice in their all black. Some of them are holding hands with each other and one of them looks a lot like an old woman all crumpled up in the arms of her husband, only it ain't her husband and it ain't a her. For some reason, it feels like I'm looking at Brian's penis again. Like I'm trying not to, but I can't help myself from staring. From seeing more. Then I remember my mom's with me and I'm wishing she'd have stayed home with Ron. I'm hoping she's not noticing any of this, though I know she is.

The preacher is holding Mr. Turner's big red bible, the one he never reads. The one that gave me all those dollars I have hid inside my Snoopy. And I start thinking about how plump my Snoopy looks and how many dollars he must have curled up in his belly. The preacher opens the big red bible and out fall three dollar bills. I want to tell him they're mine since Mr. Turner hadn't paid me for several weeks, but this ain't the time. He just leaves them on the ground and starts reading Psalm 23, which is what they pretty much read at every funeral because that's probably all that verse is good for. I don't listen to anything from the Bible. I just listen to all the old men around me sniffling and whimpering and whispering stuff to each other that I can't hear. And I watch those dollar bills get wetter from the rain. And I think about the day when I'll pack me up a little bag. When I'll tear open the Snoopy and count out all those dollar bills. When I'll leave my ma and my stepdad and all the boys at school and head out on my own. When I'll own the nighttime song all to myself.

My mom puts her arm around me and hugs me close. The pastor is finishing up the verse. "Surely goodness and mercy shall follow me all the days of my life."

Trapped

SMALL VICTORIES

Dave DeFusco

In January of 1970, a couple of months before I turned eighteen, I was thrown out of my parents' home after trying to commit suicide. I'd stolen a bottle of sleeping pills from my mother's purse and swallowed almost every tablet on a Sunday evening while they watched Mutual of Omaha's *Wild Kingdom*. A week after I returned home from the hospital, my mother sat at the edge of my bed. Her hands were balled up in her lap, her inebriated eyes a watery blue. She told me they "couldn't keep me" any longer. My father was out of work, and between his age and emphysema, the strain of caring for him and the medical bills threatening to overwhelm them, they didn't "have the energy" to deal with the challenges that beset me.

My mother, haggard and forlorn, dabbed her nose with a tissue. She didn't suggest where I'd go, nor did I ask, out of a mixture of shock and understanding. Nor did she demand that I leave immediately, but I took it to be that. Her decision seemed as spontaneous as my suicide attempt, which left doubt in my own mind whether it was a sincere attempt or a cry for help. We sat in silence, stealing glances at each other, before she announced that we were having meatloaf for dinner.

"Wash your hands," she said.

I nodded and rolled over to face away from her. When I felt her end of the bed rise, I buried my face in the crook of my elbow. She turned on the bedside lamp and gently shut the door behind her.

I slept through dinner, my body trying to shake off the lingering nausea and cramps, and was awakened by bright light streaming through the windows. I sat up and looked around for the time. My windup clock was frozen at two-twenty. She usually woke me up for school, but I could tell by the slant of light that it was late morning. I heard a commotion in the kitchen. I turned off the bedside lamp and listened by my door. My mother was chastising my father for not moving fast enough to make a doctor's appointment. I waited until they left, and then went into the kitchen. I sipped my father's warm tea and picked at his uneaten toast, and paged through his open newspaper. A headline declared Willie Mays the 1960s' player of the decade. When I reached for the butter on the Lazy Susan, I saw five twenty-dollar bills. I wiped my hands on my pants and read the accompanying note.

Dear Bobby, please understand our situation. We love you. Mom and Dad.

Before I had drifted off to sleep, a part of me hoped there would be a change of heart in the morning, that my mother, a secretary at a local insurance company thrust back into the workforce after the onset of my father's illness, was under such strain that she had briefly lost her senses. I balled up the note, threw it across the table, and retreated to my bedroom where I dug a prescription slip out of my bellbottoms for the name and phone number of the hospital's staff psychiatrist. Dr. Hamels. I left an urgent message with the secretary on his floor, then I took a shower. Afterward, I raided my mother's dresser for lipsticks and silk scarves, and packed a stationary pad filled with odes to Manny.

As I waited for Dr. Hamels to call, I flipped through a family photo album on the living room coffee table. In one photograph, I was barely three. My hair was perfectly parted and oiled. I wore a plaid flannel shirt and cuffed dungarees, and sat on my mother's lap, my father beside her. My parents, youthful and slender, held the promise of the future in their smiles. I was beaming, no doubt, from the secure embrace of my mother. I peeled away the plastic cover holding the photo in place and pocketed it as a reminder of how proud they were of me once.

When Dr. Hamels called, I told him what my mother had said. Even though I was still a minor and he was risking professional censure, he recommended I stay with a foster parent, Jane Hanley, who lived one town over. Since I was almost eighteen and would therefore be an adult under the law, he didn't think state authorities would act to remove me, or discipline him, if my mother were to have a sudden change of heart. He said he'd call ahead.

After I hung up, I scooped up the twenties and took one last look around the living room. It all seemed artificial now, the shrink-wrapped yellow couch and the high-back chairs used only by company, an amateurish oil painting of our steepled church hanging above a fireplace we never used, and an array of dishes on the mantel painted with each

Wonder of the World. I slung the bag over my shoulder, locked the door, and hurried to my car, a used gold Impala that I had bought with money saved from cutting grass for the town during the summer.

After a couple of wrong turns, I pulled up beside a rusted mailbox with its lid lying flat. *Hanley* was inscribed in black script on the side. I entered a serpentine driveway hemmed by pines. A weathered sign posted on a tree declared: "Not a public road . . . Use at your own risk." A hundred feet in, I entered a clearing overshadowed by a weathered Victorian. In the apron of the front yard, a scrub of tall weeds partially camouflaged a clawfoot bathtub, and an old tractor languished in a muddy skid on the side of the house.

I parked beside the tractor, left my bag in the car, and cautiously approached the front door. Although it was early afternoon, the unprepossessing house was cast in a pallid gray, the sun twinkling through the surrounding pine.

I rapped on the door. When I heard footsteps, I took a step back. I noticed first her gray hair, spread out in little waves down both sides of her head from a part in the middle and cascading in silvery streaks to her waist. She wore a heavy open sweater and an ankle-length skirt, and her braless nipples pressed against a thin t-shirt. Her eyes were manic, sagging under the pull of grayish pouches, her grin more sinister than welcoming. A corncob pipe dangled from the side of her mouth.

I didn't see the rifle as she swung the barrel into place and aimed, the muzzle pointing at my head. I took another step back and thrust my hands into the air.

"Who might you be?" she said.

"Didn't he call you?"

"Who's *he*?"

"Dr. Hamels."

"You're Bobby."

"Yes, ma'am."

She lowered the rifle. "Bill said you'd be calling first."

I rested my hands on my hips and exhaled.

"She wasn't loaded anyway." She was self-assured, even genial now, as if greeting every visitor at gunpoint was a necessary initiation into her world. "A woman alone out here can't take chances."

I smiled weakly.

"Hanley. Jane Hanley." She nudged open the door. "Come on in."

I stopped short of the threshold. I couldn't return home to my parents, pickled by bourbon, who raged nightly about their mutual disappointments, I being one of them. Dr. Hamels' promise that Jane would be a "safe haven" was bewildering. I wondered if he had been to the house. She stood the rifle against the wall and waved me in.

"C'mon, come in from the cold. Unless you're CIA, you're not getting hurt," she said with a wry smile.

She looked like one of those hippies I saw on television protesting the war, or slithering in the mud at Woodstock, the ones my father accused of betraying America. The house smelled of sweet pipe tobacco commingled with the aroma of cabbage steaming up from a cast-iron pot on a wood-fired stove. She led me into the living room. Bright light flooded through two tall windows with wide sashes that looked out over a sprawling, unkempt lawn.

"Welcome to my humble home." She held the bowl of the pipe as she puffed. "You want something to eat?"

I shook my head. "Where are the others?"

"The others?"

"Dr. Hamels said you were a foster parent." I looked around the room for evidence of people my age. I didn't see a television set, but there was a stereo, a couple of small speakers, and albums stacked neatly in a corner.

"People come and go here. They get what they need and leave."

"So I'm the only one?"

"For now."

She settled into a sunken leather chair, beside it a lamp with a broad shade, the chair nestled in the corner by the bookcase. Books were crammed floor to ceiling on one side of the room, and on the opposite side, a tattered American flag drooped from a drab olive-colored wall, its stars circumscribed by a green peace sign. Under the flag, two end tables sandwiched an amply cushioned couch. A sturdy coffee table held a typewriter and stacks of envelopes and paper. She encouraged me to look out the window at a brown patch beside a leaning barn. By summer, she said, it would yield rows of tomatoes, lobster mushrooms, rhubarb, and summer squash. She used yarrow for salad and tea, she said, swearing by the leaves' medicinal properties.

"Agent Orange would be no match for my immune system." She mentioned the sunchokes she had turned into liquor. "I only use real things around here."

She tapped black ash from her pipe into an empty glass, and pulled a tobacco pouch out of her pocket. She sprinkled the contents into the bowl, tamped it down, struck a match and lowered the flame. Puffs of blue smoke burst forth from the corner of her mouth. She tamped the tobacco down a second time with the match, then held the pipe, her elbow propped on the armrest, smiling serenely as smoke encircled her. Her gaze lingered, as if she were measuring me. I felt the keys in my coat and considered escaping to the car.

"This ain't some finishing school."

"Huh?"

"You called me *ma'am* outside. We're equals. Dig?" Her voice was hoarse, but strong. "Call me Jane. Take your coat off and get comfortable."

I reluctantly complied, but held onto it just in case. She asked me what I thought of Richard Nixon, as if an exchange of social pleasantries with a guest were a bourgeois luxury. She said she taught political science at Berkeley before being fired for distributing literature on feminism and Marxism.

"Don't be fooled, Bobby. Ideas are just as threatening to educated types in ivory towers as they are to Billy Graham's followers."

I nodded dumbly, distracted by my own discomfort. She had moved to Chicago and got involved with a group of demonstrators at the Democratic National Convention in 1968, but as the FBI closed in on them, she fled to the East Coast.

"What do you think should happen when politicians abuse their power?"

I thought it might be a trick question. "I don't know. Vote them out?"

An amiable condescension veiled her thin smile. "In or out, nothing really changes," she said, slowly shaking her head. "You have to force 'em to take notice, but politicians and people who benefit from the status quo, they don't want to notice."

She told me that, in a week, she would be attending a "political meeting" in Bridgeport. She and several others were planning to rush a draft board office on the anniversary of the Catonsville Nine, commandeer draft cards, and make a spectacle of burning them in the parking lot to protest the Vietnam War. The leader of the Catonsville Nine, Father Dan Berrigan, would lead the protest. She sucked on the stem of the pipe.

"It isn't enough to say you're against the war," she said. "You have to *do* something about it, or else be an accomplice to the slaughter. You in?"

I covered my ears.

Her voice softened, the righteous indignation dissipating like retreating wisps of smoke. "Are you all right?"

I needed some fresh air. "Do you mind?" I left and sat on the front step of the porch, my coat and scarf still wrapped in my arms. I stared at a stand of maple, mottled gray and undressed, their gnarled arms bent skyward. The scratch of Jane's sandals crept up on me, the door rapping shut. I was jolted out of my reverie. She sat beside me and offered a mug of cocoa steaming from its mouth. I hugged myself against the cold. We sat in silence. A flock of ravens squawking high up in the trees pierced the leaden air. I smoothed the coat over my thighs and surveyed the grounds, muddy in winter's grip.

"The quiet at first was just what I needed," Jane said, "but it gets old pretty fast. Have you ever gone days without talking to someone? You start questioning your own existence."

"It's better than not being heard by someone."

"I've lived inside my head for so long, I've forgotten my manners."

"My father said people like you are aiding the enemy," I said, embarrassed to repeat his silliness. I picked up the mug and took a sip.

"Maybe I am, Bobby," she said, "if it's to stop military aggression. Why don't you join us next week? See for yourself."

"I think I'll pass." The images on television brought the war's horror home every night, but I felt detached from its ferocity, its devastation, its futility. Anyway, I wouldn't risk my safety for a radical who had just pointed a rifle at my head. "What would burning draft cards do anyway? What *did* it do in 1968?"

"Do you always know how things will turn out? If you're motivated to right a wrong and take action, I consider that a victory, no matter how small." She patted my thigh. "Come with me."

We went inside the house. She led me to the coffee table and pointed to the letters beside the typewriter. "My civic duty. To the president expressing my outrage at our illegal war in Vietnam."

Beside the typewriter, there was a framed black-and-white photograph of a Buddhist monk who had set himself on fire. I wondered if Jane was capable of doing that to herself, or to me.

"What does that one say?" I pointed to the piece of paper rolled up in the typewriter. "Can I read it?"

She pulled it out of the typewriter and handed it to me. "Here."

Dear Mr. President,

I demand that you end this illegal, immoral war of aggression against the peoples of Southeast Asia today. You are violating their sovereignty in direct opposition to U.N. mandates and American principles codified in our Constitution, and expressed by George Washington, who warned against foreign entanglements. The B-52 bombings and the use of Agent Orange are crimes against humanity, and should you and the members of your administration persist in your aggression you would be subject to prosecution by an international tribunal for war crimes. Was not the atrocity of My Lai enough to convince you that this war is immoral, that the prosecution of it is deeply flawed, and that ultimately there are no winners in war? Are you indifferent to the rising death toll of young Americans? Do you not hear the anguished cries of mothers who have lost their children in this quagmire? Communism isn't the problem. It is men like you who mask their impotence with missiles, and the perverted incentives of Capitalism that finance perpetual war. Whether it's in the rice paddies of Vietnam or on the streets of Selma, the white man loves to use force to keep the colored man down. I'm outraged that you are interfering in a civil war and with the Vietnamese people's right to self-determination, a principle that we Americans hold as sacred. Is not our own Civil War instructive in this conflict? I beseech you to devote yourself to a just peace, to sign a treaty with Vietnam, to respect the rights of the Vietnamese people, and to immediately withdraw American troops from Southeast Asia. It is the only right and honorable thing to do.

Yours truly,
Jane Hanley
Redding, Connecticut

When I was finished, I laid the letter in my lap and watched her type another one. In the confines of that house, the war itself was her companion, her lover—animated by her passion, her anger, her sense of justice. I was just seeking refuge, quiet—time.

Jane didn't so much as type, but assault the keys of that typewriter, as if it were a telegraph and her outrage transmitted directly into the Oval Office. Only a few miles away, my parents were consumed by a different kind of rage, a bitterness that blinded them to poverty and injustice. They fully supported the war, but not because they feared the spread of communism. Military might, it seemed, was an extension of their anger over their own failures and their resentment toward black people who they thought had "more rights." But then I pictured my father struggling to breathe and their desperation to pay the bills. I felt guilty for having added to their burden and depressed at my own self-centeredness, but also mortified by their politics and the prospect of being drafted myself.

"Dr. Hamels said you took too many pills," Jane said, easing back from the typewriter.

"Not enough."

"So you really did want to kill yourself?"

"I guess I thought, 'that'll teach those assholes.'"

"Your parents?"

"Yes."

"Why not just smash the car up or get an F?"

....

Dr. Hamels had greeted me as if we had always been friends when he visited my hospital room at lunchtime. He pointed at my tray. "Thank goodness they don't make the staff eat that." He had a boyish face that smiled even at rest, with a thick mustache and beard. He gestured at the chair next to the bed. "You mind?"

I shook my head. I knew what was coming.

He clasped his hands and crossed his legs. "You're a junior, I'm told. I bet you can't wait to graduate and get away from those underclassmen."

I took a sip of orange juice, but it burned my stomach. "They're not that bad."

"Really? I have a freshman. Not a kid, but not old enough to be responsible."

I wondered how long he would try to gain my trust. I took an inordinate interest in the wilted broccoli and the gristly chicken slathered with cream-and-mushroom sauce on my plate, but I felt him looking at me.

"I'm sorry about what happened," he said. "I know this is a terrible time to be asking questions."

"Uh-huh."

"I hear you're good in school. Favorite subject? Teacher?"

My stomach hurt. I raked the corn niblets over the mash potatoes. "English."

"Excellent. You a reader or a writer?"

I stabbed the chicken on my plate and shoved it into my mouth. I was hoping I'd puke and get him to leave. He leaned forward in his chair. He seemed to be gathering his thoughts.

"Is this the first time you've tried to hurt yourself?"

"I'm not talking."

"Okay. You're not the first one who's told me that."

I dropped the fork in my plate and spit out the chicken. "Then why do you keep doing it?"

"If you let me, I think I can help."

"Bullshit."

He sat back in the chair and paused. "Okay, then. I'll make you a deal. You answer a few questions, and we both can get out of here in a jiffy."

I pushed away the tray and slid out the other side of the bed. I didn't need him. The bright sunlight felt like a ticket to freedom. I reached inside the bag that my mother had brought for me. It contained a Bible, missed homework, and baseball cards from my father, including a 1969 Tony Conigliaro and a stick of powdery bubblegum peeking out from the partially opened wrapper. I sat heavily on the side of the bed.

"You're upset," he said. "You want to tell me what it's about?"

I got up and gazed out the window. I watched cars jockey for space in the parking lot below, and Matchbox-size vehicles streaming relentlessly on a far-off stretch of highway. I wondered how I could get Manny, the boy I loved, to bring me clothes.

Dr. Hamels invited me again to call him Jeff. "I was heavy and picked on unmercifully. I wasn't much younger than you. I didn't think I had any options."

I turned around to face him. "What do you *want*, Jeff?"

"Please try not to hold your past experience against me." He pulled a folded piece of paper out of his pocket and handed it to me. "I want to help."

It was a poem I had written for Manny in a solitary moment.

I read your diary. I try not to care.
We all have a past, I say.
No problem, I say.
It is what it is, I say, I say, I say, you say.
Licking. Sucking. Blowing. Fucking. I put my face on your lover's pictures.
Your innocence,
hanging from a shoelace in your cell,

drips from your toes.
I envy your lovers,
your accusers,
your murderers. I worship the ground they walk on.
You barely kept your head above my raging river.
An angel's wings,
tied by your own hands.
I blame myself, myself, myself, you.
Now all I hear is ringing in my ears,
your private thoughts piercing my pillow.

"Where the fuck did you get this?" I shook the piece of paper at him. "Who gave you permission?"

"Your mother gave it to me. Bobby, she's trying to help."

"That's how much *you* know."

An attendant opened the door as he knocked. When he heard my raised voice, he stopped and apologized for the intrusion. The attendant said a friend had left a package with the front desk. He placed it just inside the door and apologized again for not delivering it sooner. The package was a rolled-up grocery bag. I opened it and peeked inside.

"The poem, Bobby."

I ignored him. Inside the bag were a pair of dungarees, a sweatshirt, and a clean pair of socks. But wedged beside them were a woolen dress and a silk scarf. A note inside said: "It's important to look your best even when you're not feeling your best. Love, Manny." I broke into a broad smile.

"So as I was saying before," Dr. Hamels said, "I went to a nearby swimming hole one night and jumped off a ledge. A thirty-foot drop in total darkness."

I motioned for him to turn around. When he did, I pulled on my jeans and buttoned my shirt. I left it untucked in order to "look" male and then zipped up my blue vest. I didn't bother tying my laces. I threw my gown at the chair but missed.

"Now I understand." Dr. Hamels nodded his head thoughtfully.

I picked up the bag with the woolen dress. "Understand what?"

"I'm sorry for being so slow."

"No clue."

Dr. Hamels reached for a pen in his breast pocket. "It takes work, doesn't it?"

"Stop talking in circles, will you, Jeff?"

"Your mom is afraid you're gay, which you could live with. But *this*—"

"Okay, I'm outta here."

"You can't leave until I recommend you be discharged."

"You gotta be fuckin' kidding me."

"Listen, I think I know what you're going through."

"No thanks. You're like the rest of 'em."

"Not true. I survived that jump, but it made things worse. I couldn't do anything right, I thought. Couldn't even kill myself. Sound familiar?"

"My session up?"

Dr. Hamels stood up and started scribbling on a pad.

I put the bag down and crossed my arms. "Fine. My mother thinks she's failed."

"Your mother doesn't understand you." Dr. Hamels looked up from what he was writing. "What if she never will?"

"Then I'll be all alone."

"Fair to say she's disappointed?"

"How'd you guess?" I said.

"And, of course, fathers don't pay attention to feelings."

I thought of all the times my father and I watched Red Sox games together in silence, how he yelled in ecstasy when Rico Petrocelli caught a popup that sealed the 1967 pennant, how he drove like a madman to get me to the hospital that night despite his illness. His way of expressing love.

"But moms, they're special," Dr. Hamels said. "They know us in ways no one else does. We *need* their okay."

"My mother has this idea of the perfect son who has a beautiful wife, is rich and successful, and loves God."

"Yikes! I feel her pressure. You might be rich someday, but you'll never be able to give her that daughter-in-law." He shook his head knowingly. "And your dad?"

"Never in a million years. . ."

"So you've been acting out. You feel guilty for being you and sad you've disappointed them, and you confirm that by taking pills—"

"And smoking and drinking . . ."

"If only they'd say you're all right just the way you are once in a while." He flashed a wistful smile as he finished writing. "Well, they probably will never understand you. They will never tell you they love you in the way you need them to. So how are you going to deal with it? You can't keep doing this, Bobby. You were lucky this time."

Dr. Hamels tore the piece of paper from the pad and handed it to me. "Someone I've known since my days at Berkeley. Someone you'll listen to, maybe."

"My mother thinks all I need is a teaspoon of Jesus. Grass and beer are better. If you have enough friends, you can get it free."

Dr. Hamels extended his hand. "Nice meeting you, Bobby. I have another appointment."

It wasn't a prescription. "Thanks for nothing," I muttered.

....

Jane grouped several envelopes together, put an elastic band around them, and placed the stack in a bin beside the coffee table. There were dozens of letters. "You know, in some ways personal transformation is a violent act. Think of all the New Year's resolutions made in the spirit of the moment to lose weight, or exercise, or give up smoking. Most people give up after a week. It's too hard."

"I couldn't ever give up TV. Don't you want to watch it when you're bored?"

"That's one habit I'm never letting myself get sucked into."

"Sometimes it's the only friend I have." Jane's plain-spokenness started to make me feel comfortable around her. "When my parents are fighting or I'm sick, I like just hearing it."

"The point I wanted to make is people I've known who believe Jesus was the Son of God say only a crazy man would've allowed himself to be crucified on a lie. So wouldn't it make sense if you committed yourself to looking like what you feel inside, that you're *not* crazy or screwed up in some way?"

As she inserted another piece of paper into the typewriter, she drank brown liquid from a mason jar—the "best damn whiskey" she had ever made from her moonshine still in the basement. She didn't seek my reaction to what she had said about Jesus, as if the point made was so obvious that there would unlikely be a rejoinder. I decided then to join her in the card burning. My only rebellious act up to that point was writing an inflammatory article for the school newspaper criticizing the cafeteria food. I handed her back the letter, and she slid it into the envelope and sealed it.

Jane had thick eyebrows that conspired against her femininity but could've easily been tamed to make her face more pleasing. A scar on the bottom of her chin, half an inch long, angled up the side of her jaw. I wondered if it was from a protest.

"Were you ever in love?" I said.

Jane struck a match and lowered it into the bowl of the pipe. She sucked on the stem, a ribbon of smoke curling up from her mouth.

"Sam." Her face relaxed, even glowed, as if the very thought of him transported her back to adolescence. "We met at a hootenanny. We were young and had few responsibilities besides being on time to the next hoot. We literally sang along with Pete Seeger and Bob Dylan in the Village. Amazing times."

Later, she said, he came into money and bought a record store in Greenwich Village that turned into two stores, then almost a third.

"He gave them all up one day, just like that." She snapped her finger. The glow in her face ebbed, as if she still questioned the wisdom of such a move. "He became a cabbie. He didn't want the expectations that came with money. He didn't want to manage it, or worry about it, or be captive to the things that money buys. I didn't mind. I was just along for the ride, so to speak. He thought ambition of any kind was corrupting. He said it freed him to love unconditionally."

"Why didn't you get married?"

"We decided it was an outdated social convention," she said, as if she had grown more and more unconvinced in the retelling. "Something people did out of fear of being alone."

"But sometimes you question your existence here," I pressed. "You said it yourself."

"I did. Loneliness is ever-present, whether you're with someone or not. More unions would succeed if they were entered into for the right reasons and not out of need. Sam and I, we shared everything."

"Everything?"

"Men *and* women."

I admired her worldliness, even envied it, but I couldn't imagine not belonging to anyone, living alone in a house with nothing but a typewriter and an ideal. Still, my only romantic role models were derived from the movies. Bogart and Bacall. Burton and Taylor. I had wants and desires, but they never took much shape or form.

"We thought if there was love, then you'd want each other to be happy and free." Jane sighed, then smiled and shook her head. "Naïve, weren't we?"

"Not really, if that's what both of you believed."

"We thought we could show the squares how to live and love, but we didn't know how to overcome what the ancients had warned us about—pride, jealousy, lust."

"I didn't tell you about my cousin Marty," I said.

My father, after his brother died, practically adopted him. He was four years older than me, but we were close. The night before he shipped out to Camp Lejeune, Marty jumped out from behind a bush and chased me and my friends out of our yard. When he caught up to me, he gently lowered me to the ground and tickled me. The hair from his forehead brushed against my cheeks. I smelled beer on him. Six months later, while stationed in Da Nang, he was riding in a jeep that ran over a landmine. My father started drinking heavily after that.

I leaned my head into Jane's shoulder and covered my eyes, surprised and embarrassed at the rush of emotion. Jane rested her hand on my head. I looked up at her.

"I wish I had the chance to burn Marty's card," I said, pressing the butt of my palm against my moist cheek. "I want to go with you to the protest."

....

The day before the card burning, I went home to visit my parents. I went in through the garage, past the laundry room, and into the finished basement. The TV was blaring, and my father was leaning back in the recliner, snoring almost as loudly. A couple of empty beer cans and a bag of chips were on the floor beside the recliner. I turned the TV down, draped an afghan over him, and went upstairs, pressing gingerly on the steps. I wasn't sure I wanted to see her.

She was sitting at the kitchen table, her half-glasses at the tip of her nose, poring over what looked like a stack of bills. When she looked up, her concern melted away. She got out of her chair and cradled my face, staring intently at me.

"I'm so glad you're all right." She hugged me, then asked if I was hungry. I begged off. She told me to sit down, poured herself a cup of coffee, and lit a cigarette. It kept the hunger away, she said. She asked where I was staying. With a friend, I said. My mother tapped her cigarette over a porcelain ashtray and crossed her arms, the cigarette, clinched between her fingers, smoldering beside her cheek.

"How's everything?" I asked.

"I'd feel better if you told me where you were staying."

"In a house."

She dismissed my answer with a cutting look and the wave of a hand.

"How's Dad?"

"The same." She poured milk into her coffee and stirred it. "Did you see the air purifier downstairs?"

I shook my head.

"The doctor said he's going to need one of those oxygen tanks soon." She looked at me wearily, stirring slowly, as if she was still annoyed that I wouldn't tell her where I was staying. "Now where are we going to get the money for *that*? I asked the doctor that right in front of your father. I didn't care. We're not paying his bills as it is."

"What did the doctor say?"

"He just stood there with a dumb look on his face." She snickered hoarsely. "High-priced fancy pants with the big degree didn't have an answer."

"He won't leave you hanging, Mom. He's a good doctor. What did Dad say?"

"You know your father. He still thinks he'll be back to work soon."

"Thanks for the money you left. You mind if I grab some more clothes?"

"Who's that Manny kid who keeps coming around here looking for you?"

"Just a friend."

"You sure? He looks a little—" She arched an eyebrow.

"Why, is it a problem?" I realized I was bending the corner of the placemat.

"Please have something to eat, Bobby. There's a plate of chicken in the fridge. Let me warm it up for you."

"I'm not hungry, Mom. I probably should go."

"Okay, you asked if I mind. Let me tell you a story."

She freshened her cup. "I'm a coffee drinker, you know that. I've been drinking coffee ever since I started smoking at the age of twelve." She grinned sheepishly, as if she should still be ashamed. "Every now and then, though, I like a good cup of tea. You know the secret to good tea?"

I shook my head impatiently.

"You put the tea bag in first, then pour not-quite-boiling water in the cup. Dunk it to wring out some color." She pretended to stir the mug's contents with her pinky. "Then you put in just a touch of milk—just a touch, though. You don't want it sickly sweet."

I looked at the wall clock. "Mom, what does this have to do with anything?"

"Just bear with me. I smoked my first cigarette in the woods on the last day of sixth grade. Skinny Rogers, our neighbor, stole a pack from his mother. I like a cigarette with a cup of tea or coffee. He's in that picture on the mantel. He died, Skinny, in World War II. Good man, God bless him."

I looked over my shoulder at an array of framed photographs, but I didn't see Skinny.

"My first cup of coffee came soon after." She tapped ashes into the tray. "Of course my mother wouldn't make it for me, so I'd go to the corner drugstore and pay for it with the dime I earned delivering newspapers. I drink it black, but only lately have I added milk."

I sighed softly. A flash of anger and indignation hardened her eyes.

"Just listen, and learn something."

She said my father had helped Skinny rebuild the engine of a Ford convertible, and Skinny helped replace the backseat of my father's Buick—for when they both went out dancing to meet girls. When Skinny's father died in a mill accident, she said my father's parents took Skinny in as a boarder until his mother got a job and remarried."

"Just like when Dad took in Marty."

"Exactly."

"You dated Skinny first?"

"Not really." She took a long pull on her cigarette, and the hint of a smile suggested that she preferred to dwell in the recollection of a faded memory. "We did like to dance. Skinny had thick, wavy blond hair, like James Cagney. I loved combing my fingers through it."

"So did you date Skinny or not?"

"It's not important."

I asked for a drag of her cigarette. She pulled back, as if not to corrupt her own son, but then shared it with me. "C'mon, Mom. Did Dad fight him over you?"

"Of course not. They were chums. But things changed after he found out about Skinny."

"Found out what?" I exhaled and gave her the cigarette.

She mouthed the words.

"What?"

"He liked, you know . . ." she whispered.

"No, I don't know."

She exhaled, then screwed the cigarette into the ashtray. They had been working on a car when Skinny's hand lingered too long on my father's shoulder. My father gave him a hard look and a shove, and then they scuffled. When my grandfather broke it up, they said they were just horsing around. But afterward, my father told Skinny to find someone else to work with him on the Ford.

"They stopped being friends?"

"There was an awkwardness, you understand. But when the Japs bombed Pearl Harbor, they enlisted together the same day."

They went through basic training together, worked on tank engines, and fought alongside each other in the same platoon in Europe. Toward the end of the war, they were clearing out the French village of Bayeux. After a gun battle, Skinny pried a Luger from the hand of a dead German soldier. He didn't see the sniper on the roof of a tattered bakery.

"What happened?"

My mother smiled wanly, as if it were all too much trouble.

"Your father hesitated." She fingered the crucifix looped around her neck. Her eyes were distant before they wandered up to mine when they turned grave, as if she were the one who had gotten the telegram.

"The bullet went through his heart. Your father never forgave himself. I know it's why he started drinking. He kept questioning why he didn't call out. He wondered if it was because Skinny was different in that way, you know? Worse, he didn't save one of his comrades. When Marty died, that was too much for even him—a big, strong man, always a provider.

"Then when you tried to . . ." She looked away. "He gave up."

I shot up from my seat and started pacing back and forth. "No, no. *No!* I can't be responsible. You can't put that on me." I felt a craving.

My mother lunged for my arm, but I yanked it away. "Sweetheart, please sit down. I'm not blaming you. What I guess I'm trying to say is, we're not bad people. That's all. You need to find your way in this life, Bobby. Don't wait until it's too late."

My rage ebbed, but I continued to pace.

"Please, Bobby, calm down."

"You mean it? You're not just saying that?"

She nodded pleadingly. I bent over her and hugged her fiercely around the neck. "You'll be all right?"

She lifted a bill and shrugged. "We made it through the Big One."

....

Jane and I woke before dawn on the day of the card burning. She had stayed up until well past midnight typing, the thwacking permeating my dreams and disturbing my sleep. I huddled over my coffee on the couch, trying to shake off the rust. The phone rang; Jane picked it up. The conversation was littered with murmured assents, then she looked at me and smiled.

"Dan, I've recruited another foot soldier. He's got a lot of enthusiasm." She winked, then turned her back to me and hunched into the phone. "Yes, yes, I have it. Of course I've tested it," she said in a low voice. "Yes, it *does* work. See you at nine, as we agreed." She hung up.

"That Father Berrigan?" I put the coffee on the table.

"He said he's looking forward to meeting you."

"What needed testing?"

"I'll tell you later. We have to get going. Put the letters in the truck, will you?"

As I made my way to the pickup with the bin of letters, she opened the cellar storm doors and descended. I placed the bin on the driver's seat, and went to join her at the cellar. She reappeared with a container no bigger than a gallon milk bottle.

"What's in it?"

"Napalm."

"You're kidding, right?"

"Nope." She started walking toward the truck.

"Wait." I blocked her with an outstretched arm. "What's it for?"

She scowled at my arm and then at me. "For our little meeting."

I thought of the picture of the Buddhist monk. "People will get hurt, won't they?"

"On second thought, Bobby, maybe you should stay here."

I felt betrayed. "No, I'm coming."

"I'm not sure you're old enough." She pushed past my arm and started walking toward the truck.

I followed behind her. "I think I'm old enough to protest the war they're going to make me fight in."

She nestled the gallon bottle behind thick straps in the truck bed. "Then come along, but you'll have to do what I say. Is that clear?"

"Okay, okay, I will," I said, but I resolved to stop her from using the napalm on herself even if it meant sabotaging the card burning. The truck rumbled to a start on the third try. She said it was fifty-fifty whether we'd have heat. As we waited for the truck to warm up, I covered a hole in the floor on my side with a dog-eared atlas. I drew my coat in close, my teeth chattering more from nervousness than the cold. Jane picked up on the former.

"Protest. Rally. Party. They're all the same," she said as we exited the driveway. "You just need to know how to throw a good one. Anyway, no one else knows about this but us. The plan is that once we're inside, we grab as many cards as possible and call Berrigan's friends at the local TV station. They've been instructed *not* to tip off the cops."

"What do I need to do?"

"Don't be a hero, for starters, and don't be a martyr. I'll need you to protect the container, and when I signal for it, you have to give it to me right away. Just stay cool and everything will be all right."

We rode in silence until she drove up to the front door of the post office. "They're expecting them," she said. I jumped out of the truck and placed the bin of letters by the door. By that act, it seemed I had given Jane some measure of confidence in my dependability. She said there'd only be a dozen of us, including the firebrand, Pastor Lester Wilkinson, from the Ebenezer Baptist Church, Rabbi Daniel Freed from B'Nai Birth, and Father Berrigan who was the media draw. "If I believed in God," Jane said, "I'd say She's on our side today."

We parked a couple of blocks from the draft board office on Main Street, a squat cinderblock building, and met up with a half-dozen shaggy-haired collaborators holding Styrofoam cups of coffee. Jane gave me the keys to the truck.

"In case something happens," she said.

I thought of pouring the napalm down a catch basin, but I guarded it at my feet as I was instructed. In the bitter cold, we shared highlights of the '69 Amazin' Mets and wondered whether they could repeat as world champions. The protests I saw on TV looked far bigger and more romantic. At nine o'clock, Berrigan showed up with the rabbi and the pastor in a small Dodge.

"Wait here," Jane said. "We're going in."

I started following her, but she pressed her hand against my chest.

"What did I say? Guard the container. If any fuzz show, come to the door."

I felt demoted. On high alert, we looked up and down the block for signs of the police, and patrolled the front of the building just to keep warm. I kept spying the door, not knowing what to expect. They weren't armed, but that didn't mean the staff inside weren't.

Fifteen minutes later, the four of them emerged from the building, each carrying a box, and trailed by a woman with a beehive and egg-shaped glasses who stopped at the door to watch. Jane signaled for me to bring the container. I stood paralyzed, cradling it in my arms.

"Bobby, now!"

"Are you going to use it on yourself?" I shouted.

"Bobby, there's no time for games! Bring it to me! Now!"

I reluctantly joined them at an open space in the lot as they dumped the cards into a pile, but I held fast to the napalm. Photographers and cameramen emerged from a swarm of cars and vans. One of the demonstrators keeping guard wrestled the container from me, doused the cards, and struck a match.

"Get back!" Jane shouted.

As flashbulbs popped, the pile erupted into a yellow ball of flame. Reporters who stuck microphones in Berrigan's face raised their arms in self-defense. Berrigan said that better the cards be burned than innocent children. We joined hands and started singing "We Shall Overcome."

I grabbed Pastor Wilkinson's hand and sang loudly to the heavens, hoping Marty would hear me. Almost as quickly as the eruption of the fireball, two police cars and a fire truck cordoned off the entrance. A fireman brought an extinguisher to the pile, but the flames were dogged. Embers flaked and swirled on an updraft of heat. Berrigan, Wilkinson, and Freed, as well as Jane, sat on the ground, determined to defy police orders. Reporters shouted questions and flash bulbs popped. The officers slapped cuffs on the four of them and helped them to their feet. I called out to Jane and started toward her, but an officer stiff-armed me while holding Jane's cuffed hands.

"Go home, kid," the officer said. "The party's over."

Jane's face was serene, unapologetic, as she stared at me. I was ready to drop to the ground in protest, seized by a fearlessness I had never felt before. The officer led her to a police car and pressed down on her head to ease her into the backseat. Before complying, she blurted out: "The glove box! When you get home!" She winked at me and nodded, then got into the police car.

I watched as she left the parking lot with Berrigan, Wilkinson, and Freed, then walked the two blocks to the truck. When I got inside, I opened the glove box. An envelope with my name on it. I put it on the seat and drove to Jane's house recounting what had transpired in the parking lot, hoping Jane wouldn't be mad at me for resisting her call for the napalm. When I got home, I took a beer out of the icebox, sat on the couch, and opened the letter.

January 29, 1970

Dear Bobby,
I apologize for this letter and for not having the chance to say goodbye to you properly. There are things about me and my past that I couldn't reveal, but which you will come to know soon enough. Barry Goldwater once said, "Extremism in defense of liberty is no vice. Moderation in pursuit of justice is no virtue." In all my years I think it's the only thing I've heard a Republican say that I agree with, although he'd be aghast (thankfully) at my interpretation. In my own way, I am trying to force change for the better or at least trying to force people to think of the necessity for change. Today we took a baby step, but it's a long road. The People have been pacified by failed schools, lying politicians and corporate media. They need ad men telling them how to think and what to value. Any capitalist society devalues its own people. We're just commodities that get tossed aside after we've given everything we have or when we get too old. While the People can't articulate it, they know it's true because they feel it. They're angry, but they unjustifiably turn their anger on people like you. You're a scapegoat, Bobby, because people are too afraid to confront their real oppressors—politicians, their corporate masters, their own lack of imagination and will. There's another envelope on the coffee table with a phone number to call and money to help you become the person you're supposed to be. Anything less than your self-realization would be a capitulation to fear and bigotry—to injustice! I only wish I could be present to witness your emergence, like a butterfly bursting forth from its chrysalis. I'm getting up there in years and I'm feeling my ability to change the world slipping away. Today's card burning is probably my last. If the police should question you, tell them the truth as you see it, but don't tell them about the money. It's rightfully yours. I have to go now. Know that wherever you are in life, I'll be there with you in spirit, cheering you on and fighting alongside you.
Peace be with you.
Jane

I rested the letter in my lap and stared at the thick envelope next to the phone. I was numbed by her gesture and scared by the prospect of change, having grown perversely comfortable denying who I was. Typed on the front were *Johns Hopkins Hospital* and a phone number. A sheaf of one-hundred-dollar bills bloomed out of the envelope. My parents needed it most, I tried convincing myself. I picked up the phone and dialed home. My father answered.

"Yeah?" His breathing was labored, his lungs whistling. "Who's there?"

The TV blared in the background. I closed my eyes and pressed the phone to my ear.

"Buddy, if this is some kind of joke."

I weighed the envelope in my palm and thought about the protest, of what Jane said about taking risks, taking action. I hung up, and then dialed again.

"Hello, this is Hopkins Hospital. May I help you?"

"I need to talk to someone."

DECEIVING ANGELS

C.A. Demi

Cara never missed an opportunity to bring up the night that we'd shared her bed with Angel. Cara would say she'd watched Angel and me dancing together in her living room, and that she'd gone to bed with the intention of feigning sleep in order to see if we would continue our intimacy. She would then say Angel and I had indeed started cuddling. If I protested, Cara would counter that I would get so drunk at parties back then that I shouldn't have much trust in my own memory. Angel and Cara were—and, to the best of my increasingly limited knowledge, still are—friends, and she always insisted his account of that evening verified hers.

None of the details in their collaboration are true. At least, not about the dancing or cuddling. It was a party. Cara's living room had been full of people. Things started off the way they usually did. At the beginning, the guests congregated in groups of three or four, each with a bottle of beer or mug of wine clutched, talisman-like, in his or her first. By the end most people were dancing. If not just the general shrinking of personal boundaries brought on by the enjoyment of alcohol, or even a mere coincidence, then Angel and I ending up in such close proximity to each other during this dancing was something purely of his design. Likewise, when Cara and Angel and I had settled into bed, the only reason I hadn't objected to his putting an arm around me was to avoid making a scene that would leave Cara with the impression that I wasn't cool, or that I was in some way hung-up about those kinds of things. If this innocent kind of contact had progressed to the point of cuddling, I'd have most certainly disentangled myself in such a way as to make my boundaries clear.

Cara and I hadn't yet been living together on the night of party. In fact, we'd only slept together a few times before sharing the bed with Angel. When we did finally decide to get an apartment together our lives settled down considerably. I don't think either of us felt too conflicted about leaving behind the familiar broken down, wine stained couches arranged in rooms lit with strings of holiday lights that had been the setting of so much our courtship. From time to time I did miss my former roommate's cat, but not stepping, barefooted, on the bottle tops it obsessively batted off the end table and then left in the middle of the floor.

In first year or so after moving in together we hosted a few potlucks, get togethers that can be characterized by an abundance of wheat-berry salads and a sense of boredom pretending sophistication. But, for the most part, we had few guests. Angel never came to visit. Maybe he found potlucks too quaint. Maybe it was me. He did call and, even though she would take her cellphone into another room and close the door, I could hear Cara as they reminisced about the old times. Maybe, in the moments when their voices dropped low or they slipped into speaking Spanish—him being the son of Cuban immigrants and her having studied the language and spent a semester in Montevideo—she and her friend discussed the events of the night the three of us shared a bed. Usually not long after such a call, she'd bring that night up to me, teasing me or daring me to deny it. The phone conversations between Cara and Angel became more frequent as our relationship began to deteriorate once and for all.

By the end, it became understood that I would be the one to move out of the apartment. I don't know why, but from the start I felt the need to keep the arrangements I was making for myself as a secret from her. Perhaps she suspected my furtiveness had something to do with there being another woman, a deception from which I made no effort to dispel her.

The truth is that, after repeated failed attempts to rekindle our affections, I was eager to get out of there. I found a sublet from a postgraduate student who'd be spending the summer in Spain, his home country. Having settled this only increased my desire to withhold as much information as possible from Cara, not only for the sickening pleasure I felt at the possibility she may have been feeling some kind of jealousy, but also for a certain fact of the subletter's identity.

To Cara, I referred to the man exclusively as the Spanish guy. When pressed for more information about his identity, I deflected questions by saying that there was no way she'd know a Theology PhD candidate at

Brown. There had seemed to be some reason for our breakup that Cara wasn't telling me, and it felt briefly empowering to have a secret. As far as I know, Cara never discovered that I'd found refuge in the home of a man named Angel.

The strange, and it must be said, discomforting, coincidence of the Spaniard's name notwithstanding, the sublet was nearly ideal. Since most of the furnishings of my and Cara's shared apartment had belonged to her, I happily accepted when Angel suggested that he would rather leave the setup of his apartment intact. Other than phone conversations, I only spoke in person with Angel twice. The first time had been to look at the apartment, and the second time had been when I met him to be given the keys. As such, I mostly got to know this Angel, at first, from his possessions. And in my initial impression, there was little in common between him and Cara's friend.

The apartment's furnishings were in good condition, a mix of new and well-selected second hand items, most of which I assumed Angel had procured on his arrival to the States. To be honest, his taste in decor, if not in kind then at least in general sense, put me in mind of Cara—though I was still at a stage in our breakup when most things, in one way or another, put me in mind of her. As was her penchant, the Spaniard seemed to have decorated the walls and shelf spaces and sills with items collected during travel, and which, no doubt, held some sort of sentimental value. Central among these was a rather beautiful framed stained glass mosaic, depicting a tree in the center of a garden. The mosaic hung before the bottom half of a window looking from the height of the third floor to the street below. It appeared old. I often wondered if Angel had brought the stained glass with him across the Atlantic or if he had chanced upon it during his time here. His collection included other items that would have been more practical to transatlantic relocation, such as figurines depicting the Buddha and an elephant and the Virgin, other carvings less descript, a smooth chunk of angular stone whose color led me to imagine that it had been stolen from the base of a pyramid, and even the twisted-horned skull of what I believed to be a gazelle, but which, at certain hours of certain days, when the sun sank to the west and sparked light of a glorious intensity into to the framed stained glass, became suggestive of something much more ominous. Of these mementos, one particular thing was absent in Angel's decor which in Cara's had been abundant. He had no photographs. I considered two possible reasons for this. Maybe he was the sort of person too engaged in any experience to think of stopping to retrieve a camera. Of course this failed to account for that fact that others may have taken and given him photographs, or that for certain events, such as family gatherings or graduations, some sort of visual documentation is nearly ubiquitous. The other possibility was that any pictures, rather than being absent as a result of disregard, were in fact so precious Angel had taken them back with him to Spain. I inspected the apartment for places where there may have been freestanding picture frames, but the place had been so meticulously cleaned—likely in anticipation of having a stranger come to spend the summer months—that not a single dusty silhouette existed that might reveal any such recently removed display.

The apartment was in Fox Point, near the university. It being summer, the nearby campus and surrounding streets were largely empty of traffic and people walking. Going out, I felt especially visible to anyone who might be around and didn't really like the possibility of bumping into someone I might know, and who would in turn know Cara. In this way, the Spaniard's apartment became a strange sort of refuge. Rather than being familiar, a place of my own and utterly of myself, it existed as a world completely apart, where I could feel anonymous. The only old friends made privy to the details of my arrangement with the Spaniard were those who shared no connection with my and Cara's relationship—an admittedly small number since she and I had met at a friend's house party. And, even in instances where I confided in friends, I never went so far as to extend an invitation for anyone to come by. Such was my surprise, then, when, one Saturday in the late afternoon, someone rang the doorbell.

Hoping it might be a solicitor, and not someone seeking to discover me, I chose to ignore the sound. The bell rang again and again. When I finally went to the window and, careful to not disturb the framed stained glass hanging before its lower portion, leaned forward to peer to the building's front stoop, my gaze was met over the distance of the three floors that separated us by a man dressed, surely uncomfortably given the time of day and year, in a black cardigan and black trousers. One of the man's hands clutched a rolling suitcase. The other waved excitedly as if he recognized, and was greatly relieved to see, me. I shook my head. He persisted. After a number of repetitions of this exchange, the man released his grip from the suitcase, and beckoned me with a full sweeping gesture of both arms. As I backed away from the window, he placed his hands on his hips in a manner which, as fleeting as my observance of it had been, seemed intended restore a degree dignity to his self.

Though the man spoke in slow, uncertain english, he introduced himself without a hint of embarrassment. Nor did he make an effort to veil the look of disappointment in his eyes that, me being someone other than the person whom he'd expected, such an introduction should need to be made. He seemed unbothered by the afternoon's heat. The buttoned collar of his shirt was clean and fitted perfectly around his throat. He wore his hair slicked back, and from his deeply tanned cheeks I could see that, if he did not shave with absolute regularity, the man would spring forth a thick beard, something which in the estimation of some might have only augmented his overall handsomeness.

When he first asked the whereabouts of Angel, the man, thinking I was merely telling him that Angel had come from Spain, misunderstood my description of the situation. The man stated resolutely that he too came from Spain, and, that like Angel, he was Gallego, and then demanded to know where Angel was at that moment. He became crestfallen as he began to comprehend the reality of Angel's having returned to Spain—or, Galicia as the man, as if by reflex, interrupted to correct me. I couldn't help but take pity and invited him upstairs.

Upon entering Angel's apartment, the man became overtaken a by a grief. Though he had impressed upon me that this was his first time visiting Angel in the States, it became immediately clear that the man innately recognized the rooms' arrangement and decor. This recognition did nothing to put him at ease and in short order he voiced his disapproval in a broken, angry sob. He accused me of being Angel's lover. However, whatever feelings he may have held on this point, they were secondary to the impact Angel's absence seemed to have on him. Perhaps a little later than I should have, I realized that this man and Angel had been a couple and that the man had travelled all this way to discover he'd been jilted in secret, that in fact he'd been in closer proximity to Angel at the beginning of his trip than he was at its destination.

He took a seat on the couch. Not knowing the appropriate sentiment to express in such a situation, I went to fetch him a glass of water. Upon returning, I noticed the man's eyes scanning the room, perhaps looking for evidence of what could have caused the unknown gulf between him and his former love, or maybe searching for the absent photograph of them together that would confirm they had ever been in the same place to begin with. Accepting the glass from my hand, the man's gaze fell to, and remained on, the stained glass mosaic. He never sipped from the water. I stood at the side of the couch, still uncertain of what to say. Neither of us spoke for a few minutes.

At last he indicated dissatisfaction with the water and after a stilted exchange we both came to an agreement that the situation would be ameliorated, at least marginally, with some alcohol. Embarrassed and still uncertain of my role as host, I tried to explain that I didn't happen to have anything of the sort on hand and wold just run out and around the corner to get a bottle. In doing so, I fumbled an attempt to recollect the man's name, mistakingly—and unforgivably—calling him Angel. At this error my guest restated his name, in full, Miguel Enrique Santiago de Ardá. He enunciated each syllable with a clarity and conveyance of meaning against which any utterance of my own would have seemed impoverished. I'm not sure if Miguel understood that my leaving him alone in the apartment was only to make the two minute jaunt to the Portuguese family-owned liquor store, but when I returned he seemed to have regained something of his initial composure. As I proffered the bottle for his approval on my way across the living room, Miguel regarded me—flushed from hurrying up and down the steps and around the corner, and wearing a stretched-out t-shirt that I wouldn't have normally worn into public—with an impassive gaze.

In the kitchen, I experienced a sort of crisis. Knowing that my guest's temper had been restored, as much as could be expected, I wanted to do everything I could to honor his situation, and to impress him with my hospitality. This impulse had been my sole cause for choosing to buy a bottle of sherry. However, I was not an experienced sherry drinker. And, standing before the cupboard, I began to doubt my choice, thinking that it might not be the appropriate time of day for such a liquor and not knowing which of the glasses in Angel's collection would be best suited for serving it. At first I took down two wine glasses, but they seemed too suggestive of romance or formality. When I put them back in their place they pinged against each other.

Miguel sniffed and cleared his throat in the other room.

I felt suddenly frantic. After touching each of the remaining glasses in the cupboard, I went to the drying rack beside the sink and retrieved two ceramic mugs. As well as having no pretense, I could be assured that, their being items I had brought with me when I moved, such vessels would bear no associations with the absent Angel.

I carried the mugs and the bottle into the living room and, trying not to make a show of my doing so, poured each of us a measure of the sherry. Miguel took a drink from his mug, neither reacting to the taste nor to the manner in which it had been served.

We drank from our mugs as slowly as our mutual silence permitted.

When I offered to pour him some more, Miguel accepted. He then looked into the mug and sighed. We each drank. He then broke our silence by asking if I was a student at the university. From there it did not take long for our conversation, impeded as it was by the differences in our native languages, to become intimate in the way that conversations can between strangers brought together in a strange place.

Evening came, and with it the breeze from the nearby harbor. The sherry warmed our insides and it didn't matter that the stirring of the air did little to alleviate the day's heat. I told Miguel about Cara, about her friend who was also named Angel. Miguel admitted that his coming to the States to surprise his Angel was an attempt to restore a feeling that had likely been long lost between them.

I poured another round. We drank.

We each wondered if we'd known all along that our respective loves would not last, or if they ever were love at all and not just a deception. We wondered who was the deceiver and who was the deceived. Sadness can invite a kind of philosophy which only deepens it.

Miguel refilled my mug, then his own.

The sun settled closer to the rooftops on the other side of the street. The colors in the stained glass warmed.

We made a toast.

Our mugs made a dull clunk when they came together. There was a memory in that sound. We both wept, then sought solace in an embrace. We pulled each other close. His cheek brushed against mine. Sunlight projected through the mosaic hung in the window and cast its myriad colors into the room and over our bodies. The sherry perfumed a shared breath. We could have disentangled ourselves. We didn't. The boundaries which we'd already crossed, and those which might yet have contained us, seemed diffuse and fluid as the colors overtaking the walls.

BATTER SWING

L.A Harris

All spring, our town boys sodded then coaxed the bluegrass that now spread like a rogue wave rushing the outfield. A craggy wall of backfill stepped up the hillside, shading the turf under the untouched chalked stripes and manicured edging. Our new field was ready for its debut.

Soon, they'd place the bases—first, second, third—before dropping home plate during the naming ceremony for Coach Bledsoe. In the stands, restless families gathered and buzzed hearsay as the sun dipped in a gradient descent of scarlet to coral pink. Spring was faking summer and the air hung in a gauzy curtain from the fumes of bodies set too long on low boils. The red sinking sun reminded me of when I flew Intruders over the Gulf of Tonkin, the early May air now souped a path down my back the same way it did then.

Kids milled outside the dugouts, ranking themselves into packs and haggling over candy and chili dogs. One of those smartasses mumbled *pig* when I walked past. That's where I left them, when I got the call.

Strange knee-high grasses swayed roadside as I zig-zagged down the old strip mine road, the new field in my rearview, flat-topped on a nude terrace that now mounted the shrunken mountain. Pipeline that it was, our town forged several hard hitters in the farm leagues and two journeymen that still cycled through the pros. Our young ones would now start fresh on that new field with its new grass and those new lights so the summer games could run late. Keeps them out of trouble, they'd say. But I don't know.

Siren wailing, I arrived to find the rescue squad boys lingering and already sharing a smoke outside the trailer's front door that hung crooked from one hinge. Above the pine-studded northern ridge, the lights glared and the naming ceremony boomed and crackled. Soon, those boys would square up to take cuts at the ball. It was starting and here I am with you, Lacy Jenkins. Again. Familiar after all these years.

Never one to put up much of a fuss, Lacy's fingernails were varnished pearl with the left thumbnail smudged. Brushed up against something or someone hard, I guess.

I weighed how she chose the yellow hair band that circled her blue-black hair too tight, stretching up her plucked eyebrows in a permanent surprise. Cobalt bangle bracelets stacked to her elbows, hiding a constellation of marks that ended with white scars cuffing each wrist. I shut my eyes to picture how she wiggled into that Little League jersey in her own sort of remembrance. It was her son's before we took him away to stay with Lacy's sister. That last time, he grabbed his mitt as we pulled him from Lacy's clawing hands. Lacy was never strong that way. I can still hear that low noise she made. Feral. A kind of growling that hummed guttural, forming deep in her porcelain throat.

I'd see her around town, squeezed into his little baseball shirts when she could still find them. Sometimes she'd wear one to panty dance for some quick cash over in Kentucky. Blue was her favorite color, like his. His eyes, her eyes blued and rimmed darkly like a crushed violet. But this jersey was the color of mustard. His team that year was the Pirates. It was that one from his no-hitter. A ten-year-old's no-hitter can get him through this world. I've seen it happen that year I coached him. Lacy's son was on my son's team. It still had grass stains from his slide into home. He wouldn't let Lacy wash the luck out of it.

In another spring when the heat flared too early, we lost something that now resurfaced. We were both seniors. I remember when Lacy's daddy turned her out to run with those rough boys. That was right after he gave her that bad leg. We were a bunch of schoolkids and I guess we had something to do with it. You can hobble somebody a hundred different ways, Granny'd always say. But I don't know.

Examining this display, I do know this time, Lacy fought me and them and us for her boy. Later, when he was older, I'd make sure he knew it. Blood gritted under the half-moon cusps of her pearly nails and a twist of sandy blond hair threaded her right hand. Knuckles green faded to yellow. Her body bent fetal. The blanket beneath looked like one of her mommy's star quilts gone ruined, blooming with blood from Lacy's final struggle.

I traced the lines to here and choked back the regret. In that senior year spring, I said I'd never tell and I meant it, but the others ran their mouths. I wasn't the one who fed her all that liquor. But still. I didn't stop it. Didn't stop. Word got back to Lacy's daddy but nothing much ever came of it for us. We were the team. I pitched that year and ran the school paper. Immunity granted. Probably would've been different if Lacy had brothers but she didn't. After school was done, I left and came back but Lacy stayed here. She was always here. Her hair's still the softest I've ever felt.

I took in the scenarios, this scene—the job. The samples the fluids the scrapings. Taking in the angles the approaches the retreats. Wrote it down in my black leather flipbook, scarred bone white at the edges. The one my daddy gave me before he called me a liar.

"Revisitation," I said out loud. My deputies didn't respond and I walked out alone.

Later that evening, thunderclouds bruised the narrowing sky as though the mountains lifted them up on shrugged shoulders. I cruised by the field, making the rounds on my patrol. I still needed to shake Coach Bledsoe's hand. Those new lights and that new field marked the big time for us.

July Honeycutt loitered at the fence and spat a stream that scented the air wintergreen.

"Good game, July?"

"Yessir, Sheriff. Lacy Jenkins' boy is throwing heat tonight."

DRIVING LESSONS

Christl R. Perkins

It is 6 AM. Tuesday night became Wednesday morning hours ago. You are sitting bare, exposed in K's lap in the driver's seat of his pickup truck at the top of a hill in Carson—a petro-industrial plantation in Southern California. A thin layer of sweat gives your sable skin a refined sheen. As the mist inside the truck windows begins to clear, you see inhabitants in pressed clothes and polished shoes emerging from their warm abodes, out into the morning to their cars. They can see their own breaths as they greet their neighbors across the street. You are coming down to the morning while they are waking up to it.

You'd better put on your clothes, at least your blouse, before your neighbors see you like this.

When you see your uncle, a maintenance man at the Shell Carson Refinery, emerging from the house, you duck. K quickly puts on his shirt.

The sky grows from dim to violet. You turn your head and look out over Carson from the top of the hill, the city where you grew up as that lil' tar baby girl, to see a jungle of oil refineries and clusters of industrial parks in the distance. There is no bustling financial district, no downtown high rises or sky scrapers here. Instead, the Carson skyline is an assemblage of oil derricks, tank farms, enormous metallic anthills and beehives of distillation, reforming, cracking, coking, alkylating, and blending.

The halogen glow of the street lamps dims just as the sun slowly becomes luminous, its beams spreading like liquid gold across lawns and rooftops, resting its rays against the refineries. By 10 AM the light will fully reflect the great metallic Leviathans, and the image will be so blinding that the American flag hanging like a billboard on the north side of the BP compound is rendered invisible.

Your eyes rest on Broad Acres Elementary School, which you attended about twenty years ago. It has always been virtually all Black—

except for one Korean girl and one White boy both in your class—with you as the darkest and K as the highest yellow, the two extremes of the spectrum. You used to be called the field nigga and he the house nigga. You wondered if birthright entitled you to getting your ass kicked on a weekly—sometimes daily—basis. Eventually K's family moved into a white neighborhood in Orange County and the Korean girl went to Los Angeles High School, their families were upwardly mobile. But your family stayed in the hood. So, you had to learn to fight, duck, and run.

Thus you wanted out. You wanted out so bad you took extra part time jobs to save up for a car. The running turned into cycling turned into driving, two and four wheels, and you got out. You drove very fast to the other side of the continent, all over. Running red lights, speeding. The reckless, stoned-out accidents. You didn't stop. Eventually your flagrant disregard for authority pissed the law off, and they revoked your license. When you finally escaped this environment, you fixed your insecurities and came to be about the flow.

You came back to Carson as the prodigal daughter unapologetic. It's been eight years since you have driven—enough time has elapsed so that your driving record has been wiped clean. Now it is important to get back to the flow. In order to regain your license, you must pass the test. To be on the safe side, you sign up for driving lessons, telling them you are a night person so they schedule you a short refresher course—three lessons plus vehicle rental for the DMV driving test—with their nighttime instructor. He agrees to meet you at 10 PM on Tuesdays and Thursdays. After all, everyone knows the best time to drive in Southern California is between the hours of 11 PM and 6 AM, when the traffic is limited and the way is more free.

When you meet your driving instructor for the first lesson on Tuesday, you think you recognize him, but you are not sure. He turns out to be K—the high yellow boy from Broad Acres. Back then, he was the skinny, nappy blonde—you used to call him "brace face," trying to hide your crush on him. Other kids used to call him "pretty boy" and "puddin' head." Now, you observe the man, tall and lean, athletic build, all-American smile, still fair-haired, wearing Dockers and a polo shirt—workin' that O.C. look. Some say you can run but you cannot hide. Well, you may have run, but K's the one hiding.

The way he introduces himself indicates that he doesn't remember you (and why should he? After all, you were only the darkest of a thousand little black girls at the school), so you don't mention it. Back then, he would laugh when other kids called you "skillet" and "Congo." He probably never even knew your real name. He certainly wouldn't have given a girl as dark as you the time of day.

K says, "I know you have experience and this is all review—just think of it as a refresher." You just want to pass your test and get your license back, so you listen intently as he outlines his plan. "Tonight, we will review basic car instruments and rules of the road. If we get through this quickly enough, we will go over parallel parking. That may be all we have time for tonight. Next session, we will practice on residential streets and surrounding business districts. In the last session, we will survey the freeways before doing a review of parking and a practice test."

He explains all this as he drives over to the large empty student parking lot on the south side of Cal State Dominguez looking down on the refineries. Once there, K matter-of-factly shows you the vehicle's headlight switch, windshield wipers, defroster, and emergency flashers.

You both get out of the truck. K saunters around to the front of the car, pops the hood, and points out the vehicle's internal organs: oil cap, air filter, battery. "Lil' junk in the trunk . . . Is it fully loaded?" you murmur and lean into his side.

He ignores your smart retort, instead answering a question with a question: "Do you know your arm signals and how to use the vehicle's turn signal lights?" You demonstrate, then he has you do a three-point turn in the parking lot: back up in a straight line and practice turning the vehicle around as if on a narrow two-way street to park on a hill.

You find it difficult to parallel park. In fact, it makes you wonder how the Korean girl from Broad Acres fared out. You imagine you are her, probably in Santa Monica or Silver Lake, squinting over the wheel, either starting out too forward or not forward enough, and swinging either too close or too wide, not being decisive enough. After K's demonstration and your inept execution, you see that it is around midnight. You ask K to show you the freeways, take you to the beach; he seems to be a night person too.

You are not one to cruise Crenshaw or MLK. Instead, he drives down the 110 Freeway to Long Beach to have a couple drinks at a jazz bar along Pacific Coast Highway where you sit at a booth in the back corner. Gentleman that he is, he gestures for you to sit first, then he slides in beside you and orders. When the waitress brings your shots, you toast and both drink and you feel the burn of the whiskey. The karaoke crew, raucous and unruly, filter by so you lean into him as he speaks. He tells you, "The driving instruction gig is my day job. What I really want to do is write."

You quip, "Edgar Doctorow said that writing is like driving at night in the fog. You can only see as far as your headlights, but you can make the whole trip that way." That's because to you, it is all about the flow . . . the natural instinct and control as you drive on.

"What do you mean?" he whispers in your ear, nuzzling your neck. You feel his breath calling your body and you want him to kiss you.

You prattle about the ecstasy when driving, driving into a song, warm breeze licking your skin, the upward grades and downward windy turns, the periodic road-kill which you swerve to avoid. The flow is in sunsets and dramatic skies with every cloud in place, or along the coast beside perfectly plump moons. Driving in your car alone along the Angeles Crest Highway on a late October afternoon, when the filtered light comes through the trees, you like the feeling of coming from behind in passing lanes and the feeling of arriving at your destination, your arms tired and burning. You want the song on the radio to turn into a soundtrack where every word, rhythm, and tempo makes sense.

The bartender, watching you put your hand on K's thigh as he kisses you, glares and hisses, "Get a room!" So K settles the bill, tipping the waitress well, and you both slink out. You and K walk three blocks to the pier and out to the end of it. You both snuggle under the blanket of darkness and listen to the ubiquitous lapping of the ocean upon the pier. K's lips brush back and forth on your shoulder, nibbling your neck and the nudging and touches increase as you kiss and talk more. He starts describing a short story he wants to write: "The story is about sex, but it's not about sex, it's about the ulterior motives behind sex."

You feel K's warm breath as he pauses to plant soft warm kisses on your neck. "My theory," K says, "is a mix of nature and nurture, that women are raised to know how to deal with men—how to stroke a man's ego, make him feel powerful, deal with his insecurities, not to chastise him—in order to get what she wants. At the same time, it's a biological thing: women are always trying to get what they want, and men are always trying to get what they want." His theory translates into a type of emotional materialism, a type of economics in which men are trying to reap short term profits, while women are looking towards the long term gains. The only thing is that growing up, what men learn on the streets about women really ain't about women. Women are always in control.

You suppress the urge to roll your eyes or slap him. K's comments remind you that everyday sexism prevails and you could never be content with that kind of life. But he is speaking in your ear. So while your mind registers these notions, your body registers his voice, low and lulling, his heartbeat, steady and hypnotic, his breath, warm and inviting. All of this pulls your body into a different conversation of a more primitive nature. You try to seem like you are listening carefully as K pontificates, "In my story, I want to show how a woman makes a man feel like he is independent, but it's all a ruse. The man grows to need her; he grows dependent—on the food, the sex, the care, the emotion. . .When he goes out into the world, he comes back to the woman because he needs the feeling of power and independence she provides."

While K continues, his hand creeps up your shirt, he pulls your bra up to expose your breasts and explores, fondling, squeezing your nipples. With your complexion, you wonder whether K can tell where your nipples begin except for the shape. He has you up against the pier railing, your legs apart as he grinds up against you.

When the sea breeze turns nippy, he drives you home. He parks two houses up the hill from your aunt's house and you converse, indulging in a protracted game of "Seven Minutes in Heaven."

It starts out with him in the driver's seat and you in the passenger seat but advances to the stage where you can't help but climb onto K's lap. You forget your hair, grow hot and bothered from the inside and your clothes feel sticky so you start to shed them. K helps take off your shirt and bra, continuing to kiss your breasts. You unbutton his shirt and kiss his neck and chest. You unbutton his fly and find that he is not wearing underwear. He puts his hands around your waist and begins thrusting his pelvis upwards. You are already breathing heavily, but as he keeps thrusting, you start to moan and quiver.

"Come," he whispers in your ear.

You can't believe your ears. You murmur, "K, you are driving me crazy. You are going to make me lose control."

He looks you in the eye and asks, "What's holding you back?"

His eyes are shining, the expression on his face is of arousal—animalistic, slightly diabolical. He opens his eyes wide with desire, licks his lips and repeats, "You're so sexy. I love watching you this way."

Your body takes it as a challenge. Your thrusting becomes mutual, and your shivering turns into uncontrollable shaking. You begin to call his name over and over.

You come. Trembling and gasping.

....

When you wake up, you find that the sun is yawning and stretching, people are coming out of their homes and starting up their cars to warm the engines up and go to work.

You dress. You wait until your uncle drives off, then open the passenger door to leave.

K tells you that you should be able to pass the driving test after a couple more lessons. He asks, "Still on for Thursday night?"

....

You cogitate on K's theory of Gender Economics: the study of people's behavior in the pursuit of satisfying their needs and wants in a condition of scarcity. There is the need for procreation and the desire for sex. Love is real, but there is always a price. Humanity used to operate on the barter system, but in the post-modern economy, things are just so cutthroat. This has become a market where you must have great haggling skills so you don't get ripped off. Some people pay too much. As you have gotten older, you have become conscious of the fact that love is not always such a great bargain.

You know that men have a rotation system—usually as a strategy to diversify their own supply network, sometimes as a defense to compensate for this same behavior on the part of women. When a man takes a woman home, he can usually plan everything to perfection—except how to get her to leave afterwards. After all, accidents happen. Everyone hopes for a successful trip; nobody ever plans the ending or the exit routes until it's too late. A man who doesn't take you home knows through experience; he is skeptical. Too many sour hookups have left a bad taste in his mouth—that's why he doesn't take you home.

These are all possible roads. Sure, there is chemistry now, but you may be disappointed, he may be disappointed, or for whatever reason, it just might not work out. Like the CD that begins with things that won't last: a rising sun, a couple in a car, love. The end could come too quickly. Before you know it, the sun has set, the trip has ended. You will part, hopefully on "good terms." You have been here before and foresee the imminent: feeling loss, you will take long drives. Face it, the happily-ever-after would be insufferable. You will always be as obscure as the road you travel.

You don't take it personally. After all, K's on your rotation. Picture the Production Possibility Frontier: for every widget of love produced, you must trade off a widget of freedom. Love requires an object, so you choose to love the moment.

The thought of K makes you wake up horny. You toy with memories of his hair and the freckles like raised bumps on his upper back as well as chest and legs, recall feeling each other in the dark, and mentally read his skin like brail.

....

The second lesson on Thursday night comes, you wear simply a button-down denim summer dress with cute little maroon pumps. You want to show your neckline and lean legs. After all, the kids used to call you "Cricket" because of these long legs. Now they say, "the blacker the berry, the sweeter the juice."

K drives up in a blue Celica. He apologizes, his truck had a minor breakdown and is in the shop—this will have to do. He has you get into the driver's seat. First you slink down single-lane residential streets where the homes have garages in front of their garages, you cruise among the squat buildings in the Dominguez Technology Industrial Park, the windowless buildings look like giant dice. Then you quickly graduate to making turns onto busy two-lane boulevards. You observe signs and pride yourself on being a defensive driver.

He has you turn onto a cul-de-sac at the top of a hill overlooking the refineries and pull over. You gaze out at the clusters of oil derricks lit up like a field of Eiffel Towers, the smokestacks and cooling systems, which look like a bed of jeweled nails, the labyrinth of connecting pipes joining the refinery structures, spires and steeples.

K asks, "What if chasing freedom is an entrapment: an end and not the means?" K is more practical. To him, freedom is a commodity; something you could trade in lieu of other resources. But to you, freedom, self-will, is genetic.

So, you tell him your story: When you were fifteen, your boyfriend taught you how to drive. You were in San Bernardino on Highway 215, a running, tiresome stretch of freeway. He taught you to maneuver the vehicle through the steering wheel; the steering wheel controls the direction of the car—steer left, the car goes left; steer right, the car goes right. Getting the vehicle pointed in the right direction was only part of the driving experience. You had to pay attention, adjust for road conditions: potholes, cars or small children coming out of nowhere, drunk drivers, Asian drivers, elderly drivers. To him, it seemed like driving was a continual stream of obstacles and complications to work out towards your destination. It seemed so much about control—so much depended on your control of the wheel.

But to you, driving is about flow. That is why you prefer to ride a motorcycle. To ride a motorcycle fast and well, you look and lean in the direction you want to go. Your body instinctively moves as if one with the bike to bring it to the direction you are looking. You are mentally more awake while riding a motorcycle, and naturally check out the black surface ahead for potholes and other possible hazards. You are mindful of the dangers, but you are not preoccupied with them. Being cognizant of your vulnerability, your focus is on the place you want to go.

K asks, "Chemistry, what do you think of chemistry?"

You tell him in zen-like fashion that true chemistry cannot be described, it can only be felt; it should remain a mysterious direct experience in your book. You tell him you'd rather not try to find the rules and laws, institutionalize it. You would just rather let it be, feel it.

Like now. Chemistry is being felt. He starts to finger your neckline which leads to him kissing you. His tongue is warm, the same temperature as yours. You probe gradually, striving for territory, sizing up the other team, mopping up the juices.

He puts his mouth on you. It's like being put under anesthesia, a sweet bliss. your fingers and hands clench, your body wants to grasp at something. You shudder as he moves his fingers along the small of your back.

He mumbles in your ear, "Right here, I like this spot right here; guys always miss this spot but I love this spot right here." K is touching the spot where your neck meets your shoulders, he softly bites you there.

Your driving lessons develop into a game of sexual chess. He makes the opening move with a coy nuzzle and soft caresses. Your kisses counter, you unbutton his shirt and nip his shoulders. He breaks through your defense and renders you senselessly sensual. You run your offense desperately, but he fortifies his defense. Somehow, in the end, he always checkmates and you are the one stripped of your clothes.

You are very conscious of the way he touches you. He plays you like a musical instrument; his plucks give rise to your sighs. You find yourself lying face down over the passenger seat. While K is riding you, he is mooning the moon.

That's how the second lesson ends at 6 AM, Thursday night having hours ago slipped into Friday morning.

You put on your clothes and step out of the car. You sleep for thirty minutes, shower and ride the bus to work. You work all day, no problem because you are used to all-nighters. Coffee helps.

Until next Tuesday, you muse about the texture of him, the feeling of his body around you, his mass, his breath.

....

The last lesson on Tuesday finally arrives. You wear a short linen wrap around skirt and a tight red pull over with a matching push up bra underneath. You want to show off your cleavage and nice calves.

This time, K lets you drive through downtown Los Angeles with its one-way streets and hectic intersections.

As this final lesson draws to a close, you finally park and K gives you "the talk." You had anticipated it so you don't interrupt, letting him do all the talking, speak his mind. Better he end it than you.

K says, "The last two lessons were memorable. I am not a morning person, and yet I find myself in strange and wonderful places with you." He discloses how he thinks of you when he's masturbating, reminiscing on your smell, your voice, your skin, your mouth and the look on your face, the moment when he knows you are aroused, the sounds of bodies in motion with one another, and your harmonic sighs.

He tells you he will write a story called "Love in Carson" about a man and a woman trying, simply, to make love, and being interrupted by car alarms, telephones, parking attendants, and their own nagging compulsions about what they should be doing to get ahead. They will scale down their original idea. "We don't have to make love," the woman will say, half way into the story, "Let's just fuck."

"Yes," the man will reply, "They can keep us from making love, but it takes no time or particular mood to just fuck." But they won't even be able to do that. Too many distractions. They will be played out of a good fuck.

He mistakes your relief and calm demeanor. Thinking that you don't get what he's trying to convey, he gives you another scenario: "A man and woman are intimate and have deep feeling for one another. The man loves the woman. He is recklessly taken with her. When they are together, he freely expresses his affections. It is tempting to continue. But he does not want to hurt what they have, and there are so many factors—timing, circumstances, et cetera—that are problematic. The man is not an uncomplicated person, nor is the woman, so it is something to think about. The man sets his own coping mechanisms. Admittedly, it is a bad setup; he is a failure at such things. He has no interest in controlling the woman. This is partly selfish, because to him, she is something of a symbol of freedom and he likes to keep it that way. Freedom is fuel for ascension, and while true freedom does not exist in familial relations, it does in friendships through which people are actualized. We can't let our emotions drive us."

Clearly, K sees all this turning into a sports car careening, overturning down a Mulholland Drive cliff and unable to control even the speed at which it will plummet into the brush. You find it humorous and chuckle which seems to trigger him.

He becomes accusative: "You are stronger than me, like a cat able to slink, leap, and land. Maybe you have the real control because you have enough spirit not to need to control such matters. But you are also more impetuous, and less far-sighted, in such matters. You plan not for the misfortunes of your leaps. All the while I cannot stop myself from expressing my affections for you, or from being enamored of your company. So, there it is, you now know how I feel."

Acquiescent, you sit up and face him. K slowly begins to outline your nipples beneath your shirt. He can't resist. His fingers straddle your spine as he reaches under your shirt from the back, unhooking your lacy peach bra and pulling your red shirt up. He encircles your breasts with his hands, putting one nipple in his mouth at a time. He kisses them and licks them, enveloping them in the whirlpool of his balmy mouth. It makes you shiver. In one motion, you reach over your head and pull off your shirt and bra. Then he caresses you, stroking your belly and fingering your waistline. He begins to fiddle with the knot on your linen wrap around skirt. But he is not able to untie it so he simply reaches underneath, into your panties and begins to finger you. This induces a moan. After some time, you become half conscious of the fact that the knot and skirt have somehow fallen away.

You undo his pants and reach inside to pull out his hardness, it feels warm in your hands. He leans over so that his penis is against your side.

He whispers, "I can't decide. I want to be inside of you, but maybe I just want to hold your image in my memory."

After all, you conclude, K is probably correct: this is an accident waiting to happen. You put on the brake and decelerate. Driving is a privilege, not a right. You remind yourself: the man and the woman are friends, just because they are sexual does not mean that they will or should make love.

When you first met him, you thought his eyes were brown-green. Then, perhaps because you mostly viewed them at night, you saw them as simply brown. This time, it was amazing staring into his eyes, the morning blazing sunlight brought out the bold beauty of them. You notice a bit of grey in his right, varying shades of brown throughout and yes some of that hidden green. You may never have this pleasure again, so you watch while making love that morning, glad that in this position, you are forced to gaze into his soul.

As 6 AM approaches, you get dressed, satisfied that your last driving lesson ends with very fond memories of his eyes in the reflection of the morning sunrise.

K asks, "Can I come to your house next time?"

Funny question coming from a man who won't invite you into his place. In the light of day, he would never come clean. You laugh inside as it dawns on you that you could be driving a stolen car so to speak—she jus' may have Lowjack, but you have radar love so you don't answer his question.

You tell him, "The name of that school down there is Broad Acres—sounds like a plantation, don't it. There, my darkness was an object of ridicule. I remember this high yellow brotha who enjoyed light skinned privilege."

K responds, "That light skinned brotha was always having to be the little player, always had to be the toughest and meanest, his blackness always questioned. . .until he moved into a white neighborhood."

You thank him for everything: the lessons, the conversation, the love. You remind him that your agreement includes vehicle rental for the DMV test.

He confirms and tells you to make the appointment on a Monday, Mondays are good.

The following Monday, as predicted, he drives you down to the DMV and hands over his keys to you. Everything goes as planned and you pass with flying colors.

....

About a month later, you buy a used Honda mini-SUV, a chick car. It's good on gas mileage. The front seat slides all the way back and fully reclines. The parking brake doesn't get in your way. There is even a secret compartment for condoms. You get a better job, become more mobile (upwardly and otherwise) and get your own sweet pad. Only after that do you call on K, ask him out for drinks. You drink until buzzed, bring him to your car and make love in the parking lot. You don't let your emotions drive you, so you decide not to bring him home because you can plan for everything else but how to get rid of him. And face it: if you don't master your emotions, they will make you a slave. So, you make this the last time you see him.

Since you regained your license, you've been in a few cars: the plush Lexus, the classic VW bug, the sporty Miata. . .You even had a guy in an SUV who tried to tell you what kind of car you should drive. With each of these experiences you find that guys try to act like what they drive, but that when you pop open the hood, in fact, it is seldom the case.

There are maniac drivers on the highway of love. People drive too fast. People drive while intoxicated. They don't watch where they are going. There are head on collisions, sideswipes, hit and runs. There are drive-by shootings. It's not like you can take out an insurance policy against accidents or theft. Some people get lost through no fault of their own—they were just given bad directions. A tire could blow out or you could just run out of gas. You just might need to pull over. And when you get out of your car and are buffeted by the wind, be prepared to find that the call box is out of order. Your best advice is put on your seatbelt and drive defensively.

But that's not the story here. The lesson is simple: love is out there, somewhere in this dark lonely world, and you will chase it despite the risks.

You creep along at dusk during rush hour traffic on the 10 Freeway going west past downtown, gazing, wondering at how the full moon looks like a pearl marble has been shot out of the barrel of the US Bank building. But when you look down, you notice that the lines of your own road have blurred beneath your wheels constantly in motion. In the end, you park your car and gaze intently out at the jungle of oil refineries and tangle of industrial parks to make sense of the drama found in between coming down in the morning and waking up to it.

LIES WE TELL

Kieran McBride

My words move through the room like a disembodied spirit.

"We were soulmates."

It's a small church of fifteen or twenty rows. Her parents asked for an intimate service and Brad and Denise feign surprise when several hundred arrive. Everyone is friendly in a town this size. The gatecrashers-turned-mourners stand or sit where they can—shoulder to shoulder, knee to knee—packed so tightly they've become part of the decorum. With no crevice to vanish between, my words leech on the parishioners' skin, worming into their pores.

Their hollow, black pupils collapse. Prior empathy replaced by a focused and intense fear, the invocation of the word *soul* having made the corporeal separation palpable. The congregation transfixes on me, and if anyone were to break gaze, they might catch a glimpse of Jill passing from this world to the next.

Those with seats rustle against the crushed, crimson velvet of the pews. The strained pop of wood echoes in the silence as a few reach for Kleenex. Those standing etch their shoulders along the beadboard paneled walls. A man coughs discreetly. A baby, unknowing and unconcerned, whines. The whole room, painted immaculate white, glistens in the midday sun. Something feels out of place. I expected rain.

I look down from the pulpit, each set of eyes equally clear, even those lined along the back. The elderly woman who introduced herself as Jill's elementary teacher groans when I say it, her billowing white curls bobbing in unison with her cries. She hides her nose behind a purple handkerchief that matches her outfit. Denise settles her head in Brad's chest, her chin-length, faded gold hair covering half of her face. What's visible of her lips fold downward, wrinkles forming on her forehead and chin, laboring against a tide of memories that will never exist.

Shit. When was the last time I said something?

I retrace my words:

Many of you don't know me. How could you? This is my first time in Barton.

—*My comms professor said to hook them with a joke. This is the best I could do.*

My name is Nathan Marin. I'm Jill's boyfriend.

—*Was.*

The first time I met Jill, we were at a fundraising event.

—*At a frat.*

We were manning a table together.

—*It was beer pong.*

And the enthusiasm she had . . .

—*For alcohol.*

. . . inspired me . . .

—*To keep pace.*

. . . and before I knew it we had spent the whole night talking . . .

—*Wink.*

. . . deeply.

—*Very.*

In time, we developed a friendship …

—*With benefits.*

. . . and came to understand each other's passions. That's who Jill was to me, someone who always sought to find passion in every opportunity.

—*Boy, did she.*

And then I say it, the words lingering because I've yet to replace them with anything. I never thought of her that way. Not until now. We liked to drink. We liked to screw. We liked each other. That's all I needed to know. I had nothing to think about.

Soulmates.

It sounds sweet and convincing, even if I couldn't tell you what the expression *means*. And these people could use a little convincing right now. So could I. We're in church after all.

Brad, concerned, leans forward, ready to stand. I try to move on, but the words pile up in my throat like sand and spill out in a desperate, arid gasp. I feel a wetness on my cheek. I don't know how it got there.

The pastor, a short-statured man of forty with a soul patch and thick, rimmed glasses, puts his hands assuringly on my shoulders. He lifts an arm, and the assembly rises to meet the organ's first notes. In celestial union the church joins the hymn, singing from their collective memory.

God sent His son, they called Him Jesus

He came to love, heal, and forgive

The pastor slides his hand from my shoulders to middle back, delicately guiding me to my seat. I count four steps from the podium to the floor, but they feel impossibly tall. With each foot forward, I briefly flinch the way one might when leaning over the edge of a building at the moment before the guardrail catches you.

He lived and died to buy my pardon

An empty grave is there to prove my Savior lives

Four steps. Four falls. Brad and Denise rush to meet me on the last, their arms sure and steady and wholly enveloping.

Because He lives, I can face tomorrow

Because He lives, all fear is gone

Together, we peer to our left to see her propped up on an easel, frozen and framed, surrounded by dozens of expertly manicured bouquets: lilies, mums, carnations. This girl doesn't look like my Jill. Her hair matches Denise: flat, dark, without highlights, cropped short around the jaw and with heavy bangs. Her cheeks round, young, and airbrushed to hide any acne. Her eyes uneasy, lips tensed. Inhibition where I only knew abandon. Caged. Even if forced, at least she's smiling. Jill didn't smile the night she left. A fake smile is a better way to say goodbye.

Because I know He holds the future

And life is worth the living, just because He lives

Behind the picture, precisely hidden, the silver pearl casket. Closed. Locked. Never to be reopened.

....

We're in a small basement now. Faded linoleum. Fluorescent lights. Plywood folding tables with chipped ends covered by stained white cloths. Rows of crock pots with chilis and dips and roasts. Styrofoam plates. Plastic silverware. Two liters of Coke and Sprite.

The pastor, Matt, introduces himself after the service. The slender wrist and rangy digits he presents when we shake hands reveal a frame that doesn't entirely fill his charcoal suit. His smile, faded and well-worn, imparts a nostalgic cheer like a cherished pair of blue jeans.

I ask him about the crowd.

"Jill was as serious about the church as she was about sinning, so she knew a bit of everyone."

Matt tells me he was only the youth pastor when Jill was young.

"When God saw fit to take Pastor Dan home, it was either me or shut the place down. Praise the Lord they let me keep the soul patch."

He laughs and sticks an elbow in my side. I don't understand the joke but do my best to share in the humor. I know I need to laugh, even if it feels like gravel in my belly.

"What sinning was she serious about?" I ask.

Jill lived the college life better than most, but I never regarded her a sinner.

"You and I both know that wasn't her first time," he whispers.

I didn't, but I believe him when he says it. There's a peculiar conviction about his words. Matt, struck by a memory, smiles, breaking the entrenched graveness in his face that had accumulated through the day.

"You see old Harry Gardner over there?" Matt says, pointing to a portly man who, on current evidence, does not dress up regularly. His collar narrows to a vintage '80s point, the buttons of his midsection stretch, his pants pleat heavily.

"One weekend," he begins. "Harry takes his old lady out for a nice getaway to the city. They leave the place to his boy, Ed. Ed—being a teenage boy and twenty-four cents short of a quarter—has himself a few friends over."

Matt kicks a fake one back with his thumb and pinky finger.

"That included Jill. Harry and Pat—that's Harry's wife—they're back the next afternoon in the old Cutlass. Ed? He's got the brown bottle flu in a bad way. Harry though, he didn't give a shit about any of that. He knew what Ed was planning that weekend before Ed did."

My ears have heard plenty of swearing in their life, but never in the basement of a church or from a man of the cloth. I glance Matt's way, but he doesn't see me. He's lost now, a dull glaze set over his eyes, that crocked, inebriated compulsion you get right before doing the shot that'll stick your head to the edge of a toilet for the night, your conscience suffocated in alcohol. I've seen Jill this way a time or two and, like Jill, I find myself unable to interrupt.

Matt continues, "What Hank does care about is that the truck's gone missing. Ed swears to this day that Jill was the last to leave the house that night—you probably know what that means."

This guy lays it on thick.

He winks and goes on, "Harry drags Ed half-dressed down to the Simmons house in a heat. And when he gets there, Jill's in the living room, right as rain, doing her studies."

Matt pauses and allows himself to reflect on a drama well told. He breaks the silence by patting me on the chest with the back of his hand and delivering the punchline.

"Never did find that truck though."

The awareness of his surroundings strikes him swiftly. The bedevilment in his face fading to dull pain. The pastor takes a long, heavy breath and exhales sharply, producing a barely audible rattle in the recesses of his chest. His brow furrows and the color around his sharp cheeks deepens.

"We're all sinners, Nathan," he says with the solace of a man come face to face with a debt. "But the Lord saves."

He shoves his hands in his pockets and rocks on his heels. That must mean something different for him than it does for me. Jill was just trying to get home that night. I wish the Lord had saved her.

....

The basement is somehow more uncomfortable than the sanctuary. You can barely move. People touch shoulders sitting at opposite tables. Children, giggling and oblivious, wiggle around and through the bodies. Matt has abandoned me to tend his sheep while Jill's parents lead a receiving line. Alone, I try disappearing into the crowd, wedging close to people I've yet to meet, hoping to conceal my face in a plate of deli meats and hashbrown casserole. This is a mistake. The food is heavy and unsettling, and I still stand out. I'm The Boyfriend. The Soulmate.

They feel compelled to talk to me, to tell me how my eulogy—as short as it was—moved them. They ask about her. She didn't stay long in Barton these days. Home for the holidays and family gatherings, maybe. They want to know about the Jill who lives in Libertyville, the culture of the town, what the professors at Western had to say about politics and God and abortion, probing for an impetus to explain this wholly new person I describe to them. They compliment my character.

"For Jill to have become that kind of person, you must be something."

I tell the truth: she studied marketing and waited tables at El Cantina to pay rent and save for festival tickets in the summer.

When they finish asking questions, most reminisce about a Jill they knew. The truck story is the most popular. Everyone has a theory on where it went and with who. But other legends anthologize the mythology of Jill Simmons. During open prayer, she once asked God to forgive Pastor Dan's hypocrisy for buying a new luxury car. She was only ten.

Or in middle school, when she snuck "I'll Make Love to You" by Boys II Men into the playlist of the church's annual Sadie Hawkins alternative. Outing Hoodie—that's Jack Haughton—and his small dick to the whole lunchroom in retaliation for embarrassing the kid with autism. The nose ring, immortalized in her senior portraits, she bribed some clod at the outlet mall to give her with a twenty under the table.

These conversations end the same way: "She's probably kicking up a fuss in Heaven right now."

Based on how Matt described it earlier, Heaven didn't seem like the place for that. But I agree anyway and avert my eyes. They fold their arms over my shoulders, pat me on the back, hang their heads, and wipe their tears. Many hug me as they move on. I sense their affection and do my best to capture it, hold it in, allow it to kindle, but the heat slips through me like my feeble apartment walls in the winter.

....

The bereaved leave after the food runs out. Ignoring the aura of death is difficult when you can't make conversation, and small talk is awkward when you don't have anything to put in your mouth between pauses. Some loiter. The third-grade teacher. A man my age with a ragged goatee and a vandal's eye who may have been the only person who didn't approach me. I don't catch his name, but the jealous gaze that stalks through the crowd unnerves me. But, one by one, as they make peace with Jill's passing in their mind, they leave.

At last, it's me, Denise, Brad, Matt, and the rest of the church staff, who have started piling linens in the corner. There are more hugs and thank-yous and anything-you-needs, more crying, and then a prayer. We find ourselves in a circle, arms draped over us like sacramental cloth, shielded by love, speaking to God, imploring mercies. I appeal to it, beg it to welcome her home, forgetting for a brief moment that she's still upstairs, trapped in a box.

....

Her parents and I drift red-eyed, sniffling, and anointed in prayer through the parking lot toward the family van. We wind through the splintered streets, past a neighborhood with board-window houses, patchy and weed-choked grass, and twisted chain links. Drifting over the highway interchange, near the half-occupied and terminal outlet mall, we pass underneath the giant McDonald's sign overlooking the city, flickering to life as the sun begins its descent beyond the trees. Outside the car, the spring breeze twists freshly bloomed branches of poplars and dogwoods. Inside the vehicle, the air is stale, praise and worship playing quietly on the radio, while Denise—eyes closed, head against the window—sings under her breath.

We arrive back at the house around 5:30. Matt isn't far behind. I pull my overnight bag in from outside and ask Brad to remind me where the guest room is. Down the hall. First left.

As soon as the door clicks, exhaustion seizes me. I shuck my suit coat and heave it onto the chair, loosen my tie, pull my button down from my waistline, and crawl face first like a sniffing dog toward the headboard. Soft bed. Cool sheets. A firm but forgiving pillow. This will do. My body expresses its satisfaction by easing its muscles and seeping into the mattress. Rest follows shortly after.

....

Somewhere between awake and asleep, where memories are made and remade, I roll over. Jill's not there.

I check my phone.

10:42 a.m. No texts. No calls.

I look for signs: a dress on the floor, her bra hanging on the closet door, the sound of retching in the bathroom, the blender whipping her breakfast smoothie in the kitchen.

Nothing. Only still air.

Is she at work? The Cantina opens at 11. No. We have plans to go to the lake. It won't be the last time she forgets.

Did she stay at her place? She can't be that mad at me. And she has nothing there. Her toothbrush is here, her work clothes, all her food. She only kept that place full enough so her parents wouldn't know we were living together.

I send her a text as I inspect the apartment. The shower is bone dry. Toilet unsullied. No breakfast dishes.

Fifteen minutes amble silently.

I call.

Voicemail.

Voicemail.

Voicemail.

I try Bryce. He never missed a night at the bar.

"How bad was she?" I ask.

"Not as bad as Paddy's."

"Did she get a ride?"

"I don't know."

"Who'd she leave with?"

The shifting of sheets crackles in the speaker as he sits up in bed.

"Is she not home?"

I check her email, looking for a ride receipt. I call again. I check her Facebook, her Twitter, her group chats. Nothing after she left the house.

I text.

I call.

I text her roommate.

I text her roommate again.

I text all of our friends.

I pour a cup of coffee and steal a cigarette from my roommate's dresser.

I chew down the fingernails on my pinky and forefinger.

Should I call the restaurant? Or the bar? I ask other questions I don't let myself answer. Do I meet her at the lake? The cigarette sears with every inhale, my lungs smoldering between breaths. I'm not drinking, so I feel it this time.

....

The phone finally rings. What a bitch. She'll blame this on me and force an apology. I'll have to take her out to dinner. Better pick up an extra shift this week.

....

The number is unknown. The terror strikes in a frenzy. I've felt it once before, when my cousin sat on my shoulders and pinned me to the bottom of the pool, the whole of creation undone, the grand expanse of the universe narrowing in a flash to this moment and—if I allow it—ceasing entirely. I thrashed and scraped and kicked then. I don't now. I'm stiff and cold, the world already lost.

....

If Schrödinger is right, she only dies if you pick up the phone.

....

I hang up on Denise abruptly. I have to get out of the house. Jill is everywhere.

....

I wrench the steering wheel until it stains my palms and black rubber flakes fill the blisters on my skin. The windows barely conceal my groans. Those passing by avert their eyes but find staring unavoidable. There are behaviors beyond our control.

....

My parents never met Jill. They planned a visit for the summer or renting a cabin in Colorado.

"If it works out," we all agreed.

....

Brad and Denise arrive in Libertyville early the next morning to begin the gratuitous task of reclaiming her. They identify the body, interview with the police, and sign endless forms at the coroner's office. They file for a death certificate.

I'm halfway into a handle of Jack when Bryce knocks on my door. He helps me finish and sits in the bathroom rubbing my back while I vomit.

Denise suggests we meet up for dinner that evening.

"We need to hold fast to each other," she says.

We sit outside at The Quarry and wear our sunglasses even after the sun sets. The words are sparse, like the moment before a breakup your heart accepts but your mind cannot anticipate. The world around us clueless, indulging in the blind callousness of its normalcy. Our waitress, full of well-trained and polite smiles, upsells us on the spinach dip special.

"We've already made arrangements," Brad tells me. "Obituary to run in Monday's papers, both in Libertyville and Barton. Body to arrive in Barton on Tuesday morning. Funeral at Emmanuel Community Church on Wednesday at 1:30 in the afternoon."

I didn't even know Jill went to church. Now Brad is insisting I give a eulogy at her service.

"Her mom knew her best as a child. I knew her best as a young girl. You knew her best as a woman. Maybe you can speak to that."

Before I can decline, he continues.

"Reception to immediately follow in the basement. Donations accepted at Burnley Funeral Home in the form of flowers and charitable contributions to the Youth Mission Trip. Burial the next morning at Union Hill Cemetery at 9 in the morning."

I ask myself, "How can you even plan for this?"

A voice from the present, "You and I both know that wasn't her first time."

....

The delirium comes to me in the form of a thousand tiny hands. They pummel and snatch and jerk me one way then the next, my mind churning back and forth across time in fear that if any one of these violent extremities latches on to me, I'll be lost to its abyss forever.

....

One eye opens, the other smashed shut against the pillow. My back, stiff, loosens slowly. A throb builds behind the closed right eye. My open eyelid flutters, trying to bat in enough light to flush out the fog. I scan the walls, drawing clues from unfamiliar surroundings, attempting to orient myself in place and time. On the wall opposite me, a stock, oversized canvas of the Eiffel Tower at night, the Siren in every young wanderer's ear. Above the bed, a Cranberries poster—edges pinned, stickied, and repinned to shreds—hides the decade-old pink paint. The doorknobs of the closet wrapped in scrunchies. On the shabby, sunbleached desk, old keepsakes adorn a mirror with elastic strapped corners: a cross, a corsage, several senior portraits (mostly boys in letter jackets leaning against trucks and muscle cars). The one with a heart around it: sweeping black bangs and a bass guitar. This disconcerting lack of context keeps the room spinning.

Finally, on the nightstand to my left, barely in line with my eye, I glimpse a small oval frame with ornate trim. A young girl—six or seven—holding a stuffed doll with overalls and pigtails. The girl smiles, bright and triumphant and free. Her mother hunches over, dangling the child by the underarms, matching her daughter's glow equally. The picture crops out the location, but it doesn't matter, a smile like that isn't bound by time. It could be any number of happy moments: the first day of school, a family reunion, her birthday, a recital. It could have been a few weeks ago, skipping class and lying on a hill overlooking campus, drenched in sun. The type of warmth that speaks to your bones, declaring that spring has taken root after a bitter winter.

....

That little girl is gone too, just like my Jill and long before. But here she is, still blissfully radiating through time. The world stops spinning and comes to focus as if her joy were the foundation the Earth rested on.

....

It's well past dark, and now I can't sleep. The old, digital clock reads 10:29. My phone says 10:31. Relieving my thirst and hunger and the need for a piss keeps me checking the time every few minutes. Matt, Brad, and Denise are in the kitchen, telling stories of Jill in a past but present way. I worry that my presence would break their momentary illusion that Jill is alive, on her way home from Libertyville, due to stumble through the door at any minute, and that the stranger in the guest room is supposed to be here.

I feel a sudden kinship with roadside memorials. They never asked to be placed. Their flowers could have been a garden bed, their wood a table or a chair, but every time someone passes by—even in a brief, peripheral moment—there's an awareness of gruesome horror and the inescapable permanence of death.

The bathroom can wait a little longer.

....

Classwork keeps my mind off the swollen bladder. Despite conjuring letters from both the coroner's office and Jill's parents, "girlfriend of six months" doesn't count as immediate family, so I'm on borrowed time. It's six hours from Barton to campus. If I leave right after the burial, I might be back in time for Stats.

....

More stories from the kitchen. I start to walk in place, kicking my leg every other step, Lamaze breathing. *She only made it to twenty-two, there can't be much left*, I think to myself.

....

One thing I pick up from eavesdropping is that Matt loved Jill unquestionably, ever since her earliest days at the church. Not like a pervert, although the thought crossed my mind. Like something else. His voice brightens when speaking of her, the same as her parents when a cherished memory comes to mind. I caught a glimpse of this in the church basement.

A familiar pattern emerges in the storytelling. Denise, providing the plot, spinning the yarn. Brad, cutting in, moralizes over the fated consequence. And finally, Matt, taking into consideration the breadth of her life, rationalizes Jill's motives with his secret knowledge and flair for dramatic irony.

The Three Fates of Jill Simmons.

Thank you, Western Civ.

I see why she found solace in Matt. It was Matt's obligation as her pastor to forgo judgment. That's his job, right? I wonder if Jill had any awareness he was terrible at it. I never felt a need to forgive Jill, but also lacked the practice. Maybe if I had known her as long as Matt, I would be wrong too.

....

The mood shifts in the next room over, tension as tangible and fervent as the pinch in my bladder. They no longer speak of the Past-Present Jill. She is too late arriving home and pronounced dead at 11:02 p.m. The topic changes to those that remain. I pretend to pack, alone in the room, hoping to excuse my voyeurism later.

"When will you go back to work?" Matt asks.

"Monday," Brad says. "The store gave me a week. Life insurance won't pay out for a month at least and we just . . ." His throat catches, ". . . can't."

"I didn't count it, but the offering basket was plenty full after the service, and we'll take another on Sunday," the pastor commiserates.

I hear nothing for a moment, Jill's parents gripped by an abrupt awareness of their town's corporeal pity.

Brad speaks up, "Denise has been thinking about going back too."

"*He* has," Denise bellows.

"You've always wanted to work at the church," her husband reminds her, his empathy woven with underlying selfishness. "Maybe now's the right time."

"We could use a new youth minister," Matt chimes in.

There's a loud, flat smack of a palm against the linoleum. A grim hush falls on the house, the type of silence that isn't silent at all but borne of a blunt inward trauma.

"Who the fuck do you think would trust me with their child after all of this?" Denise cries, replete with anguish and madness, her words trembling in audible vertigo.

She can hardly finish the sentence before the tears come, and I realize this is my chance to make a break for it.

....

I'd only met Brad and Denise twice before today. The first was during homecoming weekend. Jill and I had been sleeping together for a couple of months but recently made it official. It would be a short visit for her parents, but Jill was still excited to introduce me.

We went for a nice dinner at Three-One-Eight. I ordered a beer before everyone else. Jill's face flushed. I didn't understand why until Brad scolded me. He then had the waitress bring a bottle of wine for the table, much to Jill's surprise. We laughed a lot. The sun was starting to get colder but had enough left in it to keep the air warm until it dropped below the horizon. The trees had just started to show spots of orange and yellow and dying.

The second time we met was when they came to retrieve Jill, but we were different people by then.

....

The back hallway leads me outside. The unlocked patio door notwithstanding, I keep quiet enough to avoid notice. Eyeing around, I spot a heavy, well-aged oak in the corner of the yard only a few feet beyond the edge of the floodlights, the dim silhouette of the trunk impugning on the tree the appearance of an empty container waiting to be filled. Out of sight from the neighbors, I take the long overdue satisfaction of relieving myself. It is the most pleasurable thing I've done all week.

I shake, tuck myself in, and am immediately seized by a primal urge to find something to drink. I sneak along the fence, tiptoeing along the border of the light, back to a shadowed corner of the old stone house. Running my hand along the jagged limestone for guidance, I discover the spigot with my shin, taking the Lord's name, first in vain and then in praise of this blessed, holy water that I lap at like a dog.

It's all a bit degrading, slurping and pissing in the wild, but I've had enough of my higher level emotions for the day. There's self-determination in allowing my base urges to run free for a moment rather than grieving.

I continue in this feral state, prowling the exterior of the house for signs of a young Jill: a discarded toy left in the storm gutters, an etching in the stone foundation, or a handprint in the poured concrete of the driveway. Any trace that says, "Jill was here."

At the front of the house, I take a seat on the porch swing, concluding I have no way back in without discovery. The firmness of the wood pushes against my legs and back as I settle into the seat. The stiff, unyielding firmness of the natural world providing an assuring anchor after an unexpected encounter with the life beyond.

I close my eyes and begin to relax my muscles, allowing the rigid strips to act against the knots and tension built up over the week. The night breeze undulates, each wave like a burst of cold water against the skin after a full day in the sun, the filth of the heat washing away.

Barton isn't pretty, but it is quiet. The ambient creek of the swing cast a quieting spell on my mind, the jarring impressions of the last week soothed with each ebb and flow. The final thought playing in my head before the front door rasps open and Matt half steps through the frame, is Jill, her manipulation hidden behind a mask of self-pity and disappointment, chastising me for refusing to go out.

"You always do this."

....

"Love you, Denise. You too, Brad," Matt says, backing through the entryway.

"Love you too, Matt," Denise calls back, her voice weary. She sniffles. "I'm sorry I yelled."

"Already forgiven," he says, the delay in his reply, though brief, telling. "We'll see you tomorrow."

Matt closes the door gently and eases the screen into place. He walks past me, oblivious to my presence on the swing, and stops at the precipice of the porch, his hands rummaging through the pockets of his nylon jacket. The swing squeals and Matt whips around like a startled cat.

"Nate! My goodness!" He puts a hand over his heart. "I didn't expect you'd still be here."

I see in his eyes a familiar and not-so-distant fear. That of a teenage boy caught doing a naughty something alone in his room.

"I'm sorry." I don't know why I say it that way, laced with animus. Like earlier in the day, my words hang longer than they should, thick as dew in the ever-moistening air, consonants and vowels stretching over us like the joints and cartilage of a drawn, tortured soul. Matt raises his hands, palm out, just above his shoulders.

"Didn't mean nothing by it. Figured you had to head back to . . ." He snaps his fingers, searching.

"Where were you two studying again?" he asks, feigning ignorance.

I oblige, "Western."

"That's right. Over in Libertyville. The Mighty Bison."

Without breaking eye contact, his fingers creep back towards the jacket. I see his pupils dart up and down, sizing me up before slowly removing a pack of Marlboros. When I don't recoil in disgust—though I happen to prefer Spirits, I see no point in passing judgment among iniquities—Matt expertly slides out a square and slips it between his lips. The lighter appears and then vanishes behind his cupped hand in a flash of muscle memory, and before I can blink, he exhales a medley of smoke and overdue relief.

I lean back on the swing and glance through the window into the kitchen to make sure no one is watching. Brad gently rubs Denise's back between her shoulder blades, her arms crossed at the kitchen bar, her head buried. Juvenile habits but the coast is clear.

"They know," he says, releasing another thick trail of smoke. "Denise and I used to cut together."

He must see the confusion on my face.

"You thought Brad was the one who came to Jesus?"

....

Matt leans over the porch railing and ashes the cigarette, pinched firmly between his middle and index fingers, with a few upward flicks of his thumb.

"First time in Barton?" he asks.

I hate it when people do that. Try to weasel a reaction out of you by asking questions they already have answers for.

"Yes, sir."

"Not much to look at is there?"

Another one.

"No, sir."

"Sir? Jill would have died if she heard you call me that."

The mere invocation of that word casts all life from the air surrounding us. Matt smacks his lips and tilts the pack towards me in an apologetic offer. I have a suspicion this is a trick, one he plays frequently, and I'm being cultivated by this clerical double agent—an inverse Satan, posing as a demon instead of an angel, offering a smoke and then ratting you out as a fraud to the pious.

"Only when I drink," I tell him. We are now even on thoughtless comments.

"Been a while?" he says venomously, his eyes searing, blood-red and glowing behind the equally bright tip of his cigarette. He knows. He knows that Jill needed me there. That I could have cut her off, driven her home, shoved her in a cab.

No, something else.

Preacher man wanted me in that car. He wanted someone there when she went. A sinister compassion.

Matt draws from the cigarette—an immense, belligerent drag—like a demon from the past, smoldering with anger, crawling out of the deep, begging for a breath.

"How old were you when you came to know the Lord, Nate?"

He grins, the cigarette purses his lips, and I notice for the first time the narrow gap in his teeth, the slit emanating fire and smoke. I see ferocious turbulence in his eyes. This gaze fades swiftly, replaced with the delicate pastoral touch he demonstrated when I lost my nerve at the altar.

"It's a joke, son. Tell me about yourself."

"Well, I'm an Engineering major," I say, having never been one for icebreakers. "I like the idea of creating things. I'd like to design bridges maybe."

"I didn't ask what you do, I asked who you are."

"I don't know."

I feel cripplingly childish trying to sum up my person to a man twice my age. My vapid answer reminding me of petulant, grade-school replies when Mom would ask about my day.

I stumble forward anyway, "Life just rolls from one thing to the next. I figure it'll tell me who I am when it's ready."

"That sounds like Jill."

"You think?"

"You misunderstand."

Matt doesn't look at me, his eyes fixated on some unknown point beyond the horizon. A vein throbs in his neck, muscles tense, restraining the wicked spirit from before. His voice deepens again.

"Jill might as well have been my kid too, you know? Her and every other one that came up through the church for the time I've been here. These parents . . . They expect me to instill their morals, conduct their discipline, and convey the love of God when they either can't or won't. Proverbs says, 'Train children in the right way, and when old, they will not stray.' The Bible says it, Nate: 'they will not stray.' But, I've lost them all. One way or another, they all wander. Most move. Barton's a shithole, but you already know that. A few come back. They try their hand at college and can't cope with what the world throws at them. They lose sight of the Lord and return broken like clay pots, ready to be remade. But they're still not mine. Not after that. They make new families and then hand their kids off to me just as their parents did.

"That's what I thought Jill would do. I expected her back sooner than the others, not long after the first semester. She'd get a job around here as a waitress or a hairdresser. Some other fuck up would get her pregnant. They'd save themselves the headache and get married. I'd officiate and do my best not to let on that she's carrying the child or that they don't love each other.

"She would finally settle down and—how'd you put it?—let life roll from one thing to the next. And that'd be okay because she'd be safe. That could have been the two of you.

"You see, Nate, Jill knows precisely who she is. She's the Apostle Peter before the Resurrection. Impulsive. Temperamental. Truthful. Rash. Opportunistic. I could never convince her to cling to Jesus like Peter eventually would. I thought I might get the chance if she made it back.

"But she always preferred boys like you: empty, rudderless vessels she could command. I see the draw, and I don't blame you. It's like any sin. You think you've found liberation, but before you realize you're not the one in control, the sin abandons you. Then, you have nothing. No good. No bad. Only empty and left searching for how you're going to fill that hole next."

Matt turns to face me now, his eyes wet.

"Let me guess," he says. "You two hooked up a party, and you felt like you had to take her on another date?"

Another question he has the answer to.

"You're not the first guy she met like that, friend. You did last the longest though."

"I guess that makes me special."

Matt sucks a final time, taking the white wrapping all the way down to the filter.

"That's right," he says, flipping the bud onto the cracked, uneven driveway. "Soulmates."

....

I expected to find Brad and Denise in the kitchen when I came inside. The lights are still on, mugs and snack plates out, meats and cheeses half eaten, dishes piled aimlessly in the sink, but the room is a bare, ominous void—as if Jill had led a rapture and taken them home with her.

....

My hands still shake from the conversation with Matt. I stayed outside for several minutes after he left the porch waiting for my nerves to cool and only came in once my stomach started to growl.

I grab a slice of salami off one of the stranded plates and rummage through the cabinets looking for something to go with it. My first time at the parents' place and I don't have anyone to tell me the secret rules of the house. What food is safe to eat? Whose treats are off limits? Which cabinet keeps the damn water glasses? Does the ice maker work? Which has the better water: the faucet or the fridge? All mysteries. I play it safe and sneak a few potato chips, an apple, and a slice of white bread. Something inconspicuous.

With nothing to do but chew, I saunter around the kitchen pondering the family memories. On the refrigerator: a middle school honor roll sticker. Below that, a faded watercolor with the initials JS, its corners curled and yellow. Behind the painting: a group of teenagers crowded around a large wooden cross, full of hugs and smiles in their lime green t-shirts. On the top of the cabinet: that doll from little Jill's picture in the guest room, its buttons looser, the fabric a patchwork of frayed ends and stains. In the cupboard: an unopened box of Cheez-Its. Jill's favorite snack.

Ten minutes later and still no Brad or Denise. I take my dirty plate and hide it under the others at the bottom of the sink. Why am I so scared of getting caught?

In the living area, I find a row of old VHS tapes. Disney classics like Aladdin, The Lion King, and The Little Mermaid. In the hallway, her school pictures line up neatly in a row. I spend minutes with each clue—nose inch close, eyes squinted and full of pondering—interrogating them for meaning. Maybe years on, when time has worked out the equation, I'll be able to explain why she got in that damn car.

....

When I'm finished in each room, I turn the light off behind me, every switch its own little funeral over some element of Jill's past.

....

At the back of the house, I hear their wails, growing louder and more pronounced as I creep along the hallway. Their cries deep, reflexive, heaving—the type that won't end until sleep consumes them without notice, the kind they will wake up to hours later and find themselves still in the middle of. Their sobs pulse through the drywall, pound against the door, and crawl like bugs underneath the gap in the floor.

I leave the hall switch unturned, unable to do away with the light, and make my way back to the guest room without a sound.

....

I lie in bed staring at the picture of Jill, her gripping the doll, eyes untamed and alive, while the dark cries from the other woman in the picture echo in my ears. I take the picture and put it in my bag. Pulling the sack tightly against my chest, I drape one arm over its middle while the other tucks neatly underneath my head, mimicking the familiar positions we used to take. Finally comfortable, I lose myself to sleep.

....

We bury Jill the next morning at the Union Hill Cemetery at 9:00 a.m., exactly as Brad planned. Actually, the Burnley Company moved her casket above the hole where they will eventually bury her. They'll lower the body later after everyone is gone. They'll cover it with dirt, level the soil, and seed the ground. They'll water the plot, wait for the grass to grow, and mow it when it gets too tall. If not for the slab of etched granite, they'll forget Jill is there at all.

I try not to avoid looking at the box destined for life beneath the ground, choosing instead to focus on the appeal of Heaven.

There are fewer tears today. There's only so much water in the human body. Brad, Denise, aunts, uncles, and cousins—some I remember meeting yesterday, most I don't—sit in metal folding chairs a few feet from the casket. I stand behind, not wanting to deny anyone a seat.

Matt, dressed in the same, unfilled suit as the day before, reads scripture to the assembly.

The passage from Luke reads, "If your brother or sister sins against you, forgive them. Even if they sin against you seven times and seven times ask forgiveness, you must forgive them."

The others nod their bowed heads, assured the sinner Jill was walking with the Lord in Heaven, forgiven seventy-seven times over. But Matt looks up as he reads, finding my gaze, his voice contrite and gentle, peaceful in the way I experienced so profoundly the day before.

We close with a hymn, "How Great Thou Art." At least I know this one. On the last verse, we form a line, each of us taking a flower from the wreath adorning the casket, our macabre participation trophies. The flowers are young and freshly cut, dying and full of irony.

....

I leave directly from the cemetery. I'm offered the usual small town pleasantry of staying only a little bit longer for lunch. I insist that I must get going. Her parents won't say it, their reverence for whatever love Jill and I shared too precious to discard, but they need me to leave. I'm the last relic of a demonic curse; the final, terrible spirit holding possession of their lives and once I'm exorcised, they can be free.

....

Knowing Matt will spend the day supporting the family, I drive to his house on my way out of town, having pulled his address from an unused phone book I found in the kitchen drawer. It's an old listing, but I assume the people of Barton don't change houses often.

The home is well built, humble, a small single story without a hint of style. Grey, vinyl siding. White trim. Straight, concrete walkway. A couple of unpruned bushes. Yes, a single, middle-aged man lives there.

I dig out a spiral notebook from my bag, skip past my class notes, and turn to the last page. I write Matt a note. I only come up with one line:

"She was better because of you."

I rip out the piece of paper and peel off the tattered, perforated edge. I fold it in fours, walk up the short, lonely path, and tuck it gently between the frame and the glass storm door. I don't know If Jill was a better person because of Matt or in spite of him, but he's earned the right to believe it either way.

....

On the south edge of town, there's a business strip consisting of a Dollar General, a Mexican restaurant, and Bill's Bail Bonds. There's nothing for me to buy. I only stop because the tan, stucco mass is the last building I see for miles, the horizon on which Barton sets.

There are few cars in the lot. Through the window of Los Reales, a family of three shares a large plate of fajitas. An elderly woman with tennis balls on the feet of her walker scrapes the sidewalk, escorted from the store at the arm of her greying, middle-aged daughter. An oversized, mud battered pickup idles to the right of me, cab empty.

Jill and I were supposed to go to the lake that day.

What then?

The best is easy to imagine. Holding hands at graduation. Concerts under a starlit canopy, high and full of music. Floating downstream in the sun. Her smile and the way she dips her chin when she finds me staring from the other end of the couch. A trip overseas, naked and breathless, hot against each other's skin, glowing like the Parisian lights. The heightened tension and exploratory glances at a friend's wedding. Unanswered question shrouded in the mystic, sanguine luminescence of a hopeful future.

I don't love her. Not like the others. I only skipped in line, my grief unearned. But here I am, unable to leave her, clutching the picture I stole the night before, tears welling like a river at the edge of its bank after a long and weary rain. A billion tiny drops, filling the bed inch by inch until the water finally crests, the inescapable wall of dread descending in a rush of awful power. I look up from the picture, past the prefabricated building with chipped paint, towards the frontage road leading to the highway. Beyond that—if not for the posted signs—an unbound emptiness, leading nowhere at all.

Absence

AFTERNOON OF THE HERO

Claire Noonan

Pauly leaped down St. Michael's steps two at a time, relieved that the first day of school after Christmas was over. He stumbled at the last step so as not to bump the Reverend Mother Mary Anthony. Standing at the front of the two-story brick building as the children left, the old nun in her long black habit and snow-white wimple smiled and blessed those she favored with "May the Lord be with you."

She turned to Pauly and said, "Paul Francis Mooney."

"Good afternoon, Reverend Mother," he replied, dutiful in word, but uneasy about her tone.

"Take care of your mother."

Why wouldn't he care for Ma? He didn't need advice from that bossy old lady. Pauly's hair flopped over his forehead as he looked down to frown. He hated the Sister, capable of nasty whacks on the knuckles with her ruler for anyone she wished to rebuke. She'd hit him many times, but mostly he hated her for hitting Peter, dead now for two weeks, although his brother had laughed as he'd rued the punishment for passing notes. Pauly hated the Sister for her certainty that he, only ten years old, and Peter, thirteen, would spend ages in Purgatory, if not Hell, smacking his knuckles to confirm the endless number of days. He was not consoled when in an effort to ease Ma's grief the nun had come to visit the day after Peter died.

Christmas Day, the Reverend Mother smoothed his mother's hand and assured her that her son, Peter, was praying in Heaven with Jesus and Mary, and that Ma could join him when the time came. Pauly turned away in disgust, when Ma leaned into Pa's shoulder and broke into deep sobs of despair again. She had only ceased crying in the morning, her eyes empty and face stiff, as friends and relatives, one after another, had entered their front room on the holy day. Pauly feared Ma wanted to join Peter right then, except he knew such a mortal sin would consign her to Hell to burn with Satan for eternity.

The memory churned in Pauly's head. He wished to never look at or speak to the Sister again. Knowing that would never happen while he was a student at St. Michael's, he sighed and instead, headed for Hildreth Street, turning his mind to the purchase of potato chips. As he sped up, it came to him that Peter wouldn't go straight to Heaven because he had shown Pauly the pictures of naked women hidden under the desk in Uncle John's room and bought comic books where bad guys killed and drank and swore.

Beyond question, those pictures and magazines were something to confess whenever the monsignor dragged the boys to kneel one by one in the incense-laden closet, completely dark until the father flung back the screened window. Only Peter died before he could make one more confession, having been sick in bed with a stomach ache for two days. Even though the monsignor hurried to the hospital to give Extreme Unction which saved Peter from eternal Hell, Pauly was convinced his brother would be detained for an unknown amount of time in Purgatory. Not for snickering and passing notes as Sister Mary Anthony claimed, he'd be unable to sit in glory with God for years unless the living did penance for him. There was the predicament.

Pauly felt the nickel in his jacket pocket, but he wouldn't put it in the church poor box. He didn't care if the surest way to help his brother escape Purgatory and stand before St. Peter was to offer a monetary indulgence. There must be another way. Pauly had saved the nickel since New Year's just to stop at the corner shop on Hildreth Street and buy a newspaper cone of homemade potato chips after his first day back at school, like he and Peter had always done.

The poor old lady who ran the shop, who had lived there as long as Pauly had walked to and from school, could use the nickel. Pa had told him so, and Pauly accepted his father's convictions as far as he was concentrating on anything other than the salty taste of a hot crisp potato chip.

Newspaper cone in hand, Pauly dawdled in the shop, and the old lady, Mrs. McKenna, asked, "How's your ma, Pauly?"

"All right," he said, thinking, *what else could he say?* Mrs. McKenna was just trying to be kind.

"Your pa?"

"All right, too. He goes to his meetings," and the old woman nodded as if that's what fathers were supposed to do.

"And you, Pauly?"

He looked up and blurted out, "I miss my brother." The old lady clutched her throat and said she missed Peter too.

"Remember the time you and Peter came here and those bully boys waited outside the door to grab your chips because you were the smallest?"

"You remember that day?"

"Of course, and how Peter gave them his cone and said if they wanted them so bad, take them."

Mrs. McKenna said those boys looked pretty sheepish, but they'd probably confronted another little boy again when he came out with a cone of chips.

She patted his arm and said, "Come any time, Pauly. We won't forget Peter."

Pauly blinked away tears and ate chips. He counted cars that he passed along Hildreth until he reached the old cemetery and waved to the moss-covered stone for Fanny Fadden, 1701–1792, the oldest grave in the burial ground. He imagined a new stone dated 1889–1929 with his Ma's name cut into the granite because he knew she wished to be under the ground just like old Fanny and her favored son.

Running his hand along the black iron rail, Pauly stopped to look at the monument to Ben Butler, Union hero during the Civil War. He'd refused to return fugitive slaves, calling them contraband of war, while he was Major General at the Union's Fort Monroe in Virginia. Peter had told Pauly the whole story when he'd studied about the heroism of soldiers from Lowell in those fearsome battles. Pauly wished there was room for Peter next to old Ben, but the Hildreth Cemetery was long full and had been closed in the last century when it was still on the edge of town.

By now, houses had filled up streets all around the graveyard. The dead, rich and poor alike, were buried far away in the cemetery on the other side of Lowell, and each religious group had its own section. Catholics, like his brother Peter, were buried in the section named for St. Patrick, the good Irish saint.

Finally, Pauly turned onto narrow By Street. Sitting on the bottom step of her house, Irene Guinn greeted him.

"Hi, Pauly. Haven't seen you much since Peter went." She wiped away a tear. Pauly stopped and shook his head.

"Naw, I go straight home. Don't want to play."

"Yes, I miss your brother too." Pauly knew she was Peter's girlfriend. He had caught them kissing on the front porch, but he'd just watched and never said anything. Peter had said Irene's eyes were as green as Ireland, and he was smitten.

"I have a chip left. You want one?"

"Ah, no. Sure, it's how you remember him. I remember how I laughed when he told me funny stories. He was good that way, wan't he?" She fanned her face with her hand to hide the tears and jumped up. "I've to go in now to help the little ones. See you another day, maybe."

She waved and he waved his cone of chips and walked down the street and opened the screen door to his kitchen.

"Ma!" he yelled.

No answer. He went into the bathroom, peed, and washed the grease off his hands. Back in the kitchen, he tripped on the crack in the linoleum floor and steadied himself with his hand on the wall. Snatching his palm off his mother's beloved flowery wallpaper, he saw the note on the breakfast table propped up against the ceramic salt cat and pepper dog.

Gone to the cemetery. Back by 5. Ma.

It's cold outside and mucky with snow. Why's Ma over there? She could pray her rosary with the beads given to her by Reverend Mother on the nice warm couch in the front room. She'd be around when he got home so they could talk and comfort each other. Pauly's father would never sit with him. He was at the textile mill union meeting since it was Monday and he was president. Pa wouldn't be home until late. He barely spoke to Ma or Pauly anyway, spending as much time as possible at one of his poor man's clubs. Pa would want to play catch in the yard, even if it was freezing and snowy, rather than talk about Peter.

Pauly wandered into the front room, shades pulled down, dried-up needles dropping from the Christmas tree, no one willing to throw it out, put away the ornaments, or stash unopened gifts. Peter's handsome, round face in the Confirmation photograph smiled at Pauly from the coffee table and made his eyes smart.

At the bottom of the narrow steep staircase leading to his bedroom on the second floor, Pauly pressed his head down onto the banister. On the wall at the landing Jesus waited, golden halo framing the thorn crown that made blood drip onto His pale face. His tunic was pulled back and blood poured from His scarlet heart. More blood dribbled from the wound under His ribs opened from a sharp stab by the Roman soldier's spear. Pauly gagged most times, even when he sneaked past and didn't look, though his brother had never laughed or made fun of his loathing.

He could not run up to the bedroom. He squeezed his eyes to stop the teardrops. What if Peter is there? He'd piled his brother's treasures in a box, shoved them into the closet, and asked Pa to take away the extra bed, but Peter was at the desk, by the window, on the bed each time Pauly opened his eyes.

Every night Pauly had still left his bed and opened the window to take a pee so he didn't have to go down those scary stairs to the bathroom, just as Uncle John had showed the brothers when he moved into the extra bedroom a year ago. Peter had laughed at the new technique and said Pa had let Uncle John come live with them because he couldn't get over his wife's death and needed someone to take care of him. Ma, the sister-in-law, got the job.

Looking out the window, Pauly sniffed again, thinking of his brother and remembering the jokes he'd tell. Pauly was certain his brother would never have been a priest, even though his ma had long held Peter up as a model. Pauly and Peter had too much fun.

He lifted his head, held his breath, and counted to three with the intention of running up fast, throwing down his school papers, picking up the book he read to keep his mind off his brother, and searching for cookies in the kitchen. No one was home to say not to eat them.

Pauly jerked when Uncle John's telephone rang. As the long-time town councilman and current mayor, he paid for the phone. Pauly's ma and pa couldn't afford one. Now he had a different decision to make. Answer and take a message for Uncle John or ignore the phone.

He sighed, picked up the receiver, and said, "Residence of John Mooney, mayor. May I take a message?"

"Pauly, is that you?" yelled Uncle John. "Where's your father?"

"I don't know," whispered Pauly.

Wary of passing on information when Uncle John yelled, Pauly instinctively became the ignorant ten-year-old, even though he knew his father was at the union meeting. Anyway, Uncle John had a split personality about unions. John loved good Irish Democrats to help his campaigns but hated when the union insisted on a return for the favor. John and Pa often argued the issue. They were brothers after all. So, pretending he didn't know, Pauly felt no qualms about the lie, happy to have a sin for confession. Besides, he could solve the penance problem by praying for his own soul and add extra prayers to shorten Peter's days in Purgatory.

"OK, OK," shouted Uncle John. "You'll have to do. Go get your ma. Crazy woman. Jesus, Mary, and Joseph. Mrs. Connor just came into the barbershop with her son Simon. Do you know that ratty-faced kid? What kind of name is Simon? Sounds Jewish. She yakked about seeing your ma walking down the path at St. Patrick's, striking her breast, oops, sorry Pauly, I mean chest, falling down on her knees *in the snow* to crawl to Peter's grave, and saying Hail Mary's out loud for all to hear on the big white rosary beads that nun gave her.

"I'm the mayor, Pauly. Your mother may be grieving for Peter. We all are, but she can't mourn in public like that. Mrs. Connor said Sister Mary Anthony may have told your ma to do penance, but Jesus, Mary, and Joseph, Pauly, this goes too far. Your mother didn't know she shouldn't give Peter cod liver oil. How would she know he'd burst his appendix?

"Why doesn't your pa do something, Pauly? For love of God, you're the only smart one in the whole family. Be a hero. Get a dime off the dresser in my room and take the bus to the cemetery. Bring her here. I'm at the barber shop. Get her off her knees, Pauly!"

"Uncle John," said Pauly. "It'll get dark."

"I don't care," he yelled.

"She might be on the bus already."

"Pauly, go find out."

"But can't you get her?"

"My other barbers have gone. I can't leave. No one to cover for me."

"I have lots of homework, Uncle John."

"I'll write an excuse to the monsignor, Pauly. What if Mrs. Connor, the blabbermouth, tells everyone at St. Michael's? Or fat, old Sister Mary Anthony tells?"

"Sister feels sorry for Ma," said Pauly, unable to explain to himself why he was defending someone he detested.

"What do I care about that meddlesome nun, Pauly?" hollered Uncle John. "Just get the money and get to the cemetery. Be the hero."

Pauly sighed.

"OK. Good-bye, Uncle John."

Hand trembling, thinking Uncle John gets so excited when he's upset, he waited until the line disconnected. Phone back in its cradle, Pauly shoved his hands in his pockets. He was no hero. He wished Uncle John had found Pa. He didn't want to do an adult's business—even for Ma.

In any case, the decision had been made, so Pauly ran upstairs, averted his eyes from Jesus, threw his papers down, and found the dime. He grabbed some cookies and huffed up to Bridge Street to catch the bus.

Pauly settled in for the long ride across town, dreary in early January. Every gutter, every roof, every tiny garden plot, every gate had grayish snow from car exhaust. Coal-heating furnaces sent up smoke and dropped soot. Dog poo mixed into the snow. Pa didn't understand how anyone in Lowell's Centreville neighborhood could afford a pet in these penniless days, but plenty of families still clung to their animal. Pauly's spaniel had died in October, and Pa said they didn't have money for another. Pauly missed Peter above all, but his dog too.

Finishing a cookie, Pauly checked for Ma at her favorite stores—the flower shop, the bakery, the drug store. Then he closed his eyes at the street leading to St. Michael's until the bus reached the bridge across the Merrimack River.

Everyone at school had had to read some of Thoreau's memoir about the Merrimack, even though he was a free thinker. A journey by boat along the Concord River to the Merrimack until it reached the Atlantic Ocean near Marblehead. Pauly wondered why anyone thought the river was romantic. Full of ice now, but not without cracks so no one had the nerve to ice skate like Thoreau idealized. The water rolled on, filthy ice floes broke against the rocks, so fast no wonder the boy lost his footing, slipped in, and drowned last winter. He wished he hadn't thought of the dead kid because it reminded him of his own misery.

Three days before Christmas, Peter and he had played soldier in the birch woods near By Street with four other boys. They had shinnied up the thin white and brown birch trunks which bent and swooped down. The boys had howled and leaped onto each other until the snow came down so fast and heavy, they could barely see when an ambush lay in wait just above. Then Peter had complained of a stomach ache and dragged Pauly home because he was three years younger and still not allowed to stay out in the dark by himself.

Peter had climbed the stairs, holding his stomach, paying no attention to Jesus' bloody heart, and put himself to bed. Pauly wandered into the kitchen and drank a glass of milk while his mother blabbed to him about the next-door neighbor who had been visited every day around noon by the postman while her husband was at work. His ma may have been pious, but she gossiped with the best and finished with the number of prayers she had said for the woman's soul. Also, eight were now coming to Christmas dinner, including Uncle Frankie and Pa's cousin Kenny and his new wife.

Finally, Ma had said, "Where's your brother?"

Pauly reported Peter was in bed and didn't feel good. Ma immediately wheezed her way upstairs to check his temperature. He'd had polio when he was six, and Ma always panicked when he had any complaint, although he wasn't paralyzed from the polio and had recovered quickly.

Pa had come home soon after and said to wait a day as the doctor was very expensive. Peter, himself, said his stomach wasn't so bad. Then Uncle John came home, clumped up the stairs, and was surprised to find the entire family in the back bedroom standing around the bed.

He'd said, "Let's see how he is tomorrow. We can always go to the hospital."

Ma's eyes had glowed with alarm and her hands shook. Her mouth abruptly began to say a "Hail Mary" as if it would ward off evil.

Then, Uncle John said his friend was coming to take him to the city council meeting and poker game afterwards. Pa said he had a Knights of Columbus meeting. And so, Ma and Pauly had been left to watch over Peter. That night Pauly passed on Ma's gossip and Peter laughed. The next day Pauly stayed around the house and at night he helped Peter get up. At the open window, they'd stood, comparing how far they could send their streams, arcing out and down to water the rose bushes Ma was trying to save, drops sparkling like the stars between moving clouds in the dark, cold sky. Peter still had a fever and said his stomach hurt, but whispered how to beat Uncle Frankie, the old drunk, at gin rummy, which he'd show Pauly after Christmas dinner.

Christmas Eve morning, Peter, who had never before complained or admitted pain, began to cry. Ma gave him the spoonful of castor oil. An hour later she called Uncle John.

The rest of the day was fuzzy. Uncle John had picked them up in his friend's car and left Pauly at the textile mill to get Pa, while John and Ma drove Peter to the hospital. Overcome by the dusty, dark walls and noisy machines, Pauly barely remembered talking to the supervisor who, according to his father, had only excused him because he was the union president.

"But maybe your face touched that hard man," said skinny, long-legged Pa as he took Pauly's hand and strode through the streets to the Catholic hospital.

By then Pauly had been so tired he fell asleep on the chair outside the ward. He didn't know Peter was gone, his appendix burst, poison spreading through his abdomen, until his ma stumbled into the hallway, calling on the Virgin to protect her son's soul. Pauly wasn't even allowed to see Peter's body.

On Christmas Eve the family usually went to mass to celebrate the birth of their savior, but that night Ma sat on the hospital bench, weeping and whispering one after another Hail Mary while Pa, face ashen and shoulders stooped, tried to soothe her. Uncle John had finally shown up with his friend's car to drive them all home. Pauly ran through the cold air to the car, sat squished in the corner of the back seat, and looked out the car window at the dirty streets flashing by, not listening to Ma's sobs, nor the comforting words from Pa and Uncle John.

....

Pauly twitched on the bus seat and rubbed his temples to hide the leaking tears at the memory of his brother. From the bus window Pauly watched the streets going past on the other side of Lowell in the area he didn't recognize.

"Oh Lord," he prayed to himself. "Show me the cemetery stop." While he kept an eye out for the tree-covered place with carved monuments sticking up, he wondered what he, a short, tow-headed boy, was going to do to lift his ma up off her knees. She was heavy now like the Irish women her age all over Lowell. She had a square stocky body, short fat legs, and dark hair turning gray which she wore in tight curls. Peter had said she wore ugly clothes. She said she couldn't afford anything else. Pauly thought she wore them to be virtuous. Why didn't she wear pretty dresses like Irene's ma and shoes with heels and buckles instead of old black, tie shoes? Irene's family was poor too.

The first tall gravestones appeared at the next corner and Pauly jumped up. He leaned down to look through the window and hoped to see Ma at the bus stop across the street. He wouldn't even mind if she was holding her favorite beads, mouth moving, as she did most of the time since Christmas Eve. But nobody stood waiting in a long black coat and white hat with a black veil pulled down over her face, rosary in hand. Maybe if he stayed on the bus, rode to the end and came back she'd be there. He could say he'd retrieved her, but not have to go into the dismal park filled with granite markers for dead people.

Pauly's bottom fell onto the seat as the bus lurched forward. The tombstones become smaller and shorter in the new part of the cemetery, and then the bus crossed the street and continued through the neighborhood.

Chastising himself for his cowardice, wondering what Peter would have done, Pauly scrambled off at the next stop. He trotted back along three streets, the path slushy with snow and dead leaves. He came to the corner where he stopped short and fixed on the burial ground fence as if it would tell him which was quicker. Turn or go on one more block.

Turning and picking up speed, he watched for ice under the leaves, jumped over the mucky spots, and didn't see the snow fort across the roadway. A boy leaped up, snowball in hand and hollered, "Where you going, mackerel snapper? Forget your beads?"

All in a moment, he wondered how they knew he was Catholic, remembered he still had on his uniform, grabbed up some snow for a ball, and shouted back, "Your pa's a Bible thumper. At least I don't have a sure ticket to Hell."

One after another four boys stood and pelted him with snowballs. Not plain icy snowballs, but snow packed around a rock. He dodged, but one hit him squarely on the forehead, the rock inside leaving a gash. Blood dripped down his face as if he were Jesus on the landing.

Pauly took off zigzag, running fearlessly in spite of the blood. At an open gate in the fence, he cut in among gravestones, hiding from the boys who hollered more threats about him and his religion, but wandered off in the direction of their fort. He gulped for breath and hoped his brother would have been proud of him.

After wiping away the smear of blood mixed with sweat, he stared at the names of the dead Protestants on the flat stone markers. James, Hudson, Lowell. He looked around to get his bearings until a rumpled old man, clutching his jacket, stood up with flowers drooping from his hand. Pauly smothered a gasp.

"Don't be feared," said the man, "I'm just puttin' these mums on th' grave. My wife gone two years. Can't get over it."

"My ma's at my brother's grave. He's only been here two weeks," said Pauly. "I don't know where to go."

The old man tilted his head. "It's that little lady sobbin', in't it? She headed to St. Patrick's graves. You tryin' to get over there?" Pauly nodded.

"It's a riddle for sure." His hand shaking, the old man lifted the chrysanthemums. He pointed the flopping yellow flowers toward the pebbly path and said to cross the rows, watching the names carved onto the granite until he reached the Irish.

Dropping to his knees, the old man leaned down to arrange the last flowers at his wife's grave, and Pauly scuffed across the gravelly divide. Only French names on flat markers stretched in the distance as far as he could see. Houdin, Valery, Croteau, Pinard. He thought about his ma who was born in Quebec and who in a happier time called him her *petit chou*.

In June, the last time he'd seen Pa and Ma happy together, Pauly had been recruited to get twenty pennies from Ma, and if not, beg them from Pa, so he and Peter could go downtown and play penny-ante poker with Peter's friends. The afternoon sun filtered through the windows, tinting the dining room walls bright and warm. As he ran in, Ma sat in her Sunday dress, her one pretty frock with flowers. She had brushed out her hair so it looked full and curly like her wedding picture. She held a fragile china tea cup between her lips.

Pa stood over her with the newspaper in one hand, holding the teapot handle as if he wanted to pour her another cup. He wore his good suit pants, a white shirt with cuffs, and his tie. His head, framed by dark hair brushed back and bushy Irish eyebrows, was tilted as if he had just asked a question, but no querulous look on his face, rather an affectionate smile. Ma put down the cup and beamed, whispered "*Mais oui*,"and leaned back in the chair. They were happy. Pauly had felt no compunction about asking for the pennies.

Pauly padded across the markers with French names and entered the Irish section to find Collins, O'Donohue, and Shea. He looked up when he saw the Houlihan marker, knowing he was finally near his brother's grave. Ma wore black rubber galoshes with her heavy black coat and, instead of her white hat with the black veil, a white wool scarf tied over her head like the old Polish lady in the corner house on By Street. The grieving woman was still on her knees saying the rosary to the plot of dirt and snow and crushed flowers that marked Peter's grave. Ma was bent so low she almost sprawled on the dirt, picking at the bits of dead grass sticking up through the icy slush with one hand, holding the favored rosary in the other, kissing each large snowy white bead held between her fingers when she finished the Hail Mary.

She moaned to the grave, "Forgive me, son. Forgive your poor mother. I didn't know. I didn't know."

Freezing wind sifted through the tree branches, separating one last leaf from a limb and dropping it onto the grave. Pauly shifted from one cold foot to the other, shook out his fingers, then put them in his pockets, and glanced at the gloomy sky. Hunching his shoulders, sinking his neck down into his coat collar, he wondered again how he was going to lift his mother off the stinking, slushy ground and up into the air. So lonely, for a second Pauly wished he were Peter. At least everyone would be moaning and grieving for him.

Instead, he thought of the many nights when speculation came over Peter after the lights were out, and he had talked about all the places to see in the world. This past November he made Pauly promise to save every penny, and they'd buy train tickets to Boston and spend a day there next summer. They studied the map and plotted the places to see in the famous town. Now how would he get there? By himself? Then he thought he would go and dedicate the trip to Peter. That would be a good memory. And then he remembered Peter had been happy up until the last morning when he began to cry from the pain.

Ma repeated, "Holy Mary, Mother of God, pray for us sinners now and at the hour of our death." Pauly stood still and listened. The wind blew. As he brushed snowflakes from his face, it came to Pauly that Peter wasn't a sinner. He had never been a sinner. The comics were just for fun. Penny-ante poker was for fun. Pauly shook his head. Peter didn't need penance. No one needed to worry about his dead brother's soul.

He did know Peter wouldn't want Ma to be lying around on the snowy ground beating her chest and counting beads. He'd want her to know he'd been happy. Maybe Peter would have asked Ma to go to Boston with them. Maybe he should ask her.

Feeling another drop of blood oozing down his temple, Pauly wiped his forehead with his coat sleeve. Kicking snow off his shoe, he sighed and walked up to his mother, leaned over, and put his hands on her shoulders. She sat back. Through swollen red eyes, she stared at his grimy face with the seeping gash.

She grabbed his hand and said, "Pauly. Pauly, is that you?"

"Yes, Ma. I came to take you back."

CURSES

Kathleene Donahoo

"Nothing," Bel says when Mol asks what's wrong. Not here, with so many nosy people parading past their table: librarians, mothers with little kids, even some boys from their grade. She picks up a marker to fill in blanks on their geological timeline, and after a moment Mol does too.

Later they're alone in the lobby, just inside the library door, their poster rolled and tucked under Mol's arm. She turns to Bel, worry crinkling her freckled nose. But Bel just stares at the salt-smeared floormats, and when she looks up Mol's mother is on the other side of the black glass, ghost-like in her white parka. The door opens and arctic air rushes in.

"All finished, girls? Wonderful! Belinda, can't I drive you home?"

"Thanks, but my father will be here soon." She hears a commuter train screeching to a stop at the station a block away; Dad will be on the very next one. He'll come here for her, and they'll go on to pick up Cora from a birthday party.

"See ya tomorrow," Mol says. The door opens and shuts behind them.

What she really wants is to walk home. But Dad won't let her because the sidewalks are icy and the streets narrowed by mounds of snow. Even in February it still gets dark too early, he said this morning.

Which is just plain stupid. It's only six blocks. Does he really think she'd die of frostbite? Has he forgotten that she's almost fourteen?

Should have argued this morning. Would have, had she known what a shitty day it'd turn out to be. The library door swings open again, tempting her to run out into the night and let the cold air sting her lungs. Running hard and fast might loosen the knot in her stomach.

Instead Belinda trudges back into the lobby, past the Circulation desk. As she walks through Reference, the shelves of phone books catch her eye. Last year's have been replaced with new 1988 directories. Of course, this happens every February. She reaches for Albany, then yanks her hand back.

When she was young and stupid, she'd flip through each directory to the *Macs* and run her finger down the page looking for her mother. Last year she realized it was a waste of time—if Helen MacIntyre was living a new life in Albuquerque or Boston, Pensacola or Portland—it'd be under a new name. Else the police or Dad's private investigator would have found her years ago.

Besides, some listings are barefaced lies. Illinois Bell's North Shore directory still includes *MacIntyre, John & Helen*. Ten years she's been gone, and Dad still hasn't changed the home listing.

Someday Belinda will tell him that is stupid.

She hurries away from the phone books and into the Garden Room. Dad will come straight here, to her favorite armchair. But as she lowers herself onto its green upholstered seat, she feels that wetness between her legs again. Better not.

She slings her coat over the back of a wooden chair so hard that the zipper rings. On the other side of the room a man lifts his bald head from his newspaper.

Belinda pulls the botanic encyclopedia from its shelf. Plants have much more sensible reproductive systems. Pollen can be sticky, but nothing like the mess down there.

She "started" two days after Thanksgiving, two hours after Amelia pulled out of the driveway, headed back to college. No choice but to call Nana, muffling her sobs so Dad and Cora wouldn't hear. Her stomach *hurt* so much, and she *hated* the maxipads!

"Sure you don't want me to come over?" Nana said. "Such a shame your sister's gone. She could tell you some things, things I've probably forgotten. She'll be back in her dorm room tonight—why don't you call her?"

No way. Belinda could imagine Amelia's roommate squealing in the background once she figured out what they were talking about.

"Well, the first is the worst," Nana said brightly. "Five days from now, you'll have that behind you. And let's see, it's November 28th. That's perfect, sweetheart—Amelia will be home for your next one. And if you still hate the pads, she can show you how to use a tampon."

No way anyone was showing Belinda *that*.

Three weeks later, Amelia returned home for Christmas. December 28th came and went without a single cramp or spot on Belinda's underwear. Nana seemed to have forgotten all about it, and Belinda certainly wasn't going to tell Miss Big Deal, who talked endlessly about her friends and her classes, Professor This and Professor That.

Amelia went back to Ann Arbor. January ended with yet another snowstorm. The Groundhog saw his shadow. Maybe that first period had been a fluke. A trial run that wouldn't be repeated for a while. With every passing day Belinda's hope grew—until today, when her stomach clenched in social studies. She tore out of the room during a quiz, Mrs. Taylor smiling sympathy and the heat of her classmates' eyes on her back. Everyone knew.

Belinda opens the botanic encyclopedia to the page where she left a Walgreens receipt. Ah yes, last time she'd finished the C's. She runs a finger down the plant names, looking for interesting ones to copy into her little notebook. Both genus and species, careful to get the spellings right.

Daboecia azorica. Daboecia cantabrica. Heather, named for the Irish Saint Dabhoeg.

Helen MacIntyre didn't name any of her daughters for a family member, Dad said when Belinda asked. Nor, presumably, for a saint.

Dacrydium. Conifers, more than a dozen species.

Helen MacIntyre is no saint herself, that's for sure. Saints don't desert their families for going-on ten years, even by accident. Good people take care not to let things like that happen. Helen MacIntyre is guilty of carelessness, if nothing else.

Daphniphyllum. Evergreen shrubs, thirty species, too many to copy.

Belinda's never heard Dad or Nana say anything bad about HM. If she ever asks about her mother—which she tries very hard not to do—their lips go thin and straight. Wrinkles appear between Dad's eyebrows. Both Dad and Nana say something like, "Is everything okay, Belinda?", before answering her question. And even then they don't say much.

Worst thing Nana's ever said was when Belinda showed her the old picture she'd found in the basement. HM in a bandana and beads and a tie-dyed dress so short that it barely covered her underpants. "Oh my." A sad look passed over Nana's face. "Well, dear, back then your mother did fancy herself a bit of a hippie."

Back then. A stage HM passed through, on her way to something else. So maybe she has a timeline, like the one on Bel and Mol's earth science poster.

Belinda turns to a blank page and writes:

1960s—hippie, bit of

1970s—mother, mostly

1980s—??

She sighs and checks her orange Swatch. Dad's missed his train. Or it's running late—still in Chicago or stuck on the tracks somewhere. Sometimes the trains get stuck because of snow. From the Garden Room she can't hear any pulling into the station. Only the murmur of voices, the rustle of down parkas, the thud of books dropped in the return slot.

Darmera peltata. Also known as umbrella plant.

Interesting how many plants have common names, like nicknames.

"Bel"—what Mol started calling her back in third grade—isn't quite right. It means "beautiful," and she's not even the slightest bit pretty. But it's way better than "Belinda." Belinda is a name for a frilly girl, a girly-girl, the sort of girl who uses pink gel pens to dot her *i*'s with hearts. Whatever was HM thinking? Probably she picked the name ahead of time, slapped it on her second daughter without a thought, without even looking at her.

No way Belinda will ever have a baby—what you have to go through is totally gross, much grosser than having a period, absolutely the grossest thing ever.

What about Helen? Was she ever called anything else?

Dad and Nana have never used a nickname, at least not in Belinda's hearing. "Helen handled all that," Dad told Nana when the stains on Cora's ceiling were traced first to a moldy mess in the attic, and then to some missing shingles on the roof. "The roofer said Helen called him out to inspect it every year. And here it's been seven. Who knew?"

Who knew? Unfortunate for Helen that the simplest shortening is 'Hel.' Belinda's never heard anyone called that. She read a book with a Helen, called Nelly by her sisters. Of course HM didn't have siblings. But she certainly had friends.

HM's friends. Those girls who wrote in the book Belinda found in the basement. A small fabric-covered autograph book, from Helen Hawley's eighth grade year. The notes began *Dear Helen*, or *To my best pal Helen.* None addressed her as Hel, Len, Lena, or Nell. *Hope to see lots of you in High School!* someone wrote with a drippy fountain pen.

Belinda crumples HM's timeline and hurls it at a trashcan. She stares at her reflection in the glass case of antique garden books. Those bubbly little notes prove that Helen Hawley was popular, just like Cora. Not that Belinda ever doubted it. Helen was pretty, just like Cora. "Blondes have more fun," as Rod Stewart said. And more friends. Only person who'd write something like that to Belinda is Molly, and she's going off to Phillips Exeter in September. Leaving Belinda to face Lake Forest High School on her own. She shifts in her chair, trying to straighten the bunched-up pad.

Yet another way Mol's lucky—she hasn't started yet. "My mom and my sister were both almost sixteen," she said when Bel shared her bad news in November. "So I guess I have a while."

Who knew about HM, but Amelia was probably precocious at periods like she's precocious at everything else. Probably started menstruating early, just like she graduated high school and left for college a year early. If Miss Big Deal hadn't been in such a big hurry, she'd have been here last November 28th, instead of leaving her sister alone with a dusty box of maxipads. And she'd be here right now, driving Belinda home so she could finally change her yucky pad. Instead of leaving her to wait an eternity for Dad, and then wait another eternity in the car while he picks up Cora.

Come to think of it, even with starting college early, Amelia would have been home for Belinda's first period if she hadn't rushed off that Saturday after Thanksgiving. Why, when classes didn't start until Monday? What kind of person rushes off the Saturday after Thanksgiving?

Another hot surge of pain in her gut, another wet surge down below. Her pad—the last of the two the school nurse gave her—must be soaked through by now.

Dad's going to be late picking up Cora, too. Has something happened? Has he . . .

No. Belinda squeezes her eyes shut until the room goes black. No.

Probably he's just running late. Probably he's found a pay-phone and called Cora's friend's house. So they know when to expect him, where he is.

Where the hell is he?

And Hel? Where's she right now, other than in Belinda's head?

For years she's tried to cut back on HM. A bad habit, like drinking soda, which the health teacher said should be strictly limited. With soda, Belinda went cold turkey, no problem. But with HM-thoughts, she can't seem to cut back even a little.

The perfect thing to resolve for 1988, she decided. But then didn't even make it through New Year's Day. HM kept popping up, like the zits that sprout overnight on her face. She finally clears up a patch on her nose, only to discover a new crop on her forehead the very next morning. "Try not to touch your face," Nana said.

Belinda pulls her hands from her cheeks, wipes them on her jeans. Lent starts soon. Why not give up HM for Lent, like the Catholic kids give up candy? And if she makes it through the forty days, she won't gorge herself like they do. She'll keep going, right through Easter and beyond, free of Helen MacIntyre at last, forevermore. Hallelujah.

She hears laughter and turns to see two guys from her science class walking by with a blank posterboard, headed toward the Reading Room. She quickly lowers her head over the encyclopedia. *Darwinia citriodora.* They probably hadn't noticed her.

The genus *Datura* has several species and Belinda's suddenly too tired to copy any more, so she just reads instead. *Datura inoxia* is also called Angel's Trumpet, but *Datura stranomium* has more sinister nicknames. Jimson Weed. Stinkweed. Mad Seeds. She checks the top of the page. Of course, she should have known—it's a member of the *Solanacae* family, a poisonous nightshade. The photo shows a trumpet-shaped blossom, white with a bit of purple inside. And a sinister green seed-pod with sharp spines. It's also called Locoweed, Devil's Cucumber, Hell's Bells.

Hell's Bells? Belinda laughs out loud. Her new favorite expression right here in this book! The man's head jerks up again. But she can't stop laughing, won't even try. And if he doesn't like it, he can just take his cue-ball head and his newspaper into the Periodical Room where they belong.

"Hell's bells," she said last month after dropping an egg on the kitchen floor.

Cora came running over from the breakfast nook where she was setting the table. "Nana, tell her to stop cursing!"

"It's not really a curse, Cora." Nana shook her head and smiled at Belinda. "That expression is even older than I am. I haven't heard anyone use it in years."

Nana probably guessed that Belinda had picked it up from a book. A crumbly paperback in the giveaway stack at the Lake Forest beach, in fact. That crappy mystery, set in 1920's London, was a total waste of time. Except for the "hell's bells!"

Belinda uses the expression in Cora's presence as much as possible, even though she knows it's wrong to delight in needling her little sister.

Now she stares so hard at *Datura stranomium*'s entry that the letters begin to shift and dance on the page. Hell's Bells. Hel's Bells. Hel's Bel.

Hel's Bel—*that's* who she is. Hel's Bel is the person who torments Cora. Who sulked when Dad said no walking around at night. Who didn't thank Nana for bringing more maxipads last November. Or for putting that first box in her closet a year ago. Who just shrugged and walked away when Amelia asked how things were going.

Sudden pain knifes Belinda's gut and she rams a fist in her mouth. A tidal wave, the heaviest yet. Now it's probably soaking through to her jeans and onto the wooden chair. She bites her fingers. Good thing Baldy's gone. So there's no one to see her stand, pull on her parka to cover any stains on her rear, and run to the ladies' room.

Good thing there are no stalls, just a single toilet and sink. So there's no one to hear her gasp when she pulls down her pants. Taking a deep breath, she wraps the sodden pad in toilet paper and rams it in the trash. But the mess coats her underwear and the inside of her jeans. Isn't it supposed to be blood-red, like last time? This is much darker, almost black. Like the black gunk the plumber snaked out of their clogged shower drain.

"What is it?" she asked, both appalled and fascinated by what he pulled up with his metal coil. He laughed. "Just soap scum and some hair." Looking closer, Belinda made out a few of Cora's golden strands.

But *this* has come out of her.

And it's still coming, dripping onto her boots, her bunched-up jeans, the tile floor. She grabs paper towels and bends down to wipe it up.

The door handle rattles.

"Just a minute!" she calls out.

Good thing she locked it, or everyone walking by would see her bare butt in the air as she wipes the floor. And it's hopeless, hopeless, because more keeps dripping out of her.

The door handle rattles again.

Not a *literal* minute, asshole. "There's another bathroom downstairs!" she yells.

Where is Dad? If he'd let her walk, she'd be home by now, in her own bathroom with all those boxes of maxipads.

When he gets here, she'll insist that he drop her home first thing. She won't survive even the five-minute drive up to Lake Bluff. Not to mention the wait while he gabs with the friend's parents, apologizing over and over, thanking them over and over.

How much will she have to say? Maybe just a little hint. Dad's smart—he'll know what she means. They never discussed her period, but he knew. The morning after she called Nana, back in November, he put a hand on her shoulder. "Belinda, honey, how are you doing? Is everything okay? Anything I can do?" Of course she'd just shrugged off his hand, gotten away from him as fast as she could.

Her face crumples. Tears and snot drip, adding to the mess on the floor

She wipes her face with her sleeve and stares down at the splattered tile. This isn't working. She needs a new pad—maybe two or three, all crammed together in her underwear—to stop the leaking long enough that she can clean the floor.

Please deposit 25 cents, the feminine hygiene dispenser requests in prim curlicue letters. Belinda pulls coins from her jeans pocket. The first quarter gets stuck. She inserts another, and another. Fucking thing refuses to yield a single pad, even when she slams it with her fist.

The first is the worst. Nana's such a liar. This is much worse, the pain almost as bad as that time she broke her arm and Dad got them stuck in traffic on the way to the ER.

Nana said something else in January when she remembered to ask about Belinda's second period. "Be sure to take pads with you when you go to school. From what I recall—and I'm dredging up ancient history here—whenever I skipped a period, the next one was very heavy." But Belinda left the pads at home, hoping Nana was wrong, hoping she'd never menstruate ever again.

Now she's a disgusting mess. Probably stinks too. No way she can go out like this. She shoves a wad of toilet paper in her underwear and pulls up her sticky jeans. Only to discover that the gunk is now matted in the beige fur that tops her boots. Why, oh why didn't she get *black* boots? Black, to match her insides. Hurry, hurry, before Dad shows.

"Have you seen . . ." Too late—his voice out in the hallway. "She's thirteen, short brown hair. A navy coat." Dad, an anxious edge to his voice, talking faster and faster, piling on more and more details, as he does when nervous or upset. "And oh yes, she has a bright green backpack. Kelly green, actually."

Belinda scowls at her backpack, hanging from the hook on the door. Why didn't she leave it there in the Garden Room for him to find? It'd calm him and maybe shut him up for a while, just to know she's somewhere in the library.

Of course he's come *now*, at precisely the wrong moment. Not earlier, or after she's cleaned up. Now.

"And snow boots." Dad's goofy laugh. "I guess that's no help—everyone's wearing them today." A regular motor-mouth, her dad.

Belinda's about to yell out to him, then thinks better of it. Does she really want him standing in front of the ladies' room and calling through the door, *Belinda, are you okay? Honey, what's wrong?* The entire library will know she's holed up in here. Including those guys from her science class. They'll walk by Dad, smirking. By homeroom tomorrow, the entire eighth grade will know every stupid thing her father said, and exactly what she looked like when she finally emerged.

Belinda holds perfectly still. Dad's voice is gone. Probably he's walking through the building looking for her, still yacking.

She should go after him. But he's made her wait so long that this mess happened. So he can just wait until she gets herself cleaned up. She yanks out another paper towel and dabs at her boots.

She's always here, he'll be telling the librarian as they enter the Garden Room. *That's her favorite spot, right there in that chair. She's got this thing about plants, you see . . .*

Next they'll go through the Reading Room, the Art Room, Periodicals, then Fiction, upstairs to Nonfiction, downstairs to Children's and Audio-Visual. All the while, Dad talking faster and faster. *I'm going to check Fiction again. Belinda reads everything.*

Still crouched on the floor, she hurls a wad of soiled paper towels at the trash, misses.

Now he's using the library's phone. How long will he let the home phone ring before hanging up? Then fumble through his little brown book for another number, and dial it with shaky fingers. *About ninety minutes ago, maybe a little more*, Molly's mother tells him before passing the phone to Mol, who says, *Oh Mr. MacIntyre, she's got to be there. She wouldn't have just walked out. I know Bel, she just wouldn't!*

Belinda jerks upright so quickly that everything spins. She pulls on her coat, yanks it down over the rear of her jeans, grabs her backpack. Hurry, hurry! Let Dad know she's okay. Not okay, she'll never be okay ever again, but at least here. At least that much, she needs to let him know. She's here.

Still the room spins. Leaning against the wall for just a moment before she opens the door, just long enough for things to still. Leaning against the wall, she glimpses a face in the mirror. Eyes puffed to slits, hair stringy, skin shiny and dotted with red zits.

Who *is* that?

Of course. The face in the mirror nods back.

Hel's Bel.

THE WAY TO BAGHDAD

Nektaria Anastasiadou

On our quest to find the church that did not exist, we passed fields of wheat and great patches of yellow and orange pumpkins growing in sandy soil that looked like it should produce nothing at all. Forty minutes after setting out from Kayseri, we drove into Tomarza, my grandmother's village. Its buildings were mostly tile-roofed, two- and three-story cement boxes painted in washed-out pastels. Kinder, smaller versions of Kayseri's Soviet-style high-rises, but nothing comparable to the aristocratic stone mansions of my grandmother's day. The crows on the telephone lines swooping along and over the streets squawked so loudly that they could be heard above the motor. A man hauled his shopping to the third-floor balcony with a mounted winch, a rope, and a wicker basket. Withered ladies crowded on doorsteps, eating sunflower seeds, shucking beans, and staring at us in our rented Opel.

"By asking and asking you find your way to Baghdad," said Mazal, pushing down the broken electric window.

I took a deep breath of cooking oil and tomato sauce-scented air. "Meaning?"

"It's a Turkish proverb. *Sora sora Bağdat bulunur. By asking, you can find your way anywhere.*"

I let my eyes run over her dark shoulder and sweaty elbow crease to an aristocratic hand with nails painted the color of maiden Aunt Narod's pearls. Even in my grandmother's village, I wasn't so absorbed that I didn't notice the contrast between the cream of Mazal's palm and the coffee-tan of the back of her hand. Monkey paws, I'd teasingly called them when we left Istanbul. She'd been good-humored enough to laugh.

I returned my attention to the road. Up ahead was an old man in a prayer cap, blazer jacket, and tieless shirt buttoned to his Adam's apple.

Mazal waved. We'd already tried a few young fellows. They'd looked at us as if we'd asked our way not to Baghdad, but to the moon. *"Kilise mi?"* they said. "*Yok böyle bir şey.*" *Church? Nothing like that exists.*

So Mrs. Fatma had been wrong. Or perhaps she'd just *wished* the continued existence of Saints Peter and Paul. But after coming this far, I had to be sure.

The old man rattled away, two shakes straight, gesture right, gesture left. I followed his directions through potholed streets into the dusty open space that might once have been called a square. Of course I still didn't believe. But it's the journey that's important, the effort, and the fact that, after fearing travel my entire life, I was finally in Cappadocia, my ancestral lands.

I stopped the car and stared at the ramshackle stone structure. It looked like an old storage bunker.

"That's it," said Mazal.

"Don't get your hopes up," I said, not even admitting the possibility that she could be right.

....

My Armenian grandparents survived the death march of 1915 with nothing but memories. Grandpa Yetvart remembered his mother throwing him from the bedroom window so that the gendarmes wouldn't get him. He also remembered his Kangal dog, Lili, who would howl whenever the church bells tolled. Grandma Ani remembered learning to slow-cook onions without oil so that they wouldn't cause "air," but she had zero recollection of the years 1915-1918. Grandma Yeghisabet remembered her father's advice about how to treat her husband. She also remembered her father's screams as he was tortured in the village prison. Grandpa Hovhannes, for whom I was named John, remembered watching the stars from his rooftop bed during the sweltering Mersin summers, as well as marching past corpses whose hair and scalps had detached like wigs.

My grandparents were from Cilicia, Cappadocia, and Eastern Anatolia. Each was the only surviving member of a large family. After the First World War, they were rounded up from the streets of Aleppo and the camp of Der-Zor by American missionaries who de-wormed and de-liced them, taught them trades like sewing and bricklaying, unsuccessfully tried to convert them to Congregationalism, and finally put them on a ship to New York. Like other refugees, my grandparents worked night and day in garbage collection, dressmaking, and construction. Their children studied and worked just as hard. My father began his career as an accountant and eventually became a nursing home mogul, but he never stopped eating at Denny's with his doormen and janitors. When I graduated from college with a degree in art history, he turned over my inheritance.

"Do whatever you want with it," he said. "As long as it does good both to you and to others."

What I really wanted was to explore my heritage—not the death march, but the life before it. Travel would have been the thing for most people, but it wasn't for me. First, I couldn't see how it would do any good to others; second, I suffered from severe aviophobia. So I started buying Armenian art with the hope of exhibition. Pieces of the Ottoman Armenian past would arrive on my Santa Barbara doorstep in neatly wrapped packages. I'd open them with care, put on white cotton gloves, and reach into the foam peanuts like an archeologist on a dig. I'd pick up a snake-entwined liturgical staff, a silver spoon set, a copper jug engraved with crosses and fish, a cobalt and bole-red *Kütahya* plate with a portrait of the Armenian benefactor Harutyun Bezciyan, or whatever the day's prize happened to be. Then I'd brush away the foam crumbs and try to picture the people who had owned the object a century ago.

While holding a glazed ceramic ewer, I imagined my great-grandparents performing their ablutions. I wasn't religious, but I knew the prayer that accompanied the ritual: "I will wash my hands in innocence and will go around thine altar, O Lord." My great-grandfathers could have said it the Sunday before they were taken into custody. My great-grandmothers could have said it the Sunday before they were sent with their children on the road to Syria, before they saw their infants thrown into wells and their toddlers pushed down a hillside with the mules that carried them.

Was it a waste of money? Expensive self-indulgence? Maybe. But it became my profession. I extensively researched the origins of my pieces. I ordered every English language book with even the smallest reference to the Armenian communities of Turkey. I searched the internet for photographs and details missing from history books. I learned that the star piece of my collection was from Grandma Ani's home town, Tomarza, a village located on a dry plain to the east of Mount Argeus. Back then, Tomarza was an eight-hour walk from the city of Kayseri. It had good water and healthy air. It produced glue, barley, cucumbers, and watermelons. In 1915, its population consisted of about four-thousand Armenians and a couple hundred Muslim Turks. It had an important monastery dedicated to the Holy Mother of God, as well as several churches.

I thought I'd learned everything there was to know about Tomarza. That is, until Mazal Behar, assistant curator of the Paris Gallery of Middle Eastern Art, emailed to say that she wanted to see my collection during an upcoming visit to Los Angeles. Twenty-three days later, she flew into my house like a butterfly, hardly even noticing me. (Sometimes I don't think her feet touch the ground. To prove it, I have a photo of her from the same evening: she is not jumping, but hovering, feet flexed, above the surf on Santa Claus Beach.) She went straight into the living room and picked up my favorite piece: an almost life-size solid silver hand stuck for eternity in the gesture of blessing. Its thumb crossed over the tip of the ring finger. The middle and index fingers extended upward in representation of the divine and human natures of Christ. It was called, at least according to the auction catalogue, the Hand of God.

Mazal knelt on the Yörük carpet of my entryway, held the Hand up to the dust particles floating like fairies in the skylight beams, and examined the broken glass reliquary compartment on the dorsum.

"A reliquary without a relic," she said, her finger trailing over the rubies that surrounded the shattered compartment.

This had puzzled me, too, since the day FedEx had delivered the piece. Why take the bone fragment and not the rubies? Or, if you only wanted to resell the Hand, why break the reliquary at all?

Mazal set the Hand upon it upon a piece of white paper and snapped a photo. "I'd like to put it on the catalogue cover, What's the provenance?"

"I bought it from a dealer in Damascus. The dedication inscription confirms its origin."

"Yes, but before that?"

I began pacing to hide my annoyance. As calmly as possible, I replied, "You mean how did it survive the genocide? I don't even know how my own grandparents survived."

"I don't mean to be insensitive," said Mazal, still kneeling. "I was born in Turkey, but I'm Jewish. I understand the emotions this stirs up. Still, my boss will want to know."

"Listen. When Armenian art comes out of the state of Armenia, provenance is expected. But when it comes out of Turkey . . ."

I sighed. Mazal charmingly tilted her head downward and looked up into my eyes for just a second before redirecting her attention to the artifacts we were cataloguing. Her body—round and full where it ought to be—was what my Grandma Ani would have called a good thing. Her stale, rosy perfume reminded me of Aunt Narod. But Mazal didn't seem to get it. So I suggested dinner.

....

We'd already drunk two glasses of Amarone and devoured a plate of fried zucchini flowers. She playfully held her fork and knife in her fists, like a hungry cave woman, while I took her picture. Then I asked the stupid question: "Do you have children?"

Her joy melted. She glanced off toward the bar, where smartly dressed singles sat on leather bar stools, flirting over glasses of champagne and engaging in empty chitchat. I'd read somewhere that one shouldn't ask women about children, but in my desire to learn whether Mazal was attached or not, I disregarded this rule. Foolishly. A woman friend of mine had once admitted that, single and childless at forty-two, she almost wished it would all just be over.

The waiter served our main course of osso bucco. Mazal inhaled its aroma with eyes closed, perhaps in an effort to put my question out of mind. "Rosemary, thyme, and fat," she said. "I love it." She enthusiastically chewed a few bites and returned to business: "I'm not so concerned about the chalice because it's scorched. And I can overlook the lack of documentation for the gravestones, oil lamps, and worm-holed books. But the Hand of God is different. Except for the broken reliquary compartment, it's in perfect condition. Valuable, portable. It may have been stolen in a more traditional sense and kept safely, like the master paintings in Nazi vaults."

"Not exactly," I said. "Looting of Armenian goods was not so well organized. Nor so secretive. It was done haphazardly, openly. The Armenians were marched off and then their churches were pillaged and burned or turned into stables."

"Could the pieces be claimed by the Armenian government?"

"Today's Armenia doesn't include the area from which my pieces originated."

Mazal cranked her long neck toward the bar again. There was something especially sexy about that neck, despite the bump of her thyroid, enlarged on the left side. "And the Church? Does it have a claim?"

"They have neither the resources nor the time to pursue it all. Besides, they don't want to buy back what should still belong to us anyway. So much time has passed. I'm just trying to save what I can."

"But the Hand of God could have been stolen and resold by the same person, or by the descendants of the original thief. Somebody who knew that its value as art was higher than its value as precious metal."

"Perhaps. At least it could have been like that until it was sold to the Syrian who sold it to me."

Mazal glanced at her phone, which she'd set beside her plate as if it were a necessary piece of cutlery. "You'll have to contact him."

"This isn't done for Armenian artifacts originating from Turkey."

"The gallery is particular. I speak Turkish, if you need help."

....

My grandparents' language was also Turkish, but they hadn't actively tried to teach it to us. I understand fairly well. Speaking, however, is almost impossible. *Maşallah* (God has willed) and *İnşallah* (if God wills) are the words I remember best. Grandma Ani would say them with extra zest, drawing out the first *a* and the double *l*'s and holding the *h* in her throat. "*Maaaaashallllllahhh*, my son!" when I put on my Sunday suit. "*Inshaaaaallllllahhh*," when I declared I wanted to become an art history professor.

"İnşallah," I whispered to myself as I picked up the phone to call the Damascene seller, the day after Mazal's visit. İnşallah I'll get the provenance. İnşallah I'll get the exhibition. İnşallah I'll get Mazal.

But the Damascene seller had little information. He'd bought the piece from a woman in Kayseri named Fatma Yılmaz, whose number and address he gave me. I stared at the name scribbled on the note pad. Was Fatma the daughter or granddaughter of the murderers of my great-grandfathers? A dealer in the goods of the slaughtered? Did she have a house or a shop filled with things that had belonged to my people—silver bride belts, painted sewing boxes, embroidered dowry sheets? I asked a Turkish professor friend to call. He did repeatedly, but there was no answer. I messaged Mazal. She said I'd have to go in person, adding that it would be good for me.

"But I don't even have a passport," I wrote back.

"Get one."

"I'm afraid of flying." Perhaps unmanly to admit, but I didn't care. "And my father doesn't think it's a good idea. He says it's still dangerous for us over there."

"I'll meet you in Istanbul," Mazal replied.

"Deal."

....

I'd flown a few times as a kid. It wasn't that bad, apart from the excruciating earaches during landing. My experiences in the car and on boats were worse. I remember family trips with brown paper bags at my side, wrist bands with plastic nibs that were supposed to hit certain pressure points and prevent nausea, and the motion sickness pills that my father forced me to swallow without water. None of it worked. At the age of eighteen, I also developed a fear of closed spaces and heights. I decided I was never going anywhere. I could find almost anything by driving myself down to LA (no motion sickness when I was behind the wheel), and I could bring the rest to me. Except for the provenance of the Hand of God.

I went to the pill pusher and asked for sedatives. "Take one an hour before your flight, another when you get on the plane," he said, tearing the script from the pad. "And no alcohol or caffeine for eight hours."

"What happens if I have a little nightcap? Or an espresso?"

"Death or coma for the first, cytotoxicity for the latter. Take your pills, have a good meal, and drink water."

I almost considered a support group. Then I read an article about an aviophobe woman who tried one. Along with her buddies, she made it through the trial Boston to New York flight, but when it came time to board the return, she went catatonic, copped out, and took the train home to Boston. The following day she told a reporter she'd decided to focus on *why* she was so afraid of planes: on the underlying, perhaps unrelated cause. I didn't want to think about any of that. So I filled my prescription and bought a one-way ticket from LA to Istanbul, in case I had to return on the Queen Mary.

A month later, after popping two pills, traversing a fuel-stinking jet bridge, and passing through the terrifying void in the airplane's shell, I found myself face to face with a faultlessly coiffed Turkish hostess with bright red lips. She extended a tray of bubbling flutes and asked, "*Apéritif*, sir?"

What could champagne do to a man who had survived the degrading feel-up provided by the TSA to cancer opt-outs? I swilled it along with another pill, and I remember nothing else from the rest of the flight. I awoke groggy, nauseous, but on the ground. I sleepwalked through passport control, emerged from the sliding glass doors that separated international arrivals from the world outside, and somehow managed to put on my almost useless pressure-point wrist bands before getting into a taxi. Still, I wasn't able to properly enjoy the ride between the Marmara shore and the crumbling Byzantine sea walls, nor did I fully realize that I'd arrived until I stepped into the wainscoted lobby of the Pera Palace, complete with potted ferns and over-anxious bellboys.

I wandered to the back of the hotel, opened a frosted glass door, and found myself in the Bordeaux-hued Kubbeli Tea Salon. According to family gossip, my great-grandfather, the carpet merchant Vahan Aslanyan, had enjoyed afternoon tea here on his 1911 visit to Constantinople. I looked up past the brass chandeliers to the Kubbeli's six grated domes, bright in the noon light of summer, and said out loud, "I'm here, Papik." I wondered whether Vahan Aslanyan—who was arrested in July 1915, bastinadoed, and hung—could hear me.

....

Mazal and I met the following morning at Sabiha Gökçen Airport, on the Asian side of the city. I'd flown over the ocean out of necessity, but I wasn't about to fly over Turkey, where I could just as well drive. From Sabiha Gökçen, we picked up our rental, threw Mazal's well-worn carry-on into the hatchback trunk, and set out across the highways of Anatolia. Over the next ten hours we talked about our childhoods (mine in Fresno and hers in Paris), our previous marriages, khachkars, Ladino bibles, the history of Armenian printing, and the Istanbul synagogue bombings, which killed one of her cousins. I steered clear of the subject of children, but when a five-year-old girl at a highway rest stop tip-toed over to our table and gave Mazal a piece of candy, I noticed the sudden glassiness of my travel companion's black-lined eyes. She clutched that bit of orange candy as if it were a talisman and put it in her purse for safekeeping. My instinct told me to pretend I hadn't noticed, but I thought this was something I could fix.

"Your ex," I said. "Did he . . ."

"Vasectomy. I told myself it didn't matter. The things one thinks at thirty!" She took a few *leblebi*—roasted chick peas—from the bag we'd just bought and pushed them one by one through closed lips.

"Perhaps there's still time," I said.

"Highly unlikely." She rose to her feet. "Shall we get going?"

Just before sunset, we drove into a rocky moonscape of sand-colored tufa formations, dry hills that looked as if they'd been sculpted with a butter knife, and party-hat shaped caves that the locals called fairy chimneys. We were finally in Cappadocia, the land of early Christian cave monasteries, the home of Saints Basil the Great and Gregory the Illuminator, and the birthplace of Ani Gurdikyan, my maternal grandmother.

Mazal and I engaged in benign shop talk over dinner on the terrace of our Kayseri hotel. I didn't have the courage to say what I was really thinking until afterward, when we'd finished our bottle of Kavaklıdere Chardonnay and turned our chairs to face the city, so that we were sitting side by side instead of across from one another.

"Hundreds of thousands of tourists must come here every year." I looked toward snow-capped Mount Argeus, rising in the darkness behind the city lights. "But all I can think of is Grandma Ani, nine years old, being marched out."

Mazal rearranged her scarf as if she'd caught a chill. "I did the same when I went to Barcelona. I thought of my ancestors piling into boats in 1492. And every time I return to Istanbul, I think of how my family and I left. We sold almost everything, packed a few suitcases, and got on a plane to Paris with our cat in my mother's purse."

"But you weren't driven out of Turkey." I took off my sport jacket and draped it over her shoulders.

She snuggled into the warm jacket, pulling its flaps around her. "True, but we also didn't feel welcome enough to stay. No matter how hard we tried to assimilate, we couldn't win."

"Sometimes I don't think anybody can."

"What do you know about Grandma Ani?"

"As far as the genocide goes, not much. She said she didn't remember. Perhaps she'd erased the memory, or perhaps she was lying to protect herself. Either way, it was too terrible to speak of."

We sat in silence for a while before calling it a night. Although I'd been disappointed when I learned that Mazal had reserved two rooms, I was now glad of it. Something was holding me back. Perhaps it was talking about Grandma Ani: although she'd sing and laugh the loudest at family parties, she was also prone to bouts of depression that sent her out barefoot into the snow of her Brooklyn garden, wearing nothing but a nightgown. Or perhaps it was that, despite my efforts to do something constructive with my family's trauma, I still felt confined by it, as if a part of me was buried somewhere on the way to Syria. In any case, Mazal's sleeping arrangements and my melancholy helped me uphold my father's maxim: never touch a woman until the third date.

After breakfast, Mazal called Fatma Yılmaz. The plan was to knock on Fatma's door if she still didn't pick up. And I have to admit I secretly hoped that she neither picked up nor opened her door, and that Mazal would just overlook the Hand's lack of provenance. I didn't want to have anything to do with anyone connected to what had happened to my grandparents. Having Turkish academic friends was one thing. Chatting with Turkish dealers of Armenian goods was another altogether.

But this time, Fatma Yılmaz answered after just one ring. I expected her to hang up as soon as she learned we'd come about the Hand. Either that or say she was indisposed, busy, unsure, had to think about it, next week maybe, after she checked with someone . . . but no.

"Come on over, my daughter."

"When?"

"Now, of course."

It seemed weird, even to Mazal, but she'd heard, in a legendary sort of way, that provincial Turks could be like that. Fatma had plastic guest slippers ready when we arrived at her apartment. Toothless, headscarved, with a worrying sore on one cheek, she welcomed us into a modest but spotless living room, sat us down on a tatty sectional sofa beneath a portrait of Mustafa Kemal Ataturk in a tuxedo, and offered tea.

"Where are you from?" she asked.

"Istanbul," said Mazal. "John was born in Los Angeles, but—"

"How long have you been married?

"We're not. Both divorced."

"Children?"

In order to save Mazal from her secret ache, I surprised myself by digging up something from my childhood: "*İnşallah, çok geçmeden.*" *God-willing, soon.*

"İnşallah," said Fatma.

"İnşallah," echoed Mazal, glancing at me with a softness that was more than enough reward for speaking the language I'd always found embarrassing, both because of my lack of mastery and the oddity of having absorbed the tongue of the *dacikler*, which meant something like "dark ones" or "hard ones." Every genocide story my grandparents told began with this word. The dacikler were jealous. The dacikler wanted our houses and brides. The dacikler murdered our fathers. And yet my grandparents spoke the language of the dacikler, not Armenian.

"John's grandmother was from Tomarza," said Mazal.

Fatma twisted her handkerchief, looking back and forth between me and Mazal.

"She was Armenian," Mazal added.

Fatma gave her handkerchief a nervous tug.

"Why did you tell her that?" I asked in English.

Mazal gathered her wiry black hair to the nape of her neck and bound it with the elastic that she'd been wearing like a bracelet. "I wanted her to know you're from here. Or you would have been."

From here? I couldn't match Kayseri to anything I'd ever seen or heard of Ottoman Anatolia. The Turks seemed to have little knack—and hardly any legislation—for the preservation of old architecture. Outside historical Istanbul, Turkey seemed so cement, asphalt, synthetic, plastic.

"She might think I'm after something," I said. "They've dug up the floor of every Armenian house in Turkey because they think we buried our gold in them. Maybe she even dug up the Hand."

Mrs. Fatma squirted lemon-scented alcohol into our palms and brought a syrupy cake that I knew well—*revani.* Before sitting beside me on the sofa, she pinched my chin and said, "*Ye, ye!*"

Both of my grandmothers used to say that: *Eat, eat!* I took a bite. It could have been Grandma Ani's revani: semolina cake flavored with vanilla, texturized with poppy seeds, soaked with honey syrup, and garnished with ground pistachios. But that shouldn't have surprised me. Grandma Ani's village was less than an hour away.

While Mazal and I ate, Fatma hummed—and then sang—a lullaby. She mangled the words, but the haunting tune was unmistakable, sad as a dirge, yet totally effective: I'd always be sound asleep before Grandma Ani had sung the last refrain, "*Neni, neni.*" Even as an adult, the song hypnotized me. I looked at Mazal. She mouthed the question: *Armenian?* I nodded. Although Grandma Ani couldn't speak Armenian, she did sing it.

Mazal broke the silence that followed: "Aunt Fatma, your father—"

"Was a true Muslim."

"Of course. Do you know what his roots were? Which village he was from?"

Fatma fidgeted with the embroidered edge of her thin headscarf.

Mazal put her hand on Fatma's. "I'm Jewish, you know. I understand. Plenty of ours—"

"Converted," said Fatma, staring down at her knees like a child who'd been caught wrongdoing. "During the *Kesim Zamanı*."

Cutting Time. This, it seemed, was what the genocide was called in Turkey. A politically less dangerous term, yet more emotive than the g-word. When I say Cutting Time, I feel the scythe on my neck, almost as if it were a natural time of year, a harvest; a season that came, went, and will inevitably come again.

"And the Hand?" said Mazal.

"My father fasted during Ramadan and prayed five times a day, but . . . he wasn't able get rid of everything."

"Aunt Fatma," said Mazal. "The Hand was originally from a church, not a home. Do you know anything about that? We don't mean to pry, but it's important we learn the history of our pieces so that we can exhibit them properly."

Fatma took a Muslim rosary from a wall hook just beneath her religious calendars and talismans. As her fingers slid from one amber bead to the next, she repeated the Arabic word for God—Allah. Finally she said, "Before the deportation, my uncle—a priest—took a few things from a church in Tomarza, including the Hand. He hid the things in the home of a Muslim friend. Afterward they looted and destroyed everything. The monastery. The churches. Nothing remains, except for the church the Hand came from."

"The seller said the church was destroyed in 1915," said Mazal.

Fatma gathered the rosary into one hand. "A mistake. It survived the Kesim Zamanı because the Hand protected it."

"But you said the Hand wasn't inside the church during the deportation."

Fatma looked out the window, toward the blackened dome of what our concierge said was Kayseri's only remaining Armenian church. "It wasn't. But the bit of holy bone was removed and kept in the church the whole time."

Mazal looked to me. I gave her a go-ahead nod. "How did the Hand come to you?" she said.

Fatma rocked back and forth, as if she were conjuring the family story with movement. "Before my uncle died, he gave the Hand to my father, hoping it would work a miracle and bring my father back to Christianity. But my father had become Muslim in his heart."

"Do you know where the relic is?" asked Mazal.

"Perhaps stuffed between stones, perhaps buried. But I'm sure it's still there. It's the reason the church stands."

Softly, as if she were speaking to someone who had been in a coma for a long time, Mazal said, "We were told that *all* churches in the village, including Saints Peter and Paul, were destroyed. Are you sure you're not mistaken?"

Fatma nodded yes.

"Do you know the name of the friend who hid the Hand?"

"He'd be dead anyway."

"Why did you sell?"

Fatma smoothed her baggy trousers over her knees. "There just comes a time," she said, "when you must move on."

....

My legs were glued to the vinyl car upholstery. Unpeeling hurt. Mazal had been right. I shouldn't have worn shorts, not just because they betrayed my foreignness, not just because sweaty skin was itchy and uncomfortable on vinyl, but because shorts were not appropriate attire for churches.

"It *can't* exist," I said. "It's dust, like all the rest of it. That's what the books say."

Mazal went off by herself, leaving me staring.

I crossed the square for a better look. The three arches of the nave were filled in with rubble masonry. The narthex was missing. Brown grass grew from the gutters and between blackened roof tiles. But the building matched the plan and size of Saints Peter and Paul.

Mazal returned with a grizzly fellow who unlocked the low, rusty doors and waved us inside the original home of the Hand of God. The church's walls retained traces of theatrical frescoes: blue curtains with gold tassels, flamboyant acanthus leaves, and stylized scrolls. The floor was covered with debris, animal dung, and hay. The central apse was crumbling. A vintage Dodge truck was parked in the arch leading to one of the side chambers. My father had given up sending me to Sunday school when I was eight. After that I had only gone to church for weddings, baptisms, and funerals, but I loved the aesthetics of traditional Armenian churches: the incense, the bells, the chanting. Over the smell of dust and dung, it was difficult to imagine that this had once been such a place. That my grandmother might have attended liturgy here as a girl.

Mazal stuck her fingers into her nest of curls and asked the old man, "Why wasn't the church torn down?"

"They tried," he said. "But the entryway collapsed. Three men were killed. Nobody's touched it since."

"Do you know anything about a silver hand kept in the village during the deportations?"

"*What* deportations?"

"1915?" I said.

Mazal widened her eyes, surprised that I'd managed such a big number in Turkish.

The old man clicked his tongue. "I was born in 1936. Long after the Greeks were gone."

No Greeks had ever lived in the village. But we didn't bother with corrections.

"Have you heard anything about a saint's bone?" I said. "Kept here, in the church?"

The old man looked us over, trying to understand what this odd woman and her Turkish-speaking American friend could possibly want with a bit of bone. He said, "Who knows? I've heard the place is haunted. That's why we leave it alone. Someday it will fall down by itself."

"Reliquaries without relics," I said to Mazal in English. "That's what it means to be Armenian."

She stepped closer to me and slid her hand into mine. "You overcame your fear of travel. That's something."

"And I'm in Grandma Ani's hometown, which is everything." I paused, allowing the tears to fall. "What are we going to do?"

"Exhibit without provenance," Mazal said.

"They'll allow it?"

"I'll make sure they will."

We looked up toward the apse's half dome, where a painted dove hovered within a sunburst, wings outspread, ready to fly.

"And us?" she said. "What are we going to do?"

I raised my hand to the dove, as if I wanted to receive its blessing. "Exactly what he's doing."

BETWEEN MY RIBS

Riba Taylor

Her tongue slides across my palm, licks dog food from between my fingers. I cringe when I feel the edges of her teeth. They conjure memories of years before when Sofia in her terror chomped on my hand, her sharp cat teeth stabbing pain through me that had me almost passing out, sinking to the ground under the oaks outside our Hopland home. But the brown dog is gentle. She's only looking for any lingering remains of the lump of canned food she's just devoured. The other dogs have scattered, returning to the stingy shade of the small bushes that line the dusty road, or settling back beneath the rusty fender of the old red truck. The others seem to know the treats are gone, but the little brown dog looks up at me, the wiggle of her bony body all hard hope. "All gone, sweetie," I tell her. *"Es todo."* My heart sinks at the crestfallen look she gives me, but I try to ignore it. I examine the wound on her left hind leg. I've been hiding goldenseal capsules in her treat for three days now to battle the infection, and I think it might be getting better. At least, I tell myself, it isn't getting worse.

My heartbeat slows, the flurry of activity over. I like to think the dogs know me now, that they wouldn't hurt me. But each time I near this section of the road I tense for their approach. And my heart still flops about in my throat each time I hear the rustle of their bodies rising to action, the din of their barking. Today there are seven of them, six already snoozing again in the hot August afternoon. The brown dog's head droops, and she curls up by the side of the road. I wipe the dog spit on the side of my dress and make my way past them toward the open desert.

A little bit beyond what I've always thought of as the dogs' house are the "ruins" we used to dream about restoring. It was always more my dream than yours, I think, born during the year I lived here, early in our time apart. I used to climb the hill, trail a hand across the half-built red brick walls, stand at the heart of each small foundation. I would stare out across the desert toward the wolf rock and the sea beyond and dream of making it my home.

When we came here together all those years later, I think you played along with me because it was my dream, and you were being kind. And maybe, in part, you playedalong because it was romantic. You liked the idea of reviving those other people's vision we read on that hillside in the soft curve of a wall, in the rings of rock and sand with small dead trees at their centers, their belief in a future, the beginnings of a home. But I knew you weren't convinced you wanted to move to Mexico, much less to this remote stretch of Baja California Sur. And though it seemed easy to me, within our reach, I was happy just to have you back beside me after all the long years in between, content to see where our lives led us, glad to know we'd go there together. So I didn't push, didn't try to take our idle dreaming any further.

But now, four years after that awful afternoon when the gods took you away from me again, I've come back to see if I can't buy this land, can't finish building on those layered dreams. People in the States think I'm crazy, doing this at my age. But Alvaro, the man I told you about who befriended me in Ajijic when he was a young lawyer just starting his own practice, is working now on my behalf, trying to track down the deed to theproperty. I trust him, and I'm in no hurry. I am happy to stay in the *casita* Gianni and Iris were so quick to offer, glad to be again at the heart of their boisterous Italian-Mexican brood. Did I tell you they make a vegan, gluten-free pizza now at Il Giardino? I laughed when I saw it on the menu. "Just for you," Iris told me. So I am content to let the hours take me at the restaurant, sitting outside beneath the *palapa* roof, whole afternoons and evenings sliding past, only small flashes to jostle me, like remembering your expression the first time I brought you there, watching you looking around the patio, taking in the greetings, the way the family enveloped us. Now and then Iris catches a look on my face, knows I have wandered, and the quiet understanding I see in her eyes makes me want to cry.

Gianni and Iris flew up to San Francisco after you died. They tried to make me come back here with them then, but I wasn't ready. I wasn't ready to leave our home, to abandon all the living evidence of you there. I left your lunch plate on the kitchen table for weeks, the apple core turning brown and shriveled, the orange cubes of cheddar dry and crumbly, an unorthodox shrine. Once my sense of humor exerted itself, I titled it, "The Last Lunch." My laugh rang then in the empty room, tinged, I thought, with a hint of hysteria.

Without knowing, in the midst of my reverie, I've stopped walking. I'm standing in the middle of the dirt road staring at the hillside ruins, but I am kneeling on the cold tile floor of that far away kitchen, my arms wrapped around you on that awful April day. I hold you while the last warmth leaves your skin, until my arms tremble and I lay you back against the tile. I remember how wrong it seemed to let you go, to ever stop holding you, but I did. I was afraid I'd drop you. My arms just didn't have the strength. There is movement now on the dirt road, and I start. The skinny brown dog has followed me. She slinks low to the ground as she nears, ready to take to the brush. "It's okay," I say. *"Está bien."* And then, *"Quieres venir conmigo?"* Do you want to come with me? She wriggles. I walk down the road, and she follows.

I glance back at the ruins, and I see you standing halfway up the hill. You are wearing your favorite navy-blue shirt with the white stripes, open at the neck. You watch us go, hands in the pockets of your jeans. My heart flutters, and I stumble in the sand, but I don't stop. I know if I do you will disappear, the raven flying from his branch when I stop beneath the tree. So I keep moving away while I watch you watching us. "I love you, baby," I say. The dog's ears twitch, but she keeps going. She knows I'm not talking to her.

I'm getting used to having you appear. Well, "perhaps I overstate," as you would say. But it doesn't shock me anymore to see you like this. I keep watching you as I walk away, and then from one moment to the next you are gone. I keep going, and now I watch the little dog before me. She looks back from time to time, heartened, I think, to see I'm still following. I look back once more toward the hillside where you stood, and I remember all the times I pictured you appearing during our decades apart, like that Thanksgiving night in Santa Rosa when I heard a car and imagined against all logic it was you. But then that night it *was* you, walking down my driveway in the dark to find me sitting on the steps.

For years after that night I was taken in odd moments by that same wistful certainty. I'd picture you driving up to my house in Hopland while I was sitting on my wide stone porch or showing up outside my tall blue steel gate here in Todos Santos. In Ajijic I'd hear the doorbell chime in my apartment on Aldama, and I'd imagine leaning out over the balcony to see you standing in the cobblestone street below looking up at me. I'd see you coming around the corner on Avenida Ortega in Palm Springs, even winding your way through the narrow, twisting *callejones* in Guanajuato. It didn't matter in all those years apart that you didn't know where I was living. In my dreaming I knew you would find me.

And then it happened again, a good two decades past that Thanksgiving night, long years after I'd stopped dreaming of you ever leaving the woman you had chosen over me, of you ever coming to find me. I was sitting on my patio in the late afternoon, staring out across the bay toward Oakland, the sun warm across my back, and I heard footsteps on the wooden stairs that climbed my San Francisco hillside, the famed wild parrot steps. *It's him*, I thought. I must have felt you. "Don't be silly," I muttered. How could it possibly be you? But I stood anyway, moved to the north wall like a sleepwalker. I looked down, and there you were climbing the stairs, your eyes scanning the windows all along the south side. When you found me looking down at you, you stopped. I remember the way your arm grabbed the railing, the way your body swayed so that my heart lurched with the awful fear of finding you and losing you all in one long moment. But you steadied, and you smiled up at me, a big boyish grin on your old man face. Later you told me all the worries that chased you in that slow climb. What if I was married? What if I didn't want to see you? What if I didn't live there anymore? But the beaming look you turned up to me in that first moment was free of any shadows. You teased me for years, mimicking the answering grin that stretched my face that day and seemed to freeze there. Your ghoulish exaggeration used to make us laugh until we hurt.

I shake my head now at the memory, an echo of that grin tugging at my lips, and I angle my straw hat forward on my face. I hear the crunch of my sandals in the dirt, see the dog's hind legs and tail moving ahead of me. A black-throated sparrow is singing from its perch at the tip of a *cardón* cactus. I hear no other sounds. I shake my head again. I still can't think of that day in San Francisco without marveling. And I can't walk on this desert path today without remembering the last time I was here, and you walked beside me.

You reached for my hand that day, something you did often, as though you could make up for those months when we first met and loved, when you wouldn't show the world what was growing between us, before I knew you were still in love with your former wife.

That day on this path you were describing your vision, busy landscaping our hillside ruins. You grew animated, dropping my hand again and again to gesture in the air between us. Here, another low brick wall, a terraced vegetable garden. Here, a long row of mango trees, curved in an arc. There, an avocado, a trio of figs. I can't walk here today without seeing the excitement in your hazel eyes, the chip in your tooth when you smiled, without feeling the sweat when we linked hands again and grew quiet, listening for the first sound of the sea.

The sound reaches me now, and I quicken my steps. I am eager for my first sight of it, for that first moment when I emerge from the dense desert floor and come out upon the open sand. The dog must feel my eagerness. She looks back at me more often now, trotting faster, head up, no longer stopping to sniff as she goes. I climb to the crest, and I stop, hands on my hips, the desert at my back and the sea before me. There are no people in sight. I watch a V of brown pelicans skim the water's edge, their huge feathered shapes silent and swift, all elegance and grace. I remember describing this beach to you before we visited it together, before you, too, fell in love with this untouched stretch of the Pacific. I told you of my awe for the pelicans, for the sheer numbers of the other sea birds, for walking alone along the sand as if no one else had ever walked here before me. "Like prehistoric times," you whispered, your gaze unfocused, seeing the picture I had painted in your mind.

"Yes," I said. "Exactly."

The dog flirts now with the edges of the sea. The saltwater will be good for her wound, I think, and I don't stop her. But when she begins to dogpaddle I call her back, leery of the ocean's power. This is not a swimmer's beach. She comes running toward me, and I see for the first time she has white splotches on her sides, white socks on her front paws. Her coat is slick, her tongue dangling sideways from her open mouth. She looks like she's laughing, and I glimpse the puppy in her, buried but not yet banished by the harshness and neglect of her young life. She jumps on me, spraying sand everywhere. "Ay!" I call out, but I am laughing. She runs in a circle around me then takes off toward the water again, veering away from the foam and racing north across the wet sand, her snout in the wind. I laugh again, something loosening inside me, and begin walking after her. I taste the sea air, breathe sunlight on water. I watch another group of pelicans skirt the edge of the sea, lifting and melding like one creature. They rush past me, and my heart lifts with them as they race above the water.

I stop to take off my leather sandals, let them dangle from lax fingers, let each foot sink into the wet sand. For a long time I walk north in the fierce light. My ghosts are banished, and it's just me walking, the little dog always in sight. Later, she is spooked by three young men on the beach and comes running back to me, her body close to the ground. She reaches me, and I kneel in the wet sand, heedless of my dress, of the cold on my old knees. I rub my hand across her wet back, and she shivers. "It's okay, little one," I say. *"Está bien."* Her mouth is close to my face, but I don't shy away. I see nothing in her dark brown eyes to worry me. Instead, I rest my forehead against the top of her head, and she freezes. I hold still, her wet fur cool against my skin. She smells like salt and sea air, not the stink of dirty, wet dog I was braced for. She shivers again, and then I feel her warm tongue on my neck. "That tickles," I say. I am giggling despite my years, my old bones in the wet sand. She looks proud of herself now, as though she has accomplished something great against impossible odds.

"You need a name, don't you?" I say. She tilts her head at my question. Then she races off again, looping around the young men but otherwise ignoring them this time, nose to the sky. "How about Winkler?" I ask her tail, waving in the distance. "Shall I call you Winkler, little one?" She stops as though she hears me, although it doesn't seem possible. She barks three times, staring at a spot behind me on the beach, then does an about-face and runs on. I know before I turn you will be shaking your head. You are trying to control the expression on your face, so you end up scowling at me the way you did the first time we saw each other.

"Gone and lost your heart, have you?" Your voice is gravelly, the way it used to be when you struggled to contain deep emotion, and when I hear your words, I know it's true. I'll have to go hunting up the people who live near where the dog pack lurks, see if I can find her owners. "Winkler?" you ask. "What kind of a name is that for a dog?" You mumble, as though you don't really mean for me to hear. I raise my eyebrow in response, and you laugh. I blow you a kiss, and you raise your hand to your lips, press them against it. I turn north again and follow Winkler's brown and white form.

I can feel your eyes on my back as I walk away from you. I feel the warmth of your fingers against your lips as though they are my own. For a moment, it is hard to move my legs across the sand. "Wait up, Winkler," I whisper. "Wait up." And then I bring my thumb and forefinger to my mouth the way you taught me years ago. My whistle makes Winkler bounce, a marionette, her strings pulled taut. The sharp sound pierces the layers of my world, landing me back in the clear light with the crashing sea beside me, a wet dog running down the beach toward me for all she's worth, her paws pounding hard against the packed sand. I don't turn around again, don't let you see the tears on my cheeks. Instead, I kneel, and Winkler licks my face. I let her think I am crying out of gratitude for her unexpected wriggling self, already dear, and it's only half untrue. I think of the *casita*, of family waiting in the big house. "I hope Iris doesn't mind one more for dinner," I say to Winkler. We start walking again, slower now. The sun hangs low above the water, an orange ball. You are a shining seashell lodged between my ribs.

THREE FIGURES OF NEAR SILENCE

Darci Schummer

Historically not a church goer herself, Robbie's mother started attending the Bad Lake First Christian Church regularly after the shooting. At first, Robbie thought this was part of her public relations strategy, but now she is always talking Psalms this and Revelation that. He finds it funny: people never believe until something shitty happens. Then they start needing god like alcoholics. He doesn't believe, not even now, but he goes to church when she asks without saying too much. It's easier to interact with his mother this way, all surface level, two skaters gliding on thin ice.

As the reverend drones on, Robbie can't help but check. He looks back at the double doors of the church, his palms sweating as he tells himself he's being stupid. Everything is fine. He is doing what millions of people do on Sundays all across the United States of America. He tunes back in to the sermon.

"The edict 'Love thy neighbor' means to love all of our neighbors, no matter who they are, what they've done, or what we think they have done," the reverend says.

A few minutes later, Robbie surveils the room full of his neighbors again. For a second, he thinks he sees his big brother Ricky out of the corner of his eye, but when he turns his head, the apparition is gone. He digs a fingernail into his forearm. Everything would be so much easier if Ricky were there. *Never forget: abstinence makes the Church grow fondlers*, he hears Ricky say. Robbie smirks. His mother shoots him a look, and he straightens himself back into a model son.

"The reverend wants to talk to you," his mother whispers as the service concludes.

His eyes roll involuntarily. "Why?"

"You don't talk to me. You barely say anything to the people at the school." She purses her lips. "And because that's what reverends do. They talk to people." She nudges him toward the rear of the church where the reverend stands, shaking hand after hand like some robot of Christ.

"You know I hate talking," Robbie says. "Maybe you should talk to him."

"I do, a lot. He's been helping me. He's very accepting."

"When?"

"When you're supposed to be in school."

It doesn't seem to surprise anyone that Robbie is failing most of his classes. Bad Lake is a Minnesota mining town, a spec of iron ore in the upper Midwest. You didn't need a diploma to mine iron, and one wouldn't help you when the mine laid you off anyway. And now after everything, well, no one was saying he was college material.

"Fine, I'll talk to him," Robbie says, gritting his teeth. "Just this once."

"Here's the man I wanted to see," the reverend says when Robbie approaches. He plants a palm on Robbie's shoulder, his hand surprisingly heavy. "Got a minute to talk?"

Robbie nods and follows the reverend to his office. Once inside, he settles into a big leather chair, stares at the blue veins spread across the bulb of the reverend's nose, the hair on the tops of his hands, like thatches of dead weeds. The reverend sips from a coffee cup, something rumored to be whiskey. Robbie hopes the rumor is true.

"Now I wanted to ask, how are you?" the reverend says.

It's the million-dollar question. Everyone is always asking Robbie how he is. And how is he? Well, he's alive, which means he has more going for him than a myriad of others.

"Fine."

The reverend stares at him long enough that Robbie looks away, zeroing in on a picture of Jesus hanging on the cross. Blood drips from the crown of thorns atop Jesus' head, ravines across his hands and feet, trickles down his concave abdomen. His body hangs forward, head lolled off to one side. And in the background, the sunset burns red orange. *Goddamn it must hurt to die*, Robbie thinks.

"You've been through a lot, son. I'm so sorry you've had to deal with all this, and I hope you're finding comfort in the Lord and in the scripture and in the fellowship here at church. You're also lucky to have your mother. She's a good woman, a strong and faithful woman. I've enjoyed getting to know her since you have decided to join us here at the church. And," he pauses, "she's a great mother."

"I know," Robbie says. His jaw clenches. "I know she is." The last thing he wants now is his mother to have a new boyfriend butting in.

"Reporters backing off finally?"

Immediately after the shooting, his mother had to pull him through a gaggle of reporters just so they could get out of the house. Each one came standard issue with pity, an exclusive interview request, and a slew of questions.

"Yeah," Robbie says. He hated the reporters, stopped watching TV altogether.

"I want you to know I'm here for you. I've been keeping you in my thoughts and in my prayers. I'm sure many in the congregation have been praying for you, too."

"Thanks," he says, though he doesn't know how any words sent out into a void are supposed to help. But those who say them must.

"Say, there is something that has always comforted me, something gleaned from First Corinthians. Can I share it with you, son?"

"Sure." Robbie looks down, rubs his hands across the tops of his Levi's.

"God never gives you more than you can handle," the reverend says. His bloodshot blue eyes bore into Robbie's. "God never gives you more than you can handle," he repeats, his palm tapping the desk for emphasis. "The Lord always makes a way out for you."

Robbie nods, trying to sequester a howl. Then the reverend stands, the legs of his chair abruptly grating against the tile floor. His hand shoots out. Robbie looks at it, the hand that had shaken hand after hand only a little while ago. He can feel Ricky there in the room, standing just behind him. *Can you fucking believe this guy?* Ricky mutters. Robbie shoves the howl down again. As he stands, he pushes his chair back, nearly knocking it over. "Well, I guess that means god must fucking hate me," he says as shakes the reverend's hand, flashing his best school photo smile. Ricky cackles in his ears, and Robbie gets out there.

"Say, wait a minute, son. Son, wait a minute," the reverend calls after him.

His mother stands outside the office, but he breezes past her toward the church doors.

"How did it go?" she says. "Wait, Robbie—Robbie, what happened?"

The slamming of the church doors silences her, and he heads for home. Later that night when a timid knock sounds on his bedroom door,

"I'm doing homework!" he yells. It's a lie, of course, but if they both pretend it isn't, what does that matter?

....

"And how did you sleep this week?" Ms. Northbird asks on Monday morning. Even though he's counting down the months until he can drop out of school, leave behind the whole mess, Robbie still meets with the school counselor once a week. Maybe he keeps going because she's pretty. Maybe he keeps going because he's lonely. Or maybe because the school will tell his mother if he doesn't. Regardless, he keeps going.

"I managed OK," Robbie says. Ms. Northbird has this hair he can't stop looking at. It's long, all down her back. When he can't sleep, which is all the time, he imagines it falling across his face.

"How about eating? You mentioned before that sometimes you don't feel hungry. Was your appetite normal this week?"

"It was fine," he says.

"Ok." She pauses and looks at him in her way, that hair framing her oval face.

"It was normal," he says.

"I noticed you haven't attended any more of the support group sessions with the other students. You want to tell me about that?"

He stares past her and at the wall. At least the posters here are just nature scenes with sayings on them. Motivation. Hard Work. Success. It's better than walls decorated with pictures of a murder scene.

"Listen, Robbie," she leans toward him. He can smell her hair, clean and sweet. "I know how much you loved your brother. I know how much he meant to you. He left a big hole. I just want to make sure that you find something to help fill that gap. It doesn't matter what anyone else might say about him."

His eyes tighten up, and he stares at his hands, rubs his thumb over a scar from the time he and his brother tried building a fort in the woods, remembers the look of panic on his brother's face when the pocket knife slipped. His brother rushed him into the house, cleaned up the cut, bandaged it. "I'm so sorry, buddy," he said. Then they ate ice cream and watched TV, reruns of *Magnum PI* because his brother always promised they'd move to Hawaii someday. *Don't cry now. Don't crack. Not even a little*, Ricky says.

"My brother was an asshole," Robbie says. "Do you want me to fill out that form or what?"

"Robbie, I just want—"

"I'll fill out the form," he says.

"It's November sixteenth." She hands him the clipboard, holding onto it for a beat after it's in his hand. "Be honest," she says. "There is no judgment here."

The forms he fills out always have the same questions: they ask if you are eating too much, sleeping too much, drinking too much. They ask if you can concentrate, if you are interested in life, if you have crying spells, hallucinate, hear voices.

If you don't tell them shit, they'll leave you alone. Trust me, Ricky says, the smell of his breath there and then gone.

Robbie never reveals much. Ms. Northbird and the forms are just trying to uncover an answer to the same question: Can you handle what you have been given?

....

He leaves Ms. Northbird's office and starts walking toward American History, a class taught by a fat bearded teacher who lectures from the textbook, talks on and on about America and its glory ad nauseam. He is running late, and when he gets to the room, the door is already shut. All the doors lock automatically now, and he'd have to knock to get in. He doesn't want to knock, doesn't want the others staring at him, their thoughts running like ticker tape across their eyes. He stands there for a moment, watching the teacher blabber behind his podium, watching the students screw around on their cellphones beneath the desks. Then he hears something behind him, some quasi-familiar sound. *It isn't*, he tells himself, *it can't be.* But his body doesn't understand, and then he is running, running down the hall, past the bathrooms, past the math room where he swears he can still see the algebra teacher falling. He sees Ricky, too, but his brother is stoic, stationary, the light behind him so that his face is just an oval with fuzzed out edges, a bit of feedback at the end of a song. Robbie busts through the front doors and into the cold, which is a clean and welcome slap.

He runs and runs until his chest edges toward explosion and his legs burn. He stops at Black Beach, a spot on the north shore of Lake Superior that has been his refuge since everything collapsed. In February, the beach is empty and white, the birches naked to their silver pink skin. He builds a fire in the same spot he always does and lights a cigarette, watching the smoke intertwine and drift out over the water. When the wind changes direction, he holds his breath and lets the smoke blow over him. He lights another cigarette, even though he's still smoking the first, and waits for his brother to materialize, the fresh cigarette calling Ricky back from cremation. Robbie closes his eyes. *C'mon*, he thinks. *C'mon.* The fire pops. Cold water bites the black rocky shore. The wind swirls.

How was church? Was it especially touching? Ricky says.

Robbie's eyes snap open. His brother is there, no jacket, just their dad's old plaid Pendleton, the one Ricky wore constantly after their dad disappeared. He wants to reach out, to touch him somehow, but Ricky is on the other side of the fire, and Robbie doesn't want to risk crossing the smoke.

Did you suck up a lot of knowledge? Ricky says, making the universal sign for fellatio.

"You know what that fucking drunk ass reverend said to me?" Robbie says.

"Jesus, kid, tell Mom church isn't doing anything for you. You need to start standing up to her."

"He said, 'God never gives you more than you can handle.' Can you believe that shit? 'God never gives you more than you can handle.'"

Well god must fucking hate us, little brother, Ricky says.

"That's what I said."

They both start laughing. Robbie laughs so hard he almost forgets what actually happened.

No one knows the full everything of it anyway, not even Robbie. No one, save three ghosts, saw Robbie crouch behind the teacher's desk when the first shots rang across the room. No one knows that in the space beneath the desk, Robbie's eyes met his algebra teacher's as she slumped over on the asbestos tile floor, her stomach full of buckshot. No one knows Robbie saw his friend Gabe's face turn into a crimson blur and his crush crumple like a piece of paper against a set of bookshelves. No one had smelled the smell, the iron and fire. No one knows what it looked like, what it sounded like, three figures of near silence. And no knows that after the shooting stopped, Robbie caught sight of a familiar pair of hiking boots retreating. When he saw those boots, he jumped up, he yelled. What had he yelled? He can't remember; it must have been some holy utterance, like speaking in tongues. None of it made sense. Then there was just the two of them, him and Ricky, Ricky backlit by winter sunlight, the shotgun in his arms. Ricky dropped the shotgun and pulled a pistol out of his pocket and then, and then, and then . . . The rest is all stuck somewhere in Robbie, and he wants to cram it down and down until it is diamond-hard and shiny, shiny enough that if anyone looks, they'll only see them self.

C'mon, show me what you got, Ricky busts in. He puts his hands up, bobs, weaves, and jabs around the fire, disappearing and reappearing through the smoke.

Robbie tries to remember his family during some pedestrian ritual: dinner, Christmas morning, a road trip to the Twin Cities. But now these events seem arcane. What had really been happening? What had happened for him was not what had happened for his brother. They had always been separate, it occurs to him now. They didn't hate or hurt the same, not for their father leaving, nor for any slights endured in childhood—the opaque and endless wanting, the nervousness of scarcity that had stolen their father away to the oil fields of North Dakota where letters came and came and then stopped.

"Knock it off," Robbie says, his hands loose at his sides. "It wasn't that bad, was it?"

"What?"

"All of it. I don't know. School. Us, Mom and Dad."

Ricky's eyes joke across the space between them. He leans forward. *Little brother, you ever want to know what it's like to be king? Carry a shotgun.* He laughs so hard that his breath moves smoke like the wind, enveloping them both. Robbie inhales too much and starts coughing. When he comes out of it, Ricky is gone. Out of the corner of his eye, Robbie thinks he sees a flash of red plaid atop the rocky peninsula at the end of the beach. Then he thinks he sees the flash weaving in and out of the pine trees spread across it.

"Did you know?" he yells at the flash. "Did you know I had algebra then?"

But the flash disappears. Robbie shivers. The fire has died down. He finds some small branches, stacks them on top, and blows on the embers.

When the flames are going good again, he takes off his jacket and spreads it out like a blanket. He pulls his arms inside the red Pendleton he is wearing beneath and lies down. On long late winter days like these, the sun rarely shines. The gray sky stretches over Lake Superior so wide this shoreline looks like the end of the world. Robbie stares into the slate, but every so often something in his peripheral vision distracts him, hurting his chest in a way he can't explain. *Maybe that is god, maybe that is god right inside,* he thinks, squeezing and squeezing until he can just barely breathe.

Biographical Notes

NEKTARIA ANASTASIADOU's ("The Way to Baghdad") first novel is scheduled to be published by Hoopoe, the fiction imprint of the American University in Cairo Press, in Fall 2020. Her work has appeared in *The Huffington Post*, *Al-Monitor*, *Daily Sabah*,*Mashallah News*, and *The Shanghai Literary Review*. Petrou received honorable mentions in *Ruminate*'s 2015 Short Fiction Contest and *Glimmertrain*'s New Writer Contest (May/June 2017). She lives in Istanbul, Turkey.

WILLIAM BURTCH came to writing in his sixth decade after a long investment career. His work has appeared or is forthcoming in *Northwest Indiana Literary Journal*, *BULL*, *The Airgonaut*, *Barren Magazine* and others. More at: williamburtch.com.

DAVE DEFUSCO ("Small Victories") is the author of several short stories and is currently working on a novel. He holds an MFA in Creative Writing and lives in Connecticut.

C.A. DEMI ("Deceiving Angels") is a writer currently living in Providence. He received a 2016 Fellowship Award in Fiction by the Rhode Island State Council on the Arts. In addition to short fiction, which has appeared in 'Missing Providence; A Frequency Anthology' and 'Meat for Tea; The Valley Review', Craig is at work on a novel set in the forests and steel and coal towns of his native Pennsylvania.

KATHLEENE DONAHOO'S ("Curses") fiction has appeared in many journals, including *Bellevue Literary Review*, *Carolina Quarterly*, *Connecticut Review*, and *North American Review*. She has a PhD in Economics from Yale, worked at the Federal Reserve Bank of New York, and now lives with her husband in the Bay Area.

CHARLES DUFFIE ("Catalina") is a writer and designer based in the Los Angeles area where he lives with his wife and daughters. His work has been published in the Los Angeles Review of Books and Role Reboot.

MATTHEW FITCH ("Barn Find") is an attorney living and working in Hartford, Connecticut. 'Barn Find' is his first publication.

KATHLEEN FORD ("The Shabbos Goy") has published more than fifty stories in both commercial magazines, including Redbook, Ladies Home Journal, and Yankee, and literary quarterlies, including Antioch, Sewanee, Southern Review, and North American Review. "Man on the Run," a story first printed in The New England Review, was published in BEST AMERICAN MYSTERY STORIES, 1912. Kathleen's first novel was published by St. Martin's Press and she received a Christopher Isherwood Fellowship and a Hackney Literary Prize.

DAVID H. FUKS ("Distinctions") lives and writes in Portland, Oregon, where he also works as an actor. The son of Holocaust survivors, he received degrees in both English Literature and Social Work from the University of Michigan. As a writer of both humorous and poignant stories, David is often asked to read his work at public gatherings. He was a member of the successful improvisational comedy group, "Waggie and Friends." David benefits from constant correction by his wife, DeAnn.

L.A. HARRIS ("Batter Swing") was born and raised in the Appalachian mountains of Southwest Virginia with detours since through Durham, North Carolina, and Baltimore, Maryland. She currently lives and writes in Denver, Colorado, and is finishing a first novel.

JENNIFER LEE ("Kalo Livadi") is a graduate of the Johns Hopkins MA Writing Program and an editor at the Baltimore Review. Her work has appeared in Painted Bride Quarterly, Phoebe, the Bellevue Literary Review, The Greensboro Review, Monkeybicycle, and elsewhere. Her work has won the Maryland Writers' Association short fiction prize and has been nominated for a Pushcart Award. She is currently hard at work on a looming science fiction project, among other things. She lives in Baltimore, Maryland, where she teaches middle school math and pursues her interests.

RAMONA DEFELICE LONG ("Winter Grass") writes short fiction, creative non-fiction, memoir, and personal essays about women, family and culture, and the foibles and quirks of everyday life. Her work has appeared in numerous literary and regional publications, and she is happiest on retreat, at a residency, or sharing stories at open mics. She is a transplanted Southerner living in Delaware.

KIERAN MCBRIDE ("Lies We Tell") goes by 'kaɪ-rən, though this pronunciation is technically incorrect. He was born and raised in Lawrence, Kansas, graduating from the University of Kansas with a degree in Creative Writing. He currently resides in Kansas City with his wife and son. This is his first publication.

CLAIRE NOONAN ("Afternoon of the Hero") has consulted since 1985 for the **B**ay **A**rea **W**riting **P**roject; published short stories: "The Locavore's Tale"- Spring 2012, *The Writing Disorder* and "The Laundromat Friend"- October 2017, *34th PARALLEL MAGAZINE*; and writes non-fiction posts for the education blog takecareschools.com. See www.cjnoonan.com about her novel *The House on Harrigan's Hill* by C.J. Noonan, Sea-Hill Press, April 2011.

CHRISTL R. PERKINS ("Driving Lessons") is a writer currently living in Oakland, CA. She began freelance writing in 1997, having published numerous articles (under her real name as well as pseudonyms) in *Beijing Scene*, *City Weekend*, *Metro*, and *That's Shanghai*. Christl is a 2018 participant in VONA-Voices. She has earned her Certificate in Fiction from the UCLA Extension Writers Program.

JEREMY SCHNOTALA ("Surely Goodness") just finished his MFA in creative writing at Western Michigan University. He lives with his husband in Grand Rapids, MI where he has taught English and creative writing and directed theater in the public schools for twenty-five years. He was the 2018 winner of both the Saints and Sinners Literary Festival fiction contest and The Tishman Review's Tillie Olsen short story award. Other recent work can be seen in Temenos Literary Journal, Beecher's Magazine, and Chagrin River Review. Check out his website at schnotala.com for more information.

DARCI SCHUMMER ("Three Figures of Near Silence") is the author of the story collection *Six Months in the Midwest* (Unsolicited Press). Her writing has appeared in *Necessary Fiction*, *Midway Journal*, *Midwestern Gothic*, *Pithead Chapel*, *Compose Journal*, and *Synaesthesia Magazine*, among other places. She teaches writing at Fond du Lac Tribal and Community College and serves as editor for the College's literary and arts journal, *The Thunderbird Review*.

ROSANNA STAFFA ("Magician") is published by *The Sun* and *Tampa Review* among others. Her work appears in New Rivers Press's *American Fiction* Volume 15. She was selected for the shortlist for *The Masters Review* Anthology Prize, Vol. VII, was a Yemassee Contest and Lamar York Prize finalist, and was nominated for the Pushcart Prize in 2019. She has a completed novel, *The War Ends at Four.*

Through twenty years of writing **RIBA TAYLOR** ("Between My Ribs") often let her teaching work gobble up her time. She's changing that now, finishing a memoir and a novel. She found out her story was a finalist on the first of five days she'd devoted to her writing, and she's certain this gift came because she turned toward her writing in this way, an "attagirl" from the universe. She's grateful and honored and delighted it is New Rivers Press. (NoHoldsBarred.blog)

About New Rivers Press

New Rivers Press emerged from a drafty Massachusetts barn in winter 1968. Intent on publishing work by new and emerging poets, founder C.W. "Bill" Truesdale labored for weeks over an old Chandler & Price letterpress to publish three hundred fifty copies of Margaret Randall's collection *So Many Rooms Has a House but One Roof.* About four hundred titles later, New Rivers is now a nonprofit learning press, based since 2001 at Minnesota State University Moorhead. Charles Baxter, one of the first authors with New Rivers, calls the press "the hidden backbone of the American literary tradition."

As a learning press, New Rivers guides student editors, designers, writers, and filmmakers through the various processes involved in selecting, editing, designing, publishing, and distributing literary books. In working, learning, and interning with New Rivers Press, students gain integral real-world knowledge that they bring with them into the publishing workforce at positions with publishers across the country, or to begin their own small presses and literary magazines.

Please visit our website: newriverspress.com for more information.